P

Poet and novelist Michel Houellebecq   r
of two previous novels, *Whatever* (*Extension du
domaine de la lutte*) and the international bestseller
Atomised (*Les Particules élémentaires*), winner of the
Prix Novembre and the 2002 International IMPAC
Dublin Literary Award. He lives in Ireland.

Michel Houellebecq

PLATFORM

TRANSLATED FROM THE FRENCH BY
Frank Wynne

VINTAGE

Published by Vintage 2003

2 4 6 8 10 9 7 5 3

Copyright © Flammarion 2001
Translated from the French, *Plateforme*
Translation copyright © Frank Wynne

Michel Houellebecq has asserted his right under the Copyright, Designs and Patents Act, 1988 to be identified as the author of this work

First published in Great Britain in 2002 by
William Heinemann

Vintage
Random House, 20 Vauxhall Bridge Road,
London SW1V 2SA

Random House Australia (Pty) Limited
20 Alfred Street, Milsons Point, Sydney
New South Wales 2061, Australia

Random House New Zealand Limited
18 Poland Road, Glenfield,
Auckland 10, New Zealand

Random House (Pty) Limited
Endulini, 5A Jubilee Road, Parktown 2193,
South Africa

The Random House Group Limited Reg. No. 954009
www.randomhouse.co.uk

A CIP catalogue record for this book
is available from the British Library

ISBN 0 099 43788 0

Papers used by Random House are natural, recyclable products made from wood grown in sustainable forests. The manufacturing processes conform to the environmental regulations of the country of origin

Printed and bound in Great Britain by
Bookmarque Ltd, Croydon, Surrey

Plus sa vie est infâme, plus l'homme y tient; elle est alors une protestation, une vengeance de tous les instants.

Honoré de Balzac

(The more contemptible his life, the more a man clings to it; it thus becomes a protest, a retribution for every moment.)

Part One

Thai Tropic

1

Father died last year. I don't subscribe to the theory by which we only become *truly adult* when our parents die; we never become truly adult.

As I stood before the old man's coffin, unpleasant thoughts came to me. He had made the most of life, the old bastard; he was a clever cunt. 'You had kids, you fucker . . .' I said spiritedly, 'you shoved your fat cock in my mother's cunt.' Well, I was a bit tense, I have to admit; it's not every day you have a death in the family. I'd refused to see the corpse. I'm forty, I've already had plenty of opportunity to see corpses; nowadays, I prefer to avoid them. It was this that had always dissuaded me from getting a pet.

I'm not married, either. I've had the opportunity several times, but I never took it. That said, I really love women. It's always been a bit of a regret, for me, being single. It's particularly awkward on holiday. People are

suspicious of single men on holiday, after they get to a
certain age: they assume that they're selfish, and probably
a bit pervy; I can't say they're wrong.

After the funeral, I went back to the house where my
father lived out his last years. The body had been discovered a week earlier. A little dust had already settled
around the furniture and in the corners of the rooms; I
noticed a cobweb on the window frame. So time,
entropy, all that stuff, was slowly taking the place over.
The freezer was empty. The kitchen cupboards mostly
contained single-serving Weight Watchers meals-in-a-
bag, tins of flavoured protein and energy bars. I wandered
through the rooms nibbling a magnesium-enriched
biscuit. In the boiler room, I rode the exercise bike for a
while. My father was over seventy and in much better
physical shape than I was. He did an hour of rigorous
exercise every day, lengths of the pool twice a week. At
weekends, he played tennis and went cycling with people
his age; I'd met some of them at the funeral. 'He coached
the lot of us! . . .' a gynaecologist exclaimed. 'He was ten
years older than us, and on a two kilometre hill, he'd be a
whole minute ahead.' Father, father, I said to myself, how
great was your vanity! To the left of my field of vision I
could make out a weightlifting bench, barbells. I quickly
visualised a moron in shorts – his face wrinkled, but
otherwise very like mine – building up his pectorals with
hopeless vigour. Father, I said to myself, Father, you have
built your house upon sand. I was still pedalling but I was
starting to feel breathless, my thighs ached a little, though

I was only on level one. Thinking back to the ceremony, I was aware that I had made an excellent general impression. I'm always clean shaven, my shoulders are narrow and when I developed a bald spot at about the age of thirty, I decided to cut my hair very short. I usually wear a grey suit and sober ties, and I don't look particularly cheerful. With my short hair, my lightweight glasses and my sullen expression, my head bowed a little to listen to a Christian funeral-hymn medley, I felt perfectly at ease with the situation – much more at ease than I would have done at a wedding, for example. Funerals, clearly, were my thing. I stopped pedalling, coughed gently. Night was falling quickly over the surrounding meadows. Near the concrete structure which housed the boiler, you could make out a brownish stain which had been poorly cleaned. It was there that my father had been discovered, his skull shattered, wearing shorts and an 'I love New York' sweatshirt. He had been dead for three days, according to the coroner. There was the possibility, very remote, that what happened was an accident, he could have slipped in a puddle of oil or something. That said, the floor of the room was completely dry; and the skull had been broken in several places, some of the brain had even spilled on to the floor; in all probability, what we were dealing with was murder. Captain Chaumont of the Cherbourg police was supposed to come over to see me that evening.

Back in the living room, I turned on the television, a

32-inch Sony widescreen with surround sound and an integrated DVD player. There was an episode of *Xena: Warrior Princess* on TF1, one of my favourite series: two very muscular women wearing metallic bras and miniskirts made of animal hide were challenging each other with their sabres. 'Your reign has gone on too long, Tagrathâ!' cried the brunette, 'I am Xena, warrior of the Western Plains!' There was a knock at the door; I turned the sound down.

Outside, it was dark. The wind gently shook the branches dripping with rain. A girl of about twenty-five, she looked north-African, was standing in the doorway. 'I'm Aïcha,' she said, 'I cleaned for Monsieur Renault twice a week. I've just come to get my things.'

'Well . . .' I said, '. . . well.' I made a vague gesture, something intended to be welcoming. She came in, glanced quickly at the television screen: the two warriors were now wrestling right next to a volcano; I suppose the spectacle had its stimulating side, for certain lesbians. 'I don't want to disturb you,' said Aïcha, 'I'll only be five minutes.'

'You're not disturbing me,' I said, 'in fact, nothing disturbs me.' She nodded her head as though she understood, her eyes lingered on my face; she was probably gauging my physical resemblance to my father, possibly inferring a degree of *moral* resemblance. After studying me for a few moments, she turned and climbed the stairs that lead to the bedrooms. 'Take your time,' I said, my voice barely audible. 'Take all the time you need . . .' She didn't answer, didn't pause in her ascent; she had probably not even heard me. I sat down on the sofa again, exhausted by the confrontation. I should have offered to take her coat; that's what you usually do, offer to take someone's coat. I realised that the room was terribly cold – a damp, penetrating cold, the cold of a cellar. I didn't know how to light the boiler, I had no wish to try, now my father was dead. I had intended to leave straight away. I turned over to FR3 just in time to catch the last part of *Questions pour un champion*. At the moment when Nadège from Val-Fourré told Julien Lepers that she was going to risk her title for the third time, Aïcha appeared on the stairs, a small travel bag on her shoulder. I turned off the television and walked quickly towards her. 'I've always admired Julien Lepers.' I told her, 'Even if he doesn't know the actual town or village the contestant is from, he always manages to say something about the département or the region; he always knows a bit about the climate and the local beauty spots. Above all, he understands life: the contestants are human beings to him, he understands their problems and their joys. Nothing of what constitutes human reality for the contestants is entirely strange or intimidating to him. Whoever the contestant is, he manages to get them to talk about their work, their family, their hobbies – everything, in fact, that in their eyes goes to make up a life. The contestants are often members of a brass band or a choral society, they're involved in organising the local fête, or they devote themselves to some charitable cause. Their children are often there in the studio. You generally get the impression from the programme that these people are happy, and you feel better, happier yourself. Don't you think?'

She looked at me unsmilingly; her hair in a chignon, she wore little makeup, her clothes were pretty drab – a serious girl. She hesitated for a moment before saying in a low voice which was a little hoarse with shyness: 'I was very fond of your father.' I couldn't think of anything to say; it struck me as bizarre, but just about possible. The old man must have had stories to tell: he'd travelled in Colombia, Kenya or I don't know where; he'd had the opportunity to watch rhinoceros through binoculars. Every time we met, he limited himself to making ironic comments about the fact that I was a civil servant, about the job security that went with it. 'Got yourself a cushy little number, there . . .' he would say, making no attempt to hide his scorn; families are always a bit difficult. 'I'm studying nursing,' Aïcha went on, 'but since I stopped living with my parents I have to work as a cleaner.' I racked my brains to think of an appropriate response: should I enquire as to how expensive rents were in Cherbourg? I finally opted for a 'I see . . .', into which I tried to introduce a certain worldly wisdom. This seemed to satisfy her and she walked to the door. I pressed my face to the glass to watch her Volkswagen Polo do a U-turn in the muddy track. FR3 was showing some rustic made-for-TV movie set in the nineteenth century, starring Tchéky Karyo as a farm labourer. Between piano lessons, the daughter of the landowner – he was played by Jean-

Pierre Marielle – accorded the handsome peasant certain liberties. Their clinches took place in a stable; I dozed off just as Tchéky Karyo was energetically ripping off her organza knickers. The last thing I remember was a close-up of a small group of pigs.

I was woken by pain and by the cold; I had probably fallen asleep in an awkward position, my cervical vertebrae felt paralysed. I was coughing heavily as I stood up, my breath filling the glacial air of the room with vapour. Bizarrely, the television was showing *Très Pêche*, a fishing pro-gramme on TF1; I had obviously woken up, or at least reached a sufficient level of consciousness to work the remote control; I had no memory of doing so. Tonight's programme was devoted to silurids – huge fish with no scales which had become more common in French rivers as a result of global warming; they were particularly fond of the areas around nuclear power plants. The report was intended to shed light on the truth behind a number of myths: it was true that adult silurids could grow to as much as three or four metres; in the Drôme, specimens larger than five metres had been reported; there was nothing particularly improbable about this. However there was no question of the animals ever behaving carnivorously, or attacking bathers. The public suspicion of silurids seemed, to some extent, to have rubbed off on the men who fished for them; the small group of silurid anglers was not well liked by the larger family of anglers. They felt they suffered as a result and wanted to take advantage of this programme to improve their negative image. It was true they could hardly suggest gastronomy as their motive: the flesh of the silurid was completely inedible. But it was an excellent catch, intelligent and at the same time requiring sportsmanship; it was not unlike pike fishing, and deserved a wider following. I paced around the room a little, unable to get warm; I couldn't bear the idea of sleeping in my father's bed. In the end I went upstairs and brought down pillows and blankets, settled myself as best I could on the sofa. I switched off just after the credits of 'The Silurid Demystified'. The night was opaque, the silence also.

2

All things come to an end, including the night. I was dragged from my saurian lethargy by the clear, resonant voice of Captain Chaumont. He apologised, he hadn't had time to come by the previous evening. I offered him coffee. While the water was boiling, he set up his laptop on the kitchen table and hooked up a printer. This way he could have me re-read and sign my statement before he left; I made a murmur of approval. The police force was so completely snowed under with administrative work that it did not have enough time to dedicate to its real task: investigation. That at least was what I had concluded from various television documentaries. He agreed, warmly this time. This interview was getting off to a good start, in an atmosphere of mutual trust. 'Windows' started up with a cheerful little sound.

The death of my father occurred in the evening or the night of November 14th. I was working that day; I was working on the 15th, too. Obviously, I could have taken my car and killed my father, having driven there and back overnight. What was I doing on the evening or the night of November 14th? Nothing, as far as I knew, nothing significant. At least, I had no memory of anything, though it was less than a week before. I had neither a regular sexual partner nor any real close friends: in which case, how can you be expected to remember? The days go by, and that's it. I gave Chaumont an apologetic look; I would have liked to help him out, or at least point him in the right direction. 'I'll have a look in my diary . . .' I said. I wasn't expecting anything of this; but curiously, there was a mobile number written in the space for the 14th beneath a name − 'Coralie'. Who was Coralie? The diary was completely useless.

'My brain is a mess . . .' I said with a disappointed smile. 'But, I don't know, maybe I was at a private view.'

'A private view?' He waited patiently, his fingers hovering some inches above the keyboard.

'Yes, I work for the Ministry of Culture. I plan the financing for exhibitions, or sometimes shows.'

'Shows?'

'Shows . . . contemporary dance . . .' I felt completely desperate, overcome with shame.

'Generally speaking, then, you work on cultural events?'

'Yes, that's it . . . You could put it like that.' He looked at me with a compassion tinged with seriousness. He had an awareness of the existence of a cultural sector, a vague but definite awareness. He must have had to meet people from all walks of life in his profession; no area of society could be completely alien to him. Police work is a human science.

The rest of the interview proceeded more or less normally; I had watched a few made-for-TV movies, so I was prepared for this kind of conversation. Did I know any enemies my father might have? No, but no friends either, to be honest. In any case, my father wasn't *important* enough to have enemies. Who stood to gain by his death? Well, me. When did I last visit him? August, probably. There's never much to do in the office in August, and my colleagues have to go on holiday because they have children. I stay in Paris, I play solitaire on the computer and around the 15th I take a long weekend off; that was the extent of my visits to my father. On that subject, did I have a good relationship with my father? Yes and no. Mostly no, but I came to see him once or twice a year; that in itself wasn't too bad.

He nodded. I could feel my statement was coming to an end; I would have liked to say more. I felt overcome by a feeling of irrational, abnormal pity for Chaumont. He was already loading paper into his printer. 'My father was very sporty!' I said brusquely. He looked up at me enquiringly. 'I don't know . . .' I said, spreading my hands in despair, 'I just wanted to say that he was very athletic.' He shrugged disappointedly and pressed 'Print'.

After I'd signed my statement, I walked Captain Chaumont to the door. I was aware that I had been a disappointing witness, I told him. 'All witnesses are disappointing . . .' he said. I considered this aphorism for a while. Before us stretched the endless monotony of the fields. Chaumont climbed into his Peugeot 305; he would keep me informed of any developments in the investigation. In the public sector, the death of a parent or grandparent entitles one to three days' leave. As a result, I could very easily have taken my time going home, bought some local camembert; but I immediately took the motorway for Paris.

I spent the last day of my compassionate leave in various travel agencies. I liked holiday brochures, their abstraction, their way of condensing the places of the world into a limited sequence of possible pleasures and fares; I was particularly fond of the star-ratings system, which indicated the intensity of the pleasure one was entitled to hope for. I wasn't happy, but I valued happiness and continued to aspire to it. According to the Marshall model, the buyer is a rational individual seeking to maximise his satisfaction while taking price into consideration; Veblen's model, on the other hand, analyses the effect of peer pressure on the buying process (depending on whether the buyer wishes to be identified with a defined group or to set himself apart from it). Copeland demonstrates that the buying process varies, depending on the category of product/service (impulse purchase, considered purchase, specialised purchase); but the Baudrillard and Becker model posits that a purchase necessarily implies a series of signals. Overall, I felt myself closer to the Marshall model.

Back at the office I told Marie-Jeanne that I needed a holiday. Marie-Jeanne is my colleague; together we work on exhibition proposals, together we work for the benefit of the contemporary arts. She is a woman of thirty-five, with lank blond hair, her eyes are a very light blue; I know nothing about her personal life. Within the office hierarchy, she has a position slightly senior to mine; but this is something which she ignores – she likes to emphasise teamwork within the office. Every time we receive a visit from a really important person – a delegate from the Department of Plastic Arts or someone from the Ministry – she insists on this notion of teamwork. 'And this is the most important man in the office! . . .' she exclaims, walking into my office; 'He's the one who juggles the figures and the financial statements . . . I would be completely lost without him.' And then she laughs; the important visitors laugh in turn, or at least smile good-naturedly. I smile too, insofar as I can. I try to imagine myself as a juggler; but in reality it's quite enough to master simple arithmetic. Although strictly speaking Marie-Jeanne does nothing, her work is, in fact, the most complicated job: she has to keep abreast of movements, networks, trends; having assumed a level of cultural responsibility, she constantly runs the risk of being thought reactionary, even obscurantist; it is an accusation from which she must defend herself and the institution. She is also in regular contact with artists, gallery owners and the editors of obscure reviews, obscure, at least, to me; these telephone calls keep her happy, because her passion for contemporary art is real. As far as I'm concerned, I'm not actively hostile to it: I am not an advocate of *craft*, nor of a return to figurative painting; I maintain the disinterested attitude appropriate to an accounts manager. Questions of aesthetics and politics are not my thing; it's not up to me to invent or adopt new attitudes, new affinities with the world – I gave up all that at the same time I developed a stoop and my face started to tend towards melancholy. I've attended many exhibitions, private views, many performances that remain unforgettable. My conclusion, henceforth, is that art cannot change lives. At least not mine.

I had informed Marie-Jeanne of my bereavement; she greeted me sympathetically, she even put her hand on my shoulder. My request to take some time off seemed completely natural to her. 'You need to take stock, Michel,' she reckoned, 'you need to turn inward.' I tried to visualise the movement she was suggesting and I concluded that she was probably right. 'Cécilia will put the provisional budget to bed,' she went on; 'I'll talk to her about it.' What precisely was she alluding to, and who was this Cécilia? Glancing around me, I noticed the design for a poster and I remembered. Cécilia was a fat, redhead who was always gorging herself on Cadburys and who'd been in the department for two months: a temp, work experience maybe, someone pretty insignificant at any rate. And it was true that before my father's death I had been working on a provisional budget for the exhibition,

'Hands Up, You Rascals!', due to open in Bourg-la-Reine in January. It consisted of photographs of police brutality taken with a telephoto lens in Yvelines; but we weren't talking documentary here, more a process of the theatricalisation of space, full of nods to various cop shows featuring the Los Angeles Police Department. The artist had favoured a 'fun' approach rather than the social critique you'd expect. An interesting project, all in all, not too expensive nor too complicated; even a moron like Cécilia was capable of finalising the provisional budget.

Usually, when I left the office, I'd take in a peepshow. It set me back fifty francs, maybe seventy if I was slow to ejaculate. Watching pussy in motion cleared my head. The contradictory trends of contemporary video art, balancing the conservation of national heritage with support for living creativity . . . all of that quickly evaporated before the facile magic of a moving pussy. I gently emptied my testicles. At the same moment, Cécilia was stuffing herself with chocolate cake in a pâtisserie near the Ministry; our motives were much the same.

Very occasionally, I would take a private room at five hundred francs; that was if my dick wasn't feeling too good, when it seemed to me to resemble a useless, demanding little appendage that smelled like cheese. Then I needed a girl to take it in her hands, to go into raptures, however faked, over its vigour, the richness of its semen. Be that as it may, I was always home before seven-thirty. I'd start with *Questions pour un champion* which I had set my video to record; then I would continue with the national news. The mad cow disease crisis was of little interest to me, mostly I survived on Mousline instant mash with cheese. Then the evening would continue. I wasn't unhappy, I had 128 channels. At about two in the morning, I'd finish with Turkish musicals.

A number of days went by like this, relatively peacefully, before I received another phone call from Chaumont. Things had progressed significantly, they had found the alleged killer; actually, it was more than a allegation, for in fact the man had confessed. They were going to stage a re-enactment in a couple of days. Did I want to be present? Oh yes, I said, yes.

Marie-Jeanne congratulated me on this courageous decision. She talked about the grieving process, the mysteries of the father-son relationship. She used socially acceptable terms from a limited catalogue, what was more important, even surprising, was that I realized that she was fond of me, and it felt good. Women really do have a handle on affection, I thought as I boarded the Cherbourg train; even at work, they have a tendancy to establish emotional ties, finding it difficult to orient themselves, let alone thrive, in a universe completely stripped of such emotional ties, they find it difficult to thrive in such an atmosphere. This was a weakness of theirs, as the 'psychology' column of *Marie-Claire* continually reminded them: it would be better if they could clearly separate the professional from the emotional, but they simply could not do it, and the 'true stories' column of *Marie-Claire* confirmed with equal regularity. Somewhere near

Rouen, I reviewed the essential facts of the case. Chaumont's breakthrough was the discovery that Aïcha had been having 'intimate relations' with my father. How often, and how intimate? He didn't know, and it had no significance to his continuing inquiry. One of Aïcha's brothers had quickly confessed that he had come 'to demand an explanation' of the old man, things had got out of hand, and he had left him for dead on the concrete floor of the boiler room.

In principle, the re-enactment was to be presided over by the examining magistrate, a brusque, austere little man, dressed in flannel trousers and a dark polo-neck, his face permanently clenched in a rictus of irritation; but Chaumont quickly established himself as the real master of ceremonies. Briskly and cheerfully he greeted the participants, gave each a little word of welcome, and led them to their places: he seemed remarkably happy. This was his first murder case and he'd solved it in less than a week; in this whole banal, sordid story, he was the only true hero. Clearly overcome, a black band covering her face, Aïcha sat on a chair trying to look small. She barely looked up when I arrived, pointedly looking away from where her brother was standing. Her brother, flanked by two policemen, stared at the floor with an obstinate air. He looked just like a common little thug; I didn't feel the slightest sympathy for him. Looking up, his eyes met mine; no doubt he knew who I was, He knew my role, he had undoubtedly been told: according to his brutal view of the world, I had a right to vengeance, I deserved an accounting for the blood of my father. Aware of the rapport establishing itself between us, I stared at him, not turning away; I allowed hatred to overwhelm me slowly, my breathing became easier, it was a powerful, pleasurable sensation. If I had had a gun, I would have shot him without a second thought. Killing that little shit not only seemed to me a morally neutral act, but something positive, beneficial. A policeman made some marks on the floor with a piece of chalk, and the re-enactment began. According to the accused, it was very simple: during the conversation, he had become angry and pushed my father roughly; the latter had fallen backwards, his skull had shattered on the floor; he panicked, he fled.

Of course he was lying, and Chaumont had no trouble establishing this. An examination of the victim's skull clearly indicated a furious attack; there were multiple contusions, probably the result of a series of kicks. Furthermore, my father's face had been scraped along the ground, almost sufficient to force the eye from its socket. 'I don't remember . . .' said the accused man; 'I lost it.' Watching his nervous arms, his thin, horrible face, it wasn't difficult to believe him: he hadn't planned this, he was probably excited by the impact of the skull on the ground and the sight of first blood. His defence was lucid and credible, he would probably come across well in front of a jury: a two- or three-year suspended sentence, no more. Chaumont, pleased with the way the afternoon had gone, began to bring things to a conclusion. I got up from my chair and walked over to one of the picture windows. It was getting dark: a flock of sheep were bringing their day to a close. They too were stupid, possibly even more stupid than Aïcha's brother; but violence had not been programmed into their genes. On the last night of their lives they would bleat in terror, their hoofs would scrabble desperately; there would be a gunshot, their lives would seep away and their flesh would be transformed into meat. We parted with a round of handshakes; Chaumont thanked me for coming.

I saw Aïcha the following day; on the advice of the estate agent, I had decided to have the house thoroughly cleaned before it was viewed. I gave her the keys, then she dropped me off at Cherbourg station. Winter was taking hold of the farmlands, clouds of mist hung over the hedges. We were uncomfortable being together. She had been familiar with my father's genitals, which tended to create a certain misplaced intimacy. It was all rather surprising: she seemed like a serious girl, and my father was hardly a ladies' man. He must have had certain traits, certain characteristics that I had failed to notice; in fact I was finding it difficult to remember his face. Men live alongside one another like cattle; it is a miracle if once in a while they manage to share a bottle of booze.

Aïcha's Volkswagen stopped in front of the station; I was aware that it would be best to say a few words before we parted. 'Well . . .' I said. After a few seconds, she spoke to me in a subdued voice: 'I'm going to leave the area. I've got a friend who can get me a job as a waitress in Paris; I can continue my studies there. In any case, my family think I'm a whore.' I made a murmur of comprehension. 'There are a lot more people in Paris . . .' I finally ventured with difficulty; I'd racked my brains, but that was all I could think of to say about Paris. The acute poverty of my response did not seem to discourage her. 'There's no point expecting anything from my family,' she went on with suppressed fury. 'They're not only poor, they're bloody stupid. Two years ago, my father went on the pilgrimage to Mecca; since then, you can't get a word out of him. My brothers are worse: they encourage each other's stupidity. They get blind drunk on pastis and all the while they strut around like the guardians of the one true faith, and they treat me like a slut because I prefer to go out and work rather than marry some stupid bastard like them.'

'It's true, Muslims on the whole aren't up to much . . .' I said with embarrassment. I picked up my travel bag, opened the door. 'I think you'll do alright . . .' I muttered without conviction. At that moment I had a vision of migratory flows crisscrossing Europe like blood vessels; Muslims appeared as clots that were only slowly reabsorbed. Aïcha eyed me sceptically. Cold air rushed into the car. Intellectually, I could manage to feel a certain attraction to Muslim vaginas. I managed a little forced smile. She smiled in turn, a little more sincerely than I had. I shook her hand for a long time. I could feel the warmth of her fingers. I carried on shaking her hand until I could feel the gentle pulse of her blood at the hollow of her wrist. A few feet from the car, I turned around to give a little wave. We had made a connection in spite of everything; in the end, in spite of everything, something had happened.

Settling into my seat on board the intercity, it occurred to me that I should have given her money. Actually, it was better that I hadn't, it would probably have been misinterpreted. Strangely, it was at that moment that I realised for the first time that I was going to be a rich man; well, relatively rich. The money in my father's accounts had already been transferred. For the rest, I had left the sale of the car to a local garage and of the house to an estate agent; everything had been arranged as simply as possible. The value of these assets would be determined by the market. Of course there was some room for negotiation: ten per cent one way or the other, no more. The taxes that were due were no mystery either: a quick look through the carefully thought-out little brochures available from the Tax Office would be enough.

My father had probably thought of disinheriting me several times; in the end, he must have given up on the idea, considering it too complicated, too much paperwork for an uncertain result (it is not easy to disinherit your children, the law offers you very limited possibilities: not only do the little shits ruin your life, afterwards they get to profit from everything you've managed to save, despite your worst efforts). He probably thought that there was no point – after all, what the fuck did it matter to him what happened after he was dead? That's how he looked at it, in my opinion. In any case, the old bastard was dead, and I was about to sell the house in which he had spent his last years; I was also going to sell the Toyota Land Cruiser which he had used for hauling cases of Evian from the Casino Géant in Cherbourg. I live near the Jardin des Plantes, what would I want with a Toyota Land Cruiser? I could have used it to ferry ricotta ravioli from the market at Mouffetard, that's about it.

In cases of direct inheritance, death duties are not very high – even if the emotional ties aren't very strong. After tax, I could probably expect about three million francs. To me, that represented about fifteen times my annual salary. It also represented what an unskilled worker in western Europe could expect for a lifetime of work; it wasn't so bad. You could make a start with that, you could try.

In a few weeks I would surely get a letter from my bank. The train approached Bayeux. I could already imagine the course of the conversation. The clerk at my branch would have noticed a substantial credit balance on my account, which he would very much like to discuss with me – who does not need a *financial adviser* at one time or another in his life? A little wary, I would want to steer him towards safe options; he would greet this reaction – such a common one – with a slight smile. Most novice investors, as financial advisers well know, favour security over earnings; they often laugh about it among themselves. I should not misunderstand him: when it came to managing their capital, even some elderly and otherwsie worldly people behave like complete novices. For his part, he would try to steer me in the direction of a slightly different approach – while, of course, giving me time to consider my options. Why not, in effect, put two-thirds of my holdings into investments where there would be no surprises but a low return? And why not place the remaining third in investments that were a little more adventurous, but which had the potential for significant growth? After a few days' consideration, I knew, I would defer to his judgement. He would feel reassured by my support, would put together the papers with a flash of enthusiasm, and our handshake at the moment we parted company would be warm.

I was living in a country distinguished by placid socialism, where ownership of material possessions was guaranteed by strict legislation, where the banking system was surrounded by powerful state guarantees. Unless I were to venture beyond what was lawful, I ran no risk of embezzlement or fraudulent bankruptcy. All in all, I needn't worry any more. In fact, I never really had: after serious but hardly distinguished studies, I had quickly found a career in the public sector. This was in the mid-eighties, at the beginning of the modernisation of socialism, at the time when the illustrious Jack Lang was distributing wealth and glory to the cultural institutions of the State; my starting salary was very reasonable. And then I had grown older, standing untroubled on the sidelines through successive policy changes. I was courteous, well-mannered, well-liked by colleagues and superiors; my temperament, however, was less than warm and I had failed to make any real friends. Night was falling quickly over Lisieux. Why, in my work, had I never shown a passion comparable to Marie-Jeanne's? Why had I never shown any real passion in my life in general?

Several more weeks went by without bringing me an answer; then, on the morning of December 23rd, I took a taxi to Roissy airport.

3

And now, there I was on my own like an idiot, a few feet from the Nouvelles Frontières desk. It was a Saturday morning during the Christmas holidays; Roissy was heaving, as usual. The minute they have a couple of days of freedom, the inhabitants of western Europe dash off to the other side of the world, they go halfway round the world in a plane, they behave – literally – like escaped convicts. I don't blame them, I was preparing to do just the same.

My dreams are run-of-the-mill. Like all of the inhabitants of western Europe, I want to *travel*. There are problems with that, of course: the language barrier, poorly organised public transport, the risk of being robbed or conned. To put it more bluntly, what I really want, basically, is to be a *tourist*. We dream what dreams we can afford; and my dream is to go on an endless series of 'Romantic Getaways', 'Colourful Expeditions' and

'Pleasures à la Carte' – to use the titles of the three Nouvelles Frontières brochures.

I immediately decided to go on a package tour, but I hesitated quite a bit between 'Rum and Salsa' (ref: CUB CO 033, 16 days/14 nights, 11,250FF based on two sharing, single supplement 1,350FF) and 'Thai Tropic' (ref THA CA 006, 15 days/13 nights, 9,950FF based on two sharing, single supplement 1,175FF). Actually, I was more attracted by Thailand; but the advantage of Cuba is that it's one of the last Communist countries, though probably not for much longer – it has a sort of 'endangered régime' appeal, a sort of political exoticism, to put it in a nutshell. In the end, I chose Thailand. I have to admit that the copy in the brochure was very well done, sure to tempt the average punter:

A package tour with a dash of adventure, which will take you from the bamboo forests of the River Kwai to the island of Ko Samui, winding up, after crossing the spectacular isthmus of Kra, at Ko Phi Phi, off the coast of Phuket. A cool trip to the tropics.

At 8.30 a.m. on the dot, Jacques Maillot slams the door of his house on the Boulevard Blanqui in the 13th arrondissement, straddles his moped and begins a journey across the capital from east to west. Direction: the head office of Nouvelles Frontières on the Boulevard de Grenelle. Every other day, he stops at four or five of the company's agencies: 'I bring them the latest brochures, I pick up the post and generally take the temperature,' explains the boss, full of beans, always sporting an extraordinary multi-coloured tie. It's a crack of the whip for the agents: 'On the days after my visit, there's a tremendous boost in sales at those agencies . . .' he explains with a smile. Visibly under his spell, the journalist from *Capital* goes on to marvel: who could have predicted in 1967 that a small business set up by a handful of student protestors would take off like this? Certainly not the thousands of demon-strators who, in May 1968, marched past the Nouvelles Frontières office on the Place Denfert-Rochereau in Paris. 'We were in just the right place, right in front of the cameras . . .' remembers Jacques Maillot, a former boy scout and left-wing Catholic by way of the National Students Union. It was the first piece of publicity for the company, which took its name from John F. Kennedy's speech about America's 'new frontiers'.

A passionate liberal, Jacques Maillot successfully fought the Air France monopoly, making air transport more accessible to all. His company's odyssey, which in thirty years had made it the number one travel agency in France, has fascinated the business press. Like FNAC, like Club Med, Nouvelles Frontières – born at the dawn of the leisure society – might stand as a symbol of the new face of modern capitalism. In the year 2000, for the first time, the tourist industry became – in terms of turnover – the biggest economic activity in the world. Though it required only a moderate level of physical fitness, 'Thai Tropic' was listed under 'adventure tours': a range of accommodation options (simple, standard, deluxe); group numbers limited to twenty to ensure a better group dynamic. I saw two really cute black girls with rucksacks arriving, I dared to hope that they'd opted for the same tour: then I looked away and went to collect my travel documents. The flight was scheduled to last a little more than eleven hours.

Taking a plane today, regardless of the airline, regardless of the destination, amounts to being treated like shit for the duration of the flight. Crammed into a ridiculously tiny space from which it's impossible to move without disturbing an entire row of fellow passengers, you are greeted from the outset with a series of embargos announced by stewardesses sporting fake smiles. Once on board, their first move is to get hold of your personal belongings so they can put them in overhead lockers – to which you will not have access under any circumstances until the plane lands. Then, for the duration of the flight, they do their utmost to find ways to bully you, all the while making it impossible for you to move about, or more generally to move at all, with the exception of a certain number of permitted activities: enjoying fizzy drinks, watching American videos, buying duty-free products. The unremitting sense of danger, fuelled by mental images of plane crashes, the enforced immobility in a cramped space, provokes a feeling of stress so powerful that a number of passengers have reportedly died of heart attacks while on long-haul flights. The crew do their level best to maximise this stress by preventing you from combating it by habitual means. Deprived of cigarettes, reading matter and, as happens more and more frequently, sometimes even deprived of alcohol. Thank God the bitches don't do *body searches* yet; as an experienced passenger, I had been able to stock up on some necessities for survival: a few 21-mg Nicorette patches, sleeping pills, a flask of Southern Comfort. I fell into a thick sleep as we were flying over the former East Germany.

I was awoken by a weight on my shoulder, and warm breath. I sat my neighbour upright in his seat without undue manhandling; he groaned softly, but didn't open his eyes. He was a big guy, about thirty, with light brown hair in a bowl cut; he didn't look too unpleasant, nor too clever. In fact, he was rather endearing, wrapped up in the soft blue blanket supplied by the airline, his big manual labourer's hands resting on his knees. I picked up the paperback which had fallen at his feet: a shitty Anglo-Saxon bestseller by one Frederick Forsyth. I had read something by this halfwit, full of heavy-handed eulogies to Margaret Thatcher and ludicrous depictions of the USSR as the *evil empire*. I'd wondered how he managed after the fall of the Berlin Wall. I leafed through his new opus: apparently, this time, the roles of the bad guys were played by Serb nationalists; here was a man who kept up to date with current affairs. As for his beloved hero, the tedious Jason Monk, he had gone back into service with the CIA, which had formed an alliance of convenience with the Chechen mafia. Well! I thought, replacing the book on my neighbour's knees, what a charming sense of morality bestselling British authors have. The page was marked with a piece of paper folded in three, which I recognised as the Nouvelles Frontières itinerary: I had, apparently, just met my first tour companion. A fine fellow, I was sure, certainly a lot less egocentric and neurotic than I was. I glanced at the video screen, which was showing the flight path: we had probably passed Chechnya, whether or not we had flown over it; the exterior temperature was ⁻53°C, altitude 10,143 metres, local time 00.27. Another screen replaced the first: we were flying directly over Afghanistan. Through the window, you could see nothing but pitch black of course. In any case the Taliban were probably all in bed stewing in their own filth. 'Goodnight, Talibans, good night . . . sweet dreams . . .' I whispered before swallowing a second sleeping pill.

4

The plane landed at Don Muang airport at about 5 a.m. I woke with some difficulty. The man on my left had already stood up and was waiting impatiently in the queue to disembark. I quickly lost sight of him in the corridor leading to the arrivals hall. My legs were like cotton wool, my mouth felt furry; my ears were filled with a violent drone.

No sooner had I stepped through the automatic doors than the heat enveloped me like a mouth. It must have been at least 35°C. The heat in Bangkok has something particular about it, in that it is somehow *greasy*, probably on account of the pollution; after any long period outdoors, you're always surprised to find that you're not covered with a fine film of industrial residue. It took me about thirty seconds to adjust my breathing. I was trying not to fall too far behind the guide, a Thai woman whom I hadn't taken much notice of, except that she seemed reserved and well-educated – but a lot of Thai women give that impression. My backpack was cutting into my shoulders; it was a Lowe Pro Himalaya Trekking, the most expensive one I could find at Vieux Campeur; it was guaranteed for life. It was an impressive object, steel grey with snap clasps, special Velcro fastenings – the company had a patent pending – and zips that would work at temperatures of ‾65°C. Its contents were sadly pretty limited: some shorts and tee-shirts, swimming trunks, special shoes which allowed you to walk on coral (125FF at Vieux Campeur), a wash bag containing medicines considered essential by the *Guide du Routard*, a JVC HRD-9600 MS video camera with batteries and spare tapes, and two American bestsellers that I'd bought pretty much at random at the airport.

The Nouvelles Frontières coach was parked about a hundred metres further on. Inside the powerful vehicle – a 64-seat Mercedes M-800 – the air-conditioning was turned up full; it felt like stepping into a freezer. I settled myself in the middle of the coach, on the left by a window. I could vaguely make out a dozen other passengers, amongst them my neighbour from the plane. No one came to sit beside me. I had clearly missed my first opportunity to integrate into the group; I was also well on my way to catching a nasty cold.

It wasn't light yet, but on the six-lane motorway which led to downtown Bangkok, the traffic was already heavy. We drove past buildings alternately of glass and steel with, occasionally, a massive concrete structure reminiscent of Soviet architecture: the head offices of banks, chain hotels, electronics companies – for the most part Japanese. Past the junction at Chatuchak, the motorway rose above a series of ring roads circling the heart of the city. Between the floodlit buildings, we began to be able to distinguish groups of small, slate-roofed houses in the middle of wasteland. Neon-lit stalls offered soup and rice; you could see the tinplate pots steaming. The coach slowed slightly to take the New Phetchaburi Road exit. There was a moment when we saw an interchange of the most phantasmagoric shape, its asphalt spirals seemingly suspended in the heavens, lit by banks of airport floodlights; then, after following a long curve, the coach joined the motorway again.

The Bangkok Palace Hotel is part of a chain along the lines of Mercure, sharing similar values as to catering and quality of service; this much I discovered from a brochure I picked up in the lobby while waiting for the situation to unfold. It was just after six in the morning – midnight in Paris I thought, for no reason – but activities were already well under way, the breakfast room had just opened. I sat down on a bench; I was dazed, my ears were still buzzing violently and my stomach was beginning to hurt. From the way they were waiting, I was able to identify some of the group members. There were two girls of about twenty-five, pretty much bimbos – not bad-looking, all things considered – who cast a contemptuous eye over everyone. On the other hand, a couple of retirees - he could have been called *spirited*, she looked a bit more miserable – were looking around in wonderment at the interior décor of the hotel, a lot of gilding, mirrors and chandeliers. In the first hours in the life of a group, one generally observes only phatic sociability, characterised by the use of standard phrases and by limited emotional connection. According to Edmunds and White[1], the establishment of micro-groups can only be detected after the first excursion, sometimes after the first communal meal.

I started, on the point of passing out, lit a cigarette to rally my forces. The sleeping pills really were too strong, they were making me ill, but the ones I used to take couldn't get me to sleep any more; there was no obvious solution. The OAPs were slowly circling round each other. I got the feeling that the man was a bit full of himself; as he was waiting for someone specific with whom to exchange a smile, he turned an incipient smile on the world. They had to have been a couple of small shopkeepers in a previous life, that was the only explanation. Gradually, the members of the group made their way to the guide as their names were called, took their keys and went up to their rooms – in a word, they dispersed. It was possible, the guide announced in a resonant voice, for us to take breakfast now if we wished; otherwise we could relax in our rooms; it was entirely up to us. Whatever we decided, we were to meet back in the lobby for the trip along the *khlongs* at 2 p.m.

[1.] *Sightseeing Tours: A Sociological Approach*, Annals of Tourism Research, vol. 23, pp. 213–27 (1998)

The window in my room looked directly out onto the motorway. It was six-thirty. The traffic was very heavy, but the double glazing let in only a faint rumble. The street lights were off, the sun hadn't yet begun to reflect on the steel and glass; at this time of the day, the city was grey. I ordered a double espresso from room service, which I knocked back with a couple of Efferalgan, a Doliprane and a double dose of Oscillococcinium; then I lay down and tried to close my eyes.

Shapes moved slowly in a confined space; they made a low buzzing sound – like machines on a building site, or giant insects. In the background, a man armed with a small scimitar carefully checked the sharpness of the blade; he was wearing a turban and baggy white trousers. Suddenly, the air became red and muggy, almost liquid; from the drops of condensation forming before my eyes I became conscious that a pane of glass separated me from the scene. The man was on the ground now, immobilised by some invisible force. The machines from the building site had surrounded him; there were a couple of JCBs and a small bulldozer with caterpillar tracks. The JCBs lifted their hydraulic arms and brought their buckets down together on the man, immediately slicing his body into seven or eight pieces; his head, however, still seemed animated by a demonic life-force, an evil smile continued to crease his bearded face. The bulldozer in its turn advanced on the man, his head exploded like an egg; a spurt of brain and ground bone was splashed against the glass, a few inches from my face.

5

Essentially, tourism, as a search for meaning, with the ludic sociability it favours, the images it generates, is a graduated encoded and untraumatising apprehension system of the external, of otherness.

Rachid Amirou

I woke up at about noon, the air-conditioning was making a low buzzing sound; my headache was a little better. Lying across the king-size bed, I was aware of the mechanics of the tour, the issues at stake. The group, as yet amorphous, would transform itself into a vibrant community; as of this afternoon I would have to start positioning myself, for now I had to choose a pair of shorts for the trip along the *khlongs*. I opted for a longish pair in blue denim, not too tight, which I complemented with a *Radiohead* tee-shirt; then I stuffed some odds and ends into a knapsack. In the bathroom mirror, I contemplated myself disgustedly; my anxious bureaucratic face clashed horribly with what I was wearing; I looked exactly like what I was: a forty-something civil servant on holiday, trying to pretend he's young; it was pretty demoralising. I walked over to the window, opened the curtains wide. From the twenty-seventh floor, the view was extraordinary. The imposing mass of the Marriott Hotel rose up on the left like a chalk cliff, striated by horizontal black lines: rows of windows half-hidden behind balconies. The sun, at its zenith, harshly emphasised planes and ridges. Directly ahead, reflections multiplied themselves into infinity on a complex structure of cones and pyramids of bluish glass. On the horizon, the colossal concrete cubes of the Grand Plaza President were stacked on top of one another like the levels of a step pyramid. On the right, above the green, shimmering space of Lumphini Park, you could make out, like an ochre citadel, the angular towers of the Dusit Thani. The sky was a pure blue. Slowly I drank a Singha Gold while meditating on the notion of irreparability.

Downstairs, the guide was doing a sort of roll-call, so she could hand out breakfast vouchers. That's how I discovered the two bimbos were called Babette and Léa. Babette had curly blond hair – well, not naturally curly, it had probably been *waved*; she had beautiful breasts, the slut, clearly visible under her see-through top – an ethnic print from Trois Suisses, most likely. Her trousers, in the same fabric, were just as see-through; you could easily make out the white lace of her panties. Léa, very dark, was skinnier; she made up for this with the pretty curve of her bum, nicely accentuated by her black cycling shorts, and with a thrusting bust, the tips of which were squeezed into a bright yellow bustier. A tiny diamond adorned her slender navel. I stared attentively at the two sluts so that I could forget them forever.

The distribution of the vouchers continued. The guide, Sôn, called each of the group members by their first names; it made me sick. We were *adults*, for fuck's sake. I felt a ray of hope when she referred to the OAPs as 'Monsieur et Madame Lobligeois'; but immediately she added with a delighted smile 'Josette and René'. It seemed unbelievable, but true nevertheless. 'My name is René,' confirmed the old man, addressing himself to no one in particular. 'Tough . . .' I muttered. His wife shot him a look as if to say: 'Shut up, René, you're annoying everyone.' I suddenly realised that he reminded me of the character Monsieur Plus in the Bahlsen biscuit ads. It might have been him, too. I directed this question to his wife: had they, in the past, ever worked as extras? Absolutely not, she informed me, they had run a *charcuterie*. Yeah, that would probably fit too. So, this cheery jolly little fellow was a former pork-butcher (in Clamart, his wife explained); a modest establishment devoted to feeding the proletariat had been the previous theatre for his antics and quips.

Then there were two other couples, less distinctive, who seemed to be connected in some obscure way. Had they already been on holiday together? Had they met each other over breakfast? At this point in the tour, anything was possible. The first couple was also the more unappealing. The man looked a bit like a young Antoine Waechter, if you can imagine such a thing, but his hair was darker and he had a neatly trimmed beard; actually, he didn't so much look like Antoine Waechter as like Robin Hood, though he looked Swiss, or to be more precise, he had something of the Jura about him. All in all, he didn't look much like anything, but he seemed a real jerk. Not to mention his wife, wearing dungarees, serious, a good milker. It was inconceivable that these people had not yet reproduced, I thought; they'd probably left the child with their parents in Lon-le-Saulnier. The second couple, a little older, seemed rather less serene. Skinny and nervous, with a moustache, the man introduced himself to me as a naturopath, and, faced with my ignorance, went on to explain that he practised healing using plants or other natural means wherever possible. His wife, thin and curt, worked in social services, reintegrating, I don't know, first offenders or something in Alsace; they looked like they hadn't fucked for thirty years. The man seemed inclined to tell me about the benefits of natural medicines; but still dazed from this first encounter, I went and sat on a bench nearby. From where I sat, I could barely make out the last three members of the group, who were half hidden by the pork-butcher couple. There was some fifty-year-old thug called Robert, with a particularly harsh expression; a woman, of the same age, with curly black hair framing a face that was nasty, world-weary and flabby, whose name was Josiane; and another woman, a bit younger, almost unnoticeable, of about twenty-seven who followed Josiane with a sort of canine docility and whose name was Valérie. Anyway, I'll get back to them; I'll have far too much time to get back to them, I thought glumly as I walked towards the coach. I noticed that Sôn was still staring at her list of passengers. Her face was tense, words formed on her lips involuntarily; it was clear she was anxious, almost distraught. Counting, it appeared there were thirteen people in the group; and Thais are frequently superstitious, even more so than the Chinese: the numbering of storeys in a building or houses in a street often goes straight from twelve to fourteen, simply to avoid mentioning the number thirteen. I took a seat on the left-hand side about halfway down the coach. People establish points of reference pretty quickly on this kind of group outing: in order to feel relaxed, they need to find a place and stick to it, maybe leave some personal odds and ends around, actively inhabiting the space in some way.

To my great surprise, I saw Valérie take a seat beside me, even though the coach was about three-quarters empty. Two rows behind, Babette and Léa exchanged a couple of scornful words. They'd better calm down, those sluts. I discreetly fixed my attention on the young woman: she had long black hair, a nondescript face, a face that could be described as *unexceptional*: not pretty, not ugly, strictly speaking. After brief but intense consideration, I managed awkwardly: 'Not too hot?' 'No, no, here in the coach is fine,' she replied quickly, without smiling, relieved simply that I had started a conversation. Though what I'd said was remarkably stupid: actually, it was freezing in the bus. 'Have you been to Thailand before?' she went on by way of conversation. 'Yes, once.' She froze in a waiting posture, ready to listen to an interesting anecdote. Was I about to recount my previous trip to her? Maybe not right away. 'It was good . . .' I said eventually, adopting a friendly tone to compensate for the banality of what I was saying. She nodded in satisfaction. It was then that I realised that this young woman was in no way submissive to Josiane: she was just submissive *in general*, and maybe just ready to look for a new master; maybe she'd already had enough of Josiane – who, sitting two rows in front of us, was furiously leafing through the *Guide du Routard*, throwing dirty looks in our direction. Romance, romance.

Just past Payab Ferry Pier, the boat turned right into the Khlong Samsen and we entered a completely different world. Life had changed very little here since the nineteenth century. Rows of teak houses on stilts lined the canal; washing dried under awnings. Some of the women came to their windows to watch us pass, others stopped in the middle of their washing. Children splashed and bathed between the stilts; they waved at us excitedly. There was vegetation everywhere: our pirogue cut a path through masses of water-lilies and lotuses; teeming, intense life sprang up all around. Every free patch of earth, air or water seemed to be immediately filled with butterflies, lizards, carp. We were, Sôn told us, in the middle of the dry season; even so the air was completely, unrelentingly humid.

Valérie was sitting beside me; she seemed to be enveloped by a great sense of peace. She exchanged little waves with the old men who sat smoking their pipes on the balconies, the children bathing, the women at their washing. The ecologists from the Jura seemed at peace too; even the naturopaths seemed reasonably calm. Around us, only faint sounds and smiles. Valérie turned to me. I almost felt like taking her hand; for no particular reason, I didn't. The boat stopped moving entirely: we were rapt in the momentary eternity of a blissful afternoon; even Babette and Léa had shut up. They were a bit spaced out, to use the expression Léa later employed on the jetty.

While we were visiting the Temple of Dawn, I made a mental note to buy some more Viagra when I found a chemist that was open. On the way back, I found out that Valérie was Breton and that her parents had owned a farm in Trégorrois; I didn't really know what to say, myself. She seemed intelligent. I liked her soft voice, her meek Catholic fervour, the movement of her lips when she spoke; her mouth was obviously pretty hot, just ready to swallow the spunk of a true friend. 'It's been lovely, this afternoon . . .' I said finally in desperation. I had become too remote from people, I had lived alone too long, I didn't know how to go about it any more. 'Oh, yes, lovely . . .' she replied all the same; she wasn't demanding, she really was a nice girl. Even so, as soon as the coach arrived at the hotel, I ran straight to the bar.

Three cocktails later, I was beginning to regret my behaviour. I went out and walked round the lobby. It was 7 p.m.; no one from the group was around. For about four hundred baht, those who wished could have dinner and a show of 'traditional Thai dance'; those interested were to assemble at 8 p.m. Valérie would definitely be there. For my part, I had already had a vague experience of traditional Thai dance, on a trip with Kuoni three years previously: 'Classic Thailand, from the "Rose of the North" to the "City of Angels".' Not bad, really, but a bit expensive and terrifyingly cultural; everyone involved had at least a masters degree. The thirty-two positions of the Buddha in Ratanakosin statuary, Thai-Burmese style, Thai-Khmer, Thai-Thai, they didn't miss a thing. I had come back exhausted and I'd constantly felt ridiculous without a *Guide Bleu*. Right now, I was beginning to feel a serious need to fuck. I was wandering round the lobby, with a sense of mounting indecision, when I spotted a sign saying 'Health Club', indicating the floor below.

The entrance was lit by neon and a long rope of coloured lights. On the white background of an electric sign, three bikini-clad sirens, their breasts a little larger than life, proffered champagne flutes to prospective customers; there was a heavily stylised Eiffel Tower in the far distance – not quite the same concept as the fitness centres of Mercure hotels. I went in and ordered a bourbon at the bar. Behind a glass screen, a dozen girls turned towards me; some smiled alluringly, others didn't. I was the only customer. Despite the fact that the place was small, the girls wore numbered tags. I quickly chose number 7: firstly because she was cute, also because she wasn't engrossed in the programme on the television or deep in conversation with her neighbour. Indeed, when her name was called, she stood up with evident satisfaction. I offered her a coke at the bar, then we went to one of the rooms. Her name was Oôn, at least that was what I heard, and she was from the north somewhere, a little village near Chiang Mai. She was nineteen.

After we had taken a bath together, I lay down on the foam-covered mattress; I realised at once that I wasn't going to regret my choice. Oôn moved very nicely, very lithely; she'd used just enough soap. At one point, she at length caressed my buttocks with her breasts; it was a personal initiative, not all the girls did that. Her well-soaped pussy grazed my calf like a small hard brush. I was somewhat surprised to find I got hard almost immediately; when she turned me over and started to stroke my penis with her feet, I thought for a minute that I wouldn't be able to hold back. But with a supreme effort, tensing the abductor muscles in my thighs, I managed.

When she climbed on top of me on the bed, I thought I would be able to hold out for a long time yet; but I was quickly disillusioned. She might have been very young, but she knew what to do with her pussy. She started very gently with little contractions on the glans, then she slipped down an inch or so, squeezing a little harder. 'Oh no, Oôn, no! . . .' I cried. She burst out laughing, pleased with her power, then continued to slide down gently, contracting the walls of her vagina with long, slow compressions; all the while looking me in the eyes in obvious amusement. I came well before she got to the base of my penis.

Afterwards we chatted a bit, entwined on the bed; she didn't seem to be in any hurry to get back out on stage. She didn't have many clients, she told me; the hotel was aimed at groups of terminal cases, ordinary people, who were pretty much blasé. There were a lot of French people, but they didn't really seem to like body massage. Those who patronised the place were nice enough, but they were mostly Germans and Australians. A few Japanese too, but she didn't like them – they were weird, they always wanted to hit you or tie you up, or else they just sat there masturbating, staring at your shoes; it was pointless.

And what did she think about me? Not bad, but she would have liked it if I'd been able to hold out a little longer. 'Much need . . .' she said in English, gently shaking my sated penis between her fingers. Otherwise, she thought I seemed like a nice man. 'You look quiet . . .' she said. There she was somewhat mistaken, but I suppose it was true that she'd done a good job of calming me. I gave her three thousand baht, which, as far as I remembered, was a good price. From her reaction I could tell that, yes, it was a good price. 'Krôp khun khât!' she said with a big smile, bringing her hands together in front of her forehead. Then she took my hand and accompanied me to the exit; at the door we kissed each other on the cheeks several times.

As I climbed the stairs I ran into Josiane, who was apparently hesitating about whether to go downstairs. She had changed into an evening dress, a black shift dress with gold piping, but it didn't make her the least bit more appealing. Her plump, shrewd face was turned towards me, unblinkingly. I noticed that she'd washed her hair. She wasn't ugly, you might even say she was pretty – I had fancied Lebanese women like her – but her basic expression was unmistakably nasty. I could easily imagine her trotting out tired political positions; she hadn't a flicker of compassion that I could make out. I had nothing to say to her, either. I lowered my head. A little embarrassed, maybe, she spoke: 'Anything interesting downstairs?' I found her so infuriating that I nearly said: 'A bar full of hookers', but in the end I lied, it was easier. 'No, no, I don't know, some kind of beauty salon . . .'

'You didn't go to the dinner and show . . .' the bitch remarked. 'Neither did you,' I snapped back. This time her response was slower in coming, she became snotty. 'Oh no, I don't really like that sort of thing . . .' she went on, curving her arm like an actress playing Racine. 'It's all a bit touristy . . .' What did she mean by that? Everything is touristy. Once again, I stopped myself from putting my fist through her fucking face. Standing in the middle of the stairway, she was in my way; I had to show patience. A passionate letter-writer on occasion, St Jerome also knew how to display the virtues of Christian patience when circumstances called for it; that is why he is considered to be a great saint and a Doctor of the Church.

This 'traditional Thai dance' show was, according to her, just about Josette and René's level, people she thought of, in her heart of hearts, as white trash; I realised, rather uncomfortably, that she was looking for an ally. True, the tour would soon head deep inland, we would be divided into two tables at meals; it was time to take sides. 'Well . . .' I said, after a long silence. At that moment, like a miracle, Robert appeared above us. He was trying to get downstairs. I smoothly stepped aside, climbing a couple of steps. Just before rushing off to the restaurant, I turned back: Josiane, still motionless, was staring at Robert, who was walking briskly towards the massage parlour.

Babette and Léa were standing next to the trays of vegetables. I nodded in minimal acknowledgement before serving myself some water spinach. Obviously they too had decided that the 'traditional Thai dance' was *tacky*. As I went back to my table, I noticed the tarts were sitting a couple of feet away. Léa was wearing a *Rage Against the Machine* tee-shirt and a pair of tight denim shorts, Babette something unstructured in which different coloured stripes of silk alternated with transparent fabric. They were chattering enthusiastically, talking about different hotels in New York. Marrying one of those girls, I thought, that would be *radically* hideous. Did I still have time to change tables? No, it would have been a bit obvious. I took a chair opposite so that at least I could sit with my back on them, I bolted my meal and went back up to my room.

A cockroach appeared just as I was about to get into the bath. It was just the right time for a cockroach to make an appearance in my life; couldn't have been better. It scuttled quickly across the porcelain, the little bugger; I looked around for a slipper, but actually I knew my chances of squashing him were small. What was the point in trying? And what good was Oôn, in spite of her marvellously elastic vagina? We were already doomed. Cockroaches copulate gracelessly, with no apparent pleasure; but they also do it repeatedly and their genetic mutations are rapid and efficient. There is absolutely nothing we can do about cockroaches.

Before getting undressed, I once more paid homage to Oôn and to all Thai prostitutes. They didn't have an easy job, those girls; they probably didn't come across a good guy all that often, someone with an okay physique who was honestly looking for nothing more than mutual orgasm. Not to mention the Japanese – I shivered at the thought, and grabbed my *Guide du Routard*. Babette and Léa could never have been Thai prostitutes, I thought, they weren't worthy of it. Valérie, maybe; that girl had something, she managed to be both maternal and a bit of a slut, potentially at least, I mean; for the moment she was just a nice friendly, serious girl. Intelligent, too. I definitely liked Valérie. I masturbated gently so I could read in peace, producing just a couple of drips.

If it was intended in principle to prepare you for a trip to Thailand, in practice the *Guide du Routard* had strong reservations about, and as early as the preface, felt duty-bound to denounce, sexual tourism, that 'repulsive slavery'. All in all, these backpacking *routards* were belly-aching bastards whose goal was to spoil every little pleasure on offer to tourists, whom they despised. In fact, they seemed to like themselves more than anything else, if one was to go by the sarcastic little phrases scattered throughout the book, in the style of: 'Ah, my friends, if you had been there back in the hippy days! . . .' The most excruciating thing was probably their stern, dogmatic, peremptory tone, quivering with repressed indignation: 'We're far from prudish, but Pattaya we don't like. Enough is enough.' A bit further on, they laid into 'pot-bellied Westerners' who strolled around with little Thai girls; it made them 'literally puke'. Humanitarian Protestant cunts, that's what they were, they and the 'cool bunch of mates who had helped to make this book possible', their nasty little faces smugly plastered all over the back cover. I flung the book hard across the room, missing the Sony television by a whisker, and wearily picked up *The Firm*, by John Grisham. It was an American bestseller, one of the best; meaning one of those that had sold the most copies. The hero was a young lawyer with a bright future, a talented, good-looking boy who worked eighty hours a week; not only was this shit so obviously a proto-screenplay it was obscene, but you had the feeling the author had already given some thought to the casting, the part had obviously been written for Tom Cruise. The hero's wife wasn't bad either, even if she didn't work eighty hours a week; but in this case, Nicole Kidman wouldn't fit, it wasn't a part for someone with curly hair; more like someone with a blow-dry. Thank God the lovebirds didn't have any children, which meant we were spared a number of gruelling scenes. It was a suspense thriller, well, there was a little suspense: as early as Chapter Two, it was obvious that the guys running the firm were bastards, and there was no way the hero was going to die at the end; nor his wife for that matter. But, in the meantime, to prove he wasn't joking, the author was going to sacrifice a couple of sympathetic minor characters; all that was left was to find out which ones. That might make it worth a read. Maybe it would be the hero's father: his business was going through a bad patch, he was having trouble adjusting to the new matrix management; I had a feeling that this would be his last Thanksgiving.

6

Valérie had spent the early years of her life in Tréméven, a hamlet a few kilometres north of Guingamp. In the '70s and early '80s, the government and local councils had nurtured an ambition to create a massive production centre for pork products in Brittany, capable of rivalling those of Britain or Denmark. Encouraged to adopt intensive farming methods, the young farmers – including Valérie's father – became heavily indebted to the Crédit Agricole. In 1984, pork prices began to collapse; Valérie was eleven years old. She was a well-behaved girl, a bit lonely, a good student; she was about to enter her *second year* at the secondary school in Guingamp. Her older brother, also a good student, had just passed his *bac*; he had enrolled in preparatory classes in agronomy at the lycée in Rennes.

Valérie remembered Christmas 1984; her father had spent the day with the accountant from the National

Farmers' Union. He was silent for much of Christmas dinner. During dessert, after two glasses of champagne, he spoke to his son. 'I can hardly recommend that you take over the farm,' he said. 'For twenty years now I've been getting up at dawn and finishing the day at eight or nine o'clock; your mother and I, we've barely had a holiday. I'd be as well off selling the place now, with all the machinery and the farm buildings, and investing the money in tourist property: I could spend the rest of my days working on my tan.'

In the years that followed, pork prices continued to plummet. There were farmers' protests, marked by a desperate violence; tons of slurry were dumped on the Esplanade des Invalides, a number of pigs were gutted in front of the Palais Bourbon. At the end of 1986, the government announced emergency relief followed by a recovery plan for pig-breeders. In April 1987, Valérie's father sold his farm – for a little more than four million francs. With the money from the sale, he bought a large apartment in Saint-Quay-Portrieux, where he planned to live, and three studio flats in Torremolinos. He had a million francs left over which he invested in unit trusts and was even able – it was his childhood dream – to buy a small yacht. Sadly, and with some disgust, he signed the farm bill of sale. The new owner was a young guy, about twenty-three, single, from Lannion, just out of agricultural college; he still believed in the plans to revive the industry. Valérie's father was forty-eight, his wife, forty-seven; they had dedicated the best years of their lives to a hopeless task. They lived in a country where, compared to speculative investment, investment in production brought little return; he understood that now. In their first year, the rents from the studio flats brought in more money than all his years of work. He took up crosswords, took the yacht out into the bay, sometimes fishing. His wife found it easier to adapt to their new life and was a great support to him; she started to want to read again, to go to the cinema, to go out.

At the time of the sale, Valérie was fourteen, she was just starting to wear makeup; in the bathroom mirror she watched her breasts as they gradually swelled. The night before they moved out, she spent a long time walking around the farm buildings. There were still a dozen pigs in the main sty, which came up to her grunting softly. They were being picked up that night by a wholesaler and would be slaughtered in a few days time.

The summer that followed was a strange period. Compared to Tréméven, Saint-Quay-Portrieux was almost a small town. When she walked out of her door, she couldn't lie on the grass, letting her thoughts float with the clouds, flow with the river. Among the holiday-makers there were boys, who turned to look at her as she passed; she never really managed to relax. Towards the end of August, she met Bérénice, a girl from the second-ary school at Saint-Brieuc. Bérénice was a year older than she, she already wore makeup and designer skirts; she had a pretty, angular face and very long hair which was an extraordinary strawberry blond. They got into the habit of going to the beach at Saint-Marguerite together; they would get changed in Valérie's room before they set off. One afternoon, as she was taking off her bra, Valérie noticed Bérénice staring at her breasts. She knew that she had superb breasts, round and high, so swollen and firm that they looked artificial. Bérénice stretched out her hand, traced the curve and the nipple. Valérie opened her mouth and closed her eyes as Bérénice's lips approached her own; she abandoned herself completely to the kiss. She was already wet when Bérénice slipped a hand into her panties. Impatiently she took them off, fell back on the bed and parted her thighs. Bérénice knelt in front of her, placed her mouth over her pussy. Her stomach quivered with warm spasms, she felt her mind floating in the endless space of the sky; she had never imagined pleasure like this could exist.

Every day until they went back to school, they did it again. Once in the afternoon, before they went to the beach; then they would lie side by side in the sunshine. Little by little, Valérie would feel desire mounting in her skin, she would take off her top so that Bérénice could see her breasts. They would practically run back to the bedroom and make love a second time.

From their first week back at school, Bérénice began to distance herself from Valérie, avoided walking back from school with her; shortly afterwards she started going out with a boy. Valérie accepted the separation without any real sorrow – that's the way things go. She had taken to

masturbating every morning when she woke up. Each
time, in a few short minutes, she would reach orgasm; it
was something marvellous, something simple happening
within her and which began her day with joy. About boys
she had more reservations; having bought a couple of
issues of *Hot Video* at the station kiosk, she knew what to
expect from their anatomy, their organs, various sexual
practices; but she felt a slight repugnance for their body
hair, their muscles; their skin looked thick and not at all
soft. The brownish, wrinkled skin of their balls, the
brutally anatomical look of the glans when the foreskin
was retracted, red, shiny . . . none of these things was
especially attractive. In the end, however, she slept with a
boy in his final year, a tall blond guy, after spending the
night in a club in Paimpol; she did not find it particularly
pleasurable. She tried again several times with others while
she was in her last couple of years at school. It was easy to
seduce boys: all you had to do was wear a short skirt, cross
your legs, wear a low-cut or a see-through blouse that
showed off your breasts. None of these experiences
proved especially conclusive. Intellectually, she could
understand the triumphant yet gentle feeling some girls
experienced when they felt a cock pushing deep into their
pussies; but she herself felt nothing of the sort. It had to be
said that condoms didn't help; the sound the latex made,
flaccid and repetitive, constantly brought her down to
earth, prevented her from drifting into the nebulous
infinity of sensual pleasure. By the time she sat her *bac*, she
had more or less given up.

Ten years later, she still hadn't really started again, she thought sadly as she woke in the bedroom of the Bangkok Palace. It was not quite daylight. She turned on the overhead light and contemplated her body in the mirror. Her breasts were as firm as ever, they hadn't changed since she was seventeen. Her arse was amazingly round too, without a trace of fat; unquestionably she had a very beautiful body. Nonetheless, she slipped on a baggy sweatshirt and a shapeless pair of shorts before going downstairs to breakfast. Before she closed the door, she glanced at herself one last time in the mirror: her face was very average, a little rounded, nice but nothing more than that; the same was true of her limp, black hair which fell untidily on her shoulders; and her brown eyes weren't much of an asset either. No doubt she could have made more of herself, a bit of makeup, a different hairstyle, a trip to the beauty salon. Most women her age spent at least a couple of hours a week there; she didn't think it would make much difference in her case. What she was lacking, essentially, was the desire to seduce.

We left the hotel at seven; the traffic was already heavy. Valérie gave me a little nod and took a seat in the same row on the other side of the aisle. No one in the bus was talking. Slowly, the grey megalopolis woke up; mopeds carrying couples, sometimes with a baby in the mother's arms, weaved between the crowded buses. A light haze still hung in some of the alleys by the river. Soon the sun would burst through the morning clouds, it would start to get hot. At Nonthaburi, the urban fabric began to fray and we could see the first rice fields. Buffalo standing motionless in the mud followed the bus with their eyes exactly as cows would do. The ecologists from the Jura seemed a bit restless; they'd probably wanted to take a couple of pictures of the buffalo.

The first stop was Kanchanaburi, which all the guide books agree is a lively, animated city. To the Michelin, it's a 'marvellous starting point from which to explore the surrounding region'; the *Guide du Routard*, on the other hand, considers it a 'good base camp'. The tour programme indicated a journey of several miles along the 'railway of death' which snaked alongside the River Kwai. I'd never really got to the bottom of this River Kwai story, so I tried to pay attention to what the guide was saying. Luckily René, Michelin Guide in hand, was following the story, always ready to correct this point or that. In short, after they entered the war in 1941, the Japanese decided to build a railway connecting Singapore and Burma, with the long-term objective of invading India. This railway had to cross Malaysia and Thailand. Come to think of it, what were the Thais doing during the Second World War? Well, now you come to mention it, not a lot. They were 'neutral', Sôn informed me diplomatically. In reality, René explained, they'd signed a military pact with the Japanese without actually declaring war on the Allies. That was the way of wisdom. Demonstrating, once again, the celebrated 'subtlety of mind' which had made it possible for them to spend two centuries caught in a vice-like grip between the colonial powers of France and England without actually surrendering to either, and to remain the only country in South-East Asia never to have been colonised.

Be that as it may, by 1942 work had begun on the section along the River Kwai, marshalling sixty thousand English, Australian, New Zealand and American prisoners of war, as well as 'countless' Asian forced labourers. In October 1943, the railway was completed, but sixteen thousand of POW's had died – from a variety of causes including lack of food, the hostile climate and the innate viciousness of the Japanese. Shortly afterwards, an allied bombing raid destroyed the bridge over the River Kwai, a crucial element of the infrastructure – thereby rendering the railway completely useless. In short, a lot of people copped it for very little. Things have changed little since then – it is still impossible to get a decent rail connection between Singapore and Delhi.

It was in a state of mild distress that I began the visit to the JEATH Museum, built to commemorate the appalling suffering of the allied POWs. Certainly, I thought, what had happened was thoroughly regrettable; but, let's face it, worse things happened during the Second World War. I couldn't help thinking that if the prisoners had been Polish or Russian there would have been a lot less fuss.

A little later, we were required to endure a visit to the cemetery for the allied prisoners of war – those who had, in a manner of speaking, made the ultimate sacrifice. There were white crosses in neat rows, all identical; the place radiated a profound monotony. It reminded me of Omaha Beach, which hadn't really moved me either, had actually reminded me, in fact, of a contemporary art installation. 'In this place,' I said to myself, with a feeling of sadness which I felt was somewhat inadequate, 'In this place, a bunch of morons died for the sake of democracy.' That said, the cemetery at the River Kwai was much smaller, you could even imagine counting the graves; actually, I gave up pretty quickly. 'There can't be sixteen thousand graves . . .' I concluded aloud. 'You're quite right,' René informed me, still armed with his Michelin Guide. 'The number of dead is estimated at sixteen thousand; but the cemetery contains only five hundred and eighty-two graves. They are considered to be (he read, running his finger under the words) the *five hundred and eighty-two martyrs to democracy*.'

When I got my third gold star at the age of ten, I went to a pâtisserie to stuff my face with *crêpes aux Grand Marnier*. It was a little private party; I had no friends with whom I could share my joy. I was staying with my father in Chamonix, as I did every year at that time. He was an alpine guide and a committed mountaineer. His friends were like him, men who were brave and manly; I never felt comfortable around them. I've never really felt comfortable around men. I was eleven the first time a girl ever showed me her pussy; I was immediately filled with wonder, I adored this small, strange, cleft organ. She didn't have much pubic hair, she was about the same age as me; her name was Martine. For a long time, she stood with her thighs apart, holding her knickers to one side so I could look; but when I tried to move my hand towards it, she got scared, she ran off. It all seemed very recent to me; I didn't feel that I had changed much. My enthusiasm for pussy had not waned, in fact I saw in it one of my few remaining recognisable, fully human qualities; as for the rest, I didn't really know anymore.

A short while after we had boarded the coach again, Sôn spoke. We were now heading towards our accommodation for the night, which, she was keen to emphasise, was of exceptional quality. No TV, no video. No electricity, candles. No bathroom, the river. No mattresses, mats. Absolutely back to nature. Back to nature, I mentally noted, seemed to consist principally of privations; the ecologists from the Jura – who, I had discovered on the train – against my will – were called Éric and Sylvie – were drooling with excitement. 'French cuisine tonight,' concluded Sôn for no apparent reason. 'We now eat Thai. Small restaurant too, beside river.'

The place was charming. Trees shaded the tables. Near the entrance was a sunlit pool full of turtles and frogs. I watched the frogs for a long time; once again, I was struck by the extraordinary abundance of life in the tropics. White fish swam between two pools. On the surface were water-lilies and water-fleas. Insects continuously settled on the water-lilies. Turtles observed all this with a placidity characteristic of their species.

Sôn came to let me know that the meal had begun. I walked towards the dining room by the river. They had laid two tables for six; all the places were taken. I glanced around me, a little panicked, but René quickly came to my rescue. 'No problem! Come and join our table!' he called generously, 'We can add another place on the end.' So I sat at what was apparently the *established couples* table: the ecologists from the Jura, the naturopaths – who, I now discovered, answered to the names of Albert and Suzanne – and the two senior citizens and former pork-butchers. This arrangement, I quickly came to believe, was not based on any real affinity but on the urgent situation which presented itself when they were shown to the tables; the couples had instinctively banded together; all in all, lunch was nothing more than an *observation round*.

The conversation first moved to the subject of massage, a subject which seemed dear to the naturopaths. The previous evening, Albert and Suzanne, forsaking traditional dance, had enjoyed an excellent back massage. René smiled a lewd smile; Albert's expression quickly let him know that his attitude was completely inappropriate. Traditional Thai massage, he thundered, had nothing whatever to do with who knows what kind of practices; it was the expression of a centuries-old, perhaps millennia-old, civilisation and, as it happened, was completely consistent with Chinese teachings on the points of acupuncture. They practised it themselves at their surgery in Montbéliard, without, naturally, attaining the dexterity of Thai practitioners; the night before, they had had, he concluded, an excellent lesson. Éric and Sylvie listened, fascinated. René coughed slightly in embarrassment; it was true that the Montbéliard couple did not, in fact, exude even the slightest impression of lewdness. Who could possibly have proposed the idea that France was the country of *debauchery* and *libertinage*. France was a sinister country, utterly sinister and bureaucratic.

'I had a back massage too, but the girl finished on my balls . . .' I interrupted without much conviction. Since I was chewing cashew nuts at the time, no one heard, with the exception of Sylvie who shot me a horrified look. I took a mouthful of beer and looked her straight in the eyes, not in the least embarrassed: was this girl even capable of *correctly* handling a cock? That remained to be seen. In the meantime, I waited for my coffee.

'It's true they're cute, the little girls . . .' commented Josette, taking a slice of papaya and adding to the general unease. The coffee was slow in coming. What do you do at the end of a meal if you're not allowed to smoke? I sat quietly as the boredom increased. We concluded the conversation, not without difficulty, with some remarks about the weather.

I saw my father once again, confined to his bed, struck down by sudden depression – a terrifying thing in such an active man; his mountaineering friends stood around awkwardly, powerless in the face of the disease. The reason he played so much sport, he told me once, was to stupefy himself, to stop himself thinking. He had succeeded: I was convinced that he had managed to go through his whole life without ever really questioning the human condition.

7

On the bus, Sôn continued her commentary. The border region which we were about to enter was partly populated by Burmese refugees of Karen origin, but this should present no problems. Karen tribe good, deemed Sôn, brave, children good study in school, no problem. Nothing like some of the northern tribes, which we would not have the opportunity to meet on our tour; according to her, we weren't missing much. Particularly in the case of the Akha tribe, which she seemed to have something against. In spite of the government's best efforts, the Akhas seemed incapable of giving up growing opium poppies, their traditional activity. Akhas bad, Sôn stressed forcefully: apart grow poppy and pick fruit, know how to do nothing; children not good study in school. Many money spend for them, no result. They are completely useless, she concluded, demonstrating her consummate ability to summarise.

So, as we arrived at the hotel, I watched these famous

Karens curiously, as they busied themselves by the river's edge. Seen close up, I mean without machine-guns, they didn't seem particularly nasty; the most obvious thing about them was that they clearly adored their elephants. Bathing in the river, scrubbing the backs of their elephants seemed to be their greatest pleasure. It's true that these weren't Karen rebels but ordinary Karens – those who had fled the combat zone because they were sick of the whole thing and who were more or less indifferent to the cause of Karen independence.

A brochure in my hotel room gave me some information about the history of the resort, which was the product of a wonderful human adventure: that of Bertrand Le Moal, backpacker *avant la lettre* who, having fallen in love with this place, had 'laid down his pack' here at the end of the 60s. With furious energy, and the help of his Karen friends, little by little he had built this 'ecological paradise', which an international clientele could now enjoy.

It's true the place was superb. Small, beautifully sculpted chalets made of teak connected by a pathway decked with flowers, overhung the river, which you could feel pulse under your feet. The hotel was situated at the bottom of a steep valley, the sides of which were shrouded in dense jungle. When I stepped out on to the terrace there was a profound silence. It took me a moment or two to understand why: all at once every bird had stopped singing. It was the hour when the jungle readies itself for night. What sort of large predators would there be in a jungle like that? Not many, probably – two or three leopards – but there was probably no shortage of snakes and spiders. The light was fading fast. On the far bank, a lone monkey leaped from tree to tree; he gave a short call. You could feel he was fretful, anxious to rejoin his group.

I went back into the room, lit the candles. The furniture was minimal: a teak table, two rustic wooden bedsteads, sleeping bags and mats. I spent a quarter of an hour methodically rubbing myself with Cinq sur Cinq insect repellent. Rivers are all very well, but you know what they're like: they attract mosquitoes. There was a bar of citronella too, which you could melt; it seemed to me a worthwhile precaution.

When I came down to dinner, it was completely dark; garlands of multicoloured lights were strung between the houses. So there *was* electricity in the village, I noted, they simply hadn't thought it necessary to install it in the rooms. I stopped for a moment and leaned on the guard-rail to look down at the river; the moon was up and shimmered on the water. Opposite, you could vaguely make out the dark mass of the jungle; from time to time, the raucous cry of a nocturnal bird could be heard.

Human groups of more than three people have a tendency, apparently, to split into two hostile sub-groups. Dinner was served on a pontoon in the middle of the river; this time, the tables had been laid for eight. The ecologists and the naturopaths were already installed at one table; the former pork-butchers were currently all alone at the second. What could have brought about the rift? Maybe the massage discussion at lunch, which, let's face it, hadn't gone too well. In addition, that morning, Suzanne, soberly dressed in a white linen tunic and trousers – nicely cut to emphasise her angular features – had burst out laughing when she saw Josette's flower-print dress. Whatever the reason, the divisions had begun. In a rather cowardly move, I slowed my pace so as to let Lionel, my neighbour from the plane, who also had the neighbouring chalet, overtake me. He made his choice quickly, barely aware of doing so; I didn't even get the impression it was a choice based on elective affinity, more a sort of class solidarity (since he worked at Gaz de France and was therefore a civil servant, while the others had been small shopkeepers) a solidarity based on level of education. René welcomed us with evident relief. In any case, our decision was not critical at this stage of the game: had we joined the others we would have forcefully confirmed the isolation of the former pork-butchers; whereas this way, we were really only balancing out the table numbers.

Babette and Léa arrived shortly after and without a second thought sat at the neighbouring table.

Quite some time later – our first courses had already been served – Valérie appeared on the edge of the pontoon; she looked around her uncertainly. At the other table, there were still two empty places beside Babette and Léa. She hesitated a little longer, made a little start and came and sat on my left.

Josiane had taken even longer than usual getting ready; she must have had trouble putting on her makeup by candlelight. Her black velvet dress wasn't bad, a bit low cut, but not excessive. She also hesitated for a moment, then came and sat opposite Valérie.

Robert arrived last, a little unsteady. He'd probably been boozing before the meal; I'd seen him with a bottle of Mekong earlier. He dropped heavily on to the bench next to Valérie. A short but fearful cry went up from somewhere close by in the jungle; perhaps some small mammal had just breathed its last.

Sôn moved between the tables to check that everything was okay, that we had all settled in nicely. She was having dinner elsewhere, with the driver – a less than democratic arrangement which had already earned Josiane's disapproval at lunchtime. But, basically, I think it suited her just fine, even if she had nothing against us: despite her best efforts, she seemed to find long discussions in French a bit tiring.

At the next table the conversation purred happily, discussing the beauty of the location, the joy of being at one with nature, far from civilisation, the essential values, etc. 'Yeah, it's top,' confirmed Léa. 'And y'know, we're really bang in the middle of jungle . . . I can't believe it.'

Our table was having a little more difficulty finding common ground. Opposite me, Lionel was eating placidly, making no effort whatsoever. I glanced ner-vously from side to side. At one point I saw a big bearded guy coming out of the kitchens and shouting angrily at the waiters; it must be none other than the famous Bertrand Le Moal. To my mind, his greatest achievement so far was to have taught the Karens the recipe for *gratin dauphinois*. It was delicious, and the roast pork was perfectly done, crisp but tender. 'All we're missing is a drop of wine . . .' René said sadly. Josiane pursed her lips scornfully. One didn't need to ask what she thought about French tourists who couldn't leave the country without their drop of wine. A little awkwardly, Valérie came to René's defence. With Thai food, she said, you never felt the need; but right now, a little wine would be rather appropriate. In any case, she herself only drank water.

'If you go abroad,' Josiane barked, 'It is in order to eat the *local* food and to observe *local* customs! . . . If not, you might as well stay at home.'

'I agree!' shouted Robert. She paused, cut off in midflow, and looked at him hatefully.

'Sometimes I find it a bit too spicy . . .' confessed Josette timidly. 'It doesn't seem to bother you . . .' she said, addressing me, probably to ease the tension.

'No, no, I love it. The spicier it is, the better I like it. Even in Paris I eat Chinese all the time,' I hastily responded. And so the conversation was able to move on to the Chinese restaurants that had so multiplied in Paris just recently. Valérie liked to have lunch in them, they were very reasonable, much better than eating fast food, and probably much healthier too. Josiane had nothing to say on the subject, she had a staff cafeteria; as for Robert, he probably thought the subject was beneath him. In short, everything proceeded more or less peacefully until dessert.

It all came to a head over the sticky rice. It was a light golden colour, flavoured with cinnamon – I think the recipe was original. Taking the bull by the horns, Josiane decided to tackle the question of sex tourism head on. For her, it was absolutely disgusting, there was no other word for it. It was a scandal that the Thai government tolerated such things. The international community had to do something. Robert listened to her with a half-smile which I didn't think boded well. It was scandalous, but it was hardly surprising; it was obvious that most of these places (brothels, that was the only word for them) were owned by generals; that told you what kind of protection they had.

'I'm a general . . .' interrupted Robert. She was speechless, her lower jaw dropped miserably. 'No, no, I'm only joking . . .' he said with a slight grimace. 'I've never even been in the army.'

She did not find this funny in the least. She took a moment to pull herself together, then launched back into the fray with renewed energy.

'It's absolutely shameful that fat yobs can just come over here and take advantage of these girls' poverty with impunity. Of course you know they all come from the north and the northeast, the poorest regions of the whole country.'

'Not all of them . . .' he objected. 'Some of them are from Bangkok.'

'It's sexual slavery!' screamed Josiane, who hadn't heard. 'There's no other way to describe it! . . .'

I yawned a little. She shot me a black look, but went on, calling on the others to give their verdict: 'Don't you think it's disgraceful that any fat old yob can come over here and have it off with these kids for next to nothing?'

'It's hardly next to nothing . . .' I protested modestly. 'I paid three thousand baht, which is about what you'd pay in France.' Valérie turned and looked at me, surprised. 'You paid a bit over the odds . . .' observed Robert. 'Still, if the girl was worth it . . .'

Josiane's whole body was trembling, she was starting to unsettle me a little. 'Well!' she shrieked in a very shrill voice, 'It makes me sick, that any fat pig can pay to shove his cock into a kid!'

'Nobody's forcing you to come with me, madam . . .' Robert replied calmly.

She got up, trembling, her plate of rice in her hand. All conversation at the next table had stopped. I really thought she was going to chuck the plate in his face, and in the end I think it was only fear that stopped her. Robert looked at her with the most serious expression, the muscles under his polo-neck tense. He didn't look like the sort of person to let himself be pushed around; I could well imagine him punching her. She viciously slammed down her plate, which broke into three pieces, turned on her heel and vanished into the darkness, walking quickly towards the chalets.

'Tsk . . .' he said softly.

Valérie was stuck between him and me; he stood up gracefully, walked around the table and sat where Josiane had been sitting, in case Valérie, too, wished to leave the table. She, however, did nothing; at that moment, the waiter brought the coffees. After she had taken two sips, Valérie turned to me again. 'So is it true you've paid for girls? . . .' she asked gently. Her tone was intrigued, but without any real reproach.

'They're not as poor as all that, these girls,' added Robert; 'they can afford mopeds and clothes, some of them even have their tits done. It's not cheap getting your tits done. It's true they help their parents out, too . . .' he concluded thoughtfully.

At the next table, after a few whispered comments, everyone quickly left – doubtless out of solidarity. We remained the sole masters of the place, in a sense. The moon now bathed the whole pontoon, which gleamed a little. 'Are they that good, those little masseuses? . . .' asked René dreamily.

'Ah, monsieur!' exclaimed Robert, deliberately grandiloquent, but, it seemed to me, basically sincere, 'they are marvellous, positively marvellous! And you haven't been to Pattaya yet. It's a resort on the east coast . . .' he went on, '. . . completely dedicated to lust and debauchery. The Americans were the first to go there, during the Vietnam war; after that, a lot of English and Germans; now, you get a lot of Russians and Poles. There, they have something for everyone, they cater for all tastes: homosexuals, heterosexuals, transvestites . . . It's Sodom and Gomorrah combined. Actually, it's better, because they've got lesbians, too.'

'Aaah, aaah . . .' the former pork-butcher seemed thoughtful. His wife yawned placidly, excused herself and turned to her husband; she clearly wanted to go to bed.

'In Thailand,' Robert concluded, 'everyone can have what they desire, and everyone can have something good. People will talk to you about Brazilian girls, or about Cubans. I'm well-travelled, monsieur, I have travelled for pleasure and I have no hesitation in telling you: in my opinion, Thai girls are the best lovers in the world.'

Sitting opposite, Valérie listened to him earnestly. She disappeared shortly after, followed by Josette and René. Lionel, who hadn't said a word all evening, also got to his feet; I did likewise. I didn't really feel like pursuing a conversation with Robert. So I left him alone in the dark, a picture of apparent sobriety, ordering a second cognac. He seemed to have a sophisticated and subtle intelligence; unless, of course, he was a relativist, which always gives one the impression of complexity and subtlety. In front of my chalet, I said good night to Lionel. The atmosphere was heavy with the buzzing of insects; I was more or less sure that I wouldn't get a wink of sleep.

I pushed the door and lit the candle again, more or less resigned to continue reading *The Firm*. Mosquitoes flew close, some of them charred their wings in the flame, their bodies sank into the melted wax; not one of them settled on me. Despite the fact that I was filled to the dermis with nutritious, delicious blood, they automatically turned tail, unable to break through the olfactory barrier of carbonic dimethylperoxide. Roche-Nicolas laboratories, the creators of Cinq sur Cinq, were to be congratulated. I blew out the candle, relit it, watching the ever-more teeming ballet of these sordid little flying machines. On the other side of the partition, I could hear Lionel snoring gently through the night. I got up, put another block of citronella on to melt, then went for a piss. A round hole had been made in the floor of the bathroom; it flowed straight into the river. You could hear the lapping of the water and the sound of fins; I tried not to think about what might be down there. Just as I was going back to bed, Lionel let out a long series of farts. 'Too right, my boy!' I commended him enthusiastically. 'As Martin Luther said, there's nothing like farting in your sleeping bag!' My voice resounded strangely in the dark, above the murmuring of the river and the persistent drone of the insects. Simply being able to hear the real world was a torment. 'The kingdom of heaven is like unto a cotton bud!' I shouted again into the night. 'Let he who has ears to hear, hear!' In his bed, Lionel turned over and moaned gently without waking. I didn't have much in the way of choice: I'd have to take a sleeping pill.

8

Carried by the current, tufts of grass floated downriver. The birdsong started up again, rising from the light mist which swathed the jungle. Far off to the south, at the mouth of the valley, the strange contours of the Burmese mountains were silhouetted in the distance. I had seen these curved, bluish forms before, but cut through with sudden indentations. Perhaps in the landscapes of the Italian primitives, on a visit to a museum when I was at school. The group was not awake yet; the temperature was still pleasant at this hour. I had slept very badly.

After the disaster of the previous evening, a certain benevolence floated around the breakfast tables. Josette and René seemed to be in good form; on the other hand the ecologists from the Jura were in a terrible state, I noticed, as they shambled in. The proletariat of a previous generation, who had no hang-ups about enjoying modern comforts when they were available, proved to be much more resilient in truly uncomfortable circumstances than their offspring, who championed 'ecological' principles. Éric and Sylvie clearly hadn't got a wink all night; in addition, Sylvie was completely covered in red blisters.

'Yes, the mosquitoes really got me,' she confirmed bitterly.

'I've got some soothing lotion if you want. It's very good; I can go and get it.'

'That would be nice, thanks; but let's have coffee first.'

The coffee was revolting, weak, almost undrinkable; from that point of view at least, we were working to American standards. The young couple looked completely bloody stupid, it almost pained me to see their 'ecological paradise' crumbling before their eyes; but I had a feeling that everything was going to cause me pain today. I looked to the south again. 'I'm told Burma is very beautiful,' I said in a low voice, mostly to myself. Sylvie solemnly agreed: it was indeed, very beautiful, she'd also heard as much; that said, she *forbade* herself from going to Burma. It was impossible to think that one's money would go to supporting a dictatorship like that. Yes, yes, I thought, money. 'Human rights are extremely important,' she exclaimed almost despairingly. When people talk about 'human rights', I usually get the impression that they're being ironic; but that wasn't true in this case, at least I don't think so.

'Personally, I stopped going to Spain *after* the death of Franco,' interrupted Robert, taking a seat at our table. I hadn't seen him arrive. He seemed to be in excellent form, his formidable ability to infuriate well-rested. He informed us that he'd gone to bed dead drunk and consequently had slept like a log. He had almost chucked himself in the river a couple of times on his way back to the chalet; but in the end it hadn't happened. '*Insh'allah.*' he concluded in a booming voice.

After this parody of a breakfast, Sylvie walked back with me to my room. On the way, we met Josiane. She was serious, withdrawn and did not even look at us; she seemed to be far from the road to forgiveness. I discovered that she taught literature in civvy street, as René amusingly put it; I wasn't a bit surprised. She was exactly the kind of bitch who'd made me give up studying literature many years before.

I gave Sylvie the tube of soothing lotion. 'I'll bring it straight back,' she said. 'You can keep it, I don't think we'll come across any more mosquitoes; as far as I know they hate the seaside.' She thanked me, walked to the door, hesitated, turned round: 'Surely you don't approve of the sexual exploitation of children! . . .' she exclaimed anguishedly. I was expecting something of the kind. I shook my head and answered wearily: 'There's not that much child prostitution in Thailand. No more than in Europe, in my opinion.' She nodded, not really convinced, and walked out. In fact, I had access to rather more detailed information, courtesy of a strange publication called *The White Book*, which I'd bought for my previous trip. It was apparently published – no author's or publisher's name was given – by an association called Inquisition 2000. Under the pretence of denouncing sexual tourism, it gave all the addresses, country by country – each revealing chapter was preceded by a short and vehement paragraph calling for respect for the Divine plan and the reintroduction of the death penalty for sex offenders. On the question of paedophilia, *The White Book* was unequivocal: it formally advised against Thailand, which no longer had anything to recommend it. It was much better to go to the Philippines or, better still, to Cambodia – the journey might be dangerous, but it was worth the effort.

The Khmer Kingdom was at its apogee in the twelfth century, the era in which Angkor Wât was built. After that, it pretty much fell apart; since then Thailand's principal enemy had been the Burmese. In 1351, King Ramathibodi I founded the village of Ayutthaya. In 1402, his son Ramathibodi II invaded the declining Angkor empire. Thirty-two successive sovereigns of Ayutthaya marked their reigns by building Buddhist temples and palaces. In the sixteenth and seventeenth centuries, according to the accounts of French and Portuguese travellers, it was the most magnificent city in all Asia. The wars with the Burmese continued and Ayutthaya fell in 1767, after a siege lasting fifteen months. The Burmese looted the city, melted down the gold statues and left nothing but ruins in their wake.

Now, it was very peaceful; a light breeze stirred up dust between the temples. Not much remained of King Ramathibodi, apart from a couple of lines in the Michelin Guide. The image of the Buddha, on the other hand, was very much in evidence and had retained all of its significance. The Burmese had shipped in Thai craftsmen so that they could construct identical temples several hundred kilometres away. The will to power exists, and it manifests itself in the form of history; it is, in itself, radically unproductive. The smile of the Buddha continued to float above the ruins. It was three o'clock in the afternoon. According to the Michelin Guide, you needed to set aside three days for a complete visit, one day for a quick tour. We had three hours; it was time to get out the camcorders. I imagined Chateaubriand with a Panasonic camcorder at the Coliseum, smoking cigarettes – B&H probably, rather than Gauloises Lights. Faced with a religion this radical, I expect his views would have been slightly different; he would have had a lot less respect for Napoleon. I was sure that he would have been capable of writing an excellent *Génie du bouddhisme*.

Josette and René were a bit bored during the visit; I got the impression that pretty quickly they were just going round in circles. Babette and Léa were the same. The ecologists from the Jura, on the other hand, seemed to be in their element, as did the naturopaths; they deployed an impressive array of photographic equipment. Valérie was lost in thought, walking down the alleys, across the flagstones, through the grass. That's culture for you, I thought: it's a bit of a pain in the arse, but that's good; everyone is returned to his own nothingness. That said, how did the sculptors of the Ayutthaya period *do it*? How did they manage to give their statues of the Buddha such a luminous expression of understanding?

After the fall of Ayutthaya, the Thai kingdom entered a period of great stability. Bangkok became the capital and the Râma dynasty began. For two centuries (actually, up to the present day) the kingdom knew no serious foreign wars, nor any civil or religious wars for that matter; it also succeeded in avoiding any form of colonisation. There had been no famines, either, nor great epidemics. In such circumstances, when lands are fertile and bring forth abundant harvests, when sickness seems to relax its grip, when a peaceable religion extends its laws over hearts and minds, human beings grow and multiply; in general, they live happily. Now, things were different. Thailand had become part of the free world, meaning the market economy; for five years it had been suffering a terrible economic crisis which had reduced the currency to less than half its previous value and brought the most successful businesses to the brink of ruin. This was the first real tragedy to strike the country for more than two centuries.

One after another, in a silence that was pretty striking, we went back to the coach. We left at sunset. We were due to take the night train from Bangkok, destination Surat Thani.

9

Surat Thani – population 42,000 – is distinguished, according to the guidebooks, by the fact that it is of no interest whatever. It is, and this is the only thing you can say about it, an obligatory stop on the way to the Koh Samui ferry. Nonetheless, people live here, and the Michelin Guide informed us that for a long time the city has been an important centre of metallurgical industries – and that, more recently, it has played a significant role in machine assembly.

And where would we be without machine construction? Iron ore is mined in obscure regions of the country and transported here by freighter. Machine tools are then produced, mostly under the supervision of Japanese companies. Their assembly takes place in cities like Surat Thani: resulting in coaches, train carriages, ferries; all produced under licence from NEC, General Motors or Fujimori. The products serve in part to transport western tourists, such as Babette and Léa.

I was entitled to speak to them, I was a member of the same tour; I could hardly presume to be a potential lover, which limited possible conversation from the off; I had, nevertheless, purchased the same outbound ticket; I was therefore at liberty, to some extent, to make contact. Babette and Léa, it turned out, worked for the same PR agency; for the most part, they organised events. Events? Yes. For institutions or private companies keen to develop their corporate sponsorship programmes. There was certainly money to be made there, I thought. Yes and no. Nowadays, companies were more 'human rights' focused, so there had been a slowdown in investment. But it was still pretty okay. I enquired about their salaries: pretty good. They could have been better, but still pretty good. About twenty-five times the salary of a metalworker in Surat Thani. Economics is a mystery.

After we arrived at the hotel, the group broke up, at least I suppose it did; I didn't feel much like eating with the others; I was a bit fed up with the others. I drew the curtains and lay down. Curiously, I fell asleep immediately and dreamed of an Arab girl dancing in a metro carriage. She didn't look anything like Aïcha, at least I don't think so. She was standing against the central pole, like the girls in go-go bars. Her breasts were covered by a miniscule strip of cotton which she was slowly lifting. With a smile, she freed her breasts completely; they were swollen, round, copper-coloured, magnificent. She licked her fingers and stroked her nipples. Then she put her hand on my trousers, eased down my flies and took out my penis, and began to jerk me off. People crowded past us, got off at their stations. She got on all fours on the floor, lifted up her mini-skirt; she wasn't wearing anything underneath. Her vulva was welcoming, surrounded by black hair, like a gift; I started to penetrate her. The carriage was half full, but no one paid any attention to us. Such things could never happen under any normal circumstances. It was the dream of a starving man, the ludicrous dream of man already grown old.

I woke up at about five o'clock, noticed the sheets were completely covered in semen. A nocturnal emission . . . very touching. I noticed too, to my great surprise, that I still had a hard on; I put it down to the weather. A cockroach lay on its back in the middle of the bedside table; you could easily make out the detail of its legs. This one didn't have to worry any more, as my father would have said. My father, for his part, had died in late 2000; good thing too. Consequently, his existence was entirely contained within the twentieth century, of which he was a hideously representative element. I myself had survived in middling condition. I was in my forties, well, in my early forties, after all, I was only forty; I was about half way there. My father's death gave me a certain freedom; I hadn't had my last word yet.

Situated on the east coast of Ko Samui, the hotel perfectly evoked the sort of tropical paradise you see in travel agents' brochures. The hills surrounding it were covered by thick jungle. The low-rise buildings, bordered by greenery, sloped down to an immense oval swimming pool with a jacuzzi at each end. You could swim up to the bar, which was on an island in the middle of the pool. A few yards further on was a beach of white sand and the sea. I looked around warily at my surroundings; from here, I recognised Lionel in the distance splashing in the waves like a handicapped dolphin. Then I turned back and headed for the bar along a narrow bridge overlooking the pool. With studied casualness, I familiarised myself with the cocktail menu; happy hour had just begun.

I had just ordered a Singapore Sling when Babette made her appearance. 'Well, well . . .' I said. She was wearing a generously cut two-piece bathing suit, figure-hugging shorts and a wide wraparound top in a symphony of light and dark blue. The fabric seemed to be exceptionally sheer; it was a swimsuit which clearly only came into its own when wet. 'Are you not going to swim?' she asked. 'Euh . . .' I said. Léa appeared in turn, more classically sexy in a bright red vinyl one-piece, with black zips open to reveal her skin (one of them ran across her left breast, giving a glimpse of nipple), and cut very high on the thighs. She nodded to me before joining Babette at the water's edge; when she turned round, I was in a position to observe that she had perfect buttocks. The girls had been suspicious of me at the beginning; but since I had spoken to them on the ferry they had come to the conclusion that I was a harmless human being and moderately amusing. They were right: that was about it.

They dived in together. I turned round to ogle a bit. The guy at the next table was the spitting image of Robert Hue. When wet, Babette's swimsuit really was spectacular: you could easily make out her nipples and the crack of her bum; you could even see the slight swelling of her pubic hair, even though she had opted to cut it quite short. Meanwhile, people were working, making useful commodities; or sometimes useless commodities. They were productive. What had I produced in the forty years of my existence? To tell the truth, not very much. I had managed information, facilitated access to it and disseminated it; sometimes, too, I had carried out bank transfers (on a modest scale; I was generally happy to pay the smaller invoices). In a word, I had worked in the service sector. It would be easy to get by without people like me. Still, my ineffectuality was less flamboyant than that of Babette and Léa; a moderate parasite I had never been a high-flyer in *my job*, and had never felt the need to pretend to be.

After dark, I went back to the hotel lobby, where I ran into Lionel; he was sunburned from head to toe and delighted with his day. He had done a lot of swimming; he'd never dared dream of somewhere like this. 'I had to save pretty hard to pay for the trip,' he said, 'but I don't regret it.' He sat on the edge of a sofa; he was thinking about his daily life. He worked for Gaz de France in the southeastern suburbs of Paris; he lived in Juvisy. He often had to call on people who were very poor, old people whose systems weren't up to standard. If they didn't have money the to pay for the necessary modifications, he was forced to cut off their gas. 'There are people who live in conditions . . .' he said, 'you can't imagine.'

'You get to see strange things sometimes . . .' he went on, shaking his head. As for himself, things were okay. The area he lived in wasn't great, actually it was down-right dangerous. 'There are places that are best avoided,' he said. But in general, things weren't too bad. 'We're on holiday,' he concluded before heading off to the dining room. I picked up a couple of brochures and went off to my room to read them. I still didn't feel like eating with the others. It is in our relations with other people that we gain a sense of ourselves; it's that, pretty much, that makes relations with other people unbearable.

I'd found out from Léa that Ko Samui wasn't just a tropical paradise, it was also pretty phat. Every night at the full moon there was a massive rave on the tiny neighbouring island of Ko Lanta; people came from Australia or from Germany to attend. 'A bit like Goa . . .' I said. 'Much better than Goa,' she interrupted. Goa was completely *past it*; if you were looking for a decent rave now, you had to go to Ko Samui or to Lombok.

I didn't ask as much. All I wanted right now was a decent body massage, followed by a blowjob and a good fuck. Nothing too complicated on the face of it; but looking through the brochures I realised with a feeling of profound melancholy that it didn't at all seem to be the speciality of the place. There was a lot of stuff like acupuncture, massage with essential oils, vegetarian food or tai-chi; but body massage or go-go bars, *nada*. On top of everything, the place had a painfully American, even Californian, feel about it, focused on 'healthy living' and 'meditation activities'. I glanced through a letter to *What's On: Samui* from a reader, Guy Hopkins; he was a self-confessed 'health addict' and had been coming to the island regularly for twenty years, '*The aura that backpackers spread on the island is unlikely to be erased quickly by upmarket tourists,*' he concluded; it was depressing. I couldn't even set off in search of adventure as the hotel was miles from anywhere; in fact everything was miles from anywhere, since there was nothing here. The map of the island indicated no identifiable centre: several chalet resorts like ours, set on tranquil beaches. It was then that I remembered with horror that the island had had a very good write-up in the *Guide du Routard*. Here was a place where they had managed to avoid a certain moral slide: I was caught like a rat in a trap. Even so, I felt a vague satisfaction, however theoretical, at the notion that I felt up to fucking. Half-heartedly, I picked up *The Firm* again, skipped forward two hundred pages, skipped back fifty; by chance I happened on a sex scene. The plot had developed a fair bit: Tom Cruise was now in the Cayman Islands, in the process of setting up some kind of money-laundering scheme, or in the process of unmasking it, it wasn't too clear. Whatever the deal was, he was getting to know a stunning mixed-race girl, and the girl wasn't exactly backward in coming forward. 'She unsnapped something and removed her skirt, leaving nothing but a string around her waist and a string running between her legs'. I unzipped my trousers. This was followed by a weird passage that was difficult to grasp psychologically: 'Something said run. Throw the beer bottle into the ocean. Throw the skirt on to the sand. And run like hell. Run to the condo. Lock the door. Lock the windows. Run. Run. Run.' Thankfully, Eilene didn't see things quite that way: 'In slow motion, she reached behind her neck. She unhooked her bikini top, and it fell off, very slowly. Her breasts, much larger now, lay on his left forearm. She handed the top to him. "Hold this for me." It was soft and white and weighed less than a millionth of an ounce.' I was jerking off in earnest now, trying to visualise mixed-race girls wearing tiny swimsuits in the dark. I ejaculated between two pages with a groan of satisfaction. They were going to stick together; didn't matter, it wasn't the kind of book you read twice.

In the morning, the beach was deserted. I went for a swim just after breakfast; the air was warm. The sun would soon begin its ascent across the sky, increasing the risk of skin cancer in individuals of Caucasian descent. I intended to stay long enough for the maids to make up my room, then I would head back, lie beneath the sheets and put the air-conditioning on full; with the greatest serenity I contemplated this free day.

Tom Cruise, on the other hand, was still plagued with

worries about his affair with the mixed-race girl; he even considered telling his wife (who, and this was the problem, was not content simply to be loved; she wanted to be the sexiest, the most desirable woman in the world). The idiot behaved as though the future of his marriage was at stake. 'If she was cool and showed a trace of compassion, he would tell her he was sorry, so very sorry, and that it would never happen again. If she fell all to pieces, he would beg, literally beg for forgiveness and swear on the Bible that it was a mistake and would never happen again.' Obviously, it came to much the same thing; but in the end the hero's unremitting remorse, though it was of no interest whatever, began to interfere with the story – which was pretty serious; we had a bunch of extremely nasty Mafiosi, the FBI, maybe even the Russians. It was enough to make you angry, and in the end it made you sick.

I had a go with another American bestseller, *Total Control*, by David G Baldacci; but that was even worse. This time, the hero wasn't a lawyer but a young computer genius who worked a hundred and ten hours a week. His wife, on the other hand, was a lawyer and worked ninety hours a week: they had a kid. This time the bad guys were a 'European' company which had resorted to fraudulent practices in order to corner a market. Said market should have been the territory of the American company for which our hero was working. During a conversation with the bad guys from the European company, the bad guys – without the least compunction – smoked several cigarettes; the atmosphere literally stank of them, but the hero managed to survive. I made a small hole in the sand to bury the two books; the problem now was that I had to find something to read. Life without anything to read is dangerous: you have to content yourself with life and that can lead you to take risks. At the age of fourteen, one afternoon when the fog was particularly dense, I had got lost while skiing; I had had to make my way across avalanche corridors. What I remember most were the low, leaden clouds, the utter silence on the mountain. I knew the drifts of snow could shear away at any moment if I made a sudden movement, or even for no apparent reason, some slight rise in temperature, a breath of wind. If they did I would be carried with them, dragged hundreds of metres on to the rocky ridges below; I would die, probably on impact. Despite this, I wasn't in the least afraid. I was annoyed that things had turned out this way, annoyed for myself and for everyone else. I would have preferred a more conventional death, more official in a way, with an illness, a funeral, tears. Most of all, I regretted never having known my wife's body. During the winter months, my father rented out the first floor of his house; this year the tenants were a couple of architects. Their daughter, Sylvie, was also fourteen; she seemed to be attracted to me, at least she did her best to have me around. She was slender, graceful, her hair was black and curly. Was her pubic hair black and curly too? These were the thoughts that flitted through my mind as I plodded across the mountainside. I've often wondered about that, since: faced with danger, even death, I don't feel anything in particular, no rush of adrenalin. I had searched for the sensations which attract 'extreme sports' fanatics in vain. I am not remotely brave, I run away from danger if at all possible; but if push comes to shove, I greet it with the placidity of a cow. There's probably no point in searching for meaning in this, it's just a technical matter, a question of hormone levels; other human beings apparently similar to me, seem to feel nothing in the presence of a woman's body, something which plunged me, at the time and still, plunges me into a state of agitation I can't control. In most circumstances in my life, I have had about as much freedom as a vacuum cleaner.

The sun was beginning to get hot. I noticed that Babette and Léa had arrived on the beach; they had settled themselves about ten metres away from me. Today, they were topless and dressed simply, identically, in white thongs. Apparently they'd met some boys, but I didn't think they were going to sleep with them: the guys weren't bad, reasonably muscular, but not that great either; all in all, pretty average.

I got up and gathered my things. Babette had put her copy of *Elle* next to her towel. I glanced towards the sea; they were swimming and laughing with the boys. I stooped quickly and stuffed the magazine into my bag; then I walked on along the beach.

The sea was calm; the view stretched out to the east. Cambodia was probably on the other side, or maybe

Vietnam. There was a yacht, midway to the horizon; perhaps there are millionaires who spend their time sailing back and forth across the oceans of the world; a life at once monotonous and romantic.

Valérie approached, walking along the water's edge, amusing herself by taking a sidestep now and then to avoid a stronger wave. I quickly propped myself up on my elbows, becoming painfully conscious that she had a magnificent body and was very attractive in her rather sensible two-piece swimsuit; her breasts filled out the bikini top perfectly. I gave a little wave, thinking that she hadn't seen me, but in fact she was already looking in my direction; it's not easy to catch women out.

'You're reading *Elle*?' she asked, a little surprised, quietly ironic.

'Euh . . .' I said.

'May I?' she sat down beside me. Easily, with the familiarity of a regular reader, she skimmed through the magazine: a quick look at the fashion pages, another at the front pages. '*Elle* reads', '*Elle* goes out' . . .

'Did you go to another massage parlour last night?' she asked, with a sidelong glance.

'Um . . . no, I couldn't find one.'

She nodded briefly and went back to reading the cover story: 'Are you programmed to love him forever?'

'Is it any good?' I asked after a silence

'I haven't got a lover,' she replied seriously. This girl completely unsettled me.

'I don't really understand this magazine,' she continued

without a pause; 'All it talks about is fashion and new trends: what you should see, what you should read, the causes you should campaign for, new topics of conversation . . . The readers couldn't possibly wear the same clothes as the models, and why on earth would they be interested in new trends? They're mostly older women.'

'You think so?'

'I'm sure. My mother reads it.'

'Maybe the writers simply write about the things they're interested in, not what interests their readers.'

'Economically, that shouldn't be viable; normally things are done to satisfy the customer's tastes.'

'Maybe it does satisfy the customers tastes.'

She pondered, 'Maybe . . .' she replied hesitantly

'You think when you're sixty you won't be interested in new trends any more,' I insisted

'I certainly hope not . . .' she said sincerely.

I lit a cigarette. 'If I'm going to stay, I'll have to put on sunscreen,' I said in a melancholy voice.

'We're going for a swim! You can put on sunscreen after.' In a flash she was on her feet and pulling me towards the shore.

She was a good swimmer. Personally, I can't say that I know how to swim, I can float on my back for a bit but I get tired quickly. 'You get tired quickly,' she said. 'It's because you smoke too much. You should do some sport. I'm going to sort you out . . .' She twisted my bicep. Oh no, I thought, no. In the end, she calmed down and went back to sunning herself after she'd vigorously dried her hair. She was pretty like that, with her long black hair all tousled. She didn't take off her top, it was a pity; I would have really liked her to take off her top. I would have liked to see her breasts, here, now.

She surprised me looking at her breasts and smiled quickly. 'Michel . . .' she said after a moment's silence. I jumped at the use of my first name. 'Why do you feel so old?' she asked, looking me straight in the eyes.

It was a good question; I choked a little.

'You don't have to answer straight away . . .' she said gently, 'I've got a book for you,' she went on, taking it from her bag. I was surprised to recognise the yellow cover of the 'Masque' series, and a title by Agatha Christie, *The Hollow*.

'Agatha Christie?' I said, bewildered.

'Read it anyway. I think you'll find it interesting.'

I nodded like an idiot. 'Are you not coming to lunch?' she asked after a moment, 'It's one o'clock already.'

'No . . . No, I don't think so.'

'You don't much like being in a group?'

There was no point in answering; I smiled. We picked up our things, we left together. On the way, we met Lionel, who was wandering around like a lost soul; he gave us a friendly wave, but already it seemed as if he wasn't having so much fun. It isn't for nothing that single men are so rare at holiday camps. You can see them, nervously, on the periphery of the recreational activities. Most often, they turn and leave; sometimes they launch into them, and participate. I left Valérie by the restaurant tables.

In every Sherlock Holmes story you immediately recognise the characteristics of the character; but, as well as that, the author never fails to introduce some new peculiarity (the cocaine, the violin, the existence of his older brother, Mycroft, the taste for Italian opera . . . certain services rendered long ago to the crowned heads of Europe . . . the first case Sherlock Holmes ever solved when he was still an adolescent). Each new detail that is revealed casts new areas of shadow, and in the end developed a character who was truly fascinating: Conan Doyle succeeded in creating a perfect mixture of the pleasure of discovery and the pleasure of recognition. I always felt that Agatha Christie, on the other hand, put too much emphasis on the pleasure of recognition. In her initial descriptions of Poirot, she had a tendency to limit herself to a couple of stock phrases, restricted her character's most obvious traits (his mania for symmetry, his patent-leather boots, the care he lavishes on his mustachios); in the more mediocre other books, you even get the impression that the phrases had been copied directly from one novel to another.

That said, *The Hollow* was interesting for other reasons. Not simply for the ambitious character of Henrietta, the sculptor, in whom Agatha Christie tried to portray not only the agony of creation (the scene where she destroys a statue just after labouring to finish it because she senses that it is lacking something), but that suffering which is particular to being an artist; that inability to be *truly* happy or unhappy, to *truly* feel hatred, despair, ecstasy or love; the sort of aesthetic filter which separates, without the possibility of remission, the artist from the world. The author had put much of herself into her character, and her sincerity was obvious. Unfortunately, the artist, separated in a way from the world, sensing things only in a vague, ambiguous, and consequently less intense manner, became as a result a less interesting character.

Fundamentally conservative, and hostile to any idea of the social redistribution of wealth, Agatha Christie adopted very clear-cut ideological positions throughout her career as a writer. In practise, this radical theoretical engagement nonetheless made it possible for her to be frequently cruel in her descriptions of the English aristocracy, whose privileges she so staunchly defended. Lady Angkatell is a burlesque character, only barely credible and often almost terrifying. The author is clearly fascinated with her creation, who has clearly forgotten even those rules which apply to ordinary human beings; she must have enjoyed writing sentences like: 'But then one doesn't exactly *introduce* people – not when somebody had just been killed' – but her sympathies did not lie with Lady Angkatell. On the other hand, she paints a warm portrait of Midge, forced to work as a salesgirl during the week, and who spends her weekends among people who haven't the faintest idea of what work really is. Spirited, lively, Midge loves Edward hopelessly. Edward, for his part, thinks himself a failure: he hasn't succeeded at anything in his life, *not even at becoming a writer*; he writes short stories of disenchanted irony for obscure journals read only by bibliophiles. Three times he proposes marriage to Henrietta, without success. Henrietta is John's mistress, she admires his strength, his radiant personality; but John is married. His murder shatters the delicate balance of unfulfilled desire between the characters: Edward finally realises that Henrietta will never want him, that he can never measure up to John; but nor can he bring himself closer to Midge, and his life seems to be completely ruined. It is at this point that *The Hollow* becomes a strange, poignant book; these are deep waters, with powerful undercurrents. In the scene in which Midge saves Edward from committing suicide, and in which he proposes to her, Agatha Christie achieves something beautiful, a sort of Dickensian sense of wonder.

Her arms closed round him firmly. He smiled at her, murmuring:

'You're so warm, Midge – you're so warm.'

Yes, she thought, that was what despair was. A cold thing, a thing of infinite coldness and loneliness. She'd never understood until now that despair was a cold thing. She had always thought of it as something hot and passionate, something violent, a hot-blooded desperation. But that was not so. This was despair – this utter outer darkness of coldness and loneliness. And the sin of despair, that priests talked of, was a cold sin, the sin of cutting oneself off from all warm and living human contacts.

I finished reading at about nine o'clock; I got up and

walked to the window. The sea was calm, myriads of luminous specks danced on the surface; a delicate halo surrounded the circular face of the moon. I knew there was a full-moon rave party tonight at Ko Lanta; Babette and Léa would probably go, with a good many other guests. Giving up on life is the easiest thing to do, putting one's own life to one side. As preparations for the evening continued, as taxis pulled up at the hotel, as everyone began to bustle in the corridors, I felt nothing more than a sad sense of relief.

10

A narrow strip of mountainous land separating the gulf of Thailand from the Andaman sea, the isthmus of Kra, is divided to the north by the border between Thailand and Burma. At Ranong, in the far south of Burma, it measures barely twenty-two kilometres across; after that it progressively widens to become the Malay peninsula.

Of the hundreds of islands which speckle the Andaman sea, only a few are inhabited, and not one of the islands on the Burmese side is open to tourists. On the Thai side, on the other hand, the islands of Phang Nga bay bring in 43 per cent of the country's annual tourist revenue. The largest of these is Phuket, where resorts were developed in the middle of the 80s, mostly with Chinese and French capital (South-East Asia quickly became one of the key areas of expansion for the Aurore group). It is probably in the chapter on Phuket that the *Guide du Routard* reaches the pinnacle of its loathing, its vulgar élitism and aggressive masochism. 'For some,' they announce first off, 'Phuket is an island on the way up; for us, it is already on the way down.'

'It was inevitable that we'd get here in the end,' they go on, 'to this "pearl of the Indian Ocean" . . . Only a few years ago we were still singing the praises of Phuket: the sun, the unspoiled beaches, the relaxed rhythms of life. At the risk of putting a spanner in the works, we'll come clean: we don't like Phuket any more! *Patong*, the most famous of the beaches, has been covered in concrete. Everywhere the clientele has become predominantly male, hostess bars are springing up everywhere and the only smiles are the ones you can buy. As for the backpacker chalets, they've had a JCB face lift to make way for hotels destined for lonely pot-bellied Europeans.'

We were due to spend two nights at Patong Beach; I settled myself confidently on the coach, perfectly prepared to adopt my role as a lonely pot-bellied European. The end of the trip was the highlight of the tour: three days at our leisure in Ko Phi Phi, a destination usually thought of as paradise itself. 'What to say about Ko Phi Phi?' lamented the travel guide, 'It's as if you asked us about a lost love . . . We want to say something wonderful about it, but there's a lump in our throat.' For the manipulative masochist, it is not enough that he is unhappy; others must be unhappy too; I chucked my *Guide du Routard* into the bin at the service station. Western masochism, I thought. A mile or so later, I realised that I now didn't have anything to read; I was going to have to tackle the last part of the tour without a scrap of printed matter to hide behind. I glanced around me, my heartbeat had accelerated, the outside world suddenly seemed a whole lot closer. On the other side of the aisle, Valérie had reclined her seat; she seemed to be daydreaming or sleeping, her face was turned toward the window. I tried to follow her example. Outside the landscape unfolded, made up of diverse vegetation. In desperation, I borrowed René's Michelin Guide; I thus learned that rubber plantations and latex played a key role in the economy of the region: Thailand is the third largest rubber producer in the world. That muddle of vegetation, then, served to make condoms and tyres; human ingenuity was truly remarkable. Mankind can be criticised from a variety of standpoints, but that's one thing you can't take away from him: we're unquestionably dealing with an ingenious mammal.

Since the evening at the River Kwai, the seating at table had become definitive. Valérie had joined what she called the 'yob camp'. Josiane had thrown her lot in with the naturopaths, with whom she shared certain values – such as techniques for promoting calm. At breakfast, I was able to observe from a distance a veritable calm competition between Albert and Josiane, under the watchful eyes of the ecologists – who, living in their godforsaken hole in Franche-Comté, obviously had access to fewer techniques. Babette and Léa, though they were from the Île-de-France, didn't have much to say for themselves other than an occasional: 'That's cool . . .' calm was still a medium-term goal for them. All in all, they had a well balanced table, equipped with a *natural leader* of each sex, capable of fostering team spirit. On our side, things had a bit more trouble gelling. Josette and René regularly provided a commentary on the menu; they had become very familiar with the local food, Josette even intended to take home some recipes. From time to time they carped about the people at the other table, whom they considered to be pretentious, and poseurs; that wasn't going to get us very far, and I was usually impatient for the dessert to arrive.

I gave René his Michelin Guide back; Phuket was still a four-hour drive away. At the restaurant bar, I bought a bottle of Mekong. I spent the next four hours fighting back the feeling of shame that was stopping me from taking it out of my bag and quietly getting rat-arsed; shame won out in the end. The entrance to the Beach Resortel was decorated with a banner which read: WELCOME TO THE FIREMEN OF CHAZAY. 'Now that's funny,' said Josette, 'Chazay – that's where your sister lives . . .' René couldn't remember. 'It is, it is . . .' she insisted. Before I got my room-key, I just had time to hear her say: 'So, that crossing the isthmus of Kra thing was just a day wasted'; and the worst thing was, she was right. I threw myself on to the king-size bed and took a long swig of alcohol; and then another.

I woke up with an appalling headache and spent quite a while throwing up into the toilet bowl. It was five in the morning: too late for the hostess bars, too early for breakfast. In the drawer of the bedside table there was a Bible and a copy of the teachings of the Buddha, both in English. 'Because of their ignorance,' I read, 'people are always thinking wrong thoughts and always losing the right viewpoint and, clinging to their egos, they take wrong actions. As a result, they become attached to a delusive existence.' I wasn't really sure that I understood, but the last sentence perfectly described my current state; I was sufficiently relieved that I was able to wait until breakfast time. At the next table there was a group of gigantic black Americans that could easily have been mistaken for a basketball team. Further along there was a table of Hong Kong Chinese – recognisable by their filthy manners, which are difficult for Westerners to stomach, and which threw the Thai waiters into a state of panic, barely eased by the fact that they were used to it. Unlike the Thais, who behave in all circumstances with a finicky, even pernickety propriety, the Chinese eat rapaciously, laughing loudly, their mouths open, spraying bits of food everywhere, spitting on the ground and blowing their noses between their fingers – they behave quite literally like pigs. To make matters worse, that's an awful lot of pigs.

After a few minutes' walking the streets of Patong Beach I realised that everything the civilised world had produced in the way of tourists was gathered here on the two-kilometre stretch of the seafront. Before I had walked thirty metres, I'd encountered Japanese, Italians, Germans, Americans, not to mention a couple of Scandinavians and some rich South Americans. 'We're all the same, we all head for the sun,' as the girl in the travel agency had told me. I behaved like a typical, average tourist: I rented a sun-lounger with a fitted mattress, a parasol; I consumed a number of bottles of Sprite; I went for a dip, in moderation. The waves were gentle. I went back to the hotel at about five o'clock, averagely satisfied with my free day but intent nonetheless on carrying on. *I was attached to a delusive existence.* I still had the hostess bars to come, but before heading to the relevant district, I idled outside the restaurants. In front of Royal Savoy Seafood, I noticed a couple of Americans gazing at a lobster, with exaggerated concentration. 'Two mammals in search of a crustacean', I thought. A waiter came to join them, all smiles, probably praising the freshness of the produce. 'That makes three,' I continued mechnically. The crowd flowed incessantly, single men, families, couples; it all conveyed an impression of innocence.

Sometimes, when they've had a bit to drink, the German senior citizens get together in groups and intone slow, infinitely sad songs, much to the amusement of the Thai waiters, who gather round them making appreciative little cries.

Falling in step behind three chaps in their fifties, vigorously trading shouts of 'Ach' and 'Ja', I found myself, all of a sudden, in the street of hostess bars. Young girls in short skirts billed and cooed, competing with each other to try to convince me to go the Blue Nights, the Naughty

Girl, the Classroom, the Marilyn, the Venus . . . In the end I opted for the Naughty Girl. The place was still pretty empty: about ten or so Westerners, each sitting alone at their tables – young, twenty-five to thirty-year-olds, mostly English and American. On the dance floor, a dozen girls swayed gently to some sort of retro disco beat. Some of them wore white bikinis, others had taken their tops off and were wearing only G-strings. They were all about twenty, they all had golden brown skin, supple, exciting bodies. An elderly German was sitting in front of a Carlsberg at the table on my left: big belly, white beard, glasses, he looked a lot like a retired university professor. He stared at the bodies moving before his eyes, completely hypnotised; he was so still that for a moment I thought he was dead.

Several smoke machines started up, the music changed, replaced by something slow and Polynesian. The girls left the stage, to be replaced by a dozen others wearing garlands of flowers around their hips and busts. Slowly, they turned round, the garlands occasionally revealing a breast or the top of the buttocks. The old German still stared at the stage; at one point he took off his glasses to wipe them, his eyes were moist. He was in paradise.

Strictly speaking, the girls didn't solicit; but you could invite one of them to have a drink with you, talk a little and in due course pay the establishment a bar fee of five hundred baht to take the girl to your hotel, after negotiating a price. For a whole night, I think the price was about four or five thousand baht – about a month's salary for an unskilled Thai worker; but Phuket is an expensive resort. The elderly German signalled discreetly to one of the girls who was waiting, still wearing a white G-string, to go back on stage. She came over immediately, settled herself casually between his thighs. Her curved, youthful breasts were at the same level as the old man's face; he was roaring with pleasure. I heard her call him 'Papa'. I. paid for my Tequila sour and left, a little embarrassed; I had the feeling I'd witnessed one of the old man's last pleasures. It was too moving, too intimate.

Just next to the bar, I found an open-air restaurant where I sat and had a plate of crabmeat and rice. At almost every table sat a couple, always a western man and a Thai woman. Most of the guys looked Californian, the way you imagine Californians to look, at any rate they were all wearing flip-flops. Actually, they could have been Australian – it's easy to get the two mixed up; whatever they were, they looked healthy, sporty, well-fed. They were the future. It was at that point, seeing all these young, immaculate Anglo-Saxons with their brilliant futures, that I realised just how important sex tourism would be to the future of the world. At the next table, two Thai women of about thirty, shapely, generously proportioned, were chatting excitedly. Two shaven-headed English men, who looked like post-modern convicts, sat opposite; they barely sipped their beers and said nothing. A little further along, a couple of German dykes in dungarees, rather chubby, with short red hair, had treated themselves to the company of a delightful adolescent girl with long black hair and an innocent face, wearing a colourful sarong. There were also a couple of lone Arabs of indeterminate nationality, their heads wrapped in the sort of tea-towel you see Yasser Arafat wearing when he's on television. In short, all the rich or moderately wealthy world was here, all answering 'present!' to the gentle and constant roll-call of Asian pussy. The strangest thing was that you had the impression, the minute you set eyes on each couple, of knowing whether things would work out or not. More often than not, the girls were bored, wore sulky or resigned expressions, glancing around at the other tables. But some of them, their eyes turned to their companions in an attitude of loving expectancy, hung on their partners' words, responded eagerly; in such cases you could imagine things would go further, that a friendship might develop, or perhaps a more lasting relationship: I knew that marriages were not rare, especially with Germans.

Myself, I didn't much feel like striking up a conversation with some girl in a bar; in general these conversations, overly focused on the character and price of sexual services to come, were a disappointment. I preferred massage parlours, where you begin with sex, sometimes an intimacy develops, sometimes not. In certain cases you think about extending your stay at the hotel and that's when you find out that the girl isn't always keen: sometimes she's divorced, she has children who need to be looked after; it's sad, but it's good. As I finished my rice, I sketched out the plot of a pornographic adventure film called *The Massage Room*. Sirien, a young girl from northern Thailand, falls hopelessly in love with Bob, an American student who winds up in the massage parlour by accident, dragged there by his mates after a boozy evening. Bob doesn't touch her, he's happy just to look at her with his lovely, pale-blue eyes and tell her about his country – North Carolina, or somewhere like that. They continue to see each other regularly, whenever Sirien isn't working, but, sadly, Bob must return to finish his final year at Yale. Ellipsis. Sirien waits expectantly while continuing to satisfy the needs of her numerous clients. Though pure at heart, she avidly wanks and sucks paunchy, moustached Frenchmen (supporting role for Gerard Jugnot), fat, bald Germans (supporting role for some German actor). Finally, Bob returns and tries to free her from her hell; but the Chinese mafia don't see things in quite the same light. Bob persuades the American ambassador and the president of some humanitarian organisation opposed to the exploitation of young girls to intervene (supporting role for Jane Fonda). What with the Chinese mafia (mention the Triads) and the collusion of Thai generals (political angle, appeal to democratic values), there would be a lot of fight scenes and chase sequences through the streets of Bangkok. At the end of the day, Bob carries her off. In the penultimate scene, Sirien gives an honest account of the extent of her sexual experience. All the cocks she has sucked as a humble massage parlour employee, she has sucked in the anticipation, in the hope of sucking Bob's cock, into which all the others were subsumed – well, I'd have to work on the dialogue. Cross-fade between the two rivers (the Chao Phraya, the Delaware). Closing credits. For the European market, I already had a trailer in mind, sort of: 'If you liked *The Music Room*, you'll love *The Massage Room*'. It was all a bit vague, but first I would need backers. After I paid, I got up and walked a hundred and fifty metres, dodging a variety of propositions, and found myself in front of the Pussy Paradise. I pushed the door and went in. Three metres in front of me I spotted Robert and Lionel, sitting with a couple of Irish coffees. At the back, behind a glass screen, about fifty girls sat on terraced benches, each wearing a numbered tag. A waiter quickly approached me. Turning his head, Lionel saw me and looked shamefaced. Robert also turned and with a slow wave motioned to me to join them. Lionel was biting his lip, he didn't know what to do with himself. The waiter took my order. 'I'm right wing . . .' Robert said, for no apparent reason; 'but watch your step . . .' He wagged his index finger as though warning me. Since the start of the trip, I'd noticed, he had assumed I was a leftie, and had been waiting for a favourable opportunity to have a conversation with me; I had no intention of playing that little game. I lit a cigarette; he looked me up and down gravely. 'Happiness is a delicate thing,' he announced in a sen-tentious voice, 'It is difficult to find within ourselves, and impossible to find elsewhere.' After a few seconds, he added confidently, 'Chamfort'. Lionel looked at him admiringly; he seemed to be completely under his spell. I thought his quotation was debatable: if you reversed the words 'difficult' and 'impossible' we'd probably have been a little closer to the truth; but I had no desire to pursue the conversation, it seemed to me imperative for us to get back to a normal tourist situation. On top of everything, I was starting to feel a surge of desire for number 47, a slim little Thai girl, a bit skinny maybe, but with full lips and a gentle appearance; she was wearing a red miniskirt and black stockings. Aware that my attention had wandered, Robert turned to Lionel. 'I believe in truth,' he said in a low voice, 'I believe in truth and in the importance of proof.' Listening distractedly, I was surprised to discover that he had a degree in maths and that in his youth he had written a number of promising papers on Lie groups. I reacted excitedly to this news: there were, in other words, certain areas of human intelligence in which he had been the first clearly to see the truth, to discover absolute, demonstrable certainties. 'Yes . . .' he agreed almost apologetically, 'Of course, it was all proved again in more general terms.' After that he had been a teacher, mostly teaching candidates for the Grandes Écoles; he had derived little pleasure from spending his mature years coaching a bunch of young arseholes obsessed with getting into the École Polytechnique, or the École Centrale – and even then, only the most talented of them. 'In any case,' he added, 'I didn't have the makings of a creative mathematician. It is a gift given to very few.' Towards the end of the seventies, he sat on a government

committee on the reform of maths teaching – a load of
bullshit, by his own admission. Now, at fifty-three, having
taken retirement three years earlier, he devoted himself to
sex tourism. He had been married three times. 'I'm racist
. . .' he said cheerfully. 'I've become racist . . . One of the
first effects of travel,' he added, 'is to reinforce or create
racial prejudice; because how do you imagine other
people before you meet them? You imagine they are just
like you, it goes without saying; it's only little by little that
you realise that the reality is somewhat different. When he
can, a Westerner *works*; he often finds his work frustrating
or boring, but he pretends to find it interesting: this much
is obvious. At the age of fifty, weary of teaching, of maths,
of everything, I decided to see the world. I had just been
divorced for the third time; as far as sex was concerned, I
wasn't expecting much. My first trip was to Thailand;
immediately after that I left for Madagascar. Since then, I
haven't fucked a white woman, I've never even felt the
desire to do so. Believe me,' he added placing a firm hand
on Lionel's forearm, 'you won't find a white woman with
a soft, submissive, supple, muscular pussy any more; that's
all gone now.' Number 47 noticed that I was staring at
her; she smiled at me and crossed her legs high up,
revealing a pair of red suspenders. Robert continued to
expound his theory. 'At the time when the white man
thought himself superior, racism wasn't dangerous. For
colonials, missionaries and lay teachers in the nineteenth
century, the Negro was a big animal, none too clever, a
sort of slightly more evolved monkey. At worst, they

considered him a useful beast of burden, capable of performing complex tasks; at best a frustrated soul, coarse, but, through education, capable of elevating himself to God – or at least western reason. In both cases, they saw in him a 'lesser brother', and one does not feel hatred for an inferior – at most a sort of cordial contempt. This benevolent, almost humanist racism has completely vanished. The moment the white man began to consider blacks as *equals*, it was obvious that sooner or later they would come to consider them to be *superior*. The notion of equality has no basis in human society,' he went on, lifting his index finger again. For a moment, I thought he was going to cite sources – La Rochefoucauld or I don't know whom – but in the end, he didn't. Lionel furrowed his brow. 'Once white men believed themselves to be inferior,' Robert went on, anxious that he be clearly understood, 'the stage was set for a different type of racism, based on masochism: historically, it is in circumstances like these that violence, inter-racial wars and massacres break out. For example, all anti–Semites agree that the Jews have *a certain* superiority: if you read anti-Semitic literature, you're stuck by the fact that the Jew is considered to be more intelligent, more cunning, that he is credited with having singular financial talents – and, moreover, greater communal solidarity. Result: six million dead.'

I glanced at number 47 again: anticipation is exciting, something you'd like to prolong; but there's always the risk that the girl will go off with another customer. I signalled discreetly to the waiter. 'I am not a Jew!' exclaimed Robert, thinking I was about to object. I could, in fact, have made several objections: we were in Thailand, after all, and the yellow races have never been considered by the White man to be 'lesser brothers', but to be civilised peoples, members of different, complex, possibly dangerous civilisations; I could also have pointed out that we were here to fuck and that these discussions were wasting time; in fact, that was my primary objection. The waiter came over to our table; with a swift gesture, Robert motioned to him to bring another round of drinks. 'I need a girl,' I said in English, my voice shrill, 'girl forty-seven'. He leaned towards me, his face anxious, quizzical; a Chinese group had just sat down at the next table, they were making an appalling racket. 'The girl number four seven!' I shouted, enunciating each syllable. This time he understood, smiled broadly and went to the microphone where he uttered a few words. The girl got up, stepped down and walked towards a side door smoothing her hair. 'Racism,' Robert went on, giving me a quick glance, 'seems to be characterised firstly by an accumulation of hostility, a more aggressive sense of competition between males of different races; but the corollary is an increased desire for the females of the other race. What is really at stake in racial struggles,' Robert said simply, 'is neither economic nor cultural, it is brutal and biological: it is competition for the cunts of young women.' I sensed that it wouldn't be long before he moved on to Darwinism; at that moment, the waiter came

back to our table accompanied by number 47. Robert
looked up at her, considered for a moment. 'Good choice
. . .' he concluded soberly, 'she has something of the slut
about her.' The girl smiled shyly. I slipped a hand under
her skirt and stroked her arse as though to protect her. She
snuggled against me.

'It's true that round my way, it's not the whites that
make the law any more . . .' Lionel said, for no apparent
reason.

'Exactly,' agreed Robert forcefully. 'You're scared,
and you're right to be scared. I predict an increase in
racial violence in Europe in years to come; it will all end
in civil war,' he said, frothing at the mouth a little; 'It will
all be settled with Kalashnikovs.' He gulped back his
cocktail; Lionel began to look at him a little nervously. 'I
don't give a fuck about any of it anymore!' Robert added,
slamming his glass down on the table. 'I'm a Westerner,
but I can live wherever I want, and for the time being,
I'm still the one with the money. I've been in Senegal,
Kenya, Tanzania, the Ivory Coast. It's true the girls are
less expert than Thai girls, they're less gentle, but they're
nicely curved and they have a sweet-smelling snatch.' He
was obviously lost in his memories for a moment as he
suddenly fell silent. 'What is your name?' I took the
opportunity to ask number 47. 'I am Sin,' she said. The
Chinese at the next table had made their choices, they
headed upstairs, chuckling and laughing; relative silence
was restored. 'They get on all fours, the little nigger girls,
show you their pussies and their arses,' Robert continued

thoughtfully; 'and inside, their pussies are completely pink . . .' he murmured. I also got to my feet. Lionel shot me a grateful look; he was visibly happy that I was the first to leave with a girl, it made things less embarrassing for him. I nodded to Robert to take my leave. His dour face, fixed in a bitter rictus, scanned the room – and beyond, the human race – without a hint of affability. He had made his point, at least he had had the opportunity; I sensed that I was going to forget him pretty quickly. All of a sudden he seemed to me to be finished, a broken man; I had the impression that he didn't even want to make love to these girls any more. Life can be seen as a process of gradually coming to a standstill, a process evident in the French bulldog – so frisky in its youth, so listless in middle age. In Robert, the process was already well advanced: he possibly still got erections, but even that wasn't certain. It's easy to play the smart aleck, to give the impression that you've understood something about life; the fact remains that life comes to an end. My fate was similar to his, we had shared the same defeat; but still I felt no active sense of solidarity. In the absence of love, nothing can be sanctified. On the inside of the eyelids patches of light merge; there are visions, there are dreams. None of this now concerns man, who waits for night; night comes. I paid the waiter two thousand baht and he escorted me to the double doors leading upstairs. Sin held my hand; she would, for an hour or two, try to make me happy.

Obviously, it's rare to come across a girl in a massage parlour who wants to make love. As soon as we were in the room, Sin went down on her knees in front of me, took down my trousers and my underpants and took my penis between her lips. I immediately started to get hard. She brought her lips closer, slowly pushed back the foreskin with short thrusts of her tongue. I closed my eyes, I felt a dizzying rush, I thought I was going to come in her mouth. She stopped suddenly, undressed, smiling as she did so, folded her clothes and placed them on a chair. 'Massage later . . .' she said, lying on the bed; then she parted her thighs. I was already inside her, and I was thrusting forcefully in and out when I realised I'd forgotten to put on a condom. According to reports by *Médecins du monde*, one third of all prostitutes in Thailand are HIV positive. Even so, I can't say that I felt a shudder of fear; I felt slightly annoyed, no more. Clearly those ad campaigns warning us about AIDS had been a complete failure. I went a bit limp, even so. 'Something wrong?' she was worried, she propped herself up on her elbows. 'Maybe . . . a condom,' I said, embarrassed. 'No problem, no condom . . . I'm OK!' she told me cheerfully. She took my balls in the palm of one hand, slipping the other palm on to my prick. I lay down on my back, surrendering myself to the caress. The movement of her palm quickened, I felt the blood rush back to my penis. Anyway, they probably had medical check-ups or something. As soon as I was hard, she climbed on top and went straight down on me. I laced my hands behind her back;

I felt invulnerable. She started to move her pelvis slowly, her pleasure mounted, I parted my thighs to penetrate her more deeply. The pleasure was intense, almost intoxicating, I breathed very slowly to hold myself back, I felt reconciled. She lay down on top of me, rubbing her pubis hard against mine; I moved my hands to stroke the nape of her neck. At the moment of orgasm, she became still, gave a long moan and then collapsed on my chest. I was still inside her, I could feel her pussy contracting. She had a second orgasm, a very powerful contraction from deep inside her. Involuntarily, I hugged her to me and ejaculated with a roar. She stayed motionless, her head on my chest, for about ten minutes; then she got up and suggested I take a shower. She dried me very delicately, patting me with the towel as you would a baby. I sat down on the sofa and offered her a cigarette. 'We have time . . .' she said 'we have a little time . . .'. I learned that she was thirty-two. She didn't enjoy her work, but her husband had abandoned her, leaving her with two children. 'Bad man,' she said, 'Thai men, bad men.' I asked her if she had any friends among the other girls. Not really, she told me; most of the girls were young and brainless, they spent everything they earned on clothes and perfume. She was not like that, she was serious, she put her money in the bank. In a couple of years she would be able to give this up and go back to live in her village; her parents were old now, they needed help.

As I was leaving, I gave her a two thousand baht tip; it was ridiculous, it was far too much. She took the money incredulously, and bowed to me several times, her hands together over her chest. 'You good man,' she said. She slipped on her mini skirt and her stockings; she had two hours left before they closed. She accompanied me to the door, bowed again, her hands together. 'Take care,' she said again; 'be happy.' I walked back out into the street, a little pensive. The following morning we were due to leave at eight o'clock for the last leg of the trip. I wondered how Valérie had spent her free day.

11

'I bought some presents for my family,' she said. 'I found some beautiful shells.' The boat sped through the turquoise waters, between chalk crags covered with thick jungle; it was exactly how I imagined the scenery of *Treasure Island*. 'When all's said and done, nature is, well . . .' I said. Valérie turned an attentive face towards me; she had tied her hair up in a chignon, but a couple of stray curls fluttered in the wind on either side of her face. 'In the end, nature sometimes . . .' I went on, discouraged. Theree should be lessons in *conversation*, the way there are ballroom dancing lessons; I'd probably spent too much time doing accounting, I had lost the knack. 'You realise that it's December 31st . . .' she observed, unruffled. I looked around on all sides at the endless azure, the turquoise ocean; no, I really hadn't realised. Human beings must have had a lot of courage to colonise cold regions.

Sôn stood up to address the group: 'We now approaching Ko Phi Phi. I tell you before, here cannot go. You put swimsuit on, go now? Walk, not deep, walk. Walk in water. Not take luggage, luggage later.' The pilot rounded a headland and cut the engine, the boat continued to drift into a small cove which carved a curve into the middle of cliffs shrouded in jungle. The clear green water broke on a beach of white sand so perfect it seemed unreal. In the middle of the jungle, before the first slopes, you could make out wooden huts built on stilts, their roofs thatched with palm leaves. The group fell silent for a moment. 'Earthly paradise . . .' said Sylvie softly, choked with genuine emotion. It was hardly an exaggeration. That said, she was no Eve. I was no Adam either.

One by one the group members got up, stepped over the edge of the boat. I helped Josette down to her waiting husband. She had hitched her skirt up to her waist and was having trouble getting over the side, but she was thrilled, she was virtually wetting herself with excitement. I turned round; the Thai boatman waited, leaning on his oar, for all the passengers to disembark. Valérie sat with her hands crossed in her lap; she shot me a sidelong glance and smiled in embarrassment. 'I forgot to put on my swimsuit . . .' she said at last. I lifted my hands slowly in a gesture of helplessness. 'I can go . . .' I said stupidly. She bit her lips in irritation, got up, took off her trousers in a single movement. She was wearing lace panties, very sheer, not at all in the spirit of the trip. Her pubic hair peeked out at the sides, it was quite thick, very black. I didn't turn away, that would have been stupid, but nor was my gaze insistent. I got out of the boat on the left-hand side, offered her my arm to help her down; she jumped down from the boat. We were in up to our waists in the water.

Before going to the beach, Valérie looked again at the shell necklaces she was taking back for her nieces. Immediately after graduation, her brother had got a job as a research engineer with Elf. After a few months of on-site training, he had left for Venezuela – his first assignment. A year later, he married a local girl. Valérie had the impression he hadn't had much previous sexual experience; at least he had never brought girls home. That's often the way with boys who study engineering; they haven't got time to go out, to have girlfriends. They spend their free time on trivial hobbies, complex role-playing games or chess on the internet. They get their degrees, find themselves their first jobs and discover everything at once: money, professional responsibility, sex; if they are posted to a tropical country, it's rare for them to resist. Bertrand had married a very dark mixed-race girl with a superb body; several times when they were on holiday at her parents, on the beach at Saint-Quay-Portrieux, Valérie had felt a violent surge of desire for her sister-in-law. She found it difficult to imagine her brother making love. Still, they had two children now and seemed to be a happy couple. It wasn't difficult to buy presents for Juana, she adored jewellery, and pale stones stood out beautifully against her dark skin. On the other hand, she hadn't found anything for Bertrand. When men have no vices, she thought, it's very difficult to guess what might make them happy.

I was leafing through a copy of *Phuket Weekly* I'd found in the hotel lobby when I saw Valérie walking along the beach. Further along, a group of Germans were swimming in the nude. She hesitated for a moment, then walked towards me. The sun was dazzling; it was about midday. One way or another, I would have to learn to play the game. Babette and Léa walked past wearing shoulder-bags but otherwise they too were completely naked. I registered this information without reacting. By contrast, Valérie's eyes followed them for a while with shameless curiosity. They settled themselves not far from the Germans. 'I think I'll go for a swim . . .' I said. 'I'll go in later,' she replied. I entered the water effortlessly. It was warm, translucent, deliciously calm; tiny silver fish swam close to the surface. The slope was very gentle, I could still touch bottom a hundred metres from shore. I slipped my cock out of my trunks, closed my eyes and visualised Valérie's vagina as I had seen it that morning, half exposed through her lace panties. I was hard, that in itself was something; it could be considered motive enough in itself. Besides, you have to live, you have to relate to other people; I was generally too uptight, and had been so for far too long. Perhaps I should have taken up some hobby in the evenings – badminton, choral singing or something. Even so, the only women I was still able to remember were the ones I'd fucked. That's not nothing either; we build up memories so that we will feel less alone at the moment of death. I shouldn't think like that. 'Think positive', I murmured in English to myself, panicked, 'think different'. I made my way back to the beach, stopping every ten strokes, breathing deeply to try and calm myself. The first thing I noticed as I stepped on to the sand was that Valérie had taken off her bikini top. At that moment, she was lying on her stomach, but she would turn over, it was as inexorable as the movement of the planets. Where was I exactly? I sat down on my towel, hunched over slightly. 'Think different', I reminded myself. I had seen breasts before, I had stroked them, licked them; nonetheless, I found myself in a state of shock. I was sure that she had magnificent breasts; but it was worse than I had imagined. I couldn't tear my eyes from the nipples, the areolas; it was impossible for her not to notice me staring – even so, she said nothing for what seemed to me several long seconds. What exactly does go on in women's heads? They adapt to the rules of the game so easily. Sometimes, when they look at themselves naked in a full-length mirror, you can see a sort of realism in their eyes, a dispassionate assessment of their personal powers of seduction which no man could ever achieve. I was the first to lower my eyes.

After that, an indeterminate period of time elapsed; the sun was still directly overhead, the light extremely bright. I was staring at the white, powdery sand. 'Michel . . .' she said softly. I looked up quickly as though I'd been struck.

Her exceptionally brown eyes stared deeply into mine. 'What have Thai girls got that Western women don't?' she asked plainly. Yet again I was unable to hold her gaze. Her chest rose and fell to the rhythm of her breathing; I thought I saw her nipples harden. Right there, right then, I wanted to reply: 'Nothing'. Then I had an idea; not a very good idea.

'There's an article in English about it in here, sort of an advertorial'; I handed her the copy of *Phuket Weekly*. 'Find your longlife companion . . . Well-educated Thai ladies, that one?' 'Yes, a bit further on there's an interview.' Cham Sawanasee, smiling, black suit and dark tie, answered the 'Ten questions you could ask' on the working of the Heart to Heart agency which he managed.

'There seems to be,' noted Mr Sawanasee, 'a near-perfect match between the Western men, who are unappreciated and get no respect in their own countries, and the Thai women, who would be happy to find someone who simply does his job and hopes to come home to a pleasant family life after work. Most Western women do not want such a boring husband.

'One easy way to see this,' he went on, 'is to look at any publication containing "personal" ads. The Western woman wants someone who looks a certain way, and who has certain "social skills", such as dancing and clever conversation, someone who is interesting and exciting and seductive. Now go to my catalogue, and look at what the girls say they want. It's all pretty simple, really. Over and over they state that they are happy to settle down

FOREVER with a man who is willing to hold down a steady job and be a loving and understanding HUSBAND and FATHER. That will get you exactly nowhere with an American girl!

'As Western women do not appreciate men,' he concluded, not without a certain cheek, 'as they do not value traditional family life, marriage is not the right thing for them. I'm helping modern Western women to avoid what they despise.'

'What he's saying makes sense . . .' Valérie remarked sadly, 'There's a market there, all right . . .' She put down the magazine, still thoughtful. At that moment Robert passed in front of us; he was walking along the beach, hands clasped behind his back, looking serious. Valérie abruptly turned to look the other way.

'I don't like that guy . . .' she whispered angrily.

'He's not stupid . . .' I made a rather noncommittal gesture.

'He's not stupid, but I don't like him. He goes out of his way to shock people, to make himself unpleasant; I don't like that. At least you try to fit in.'

'Really?' I shot her a surprised look.

'Yes. It's obvious you don't find it easy, you're not cut out for this kind of holiday; but at least you make an effort. Deep down, I think you're rather a nice boy.'

At that moment I could have, I should have, taken her in my arms, stroked her breasts, kissed her lips; stupidly, I didn't. The afternoon dragged on, the sun moved over the palms; we said nothing of any significance.

For dinner on New Year's Eve, Valérie wore a long dress of sinuous, slightly transparent green material, the top of which was a bustier which showed off her breasts. After dessert, there was a band out on the terrace. A weird old singer did slow-rock cover versions of Bob Dylan songs in a nasal whine. Babette and Léa had apparently joined the German group; I heard shouts coming from their end. Josette and René danced together in a tender embrace like the nice little proles they were. The night was hot; emerald moths clustered around the multi-coloured paper lanterns which hung from the balustrade. I felt suffocated; I drank whisky after whisky.

'What that guy was saying, the interview in the magazine . . .'

'Yes? . . .' Valérie looked up at me; we were sitting side by side on a rattan bench. Under her bustier, her breasts were more rounded, as though they were being offered in their own little shells. She had put on makeup; her long hair was free and floated about her shoulders.

'It's mostly true of American women, I think. For Europeans, it's less clear cut.'

She pulled a face, clearly unconvinced, and said nothing. Obviously, I should have just asked her to dance. I drank another whisky, leaned back on the bench and took a deep breath.

When I woke, the room was almost empty. The singer was still humming in Thai, half-heartedly accompanied by the drummer; no one was listening any more. The

Germans had disappeared, but Babette and Léa were deep in conversation with two Italians who had appeared from who knows where. Valérie had left. It was three in the morning local time; 2001 had just begun. In Paris, it would officially begin in three hours' time; it was exactly midnight in Teheran, five in the morning in Tokyo. Humanity in all its different forms was entering the third millennium; for my part, I had pretty much blown my entrance.

12

I went back to my cabin, mortally ashamed; laughter was coming from the garden. I came across a small grey toad, sitting stock still in the middle of the sandy path. It did not hop away, it had no defensive reflex. Sooner or later someone would accidentally step on it; its spinal column would snap, its pulped flesh would seep into the sand. The walker would feel something soft beneath his foot, utter a blunt curse, wipe off his shoes, rubbing them on the ground. I pushed the toad forward with my foot: unhurried, he made his way to the edge of the path. I pushed him again: he regained the relative safety of the lawn; I had probably prolonged his survival by a few hours. I felt I was barely better off than he was: I hadn't grown up sheltered by the cocoon of a family, nor by anything that might have concerned itself with my fate, supported me in times of misery, enthused about my adventures and my successes. Nor had I established a unit of that sort: I was single, childless; no one would have thought to come and seek support on my shoulder. Like an animal, I had lived and I would die alone. For several minutes I wallowed in gratuitous self-pity.

From another point of view, I was a compact, resilient object, of a larger size than the average animal; my life expectancy was comparable to that of an elephant, or of a crow; I was much more difficult to destroy than a small batrachian.

For the two days that followed, I remained holed up in my cabin. From time to time I went out, hugging the walls, as far as the mini-market to buy pistachios and some bottles of Mekong. I couldn't face running into Valérie again at the breakfast buffet or on the beach. There are some things that one can do, others that seem too difficult. Gradually, everything becomes too difficult: that's what life comes down to.

On the afternoon of January 2nd, I found a Nouvelles Frontières customer satisfaction questionnaire slipped under my door. I filled it out scrupulously, generally ticking the boxes marked 'Good'. It was true, in some sense, that everything had been good. My holiday had 'gone smoothly'. The tour had been 'cool' but with a hint of adventure; it lived up to the description in the brochure. In the 'personal comments' section, I wrote the following quatrain:

Shortly after waking, I feel myself transported

To a different universe, its contours ruled and picked
I know about this life, its details are all sorted
It's very like a questionnaire, with boxes to be ticked

On the morning of January 3rd, I packed my suitcase. When she saw me on the boat, Valérie suppressed an exclamation; I looked away. Sôn said her goodbyes at Phuket airport; we were early, the plane would not leave for three hours. After the check-in formalities, I wandered around the shopping arcade. Even though the departures hall was completely roofed-over, the shops were built in the form of huts, with teak uprights and roofs thatched with palm leaves. The choice of products ranged from international standards (scarves by Hermès, perfumes by Yves Saint-Laurent, bags by Vuitton) to local products (shells, ornaments, Thai silk ties); every item had a barcode. All in all, airport shops still form part of the national culture; but a part which is safe, attenuated, one which fully complies with international standards of commerce. For the traveller at the end of his journey it is a halfway house, less interesting and less frightening than the rest of the country. I had an inkling that, more and more, the whole world would come to resemble an airport.

Passing the Coral Emporium, I suddenly had the urge to buy a present for Marie-Jeanne; after all, she was all I had in the world. A necklace, a brooch? I was rummaging in a tray when I noticed Valérie a couple of metres away from me.

'I'm trying to choose a necklace . . .' I said hesitantly.

'For a brunette or a blonde?' There was a trace of bitterness in her voice.

'Blonde, blue eyes.'

'In that case, you'd be better off with a pale coral.'

I handed my boarding card to the girl at the counter. As I was paying, I said to Valérie in a rather pitiful tone of voice: 'It's for a colleague at work . . .' She gave me a strange look as though she were in two minds whether to slap me or burst out laughing; but she walked a little way with me to the shop entrance. Most of the group were sitting on benches in the hall; apparently they had done their shopping. I stopped, took a long breath, turned to Valérie.

'We could see each other in Paris . . .' I said finally.

'You think so?' she said scathingly.

I didn't reply, I simply looked at her again. At one point I intended to say, 'It would be a pity . . .' but I'm not sure whether I actually uttered the words.

Valérie looked around, saw Babette and Léa on the nearest bench and turned away in irritation. Then she took a notepad out of her bag, tore off a page and quickly wrote something on it. As she gave me the piece of paper, she started to say something, gave up, and turned and rejoined the group. I glanced at the piece of paper before pocketing it: it was a mobile phone number.

Part Two

Competitive Advantage

1

The plane landed at Roissy at eleven o'clock; I was one of the first to collect my luggage. By half-past twelve I was home. It was Saturday; I could go out and do some shopping, buy some ornaments for the house, etc. An icy wind swept down the Rue Mouffetard and nothing really seemed worth the effort. Animal rights militants were selling yellow stickers. After Christmas, there's always a slight fall-off in domestic food consumption. I bought a roast chicken, two bottles of Graves and the latest copy of *Hot Video*. It was hardly an ambitious selection for my weekend, but it was all I deserved. I devoured half the chicken, the skin was charred and greasy, slightly revolting. Shortly after three o'clock I phoned Valérie. She answered on the second ring. Yes, she was free this evening; for dinner, yes. I could collect her at eight; she lived on the Avenue Reille, near the Parc Montsouris.

She answered the door wearing a pair of white tracksuit

bottoms and a short tee-shirt. 'I'm not ready . . .' she said, pulling her hair back. The movement raised her breasts; she wasn't wearing a bra. I put my hands on her waist, leaned my face closer to hers. She parted her lips, immediately slid her tongue into my mouth. A wave of violent excitement shuddered through me; I almost fainted, immediately got a hard on. Without moving her pubis from mine, she pushed the front door, which closed with a dull thud.

The room, lit by a single lamp, seemed huge. Valérie took me by the waist and, feeling her way, led me to her bedroom. By the bed, she kissed me again. I lifted her tee-shirt to stroke her breasts; she whispered something I didn't catch. I knelt in front of her, slipping down her tracksuit bottoms and her panties, then pressed my face to her sex. The slit was damp, the labia parted, she smelled good. She let out a moan and fell back on the bed. I undressed quickly and entered her. My penis was on fire, spasms of intense pleasure coursed though it. 'Valérie,' I said, 'I'm not going to be able to hold out for long, I'm too excited.' She pulled me to her and whispered in my ear: 'Come . . .' At that moment, I felt the walls of her pussy close on my penis. I felt as though I was disappearing into space, only my penis was alive, a wave of extraordinarily intense pleasure coursing through it. I ejaculated lengthily several times; right at the end, I realised I was screaming. I could have died for such a moment.

Blue and yellow fish were swimming around me. I was

standing in the water, balancing a few metres beneath the sunlit surface. Valérie was a little way off; she too was standing, a coral reef in front of her, she had her back to me. We were both naked. I knew that this weightlessness was due to a change in the density of the ocean, but I was surprised to discover that I could breathe. In a few short strokes I was beside her. The reef was stippled with star-shaped organisms of phosphorescent silver. I placed a hand on her breasts, the other on her lower abdomen. She arched herself, her buttocks brushed against my penis.

I awoke precisely in that position; it was still dark. Gently, I parted Valérie's thighs so I could penetrate her. At the same time, I wet my fingers so I could rub her clitoris. I realised she was awake when she began to moan. She pushed herself on to her knees on the bed. I started to push into her harder and harder – I could tell she was about to come, her breaths came faster and faster. At the moment of orgasm she jerked and let out a heart-rending cry; then she was still, as though exhausted. I withdrew and lay beside her. She relaxed and wrapped herself around me; we were bathed in sweat. 'It's nice to be woken by pleasure . . .' she said, putting a hand on my chest.

When I woke again, it was daylight; I was alone in the bed. I got up and crossed the room. The other room was as vast as I had imagined, with a high ceiling. Above the sofa, bookshelves ran along a mezzanine. Valérie had gone out; on the kitchen table she had left some bread, cheese, butter and jam. I poured myself a coffee and went back to lie down. She returned ten minutes later with croissants and *pains au chocolat* and carried a tray into the bedroom. 'It's really cold out . . .' she said, getting undressed. I thought about Thailand.

'Valérie,' I said hesitantly, 'what do you see in me? I'm not particularly handsome, I'm not funny; I find it difficult to understand why anyone would find me attractive.' She looked at me and said nothing; she was almost naked, she had kept only her panties on. 'It's a serious question,' I insisted. 'Here I am, some washed-up guy, not very sociable, more or less resigned to his boring life. And you come to me, you're friendly, you're affectionate and you give me so much pleasure. I don't understand. It seems to me you're looking for something in me that isn't there. You're bound to be disappointed.' She smiled, I got the impression she was about to say something; then she put her hand on my balls, brought her face towards me. Immediately I was hard again. She wound a lock of hair around the base of my penis, then started to jerk me off with her fingertips. 'I don't know . . .' she said, without stopping what she was doing. 'It's nice that you're unsure of yourself. I wanted you so badly when we were on the trip. It was awful, I thought about it every day.' She pressed harder against my balls, enveloping them in the palm of her hand. With her other hand she took some raspberry jam and spread it on my penis; then she began conscientiously to lick it off with wide sweeps of her tongue. The pleasure was becoming more and more intense, I parted my legs in a desperate effort to hold myself back. As though it was a game, she started to jerk me off more quickly, pressing my cock to her mouth. When her tongue touched the tip of the glans, I ejaculated violently into her half-open mouth. She swallowed with a little moan, then wrapped her lips around the head of my penis to get the last drops. I was flooded with unbelievable serenity, like a wave coursing through each of my veins. She took her mouth away and lay down beside me, coiling herself around me.

'I almost knocked on your bedroom door that night, New Year's Eve, but in the end I didn't have the nerve. By then, I was convinced that nothing would happen between us; the worst thing was that I couldn't even bring myself to hate you for it. On package tours people talk to each other a lot, but it's a forced camaraderie; they know perfectly well they'll never see each other again. It's very rare for them to have a sexual relationship.'

'You think so?'

'I know so; there have been studies on the subject. It's even true of 18–30 holiday clubs. It's a big problem for them, because that's their whole selling point. Numbers have been falling consistently for ten years now, even though prices are dropping. The only possible explanation is that it's become more or less impossible to have a sexual relationship on holiday. The only destinations making any money are the ones with a large homosexual clientele like Corfu or Ibiza.'

'You're very up on all this . . .' I said, surprised.

'Of course, I work in the tourist industry.' She smiled. 'That's another thing about package tours, people don't talk about their professional lives much. It's a sort of recreational parenthesis, completely focused on what the organisers call the "pleasure of discovery". Tacitly, every-one agrees not to talk about serious subjects like work and sex.'

'Where do you work?'

'Nouvelles Frontières.'

'So you were there in a professional capacity? To do a report or something like that?'

'No, I really was on holiday. I got a big discount, obviously, but I took it as holiday time. I've been working there for five years and this was the first time I've been away with them.'

As she made a tomato and mozzarella salad, Valérie talked to me about her work. In March 1990, three months before her *bac*, she started to wonder what she was going to do with her education – and, more generally, with her life. After much effort, her brother had managed to get a place on a geology course at Nancy; he had just got his degree. His career as a geological engineer would probably take him into the mining sector or the oil rigs; either way, he'd be a long way from France. He was keen on travelling. She too was keen on travelling, well, more or less; eventually she decided to take a BTS diploma in tourism. She didn't really think the intellectual commitment necessary for university was in her nature.

It was a mistake and one that she quickly realised. The level of her BTS class seemed extremely low to her, she passed her continuous assessment without the slightest effort and could reasonably have expected to get her diploma without even thinking about it. At the same time, she enrolled in a course which would give her the equivalent of a DEUG university diploma in literature and human sciences. Once she had passed her BTS, she began a masters' in sociology. Here too she was quickly disappointed. It was an interesting field, there must have been discoveries to be made; but the methodologies suggested to them and the theories advanced seemed to her to be ridiculously simplistic: the whole thing smacked of ideology, imprecision and amateurism. She quit her course halfway through the academic year without a qualification and found a job as a travel agent at a branch of Kuoni in Rennes. After a couple of weeks, just as she was about to rent a studio flat, she realised: the trap was sprung; from now on she was in the world of work.

She stayed a year at the Rennes branch of Kuoni, where she proved to be a very good saleswoman. 'It wasn't difficult,' she said, 'All you had to do was get the customers to talk a bit, take an interest in them. It's pretty rare, in fact, people who take an interest in others.' Then the management had offered her a position as assistant tour planner at their head office in Paris. It involved working on concepts for the tours, preparing the itineraries, the excursions, negotiating rates with hoteliers and local contractors. She had proved to be pretty good at this too.

Six months later she replied to a Nouvelles Frontières ad offering a similar sort of position. It was at that point that her career really took off. They had put her in a team with Jean-Yves Frochot, a young business graduate who basically knew nothing at all about tourism. He took to her immediately, trusted her and although in theory he was her boss, he gave her a lot of room for initiative.

'The good thing about Jean-Yves is that he was ambitious on my behalf? Every time I've needed to negotiate a pay rise or a promotion, he's negotiated it for me. Now, he's Head of Products worldwide – he's responsible for supervising the entire range of Nouvelles Frontières tours and I'm still his assistant.'

'You must be pretty well paid.'

'Forty thousand francs a month. Well, it's calculated in euros now. A bit more than six thousand euros.'

I looked at Valérie, surprised, 'I wasn't expecting that . . .' I said.

'That's because you've never seen me in a suit.'

'You have a suit?'

'There's not much point, I do almost all my work by phone. But, if I need to, yes, I can wear a suit. I even have a pair of suspenders. We can try them out some time, if you like.'

It was then, somewhat incredulously, that I realised that I was going to see Valérie again, and that we would probably be happy together. It was so unexpected, this joy, that I wanted to cry; I had to change the subject.

'What's he like, Jean-Yves?'

'Normal. Married, two kids. He works a lot, he takes work home at weekends. I suppose he's a typical young executive, pretty intelligent, pretty ambitious; but he's nice, not at all fucked up. I get along well with him.'

'I don't know why, but I'm glad you're rich. It's not important, really, but it makes me happy.'

'It's true I'm successful, I have a good salary; but I pay 40 per cent tax and my rent is ten thousand francs a month. I'm not so sure I've done all that well: if my results fall off, they wouldn't think twice about firing me; it's happened before. If I had shares, then yes, I really would be rich. In the beginning, Nouvelles Frontières was just a discount flight agency. If they've become the biggest tour operator in France, it's thanks to the concepts and the value-for-money of the tours; to a large extent to our work, Jean-Yves's and mine. In ten years, the value of the company has increased twenty-fold; since Jacques Maillot still holds a 30 per cent share, I can honestly say that he's grown rich because of me.'

'Have you ever met him?'

'Several times; I don't like him. On the face of it, he's a stupid trendy Catholic populist, with his multi-coloured ties and his mopeds; but deep down he's a ruthless, hypocritical bastard. Jean-Yves had a call from a head-hunter before Christmas; he's probably met up with him by now to find out more. I promised I'd call him when I got back.'

'Well call him then, it's important.'

'Yes . . .' she seemed a bit doubtful, the mention of Jacques Maillot had depressed her. 'My life is important too. Actually, I feel like making love again.'

'I don't know if I'll be able to get it up straight away.'

'Then go down on me. It'll do me good.'

She got up, took off her panties and settled herself on the sofa. I knelt in front of her, parted her lips and started to lick her clitoris gently. 'Harder . . .' she murmured. I slipped a finger into her arse, pressed my face to her and kissed the nub, massaging it with my lips. 'Oh, yes . . .' she said. I increased the force of my kisses. Suddenly, without my expecting it, she came, her whole body shuddering violently.

'Come here to me . . .' I sat on the sofa. She snuggled against me, laying her head on my thighs. 'When I asked you what Thai women have that we don't, you didn't really answer; you just showed me that interview with the director of the marriage bureau.'

'What he said was true: a lot of men are afraid of modern women, because all they want is a nice little wife to look after the house and take care of the kids. That sort of thing hasn't disappeared really, it's just that in the West it's become impossible to express such a desire; that's why they marry Asian girls.'

'Okay . . .' She thought for a moment. 'But you're not like that; I can tell that it doesn't bother you at all that I have a high-powered job, a large salary; I don't get the impression that that scares you at all. But still you went off to the massage parlours and you didn't even try to pick me up. That's what I don't understand. What have the girls over there got? Do they really make love better than we do?'

Her voice had changed slightly on these last words; I was rather touched and it took me a minute before I could answer. 'Valérie,' I said at last, 'I have never met anyone who makes love as well as you; what I've felt since last night is almost unbelievable.' I said nothing for a moment before adding: 'You can't possibly understand, but you're an exception. It's very rare now to find a woman who feels pleasure and who wants to give pleasure. On the whole, seducing a woman you don't know, fucking her, has become a source of irritations and problems. When you think of all the tedious conversations you have to put up with to get a girl into bed, only to find out that she's a second-rate lover who bores you to fuck with her problems, goes on at you about her exes – incidentally giving you the impression that you're not exactly up to scratch – and with whom you absolutely must spend the rest of the night at the very least, it's easy to see why men might prefer to save themselves the trouble by paying a small fee. As soon as they're a bit older or a bit more experienced, men prefer to steer clear of love; they find it easier just to go and find a whore. Actually, not a Western whore, they're not worth the effort, they're real human debris, and in any case, most of the year the men haven't got time, they've got too much work. So, most of them do nothing; and some of them, from time to time, treat themselves to a little sex tourism. And that's the best possible scenario: at least there's still a little human contact in going to visit a whore. There're also all those guys who find it easier just to jerk off on the internet or watching porn films. As soon as your cock has shot its little load, you're perfectly happy.'

'I see . . .' she said after a long silence. 'I see what you're saying. And you don't think that men or women are capable of changing?'

'I don't think we can go back to the way things were, no. What will probably happen is that women will become much more like men. For the moment, they're still very hung up on romance; whereas at heart, men don't give a shit about romance, they just want to fuck. Seduction only appeals to a few guys who haven't got particularly exciting jobs and nothing else of interest in their lives. As women attach more importance to their professional lives and personal projects, they'll find it easier to pay for sex too; and they'll turn to sex tourism. It's possible for women to adapt to male values; they sometimes find it difficult, but they can do it; history has proved it.'

'So, all in all, things are in a bad way.'

'A very bad way . . .' I agreed solemnly.

'So, we were lucky.'

'I was lucky to meet you, yes.'

'Me too . . .' she said, looking me in the eyes. 'I was lucky too. The men I know are a disaster, not one of them believes in love; so they give you this big spiel about friendship, affection, a whole load of stuff that doesn't commit them to anything. I've got to the point where I can't stand the word 'friendship' any more, it makes me physically sick. Or there's the other lot, the ones who get married, who get hitched as early as possible and think about nothing but their careers afterwards. You obviously weren't one of those; but I also immediately sensed that you would never talk to me about friendship, that you would never be that vulgar. From the very beginning I hoped we would sleep together, that something important would happen; but it was possible that nothing would happen, in fact it was more than likely.' She stopped and sighed in irritation. 'Okay . . .' she said wearily 'I'd probably better go and call Jean-Yves.'

I went into the bedroom to get dressed while she was on the phone. 'Yeah, the holiday was great . . .' I heard her say. A little later she yelled: 'How much? . . .' When I came back into the room she was holding the receiver looking thoughtful; she had not yet dressed.

'Jean-Yves met the guy from the recruitment agency,' she said. 'They've offered him a hundred and twenty thousand francs a month. They're prepared to take me as well; according to him, they're prepared to go as high as eighty thousand. He has a meeting tomorrow to discuss the job.'

'Where would you be working?'

'It's with the leisure division of the Aurore group.'

'Is it a big company?'

'Too right it is; it's the biggest hotel chain in the world.'

2

Being able to understand a customer's behaviour in order to categorise him more effectively, offering him the right product at the right time, but above all persuading him that the product he is offered is adapted to his needs: that is what all companies dream of.

Jean-Louis Barma, *What Companies Dream Of*

Jean-Yves woke at five in the morning, looked over at his wife who was still sleeping. They had spent a terrible weekend with his parents – his wife couldn't stand the countryside. Nicolas, his ten-year-old son, loathed the Loiret too, as he couldn't bring his computer there; and he didn't like his grandparents, he thought they smelled. It was true that his father was slipping, increasingly, it seemed he was unable to look after himself, scarcely interested in anything apart from his rabbits. The only tolerable aspect of these weekends was his daughter, Angélique: at three, she was still capable of going into raptures over cows or chickens; but she was teething at the moment and had spent the greater part of the nights crying and whimpering. Once they got back, after three hours stuck in traffic jams, Audrey had decided to go out with some friends. He had heated up something from the freezer while he watched some mediocre American film about an autistic serial killer – it was apparently based on a true story. The man had been the first mentally ill person to be executed in the state of Nebraska for more than sixty years. His son hadn't wanted any dinner, he had immediately launched himself into a game of *Total Annihilation* – or maybe it was *Mortal Kombat II*, he got them mixed up. From time to time, he went into his daughter's room to try and quieten her howls. She fell asleep around one o'clock; Audrey still wasn't home.

She had come home in the end, he thought, making himself a coffee at the espresso machine; this time, at least. The law firm she worked for numbered *Libération* and *Le Monde* among its clients; one way or another she had started hanging out with a group of journalists, television presenters and politicians. They went out quite a lot, sometimes to strange places – once when he was leafing through one of her books he came across a card for a fetish bar. Jean-Yves suspected that she slept with some guy once in awhile; in any case she and Jean-Yves didn't sleep together any more. Curiously, for his part, he didn't have affairs. Although he was aware he was handsome in a blond, blue-eyed way more common in Americans, he never really felt like taking advantage of the opportunities which might have presented themselves – in any case they were pretty rare: he worked twelve to fourteen hours a day and at his level of seniority you didn't really meet many women. Of course there was Valérie; he had never thought of her other than as a colleague before. It was odd to think of her in this new light; but he knew it was an unimportant daydream: they had been working together for five years now and in situations like that things happened straight away, or they didn't happen at all. He admired Valérie a lot, her astonishing organisational abilities, her infallible memory; without her, he realised, he would never have got to where he was – or at least not as quickly as he had. And today, he might well be about to take a decisive step. He brushed his teeth, shaved carefully, before picking out a rather sober suit. Then he pushed open the door to his daughter's room; she was asleep, blonde like he was, in a pair of pyjamas decorated with chicks.

He walked to the République Fitness Club, which opened at seven. He and Audrey lived on the Rue du Faubourg-du-Temple, a rather trendy area which he hated. His meeting at the head office of the Aurore group was not until ten o'clock. Audrey could take care of getting the children dressed and driving them to school for once. He knew that when he got home tonight he would have a half-hour of nagging coming to him; as he walked along the wet pavement among the empty boxes and the vegetable peelings, he realised that he couldn't care less. He realised, also, for the first time with absolute clarity, that his marriage had been a mistake. This kind of realisation, he knew, usually precedes divorce by about two or three years – it's never an easy decision to take.

The big black guy at reception gave him a not very convincing 'How's things, boss?'. He handed him his membership card, nodded and took a towel. When he had met Audrey, he was only twenty-three. Two years later they got married, partly – but only partly – because she was pregnant. She was pretty, stylish, she dressed well – and she could be very sexy when she wanted to. Besides, she had ideas. The emergence of American-style judicial proceedings in France did not seem to her to be a regression, on the contrary, she thought it was progress, towards better protection for citizens and civil liberties. She was capable of expounding fairly lengthily on the subject, she was just back from doing work experience in the United States. In a nutshell, she had conned him. It was strange, he thought, how he had always felt the need to be impressed by women intellectually.

He started off with half-an-hour working through different levels on the Stairmaster, then twenty lengths of the pool. In the sauna, which was deserted at this time of day, he started to relax – and took the opportunity to run through in his mind what he knew about the Aurore group. Novotel-SIEH had been founded in 1966 by Gérard Pélisson and Paul Dubrule – one a graduate of the École Centrale, the other completely self-taught – using capital borrowed entirely from family and friends. In August 1967, the first Novotel opened its doors in Lille. It already included many of the characteristics which were to emerge as the hallmarks of the group: the rooms highly standardised, locations on the outskirts of cities – to be more precise, off the motorway, at the last exit before the city itself, above average standards of comfort for the time – Novotel was one of the first chains routinely to offer en-suite bathrooms. It was an immediate success with business travellers: in 1972, the chain already numbered thirty-five hotels. This was followed in '73 by the creation of Ibis, the takeover of Mercure in '75 and of Sofitel in '81 At the same time, the group prudently diversified into catering, acquiring the Courtepaille chain and the Jacques Borel International group, already well established in the group-catering and self-service restaurant sectors. In 1983, the company changed its name to become the Aurore group. Then, in '85, they created the Formules 1 – the first hotels with absolutely no personnel and one of the greatest successes in the history of the hotel business. Already well established in Africa and the Middle East, the company got a foothold in Asia and set up its own training centre – the Aurore academy. In 1990, the acquisition of Motel 6, comprising 650 locations throughout the United States, made the group the largest in the world; it was followed in '91 by a successful takeover bid for the Wagons Lits group. These acquisitions were costly and in '93, Aurore faced a crisis: the shareholders considered the company's debts to be too high, and the buyout of the

Méridien chain fell through. Thanks to the transfer of a number of assets and a recovery plan for Europcar, Lenôtre and the Societé des Casinos Lucien Barrière, the situation was turned around by the 1995 financial year. In January '97, Paul Dubrule and Gérard Pélisson resigned the presidency of the group which they ceded to Jean-Luc Espitalier, a graduate of the *École Normale d'Administration*, whose career was described by the financial magazines as 'atypical'. However they remained members of the supervisory board. The transition went well and, by the end of 2000, the group had reinforced its position as world leader, consolidating its lead over Marriott and Hyatt, numbers two and three respectively. Of the ten largest hotel chains in the world, nine were American and one French – the Aurore group.

At nine-thirty, Jean-Yves parked his car in the car park of the group head office at Évry. He walked for a while in the frosty air, to unwind while waiting for the appointed time. At ten o'clock precisely, he was shown into the office of Éric Leguen, executive vice-president for hotels and member of the board of directors. He was forty-five, a graduate of the École Céntrale, with a degree from Stanford.

Tall and sturdy, with blond hair and blue eyes, he looked a little like Jean-Yves – though ten years older and with something more confident in his attitude.

'M Espitalier, our president, will meet with you in fifteen minutes,' he began. 'In the meantime, I'll explain why you're here. Two months ago, we bought the

Eldorador chain from Jet Tours. It's a little chain of about a dozen beach hotel/holiday clubs spread over the Maghreb, black Africa and the West Indies.'

'It's showing a loss, I believe.'

'No more than the sector as a whole.' He smiled briefly. 'Well, yes, actually, a bit more than the sector as a whole. To be quite frank, the purchase price was reasonable, but it wasn't peanuts; there were a number of other groups in the running: there are still a lot of people in the industry who believe that the sector will pick up again. It's true that, at the moment, Club Med is the only one managing to hold its own; strictly confidentially, we had actually thought of making a takeover bid for Club Med. But the prey was a little too large, the shareholders would never have gone with it. In any case, it wouldn't have been a very friendly thing to do to Philippe Bourguignon, who is a former employee . . .' He gave a rather phony smile, as though he was trying to suggest that this was perhaps – but not definitely – a joke. 'Anyway,' he went on, 'what we are proposing is that you take over the management of all of the Eldorador resorts. Your objective, obviously, being to bring them back quickly to breakeven and then to make them profitable.'

'That's not an easy task.'

'We're very aware of that; we feel that the level of remuneration offered is sufficiently attractive. Not to mention the career prospects within the group, which are huge: we have offices in 142 countries, we employ more than a hundred and thirty thousand people. On top of that, most of our senior executives quickly become shareholders in the group: it's a system we firmly believe in. I've written up some details for you with some sample calculations.'

'I would also need more detailed information on the circumstances of the hotels in the group.'

'Of course; I'll give you a detailed dossier a little later. This is not simply a tactical acquisition; we believe in the potential of the organisation: geographically the resorts are well sited, the general condition excellent – there's very little in the way of improvements to be made. At least, that's my opinion, but I don't have any experience of the leisure sector. We'll be working together, obviously; but you will make the decisions on these matters. If you want to get rid of a hotel or acquire another, the final decision in the matter is yours. That's how we work at Aurore.'

He thought for a moment before going on: 'Of course, it's no accident that you're here. The industry has carefully followed your career at Nouvelles Frontières; you might even say you have something of a following. You haven't systematically sought to offer the lowest prices, nor the highest level of service; in each case you've matched a price that is acceptable to customers very closely with a certain level of service; that's exactly the philosophy we follow within every chain in the group. And something equally important, you've had a hand in creating a brand with a very strong image; that's something we haven't always been able to do at Aurore.'

The telephone on Leguen's desk rang. The conversation was very brief. He got up and led Jean-Yves along the beige-tiled corridor. Jean-Luc Espitalier's office was vast, it must have been at least twenty metres wide; the left-hand side was taken up by a large conference table with some fifteen chairs. As they approached, Espitalier stood and welcomed them with a smile. He was a small man, quite young – certainly no older than forty-five – his hair receding at the front, he looked oddly unobtrusive, almost retiring, as though he was trying to soften the importance of his role with irony. You probably shouldn't count on it, thought Jean-Yves; ENA graduates are often like that, they develop a veneer of humour which turns out to be deceptive. They settled themselves in armchairs around a low table in front of his desk. Espitalier looked at him for a long time with his curious, shy smile before beginning to speak.

'I have a lot of respect for Jacques Maillot,' he said eventually; 'He's built up a first-rate company, very original and with a real ethos. It doesn't happen often. That said – and I don't want to play the prophet of doom here – I think French tour operators need to prepare themselves for a rough ride. Very soon – it's inevitable at this stage, and in my opinion it's only a matter of months – British and German tour operators are going to make inroads into the market. They have two to three times the level of financial backing, and their tours are 20 to 30 per cent cheaper, for a comparable or a better standard of service. Competition will be tough, very tough. To be blunt, there will be casualties. I'm not saying Nouvelles Frontières will be one of them; it's a group with a strong identity and level-headed shareholders, it can weather this. Nevertheless, the years ahead are going to be tough for everyone.

'At Aurore, we don't have that problem at all,' he went on with a little sigh, 'we are the uncontested world leader in the business hotel sector, which fluctuates very little; but we are still poorly established in the leisure hotel sector, which is more volatile, more sensitive to economic and political fluctuations.'

'As a matter of fact,' interrupted Jean-Yves, 'I was rather surprised by your acquisition. I thought your main development priority was still business hotels, particularly in Asia.'

'That is still our main priority,' replied Espitalier calmly. 'In China alone, for example, there is extraordinary potential in the business hotel sector. We have the experience, we have the know-how: imagine concepts like Ibis and Formule 1 rolled out across the country? That said . . . how should I put this?' He thought for a moment, looked at the ceiling, at the conference table to his right before looking back at Jean-Yves. 'Aurore is a discreet group,' he said at length; 'Paul Dubrule used to say that the sole secret of success in the market was to be timely. Timely means not too early: it's very rare for true innovators to reap the full profits of their innovation – that's the story of Apple and Microsoft. But obviously, it also means not too late. That's where our discretion has served us well. If you do your development work in the shadows, without making waves, by the time your competitors wake up and decide to move on to your patch, it's too late: you have your territory sewn up, you have acquired a crucial competitive advantage. Our reputation has not kept pace with our actual significance; for the most part, this has been done deliberately.

'That time is gone,' he went on with another sigh; 'Everyone now knows that we are number one in the world. At that point it becomes useless – even dangerous – to count on our discretion. It's essential for a group of Aurore's size to have a public image. The business hotel sector is a dependable market, which generates guaranteed regular, substantial, revenues. But it's not, how shall I put it, it's not really *fun*. People rarely talk about their business trips, there's no pleasure in telling people about them. To build a positive image with the general public there are two possibilities open to us: tour operating or 18–30-style holiday clubs. Becoming a tour operator is further from our core business, but there are a number of very healthy businesses likely to change hands in the near future – we very nearly went down that road. And when Eldorador presented itself, we decided to seize the opportunity.'

'I'm just trying to understand your objectives,' said Jean-Yves. 'Are you more focused on profit or public image?'

'That's a complex issue . . .' Espitalier hesitated, shifting slightly in his chair. 'Aurore's problem is that it has a very weak shareholder base. That, in fact, is what started the

rumours of a takeover bid in 1994 – I can tell you now,'
he went on with a confident gesture, 'that they were
completely unfounded. That would be even more true
now: we have no debt whatever, and no international
company, even outside the hotel business, is large enough
to mount a bid. What remains true is that, unlike
Nouvelles Frontières for example, we do not have a
coherent shareholder base. At heart, Paul Dubrule and
Gérard Pélisson were less capitalists than they were
entrepreneurs – and great entrepreneurs in my opinion,
among the greatest the century has produced. But they
did not seek to keep a controlling share in their business;
it is this which puts us in a delicate position today. You
know as well as I do that it is occasionally necessary to
sanction prestige spending, something which will improve
the strategic position of the group without making a
positive impact on revenues in the short term. We also
know that it is sometimes necessary to temporarily shore
up a loss-making sector because the market hasn't
matured or because it is going through a short-term crisis.
This is something that the new generation of shareholders
finds difficult to accept: the focus on rapid returns on
investment has been deeply unconstructive and
damaging.'

He raised his hand discreetly, seeing that Jean-Yves was
about to interrupt. 'Mind you,' he went on, 'our shareholders are not imbeciles. They are perfectly aware that in
the current climate it would not be possible to bring a
chain like Eldorador back to breakeven in the first year –

probably not even in two years. But come the third year they'll want to look very hard at the figures – and they won't be long in coming to their conclusions. At that point, even if you have a magnificent plan, even if the potential is vast, I won't be able to do anything.'

There was a long silence. Leguen sat motionless, he had lowered his head. Espitalier stroked his chin sceptically. 'I see . . .' Jean-Yves said at last. After a couple of seconds he added calmly: 'I'll give you my answer in three days.'

3

I saw a lot of Valérie over the two months that followed. In fact, with the exception of a weekend she spent at her parents, I think I probably saw her every day. Jean-Yves had decided to accept the Aurore group's offer; she had decided to follow him. The first thing she said to me, I remember, was: 'I'm about to move into the 60 per cent tax bracket.' She was right: her salary was going from forty thousand francs a month to seventy-five thousand; after tax, the increase was less spectacular. She knew that she would have to put a lot of work in from the moment she took up her job at the group early in March. For the time being, at Nouvelles Frontières, everything was fine: they had both tendered their resignations, they were gradually handing over the reins to their successors. I advised Valérie to save, to open a savings account or something; in fact, we didn't think about it much. Spring was late, but that was of no importance. Later, thinking about this happy time with Valérie, a time of which, paradoxically, I have so few memories, I would say that man is clearly not intended to be happy. To truly arrive at the practical possibility of happiness, man would have to transform himself – transform himself *physically*. What can one compare with God? In the first place, obviously, a woman's pussy; but also perhaps the steam in a hammam. Something, at any rate, in which spirit becomes possible, because the body is sated with contentment, with pleasure, and all anxiety is abolished. I now know for certain that the spirit is not born, that it needs to be brought forth, and it will be a difficult birth, something of which we now have only a vague and harmful idea. When I brought Valérie to orgasm, when I felt her body quiver under mine, I sometimes had the impression – fleeting but irresistible – of attaining a new level of consciousness, where every evil had been abolished. In those moments of suspension, almost of motionlessness, when the pleasure in her body mounted, I felt like a god on whom depended tranquillity and storms. It was the first joy – indisputable, perfect.

The second joy which Valérie brought me was the extraordinary gentleness, the natural goodness of her nature. Sometimes, when she had been working long hours – and over the months they would become longer and longer – I felt that she was tense, emotionally drained. Never once did she turn on me, never once did she get angry, never once did she lapse into the unpredictable hysterics which sometimes make the company of women so oppressive, so pathetic. 'I'm not ambitious, Michel . . .'

she would tell me sometimes. 'I feel happy with you, I think you're the love of my life, and I don't ask for anything more than that. But that's not possible: I have to ask for more. I'm trapped in a system from which I get so little, which I know is futile; but I don't know how to get out. Just once, we should take time to think; but I don't know when we'll be able to take time to think.'

For my part, I was doing less and less work, at least I was doing my work only in the strictest possible sense. I was home in plenty of time to watch *Questions pour un champion* and shop for dinner; I spent every night at Valérie's place. Curiously, Marie-Jeanne didn't seem to hold my flagging professional attention against me. True, she enjoyed her work and was more than happy to take on her share of overtime. What she wanted more than anything, I think, was for me to be nice to her – and I was nice through all those weeks, I was gentle and peaceful. She had liked the coral necklace I had brought her from Thailand, she wore it every day now. As she worked on the files for the exhibitions she would sometimes look at me in a way that was strange and difficult to decipher. One morning in February – I remember it very well, it was my birthday – she said to me straight out: 'You've changed, Michel . . . I don't know, you seem happy.'

She was right; I was happy, I remember that. Of course there are lots of things, a whole series of inevitable troubles, decline and death, of course. But remembering those months, I can bear witness: I know that happiness exists.

Jean-Yves, on the other hand, was not happy, that was obvious. I remember the three of us having dinner together in an Italian, or rather a Venetian, restaurant, something pretty trendy anyway. He knew that we would go home later and fuck, and we could fuck with love. I didn't really know what to say to him – everything there was to be said was too obvious, too blunt. His wife obviously didn't love him, she had probably never loved anyone; and she would never love anyone, that too was patently clear. He hadn't had much luck, that was all. Human relationships aren't nearly as complicated as people make out: they're often insoluble but only rarely complicated. Now, of course, he would have to get a divorce; it wouldn't be easy but it had to be done. What else could I possibly say? The subject was dealt with long before we finished the *antipasti*.

Afterwards they talked about their careers within the Aurore group: they already had some ideas, a number of possible objectives for the Eldorador takeover. They were intelligent, competent, much-admired in their industry; but they could not afford to make a mistake. To fail in this new position would not be the end of their careers: Jean-Yves was thirty-five, Valérie, twenty-eight; they would be given a second chance. But the industry would not forget that first blunder, they would have to start again at a significantly lower level. In the society we lived in, the most important consideration in any position was represented by the *salary*, and more generally the financial benefits; the prestige and distinction of the post tended nowadays to occupy a much less significant position. There existed, however, a highly developed system of fiscal redistribution which allowed the useless, the incompetent and the dangerous – a group of which, in some sense, I was a part – to survive. In short, we were living in a mixed economy which was slowly evolving towards a more pronounced liberalism, slowly overcoming the prejudice against usury - and in more general terms, against money – which persists in traditionally Catholic countries. They could expect no real benefits from such a change. A number of young Hautes Études Commerciales business graduates, much younger than Jean-Yves – some of them still students – had thrown themselves headlong into market speculation without ever considering looking for paid employment. They had computers connected to the internet, sophisticated market-tracking software. Quite frequently, they formed groups or clubs in order to be able to make more substantial investments. They lived with their computers, worked in shifts twenty-four hours a day, never took holidays. The goal of each and every one was extraordinarily simple: to become billionaires before they turned thirty.

Jean-Yves and Valérie were part of an intermediary generation for whom it still seemed difficult to imagine a career outside business, or possibly the public sector; a little older than they were, I was in more or less the same position. The three of us were caught up in a social system like insects in a block of amber; there wasn't the slightest possibility that we could turn back.

On the morning of March 1, Valérie and Jean-Yves officially took up their positions at the Aurore group. A meeting had already been scheduled for March 4 with the principal executives who would be working on the Eldorador project. Senior management had requested a long-term study of the future of holiday clubs from Profiles, a well-known consultancy working in the field of behavioural sociology.

Despite himself, as he walked into the 23rd floor conference room for the first time, Jean-Yves was quite impressed. There were about twenty people there, every one of whom had several years' experience with Aurore behind them; and it was now up to him to lead the group. Valérie sat immediately to his left. He had spent the weekend studying the files; he knew the names, precise responsibilities and professional history of every person sitting at the table; yet he could not help feeling a little anxious. A grey day settled over the graceful suburbs of Essonne. When Paul Dubrule and Gérard Pélisson had decided to set up their head office in Évry, they had been influenced by cheap land and the proximity of the motorway to Orly Airport and the south; at the time, it was a quiet suburb. Now, the local communities had the highest crime rate in all France. Every week, there were attacks on buses, police cars, fire engines; there was not even an exact figure for assaults or robberies; some people estimated that to get the true figure, you had to multiply the number of reported crimes by five. The company premises were watched over twenty-four hours a day by a team of armed guards. An internal memo advised that public transport was best avoided after a certain time. For employees who had to work late and who did not have their own cars, Aurore had negotiated a discount with a local taxi firm.

When Lindsay Lagarrigue, the behavioural sociologist, arrived, Jean-Yves felt he was on familiar territory. The guy was about thirty, with a receding hairline, his hair tied back in a ponytail; he wore an Adidas tracksuit, a Prada tee-shirt and a pair of battered Nikes: in short, he looked like a behavioural sociologist. He began by handing out copies of a very slim file, mostly made up of diagrams with arrows and circles; his briefcase contained nothing else. The front page was a photocopy of an article from the *Nouvel Observateur*, more precisely, it was an editorial from the travel section, entitled 'Another Way to Travel'.

'In the year 2000,' Lagarrigue began, reading the article aloud, 'mass tourism has had its day. We dream of travel as of individual fulfilment, but we have ethical concerns.' This opening paragraph seemed to him symptomatic of the changes that were occurring. He talked about this for a few minutes, then asked those present to concentrate on the following sentences: 'In the year 2000, we worry about whether tourism is respectful of others. Being affluent, we want our travels to be more than simply selfish pleasures, we want them to bear witness to a certain sense of solidarity.'

'How much did we pay this guy for the study?' Jean-Yves asked Valérie discreetly.

'A hundred and fifty thousand francs.'

'I don't believe it . . . Is this asshole just going to read out a photocopy of an article from the *Nouvel Obs*?'

Linsday Lagarrigue went on, loosely paraphrasing the article, then he read a third passage, in an absurdly emphatic voice: 'In the year 2000,' he declared, 'we want to be nomads. We travel by train or by ship, over rivers and oceans; in an age of speed, we are rediscovering the pleasures of slothfulness. We lose ourselves in the silent infinities of the desert, and then, without a break, plunge into the tumult of great cities. But always with the same passion . . .' Ethical, individual fulfilment, solidarity, passion: these, according to him, were the key words. In this new mood, it was hardly surprising that the holiday club, based on selfish isolation, on the standardisation of needs and desires, was beset by chronic problems. The days of the *sun worshippers* were over: what travellers today were looking for was authenticity, discovery, a sense of sharing. More generally, the Fordist production-line model of leisure travel – typified by the famous '4 S': Sea, Sand, Sun . . . and Sex – was doomed. As the work of Michky and Braun had shown so spectacularly, the industry as a whole would have to begin to consider its activities from a post-Fordist perspective.

The behavioural sociologist clearly knew his job; he could have gone on for hours. 'Excuse me . . .' Jean-Yves interrupted him in a tone of barely suppressed irritation.

'Yes . . .' the behavioural sociologist gave him a winning smile.

'I think that every person at this table, without

exception, is aware that the holiday-club model is undergoing some problems at the moment. What we want from you isn't so much an endless description of the nature of those problems, but rather an attempt, however slight, to indicate the beginnings of a solution.'

Lindsay Lagarrigue was open-mouthed; he had not anticipated an objection of this kind. 'I think . . .' he mumbled eventually, 'I think that in order to solve the problem it is important to define it and to have some sense of what has caused it.' Another empty phrase, thought Jean-Yves furiously; not only empty, but, as it happened, untrue. The causes were clearly part of general shifts in society which were beyond their powers to change. They had to adapt to this new business climate, that was all. How could they adapt to it? This moron clearly hadn't the faintest idea.

'What you're telling us, broadly speaking,' went on Jean-Yves, 'is that the holiday-club model is obsolete.'

'No, no, not at all . . .' The behavioural sociologist was beginning to lose his footing. 'I think . . . I simply think that it requires thought.' 'And what the hell are we paying you for, asshole?' retorted Jean-Yves under his breath before addressing all those present:

'All right, we'll try to give it some thought. I'd like to thank Monsieur Lagarrigue for his contribution; I don't think we'll be needing you again today. I suggest we break for ten minutes for coffee.'

Piqued, the behavioural sociologist packed away his

diagrams. When the meeting resumed, Jean-Yves picked up his notes and began:

'Between 1993 and 1997, as you know, Club Med went through the worst crisis in its history. Competitors and imitators had multiplied, they had ripped off the Club formula wholesale while undercutting the Club considerably: numbers were in freefall. How did they manage to turn the situation around? Chiefly, by dropping their prices. But they didn't drop them to the same level as their rivals: they knew that they had the advantage of being the original, they had a reputation, an image; they knew their customers would accept a certain price differential – which they set, according to destination, and after meticulous research, at between 20 and 30 per cent – for the real Club Med experience, the 'original' if you like. This is the first idea I propose that we explore in the coming weeks: is there room in the holiday-club sector for something different from the Club Med formula? And, if so, can we begin to visualise what that something might be, what its target market might look like? The question is far from simple.

'I've come,' he went on, 'as you probably know, I've come here from Nouvelles Frontières. And, although it's not what the group is best known for, we also had a stab at the holiday-club sector: the Paladiens. We began to experience problems with the clubs at about the same time as Club Med; we resolved those problems very quickly. How? Because we were the largest tour operator in France. At the end of their discovery tour of the country, our customers, for the most part, wanted to spend some time at the beach. Our tours often have the reputation, justifiably, of being tough, of requiring a high level of physical fitness. Having won their stripes as 'travellers' the hard way, our customers were generally delighted to be back in the shoes of ordinary tourists for a while. In fact, the formula was so successful that we decided to include a beach supplement as standard in most of the tours – which allowed us to bump up the length of the tours; as you all know, a day at the beach is much less expensive than a travel day. Given this, it was easy for us to favour our own hotels. This is the second thing I propose we consider: it's possible that the future of holiday clubs depends on closer links with tour operators. You'll have to use your imaginations here, too, and don't limit yourselves to the players currently operating in the French market. I'm asking you to explore a new field; we may have a lot to gain from alliances with the major Northern European tour-operators.'

At the end of the meeting, a woman of about thirty, blonde, pretty face, approached Jean-Yves. Her name was Marylise Le François, she was the marketing manager. 'I wanted to tell you how much I appreciated your intervention . . .' she said. 'It had to be done. I think you've managed to remotivate people. Now everyone knows that there is somebody at the controls, we'll really be able to get back down to work.'

4

It quickly became apparent that it would not be quite so simple. Most of the British and particularly the German tour operators already had their own chains of holiday clubs and they weren't interested in allying themselves to another group. All attempts in that direction proved futile. On the other hand, the Club Med seemed to have hit on the definitive formula for a holiday club; since their inception, none of their rivals had proved able to offer anything really new.

Two weeks later, Valérie finally had an idea. It was almost 10 p.m.; she had collapsed into an armchair in the middle of Jean-Yves's office and was sipping a hot chocolate before heading home. They were both exhausted, they had spent the whole day working on the financial report on the clubs.

'You know,' she sighed, 'I think we might be making a mistake in trying to separate the tours from the relaxation.'

'What do you mean?'

'Remember at Nouvelles Frontières: even before we added the beach supplements to the end of the holiday, whenever there was a day at the beach in the middle of a tour, the customers always enjoyed it. And the thing people complained about most often was having to change hotels all the time. What we really want, in fact, is to alternate the excursions with time at the beach – a day touring, a day relaxing and so on. Coming back to the hotel every night, or the following night if the excursion is long, but not having to pack or check out of your room.'

'Resorts already offer additional excursions; and I'm not sure they have much take-up for them.'

'Yes, but there's a supplement, and the French hate paying supplements. On top of that, you have to make the reservation after you get there: people hesitate, they dither, they can't decide, and in the end they do nothing. Actually, they like the excursions as long as you do all the work for them; and above all they love things that are *all-inclusive*.'

Jean-Yves thought for a moment. 'You know, what you're suggesting is not a bad idea. 'On top of that, we should be able to get it under way pretty quickly: this summer, I think. We could offer the new formula as a complement to the ordinary packages. We could call it Eldorador Discovery, something like that.'

Jean-Yves consulted Leguen before implementing the idea; he quickly realised that the other man had no desire to express an opinion one way or the other. 'It's your responsibility,' Leguen said solemnly. Listening to Valérie tell me how she spent her days, I realised I didn't know very much about the world of the senior executive. Her double act with Jean-Yves was in itself remarkable. 'Under normal circumstances,' she told me, 'his assistant would be some girl who dreamed of getting his job. That complicates office politics: it means that sometimes its better to fail, as long as you can pass the blame on to somebody else.' In this case, they were in a healthier position; no one in the group wanted their jobs; most of the executives thought the takeover of Eldorador had been a mistake.

For the rest of the month, she spent a lot of time working with Marylise Le François. The catalogues for the summer holidays had to be ready by the end of April at the very latest, in fact even that was cutting it fine. She rapidly realised that the Jet Tours marketing for the resorts had been absolutely appalling. 'An Eldorador holiday is like that magical moment in Africa, when the heat begins to fade and the whole village gathers around the talking-tree to listen to the elders . . .' she read aloud to Jean-Yves. 'Honestly, can you believe this stuff? With photos of the holiday reps leaping about in their ridiculous yellow uniforms. It's complete rubbish.'

'What do you think of the slogan, "Eldorador, live life more intensely"?'

'I don't know; I don't know what to think anymore.'

'It's too late for the standard packages, the catalogues

have already gone out. One thing's for sure though, we'll have to start from scratch with the "Discovery" catalogue.'

'What I think we need to do,' interrupted Marylise, 'is to play up the contrast between physical effort and luxury. Mint tea in the middle of the desert, but on priceless carpets . . .'

'Yeah, the magical moments . . .' said Jean-Yves jadedly. He got up from his chair with effort. 'Don't forget to put "magical moments" in there somewhere; oddly enough it works every time. Okay, I'll leave you to it; I have to get back to my fixed costs . . .'

Valérie was well aware that there was no question but that Jean-Yves had the most thankless aspects of the work. She herself knew very little about hotel management – it simply brought back vague memories of studying for her BTS. 'Edward Yang owns a three-star hotel and restaurant and believes that it is his responsibility to satisfy his customers to the best of his ability; he is constantly seeking to innovate and to respond to customer needs. From experience, he knows that breakfast is very important, the most important meal of the day, and plays a decisive role in establishing the image of the hotel.' This had been part of a written test in her first year. Edward Yang arranges for a statistical analysis of his customers, focusing particularly on the number of guests per room (single people, couples, families). You had to break down the analysis, calculate chi squared; the section concluded with the following question: 'To sum up, do family circumstances correlate with the consumption of fresh fruit at breakfast?'

Rummaging through her files, she managed to find a BTS question which corresponded pretty closely to their present situation.

'You have just been appointed marketing manager of the international arm of the South America group. The company has recently purchased a hotel-restaurant in the West Indies, a four-star establishment with 110 rooms on the sea-front in Guadeloupe. Opened in 1988 and renovated in 1996, it is currently experiencing serious problems. The occupancy rate is only 45%, far below the anticipated breakeven point.'

Her answer was marked 18/20, which seemed to be a good sign. At the time, she remembered, it all seemed like a fairytale to her, and not a very plausible one. She couldn't imagine herself as marketing director of *South America*, or of anything else for that matter. It was a game, an intellectual game that was neither very interesting nor very difficult. Now, it was no longer a game; or perhaps it was, but their careers were the stakes.

She would come back from work so exhausted that she hadn't the energy to make love, barely enough energy to suck me off; she would be half asleep with my penis still in her mouth. When I penetrated her, it was usually in the morning when we woke. Her orgasms were more muted, more restrained, as though muffled by a curtain of fatigue; I think I loved her more and more.

At the end of April the catalogues were printed and distributed to five thousand travel agents – almost the entirety of the French network. Now, they needed to deal with the infrastructure for the tours so that everything would be ready for July 1. Word of mouth was very important in launching a new product of this kind: a tour cancelled or poorly organised could mean a lot of lost customers. They had decided not to invest in a major advertising campaign. Curiously, although Jean-Yves had specialised in marketing, he hadn't much faith in advertising. 'It can be useful for refining your image,' he said, 'but we're not at that point just yet. For the moment, the most important thing is for us to get good distribution and ensure the product has a reputation for reliability.' On the other hand, they invested hugely in information for the travel agents; it was crucial that they offer the product quickly and spontaneously. Valérie took most of the responsibility for this; it was familiar territory for her. She remembered the sales-pitch mnemonic SURE – Strategic Planning, Understanding, Response management, Execution excellence; she remembered too the reality, which was infinitely more simple. But most of the salesgirls were very young; most of them had barely passed their BTS diploma; it was easier to speak to them in their own language. Talking to some of the girls, she realised that Jean-Louis Barma's typology was still being taught in colleges. (*The technician consumer*: product centred, sensitive to quantitative aspects, attaches great importance to technical aspects of the product. *The devout consumer*:

trusts the salesperson blindly because he does not understand the product. *The complicit consumer*: happy to focus on points he has in common with the salesperson if the latter knows how to establish a good interpersonal relationship. *The manipulative consumer*: a manipulator whose strategy is to deal directly with the supplier and so get the best deal. *The developing consumer*: attentive to the salesperson, whom he respects, to the product offered, aware of his needs, he communicates easily.) Valérie was five or six years older than these girls; she had long risen above their current level and she had achieved a degree of professional success which most of them hardly dared dream of. They looked at her with a sort of childlike admiration.

I had the key to her apartment now; in general, while I was waiting for her in the evenings, I read August Comte's *Course in Positive Philosophy*. I liked this tedious, dense book; often I would reread a page three or four times. It took me almost three weeks to finish Lesson Fifty: 'Preliminary Considerations on Social Statics, or the General Theory of the Spontaneous Order of Human Society'. I certainly needed some sort of theory to help me take stock of my social status.

'You work far too much, Valérie . . .' I told her one evening in May as she was lying, huddled up with exhaustion, on the living-room sofa. 'You have to get something out of it. You should put some money aside, otherwise one

way or the other you'll just end up spending it.' She
agreed that I was right. The following morning, she took
two hours off and we went to Porte d'Orléans branch of
the Crédit Agricole to open a joint account. She gave me
power of attorney and the following day I went back to
talk to a financial adviser. I decided to put aside twenty
thousand francs a month from her salary, half of it in a life
assurance policy, the other half into a savings account. I
was at her place pretty much all the time now; it made no
sense to hang on to my apartment.

It was she who made the suggestion at the beginning of
June. We had made love most of the morning, taking long
breaks curled up together between the sheets. Then she
would wank me or suck me off and I would penetrate her
again; neither of us had come. Each time she touched me
I quickly got a hard on, her pussy was constantly wet. She
was feeling good, I could see calm flooding her face. At
about nine o'clock, she suggested we have dinner in an
Italian restaurant near the Parc Montsouris. It wasn't quite
dark yet; it was a warm evening. I had to go to my place
afterwards, if I intended to go to work in a shirt and tie as
I usually did. The waiter brought us two house cocktails.

'You know, Michel . . .' she said as soon as he had gone,
'You could just move into my place. I don't really think
we need to go on playing at being independent. Or, if you
prefer, we can get a flat together.'

In point of fact, yes, I did prefer; let's say it gave me a
greater sense of this as a new beginning. A first beginning

in my case, truth be told; and in her case too, I suppose. It becomes habit, being alone, being independent; it's not always a good habit. If I wanted to live something that resembled the conjugal experience, now, evidently, was the time. Of course I knew the drawbacks of the set-up; I know that desire becomes dulled more quickly when couples live together. But it becomes dulled anyhow, that's one of the laws of life; only then does it become possible for the union to move on to a different level – so many people have believed. But that evening my desire for Valérie was far from dulled. Before leaving her, I kissed her on the mouth; she opened her lips wide, abandoning herself completely to the kiss. I slipped my hand into her tracksuit bottoms, into her panties, put my hand on her buttocks. She leaned her head back, looked left and right, the street was completely quiet. She knelt down on the pavement, opened my flies, took my penis into her mouth. I leaned against the park railings. Just before I came, she moved her mouth away and continued to masturbate me with two fingers, slipping her other hand into my trousers to stroke my balls. She closed her eyes; I ejaculated over her face. At that moment I thought she was going to burst into tears; but she didn't, she simply licked at the semen trickling down her cheeks.

The very next morning, I started going through the small ads; somewhere in the southern *arrondissements* would be best for Valérie's work. A week later, I had found it: it was a large two-bedroom on the thirtieth floor of the Opale tower near the Porte de Choisy. I had never had a beautiful view of Paris before; I had never really looked for one, to be honest. When we were about to move in, I realised that I didn't feel the least attachment to anything in my apartment. I could have felt a certain joy, something like intoxication, at this freedom; on the contrary, I felt slightly scared. I had managed, it seemed, to live for forty years without forming the most tenuous of attachments to a single object. All told, I had two suits which I wore alternately. Books, sure, I had books; but I could easily have bought them again, not one of them was in any way precious or rare. Several women had crossed my path; I didn't have a photograph or a letter from any of them. Nor did I have any photos of myself: I had no memory of what I might have been like when I was fifteen, or twenty or thirty. I didn't really have any personal papers: my identity could be contained in a couple of files which would easily fit into a standard-size cardboard folder. It is wrong to pretend that human beings are unique, that they carry within them an irreplaceable individuality; as far as I was concerned, at any rate, I could not distinguish any trace of such an individuality. As often as not it is futile to wear yourself out trying to distinguish individual destinies and personalities. When all's said and done, the idea of the uniqueness of the individual is nothing more than pompous absurdity. We remember our own lives, Schopenhauer wrote somewhere, a little better than a novel we once read. That's about right: a little, no more.

5

Valérie was again overwhelmed with work in the last two weeks of June; the problem with working with a number of countries is that with the time differences you could almost be working twenty-four hours a day. The weather became increasingly warmer, heralding a magnificent summer; until now, we had had little opportunity to take advantage of it. After work, I liked to go and wander round Tang Frères, I even made an attempt to take up Eastern cooking. But it was too complicated for me, there was a completely new balance to understand between ingredients, a special way of chopping vegetables, it was almost a different mind-set. In the end I settled for Italian, something which was much more my level. I would never have believed that some day I would take pleasure in cooking. Love sanctifies.

In his fiftieth sociology lesson, Auguste Comte tackles that 'strange metaphysical aberration' which conceives the family as the template for society. 'Founded chiefly upon attachment and gratitude, the domestic union satisfies, by its mere existence, all our sympathetic instincts quite apart from all idea of active and continuous cooperation towards any end unless it be that of its own institution. When, unhappily, the coordination of employments remains the only principle of connection, the domestic union degenerates into mere association, and in most cases will soon dissolve altogether.' At the office I continued to do the bare minimum; all the same, I had two or three important exhibitions to organise; I got through them without any difficulty. Office work isn't very difficult – you simply have to be reasonably meticulous and be decisive. I had rapidly realised that you did not necessarily have to make *the right decision,* it was sufficient, in most cases, to make *any old decision*, as long as you made it quickly – if you work in the public sector, at least. I binned some projects and green lighted others: I did this based on insufficient information. In ten years, not once had I asked for additional information and, in general, I didn't feel the slightest remorse. Deep down, I had pretty little respect for the contemporary art scene. Most of the artists I knew behaved exactly like entrepreneurs: they carefully reconnoitred emerging markets, then tried to get in fast. Just like entrepreneurs, they had been at the same few colleges, they were cast from the same mould. There were some differences, however: in the art market, inno-vation was at a greater premium than in most other professional sectors; moreover, artists often worked in packs or networks, in contrast to entrepreneurs who were solitary beings surrounded by enemies – shareholders ready to drop them at a moment's notice, executives always ready to betray them. But in the artists' proposals I dealt with, it was rare for me to come across a sense of genuine inner desire. At the end of June, however, there was the Bertrand Bredane exhibition, which I had passionately supported from the outset – to the great surprise of Marie-Jeanne, who had become accustomed to my meek indifference and was herself repelled by works of that nature. He was not exactly a young artist, he was already forty-three and, physically, he was knackered – he looked a little like the alcoholic poet in *Le Gendarme de Saint-Tropez*. He was chiefly famous for leaving rotting meat in young girls' panties, or breeding flies in his own excrement and then releasing them into the galleries. He had never been really successful, he didn't have the right connections, and he stubbornly persisted in a rather dated 'trash' aesthetic. I sensed in him a certain authenticity, but maybe it was simply the authenticity of failure. He seemed a little unbalanced. His most recent project was even worse – or better, depending on one's point of view – than his earlier work. He had made a video following the fate of the bodies people donate to medical science after their death – being used for dissection practice in medical schools, for example. A number of genuine medical students were to mingle with the audience and from time to time, flash a severed hand or an eyeball that had been gouged out – to play, in fact, the kind of practical jokes of which medical students are apparently so fond. I made the mistake of taking Valérie to the opening even though she'd had an exhausting day. To my surprise, it was pretty well attended and the crowd included a number of major celebrities: could it be that Bertrand Bredane's moment had arrived? After about half an hour, Valérie had had enough and asked me if we could leave. A medical student rushed up to her holding a severed dick in his hand, the testicles still fringed with hair. She turned her head away, sickened, and led me to the exit. We sought refuge in the Café Beaubourg.

Half an hour later, Bertrand Bredane made his entrance, accompanied by two or three girls and some other people, among whom I recognised the director of sponsorship at a major venture capital firm. They took the table next to us; I couldn't not go and say hello to them. Bredane was visibly pleased to see me, it was true that that evening I'd given him a particularly warm handshake. The conversation dragged on, Valérie came and sat with us. I don't know who suggested we go for a drink at Bar-Bar; probably Bredane himself. I made the mistake of accepting. Most of the partner-swapping clubs which had tried to introduce an S&M night had failed. Bar-Bar, on the other hand, had specialised in sadomasochistic practices since it opened, and, though it didn't have a particularly strict dress code – except on certain nights – had been packed from the start. As far as I was aware, the S&M scene was a pretty particular milieu, made up of people who were no longer really interested in ordinary sexual practices, and consequently disliked going to regular orgy clubs.

Near the entrance, a chubby-faced woman of fifty-something, gagged and handcuffed, swung in a cage. Looking more closely, I discovered she was shackled, her heels attached to the bars of the cage with metal chains; she was wearing nothing but a leatherette corset on to which spilled her large sagging breasts. She was, as was the custom of the place, a slave whose master was going to auction her off for the evening. She didn't seem to find it terribly amusing. I noticed that she turned this way and that, trying to hide her arse, which was completely riddled with cellulite; but it was impossible – the cage was open on all four sides. Maybe she did this for a living; I knew it was possible to make between one to two thousand francs a night by renting yourself out as a slave. My impression was that she was a junior white-collar worker, maybe a switchboard operator for the Social Security, who was doing this to make ends meet.

There was only one table free, near the entrance to the first torture chamber. Immediately we sat down, a bald, pot-bellied middle-manager in a three-piece suit came by on a leash, led by a black, bare-arsed dominatrix. She stopped at our table and ordered him to strip to the waist. He obeyed. She took a pair of metal clamps from her bag; for a man, his breasts were pretty fat and flabby. She closed the clamps on his nipples, which were red and distended. He winced in pain. She tugged on his leash; he got back on all fours and followed her as best he could; the pasty folds of his belly wobbled in the dim light. I ordered a whisky, Valérie an orange juice. She stared stubbornly at the table, not watching what was going on around her, nor taking part in the conversation. In contrast, Marjorie and Géraldine, the two girls I knew from the Plastic Arts Delegation, seemed to be very excited. 'It's tame tonight, very tame . . .' muttered Bredane, disappointed. He went on to explain to us that, some nights, customers had needles pushed through their balls or the heads of their cocks; once he'd even see a guy whose dominatrix had torn out a fingernail with a pair of pliers. Valérie flinched in revulsion.

'I find the whole thing completely disgusting . . .' she said, unable to contain herself any longer.

'Why *disgusting*?' Géraldine protested. 'As long as the participants are freely consenting, I don't see the problem. It's a contract, that's all.'

'I don't believe you can *freely consent* to humiliation and suffering. And even if you can, I don't think it's reason enough.'

Valérie was really angry. For a moment I thought about moving the conversation on to the Arab–Israeli war, then I realised that I didn't give a shit what these girls thought; if they never phoned me again, it would simply reduce my workload. 'Yeah, I find these people a little disgusting . . .' I upped the ante, 'And I find you disgusting too . . .' I said more quietly.

Géraldine didn't hear, or she pretended not to hear. 'If I'm a consenting adult,' she went on, 'and my fantasy is to suffer, to explore the masochistic part of my sexuality, I don't see any reason why anyone should try and stop me. We are living in a democracy . . .' She was getting angry too, I could sense that it wouldn't be long before she mentioned human rights. At the word 'democracy', Bredane shot her a slightly contemptuous look; he turned to Valérie. 'You're quite right . . .' he said gravely, 'it's completely disgusting. When I see a man agreeing to have his nails torn out with a pair of pliers, then have someone shit on him, and eat his torturer's shit, I find that disgusting. But, it's precisely what is disgusting in the human animal that interests me.'

After a few seconds, Valérie asked in an agonised voice: 'Why? . . .'

'I don't know,' Bredane answered simply. 'I don't believe we have a dark side, because I don't believe in any form of damnation, nor in benediction for that matter. But I have a feeling that as we get closer to suffering and cruelty, to domination and servility, we hit on the essential, the intimate nature of sexuality. Don't you think so? . . .' He was talking to me now. No, actually, I didn't think so. Cruelty is a primordial part of the human, it is found in the most primitive peoples: in the earliest tribal wars, the victors were careful to spare the lives of some of their prisoners to let them die later, suffering hideous tortures. This tendency persisted, it is constant throughout history, it remains true today: as soon as a foreign or civil war begins to erase ordinary moral constraints, you find human beings – regardless of race, people, culture – eager to launch themselves into the joys of barbarism and massacre. This is attested, unchanging, indisputable, but it has nothing whatever to do with the quest for sexual pleasure – equally primordial, equally strong. So, all in all, I didn't agree; but I was aware, as always, that the discussion was pointless.

'Let's take a look round . . .' said Bredane after he'd finished his beer. I followed him, along with the others, into the first torture chamber. It was a vaulted cellar, the brickwork exposed. The atmospheric music consisted of a series of very deep chords on an organ, overlaid with the shrieks of the damned. I noticed that the bass speakers were huge; there were red spotlights all over the place, masks and torture implements hung from iron racks; the conversion must have cost them a fortune. In an alcove, a bald, almost fleshless guy was chained by all four limbs, his feet trapped in a wooden contraption which kept him about a foot off the ground, his arms were raised by a pair of handcuffs attached to the ceiling. A booted, gloved dominatrix, dressed completely in black latex, circled him armed with a whip of fine lashes encrusted with precious stones. First, and for a long time, she thrashed his buttocks with heavy strokes; the guy was facing us, completely naked; he screamed in pain. A small crowd gathered around the couple. 'She must be at level two . . .' Bredane whispered to me. 'Level one is where you stop when you see first blood.' The guy's cock and balls hung down, stretched and almost contorted. The dominatrix circled round him, rummaged in a bag on her belt and took out a number of hooks which she stuck into his scrotum; a little blood beaded on the surface. Then, more gently, she began to whip his genitals. It was a very close thing: if one of the lashes caught on a hook, the skin of the scrotum could rip. Valérie turned her head and pressed herself against me. 'Let's go . . .' she said, her voice pleading; 'let's go, I'll explain later.' We went back to the bar; the others were so fascinated by the spectacle that they didn't notice us leave. 'The girl who was whipping that guy . . .' she told me quietly, 'I recognised her. I've only ever seen her once before, but I'm sure it's her . . . It's Audrey, Jean-Yves's wife.'

We left immediately. In the taxi Valérie was silent, devastated. She remained silent in the lift and until we reached the apartment. It was only when the door closed behind us that she turned to me:

'Michel . . . you don't think I'm too conventional?'

'No, I hate that stuff too.'

'I can understand that torturers exist: I find it disgusting, but I know there are people who take pleasure in torturing others; what I don't understand is that victims exist. It's beyond me that a human being could come to prefer pain to pleasure. I don't know – they need to be re-educated, to be loved, to be taught what pleasure is.'

I shrugged my shoulders as if to suggest that the subject was beyond me – something which now happened in almost every aspect of my life. The things people do, the things they are prepared to endure . . . there was nothing to be made of all this, no overall conclusion, no meaning.

I undressed in silence. Valérie sat on the bed beside me. I sensed that she was still tense, preoccupied by the subject.

'What scares me about it all,' she said, 'is that there's no physical contact. Everyone wears gloves, uses equipment. Skin never touches skin, there's never a kiss, a touch or a caress. For me, it's the very antithesis of sexuality.'

She was right, but I suppose that S&M enthusiasts would have seen their practices as the apotheosis of sexuality, its ultimate form. Each person remains trapped in his skin, completely given over to his feelings of individuality; it was one way of looking at things. What was certain, in any case, was that that kind of place was increasingly fashionable. I could easily imagine girls like Marjorie and Géraldine going to them, for example; although I had trouble imagining them being able to abandon themselves sufficiently for penetration, or indeed any kind of sexual scenario.

'It's more straightforward than you might think . . .' I said at length. 'There's the sexuality of those who love each other, and the sexuality of those who don't love each other. When there's no longer any possibility of identifying with the other, the only thing left is suffering – and cruelty.'

Valérie pressed against me. 'We live in a strange world . . .' she said. In a sense, she was still innocent, protected from human reality by her insane working hours, which left her barely enough time to do the shopping, sleep, start again. She added: 'I don't like the world we live in.'

6

It became apparent from our research that consumers have three major expectations: the desire to be safe, the desire for affection and the desire for beauty.

Bernard Guilbaud

On June 30, the reservation figures from the travel agencies arrived. They were excellent. Eldorador Discovery was a success, it had immediately achieved better results than Eldorador Standard – which continued to slide. Valérie decided to take a week's holiday: we went to her parents at Saint-Quay-Portrieux. I felt rather old to be playing the role of the fiancé brought to meet the parents; after all, I was thirteen years older than she was, and this was the first time I had ever been in such a situation. The train stopped at Saint-Brieuc, her father was waiting for us at the station. He kissed his daughter warmly and hugged her to him for a long time; you could see that he missed her. 'You've lost a bit of weight . . .' he told her. Then he turned to me and offered me his hand, without really looking at me. I think he was intimidated too: he knew I worked for the Ministry of Culture, while he was just a farmer. Her mother was much more talkative; she grilled me at length about my life, my work, my hobbies. In the event, it wasn't so difficult. Valérie was at my side; from time to time she answered for me and we would exchange looks. I couldn't imagine how I might behave in a situation like this if one day I had children; I couldn't really imagine much about the future.

The evening meal was a real feast: lobster, saddle of lamb, several cheeses, a strawberry tart and coffee. For my part, I was tempted to see this as evidence of acceptance, although obviously I knew that the menu had been planned in advance. Valérie took the brunt of the conversation, mostly talking about her new job – about which I knew just about everything. I let my gaze wander over the curtain material, the ornaments, the family photos in their frames; it was touching and a little frightening.

Valérie insisted on sleeping in the room she had had as a teenager. 'You'd be better off in the guest room,' her mother insisted; 'two of you will be pushed for space.' It was true the bed was a little narrow, but I was very moved, as I pushed Valérie's panties down and stroked her pussy, to think that this was where she slept when she was only thirteen or fourteen. Wasted years, I thought. I knelt at the foot of the bed, took off her pants completely and turned her towards me. Her vagina closed over the tip of my penis. I pretended to penetrate her, going in a couple of inches and pulling back in quick, short thrusts, squeezing her breasts between my hands. She came with a muffled cry, then burst out laughing. 'My parents . . .' she whispered, 'they're not asleep yet.' I penetrated her again, harder this time so that I could come. She watched me, her eyes shining, and placed a hand over my mouth just as I came inside her with a hoarse moan.

Later, I studied the furniture in the room curiously. On a shelf, just above the *Bibliothèque Rose* series, there were several little exercise books, carefully bound. 'Oh, those,' she said; 'I used to do them when I was about ten, twelve. Have a look if you like. They're Famous Five stories.'

'How do you mean?'

'Unpublished Famous Five stories, I used to write them myself, using the same characters.'

I took them down: there was *Five in Outer Space, Five on a Canadian Adventure*. I suddenly had an image of a little girl full of imagination, a rather lonely girl, whom I would never know.

In the days that followed, we didn't do much beyond going to the beach. The weather was beautiful, but the water was too cold to swim in for long. Valérie lay in the sun for hours at a time; she was recovering gradually: the last three months had been the hardest of her working life. One evening, three days after our arrival, I talked to her about it. It was at the Oceanic Bar; we'd just ordered cocktails.

'You won't have so much work now, I suppose, now that you've launched the package?'

'In the short term, no,' she smiled cynically. 'But we'll have to come up with something else pretty quickly.'

'Why? Why not just stop at that?'

'Because that's how the game goes. If Jean-Yves were here he'd tell you that that's the capitalist principle: if you don't move forward, you're dead. Unless you have a decisive competitive advantage which you can bank on for a couple of years; but we're not there yet. The principle of Eldorador Discovery is good – it's clever, canny if you like, but it's not really innovative, it's just a good mix of other concepts. The competition will see that it works and before you know it, they'll be doing the same thing. It's not that difficult to do; the hard part was setting it up in so little time. But I'm sure that Nouvelles Frontières, for example, would be able to offer a similar package by next summer. If we want to keep our advantage, we have to innovate again.'

'And it never ends?'

'I don't think so, Michel. I'm well paid, I work in an industry I understand; I accept the rules of the game.'

I must have looked serious; she put her hand on my neck. 'Let's go and eat . . .' she said. 'My parents will be waiting for us.'

We went back to Paris on Sunday evening. Valérie and Jean-Yves had a meeting with Éric Leguen on Monday morning. He made a point of personally expressing the group's satisfaction with the first results of their recovery plan. As a bonus, the board of directors had unanimously decided to allocate shares to each of them, exceptional for executives who had been with the company less than a year.

That evening, the three of us had dinner in a Moroccan restaurant on the Rue des Écoles. Jean-Yves was unshaven, his head was nodding and he looked a little puffy. 'I think he's started drinking,' Valérie said to me in the taxi. 'He had a dreadful holiday with his wife and kids on the Île de Ré. They were supposed to be there for two weeks, but he left after a week. He told me he couldn't bear his wife's friends any more.'

It was true he didn't look at all well: he didn't touch his tagine, he constantly poured himself more wine. 'Here we go!' he said sarcastically, 'Here we go! We're getting into serious money now!' He shook his head, drained his wineglass, 'Sorry . . .' he said pitifully, 'sorry, I shouldn't talk like that.' He placed his hands, trembling slightly, on the table, waited; slowly he stopped trembling. Then he looked Valérie straight in the eye.

'You know what happened to Marylise?'

'Marylise Le François? No, I haven't seen her. Is she sick?'

'Not sick, no. She spent three days in hospital on tranquillisers, but she's not sick. Actually, she was attacked, raped on the train to Paris, on her way home from work last Wednesday.'

Marylise returned to work the following Monday. It was obvious she had been badly shaken; her movements were slow, almost mechanical. She told her story easily, too easily, it didn't seem natural: her voice was neutral, her face expressionless, rigid, it was as if she was unthinkingly repeating her police statement. Leaving work at 10.15 p.m., she had decided to take the 10.21 p.m. train, thinking it would be quicker than waiting for a taxi. The carriage was three-quarters empty. Four guys came up to her and immediately started insulting her. As far as she could tell, they were West Indian. She tried to talk to them, make a joke; for her trouble she got a couple of slaps which knocked her half-unconscious. At that point, they jumped her, two of them holding her down on the floor. Violently, brutally, they penetrated her every orifice. Every time she tried to make a sound, she was punched or slapped. It had gone on for a long time, the train had stopped at several stations; passengers got off, warily changed carriages. As the guys took turns raping her, they continued to taunt and insult her, calling her a slut and a douche-bag. By the end there was no one in the compartment. They ended up in a circle around her, spitting and pissing on her, then they shoved her with their feet, until she was half-hidden under one of the seats, then they calmly got off the train at the Gare de Lyon. Two minutes later, the first passengers to board called the police, who arrived almost immediately. The superintendent wasn't really surprised; according to him she'd been relatively lucky. Quite often when they had used the girl, these guys would end up shoving a piece of wood studded with nails into her vagina or her anus. The line was classed as dangerous.

An internal memo reminded employees of the usual safety measures, repeated that taxis were at their disposal should they need to work late and that fares would be entirely covered by the company. The number of security guards patrolling the grounds and the car park was increased.

That evening, as her car was being repaired, Jean-Yves drove Valérie home. As he was stepping out of his office, he looked out over the chaotic landscape of houses, shopping centres, tower-blocks and motorway interchanges. Far away, on the horizon, a layer of pollution lent the sunset strange tints of mauve and green. 'It's strange,' he said to her, 'here we are inside the company like well-fed beasts of burden. And outside are the predators, the savage world. I was in São Paulo once, that's where evolution has really been pushed to its limits. It's not even a city any more, it's a sort of urban territory which extends as far as the eye can see, with its favelas, its huge office blocks, its luxury housing surrounded by guards armed to the teeth. It has a population of more than twenty million, many of whom are born, live and die without ever stepping outside the limits of its terrain. The streets are dangerous there: even in a car someone might pull a gun on you at a traffic light, or you might wind up being tailed by a gang; the really well-equipped gangs have machine-guns and rocket launchers. Businessmen and rich people use helicopters to get around almost all the time; there are helipads pretty much everywhere, on the roofs of banks and apartment blocks. At ground level the street is left to the poor – and the gangs.'

As he turned on to the motorway heading south, he added in a low voice: 'I've been having doubts lately. More and more now I have doubts about the sort of world we're creating.'

A couple of days later, they returned to the subject. After he had parked on the avenue de Choisy, Jean-Yves lit a cigarette; he was silent for a moment, then he turned to Valérie: 'I feel really terrible about Marylise . . . the doctors said she could go back to work, and it's true that in a sense, she's back to normal, she's not having panic attacks. But she never takes the initiative, it's as if she's paralysed. Every time there's a decision to be made, she comes and asks me; and if I'm not there, she's capable of waiting for hours without lifting a finger. For a marketing manager, it's not good enough; it can't go on like this.'

'You're not going to fire her?'

Jean-Yves stubbed out his cigarette, stared out of the car for a long time; he gripped the steering wheel. He seemed to be more and more tense, unsettled; Valérie noticed that even his suit was sometimes stained nowadays.

'I don't know,' he whispered at last, with difficulty. 'I've never had to do anything like this. I couldn't fire her, that would be really shitty; but I'll have to find her another job where she has fewer decisions to make, fewer dealings with people. To make matters worse, ever since it happened, she's become more and more racist in her reactions. It's understandable, it's not hard to understand, but in the tourist industry it's just not acceptable. In our advertising, our catalogues, all our marketing material, we portray the locals as warm, welcoming, friendly people. That's the way it is: it really is a professional obligation.'

The following day, Jean-Yves broached the subject with Leguen, who had fewer qualms, and, a week later, Marylise was transferred to the accounts department to replace an employee who had just retired. Another marketing manager needed to be found for Eldorador. Jean-Yves and Valérie handled the job interviews together. After they had seen about ten candidates, they had lunch in the company cafeteria to discuss the appointment.

'I'd be quite tempted to go with Noureddine,' said Valérie. 'He's incredibly talented, and he's already worked on quite a variety of projects.'

'Yes, he is the best of the bunch; but I wonder if he might be a bit overqualified for the job. I can't really see him doing marketing for a travel company, I see him in something more prestigious, more *arty*. He'll get bored here, he won't stay. Our target market really is middle-of-the-road. And his parents being *beurs*, that could cause problems. To appeal to people, we have to use a lot of clichés about Arab countries: the hospitality, the mint tea, the festivals, the Bedouins . . . I've found that kind of thing doesn't really go down too well with Arabs here; in fact a lot of them don't really like Arab countries.

'That's racial discrimination . . .' Valérie said sardonically.

'Don't be stupid!' Jean-Yves was getting angry; since he had come back from holiday, he was clearly overstressed, he was beginning to lose his sense of humour. 'Everyone does it. A person's origins are part of their personality, you have to take them into consideration, it's obvious. For example, I'd happily take a Moroccan or Tunisian immigrant – even one much more recent than Noureddine – to handle the negotiations with local suppliers. They have a foot in both camps which is a real advantage – the people they deal with are always wrong-footed. On top of that, they come across as someone who's made it in France, so the guys respect them immediately, they don't think they're going to be ripped off. The best negotiators I've ever had have always been people like that. But here, for this job, I'd be more tempted to take Birgit.'

'The Danish girl?'

'Yes. Purely as a designer; she's also very talented. She's really anti-racist – I think she lives with a Jamaican guy – she's a bit stupidly enthusiastic about anything exotic, on principle. She has no intention of having children just yet. All in all, I think she's the right fit.'

There was perhaps another reason, too, Valérie realised some days later when she surprised Birgit putting her hand on Jean-Yves's shoulder. 'Yeah, you're right . . .' he admitted as they had coffee by the vending machine, 'my rap-sheet is getting worse, now I'm getting into sexual harassment . . . Look, it's only happened once or twice and it won't go any further than that – in any case, she's got a boyfriend.' Valérie looked at him quickly. He needed a haircut. 'I wasn't having a go at you . . .' she said. Intellectually, he hadn't slipped at all: he was still capable of flawless assessments of situations and people, had an excellent eye for a financial set-up; but he seemed increasingly like a man who was unhappy, adrift.

They began to assess the customer-satisfaction surveys; a large number had been filled in, thanks to a prize draw in which the first fifty won a week's holiday. At first glance, the reasons for their dissatisfaction with Eldorador Standard were difficult to establish. The customers were satisfied with the accommodation and the location, satisfied with the food, satisfied with the activities and the sports offered; but that said, fewer and fewer of them were returning customers.

By chance, Valérie happened on an article in *Tourisme Hebdo* analysing consumers' new values. The author claimed to use the Holbrook and Hirschman model, which focuses on the emotion the consumer feels when faced with a product or service; but the conclusions were nothing new. The 'new consumers' were described as being less predictable, more eclectic, more sophisticated, more concerned with humanitarian issues. They no longer consumed to 'seem', but to 'be': *more serenity*. They had balanced diets, were careful about their health; they were slightly fearful of others and of the future. They demanded the right to be unfaithful out of curiosity, out of eclecticism;

they favoured things which were solid, durable, authentic.
They had ethical leanings: *more solidarity*, etc. She had read
all these things a hundred times: behavioural psychologists
and sociologists transplanted the same words from one
article to another, one magazine to another. In any case,
they had already taken all these factors into account. The
Eldorador villages were built of traditional materials,
following the architectural traditions of the host country.
The self-service menus were balanced, with ample room
given over to selections of fresh vegetables, fruit, the Cretan
diet. Among the activities on offer were yoga, relaxation
therapy and Tai Chi. Aurore had signed the ethical tourism
charter, gave regularly to the WWF. None of these things
seemed sufficient to halt the decline.

'I think people are just lying,' said Jean-Yves, having
reread the summary of the customer surveys a second
time. 'They say they're satisfied, they tick the box marked
"Good" every time, but in reality they've been bored stiff
for the whole holiday and they feel too guilty to admit it.
I'm going to end up selling off all the resorts we can't
convert to the Discovery formula and really go for it on
the activity holidays: add four-by-fours, hot air balloon
trips, traditional feasts in the desert, trips in dug-out
canoes, scuba diving, white-water rafting, the works . . .'

'We're not the only ones in the market.'

'No . . .' he agreed, disheartened.

'We should try spending a week at one of the clubs,
incognito, not for any particular reason, just to see what
the atmosphere is like.'

'Yeah . . .' Jean-Yves sat up in his armchair, took a sheaf of listings. He flicked quickly through the pages. 'Djerba and Monastir are a disaster, but I think we're going to drop Tunisia altogether anyway. It's already too built-up, the competition are prepared to drop their prices to ludicrous levels; given our positioning, we could never follow them.'

'Have you got any offers to buy?'

'Oddly enough, yes. Neckermann are interested. They want to get into the Eastern European market: Czechoslovakia, Hungary, Poland . . . very bottom of the market, but the Costa Brava is already saturated. They're interested in our Agadir resort as well; it's a reasonable offer. I'm quite tempted to sell to them; even with southern Morocco, Agadir isn't taking off – I think people will always prefer Marrakech.'

'But Marrakech is awful.'

'I know . . . The strange thing is that Sharm-el-Sheikh isn't doing all that well. It's got a lot going for it: the most beautiful coral reefs in the world, trips to the Sinai desert . . .'

'Yeah, but it's in Egypt.'

'And . . .?'

'I don't think people have forgotten the terrorist attack in Luxor in 1997. After all, there were fifty-eight dead. The only way you're going to sell Sharm-el-Sheikh is to take out the word "Egypt".'

'What do you want to put in its place?'

'I don't know, "The Red Sea" maybe?'

'OK, "The Red Sea" it is.' He made a note and went back to leafing through the figures. 'Africa is doing well . . . that's strange. Cuba comes rather low. But Cuban music, that whole Latin vibe is hip isn't it? The Dominican Republic is always full for example.' He read the description of the Cuban resort: 'The Guardalavaca hotel is almost new, it's competitively priced. Not too sporty, not too family-oriented. "Live the magic of Cuban nights to the wild rhythms of salsa . . ." Numbers are down 15 per cent. Maybe we could go and have a look at the place: either there or Egypt.'

'Wherever you want, Jean-Yves . . .' she answered wearily. 'In any case, it will do you good to get away without your wife.'

August had settled over Paris; the days were hot, almost stifling, but the good weather didn't last: after a day or two a storm would come, the air would suddenly become cool. Then the sun would come out, the mercury in the thermometer, and the pollution index, would begin to rise again. To tell the truth, it was of limited interest to me. I had given up on peep-shows since I had met Valérie; I had also given up, many years ago, on the urban adventure. Paris had never been a moveable feast for me, and I could think of no reason why it should become one. Still, ten or twelve years ago, when I was starting out in the Ministry of Culture, I used to go out to clubs and bars that were 'unmissable'; all I remember was a slight but persistent feeling of unease. I had nothing to say, I felt completely incapable of starting a conversation with anyone at all, I didn't know how to dance either. It was in such circumstances that I started to become an alcoholic. Alcohol didn't let me down, never once in my life: it has been a constant support to me. After about ten gin-and-tonics, I occasionally – pretty rarely, all in all it must have happened four or five times – managed to find the requisite energy to ask a girl to share my bed. The results, in general, were pretty disappointing: I couldn't get it up, and I usually fell asleep after a couple of minutes. Later, I discovered the existence of Viagra; elevated blood-alcohol levels limited its effectiveness a lot, but if you boosted the dosage, you could still get somewhere. The game, in any case, wasn't really worth the candle. In fact, before Valérie, I had never met a single girl who could come close to a Thai prostitute; or maybe when I was very young, I managed to feel something when I was with girls of sixteen or seventeen. But in the world I moved in it was a complete disaster. The girls weren't remotely interested in sex, only in seduction – and even then it was a kind of élitist, trashy, bizarre seduction that was not the least bit erotic. In bed, they were simply incapable of the least thing. Either that, or they needed fantasies, a whole lot of fastidious, kitschy scenarios, the mere mention of which was enough to make me sick. They liked to talk about sex, that much was true, in fact it was their only real topic of conversation; but they didn't have the slightest sensual innocence. Actually, the men weren't much better. In any case, the French have a penchant for talking about sex at every possible opportunity without ever doing anything; but it was seriously starting to depress me.

Anything can happen in life, especially nothing. But this time at least something had happened in my life: I had found a lover and she made me happy. Our August was very quiet. Espitalier, Leguen and most of the other senior executives at Aurore had gone away on holiday. Valérie and Jean-Yves had decided not to make any important decisions before the Cuba trip at the beginning of September; it was a break, a period of calm. Jean-Yves was a bit better. 'He finally decided to go see a whore,' I learned from Valérie; 'He should have done it long ago. He's drinking less now, he's calmer.'

'All the same, from what I remember, hookers aren't up to much.'

'Yeah, but this is different, these girls work via the internet. They're pretty young, some of them are still students. They don't take many clients, they pick and choose, they don't do it just for the money. At least, he told me it's pretty good. If you want we can try it sometime. A bisexual girl for the two of us: I know men are turned on by all that and, actually, I like girls too.'

We didn't do it that summer; but the simple fact that she had suggested it was tremendously exciting. I was lucky. She knew the different things that kept male desire alive – well, not completely, that was impossible, but let's say enough to make love from time to time, while waiting for everything to come to an end. In fact, being aware of such things is nothing, it's so easy, so pathetic and easy; but she enjoyed doing these things, she took pleasure in them, she enjoyed seeing the desire rising in my eyes. Often, in a restaurant, when she came back from the toilet, she would place the panties she had just taken off on the table. Then she liked to slip a hand between my legs to make the most of my erection. Sometimes she would open my flies and jerk me off right there, hidden by the tablecloth. In the mornings, too, when she woke me with fellatio and handed me a cup of coffee before taking me into her mouth again, I would feel a dizzying rush of gratitude and gentleness. She knew how to stop just before I came, she could have kept me on the brink for hours. I lived inside a game, a game which was tender and exciting, the only game left to adults; I moved through a universe of gentle desires and limitless moments of pleasure.

7

At the end of August, the estate agent in Cherbourg phoned to tell me he had found a buyer for my father's house. The guy wanted me to drop the price a little, but he was prepared to pay cash. I accepted immediately. Very shortly, I would, therefore, receive a little more than two million francs. At the time, I was working on a proposal for a touring exhibition in which frogs were to be released onto playing cards spread out in a mosaic-tiled enclosure – some of the tiles had been engraved with the names of great men of history, such as Dürer, Einstein or Michelangelo. The lion's share of the budget was allocated to buying the decks of cards: they needed to be changed fairly frequently; the frogs had to be changed too, from time to time. The artist wanted, at least for the inaugural exhibition in Paris, to use Tarot cards; in the provinces, he was prepared to make do with ordinary playing cards. I decided to go to Cuba for a week with

Valérie and Jean-Yves in early September. I had intended to pay my way, but she told me she would sort things out with the group.

'I won't get in the way of your work . . .' I promised.

'We're not really going to work, you know, we'll just behave like ordinary tourists. We're not going to do anything much, but that in itself is very important: we're going to try and work out what's going wrong, why there's no atmosphere at the resort, why people don't come back thrilled from their holidays. You won't be in the way at all; on the contrary, you could be very useful.'

We took the mid-afternoon flight to Santiago de Cuba on Friday September 5. Jean-Yves hadn't been able to stop himself bringing along his laptop, but he seemed relaxed in his pale-blue polo neck, ready for a holiday. Shortly after take-off, Valérie put her hand on my thigh; she relaxed, her eyes closed. 'I'm not worried, we'll work out what's wrong . . .' she'd said to me as we were leaving.

The transfer from the airport took two and a half hours. 'Negative number one . . .' noted Valérie; 'we must check and see if there's a flight into Holguin.' In front of us in the coach, two little old ladies of about sixty, with blue-grey perms, twittered constantly, pointing out items of interest as we passed: men cutting sugar cane, a vulture wheeling over the fields, two cows returning to their byre . . . They had the air of ladies determined to be interested in everything, they seemed dry and difficult; I got the impression they wouldn't be easy customers. Sure enough, when the rooms were being allocated, twitterer A doggedly insisted on having a room next door to twitterer B. This sort of demand had clearly not been anticipated, the receptionist couldn't understand at all, the resort manager had to be sent for. He was about thirty, with a head like a ram and a stubborn air, his narrow brow furrowed with worry lines, in fact he looked a lot like the actor Nagui. 'No problem, okay . . .' he said when the issue had been explained to him; 'No problem, okay, my dear lady. This evening is not possible, but tomorrow we have some people leaving and we will change your room.'

A porter took us to our ocean-view chalet, turned on the air conditioning and left with a dollar tip. 'There we go . . .' said Valérie sitting down on the bed. 'The meals are served buffet style. It's an all-in package including snacks and cocktails. The disco opens at eleven. There's a supplement for massages and for lighting the tennis-courts at night.' The aim of tourist companies is to make people happy, for a specified price, for a specified period. The task can be an easy one, or it can prove impossible – depending on the nature of the people, the services offered and other factors. Valérie took off her trousers and her blouse. I lay down on the other twin bed. A source of permanent, accessible pleasure, our genitals exist. The god who created our misfortune, who made us short-lived, vain and cruel, has also provided this form of meagre compensation. If we couldn't have sex from time to time, what would life be? A futile struggle against joints that stiffen, caries that form. All of which, moreover, is as uninteresting as humanly possible – the collagen which makes muscles stiffen, the appearance of microbic cavities in the gums. Valérie parted her thighs above my mouth. She was wearing a pair of sheer tanga briefs in purple lace. I pushed the fabric aside and wet my fingers in order to stroke her labia. For her part, she undid my trousers and took my penis in the palm of her hand. She began to massage my balls gently, unhurriedly. I grabbed a pillow so my mouth would be at the same level as her pussy. At that moment, I saw a maid sweeping the sand from the terrace. The curtains and the window were wide open. As her eyes met mine, the girl burst out laughing. Valérie sat up and motioned to her to come in. She stayed where she was, hesitant, leaning on her broom. Valérie got up, walked towards her and held out her hands. As soon as the girl was inside, she started to open the buttons of her blouse: she was wearing nothing underneath but a pair of white cotton panties; she must have been about twenty, her body was very brown, almost black, she had a firm little bust and finely curved buttocks. Valérie drew the curtains; I got up in turn. The girl's name was Margarita. Valerie took her hand and placed it on my penis. She burst out laughing again, but started to jerk me off. Valérie quickly took off her bra and panties, lay down on the bed and started to stroke herself. Again, Margarita hesitated for a moment, then she took off her panties and knelt between Valérie's thighs. First she looked at her pussy, stroking it with her hand, then she brought her mouth closer and began to lick it. Valérie put her hand on

Margarita's head to guide her as she continued to jerk me off with her other hand. I felt that I was going to come; I backed off and went to look for a condom in my wash bag. I was so excited that I had trouble finding one. As I put it on, my vision seemed almost blurred. The little black girl's arse rose and fell as she bobbed over Valérie's pubis. I penetrated her in one thrust, her pussy was open like a fruit. She moaned quietly, pushed her buttocks towards me. I started to thrust in and out of her any old how, my head was spinning, shudders of pleasure coursed through my body. It was getting dark, you could hardly see anything in the room now. From far, far away, as though from another world, I heard Valérie's rising cries. I pressed my hands hard against Margarita's arse, thrusting into her harder and harder. At the moment Valérie screamed, I came in turn. For a second or two I had the impression of weightlessness, of floating in space. Then the feeling of gravity returned, I suddenly felt exhausted. I collapsed on the bed into their arms.

Later, I vaguely saw Margarita getting dressed. Valérie rummaged in her bag to give her something. They kissed on the doorstep; outside, it was dark. 'I gave her forty dollars . . .' said Valérie lying down again beside me; 'That's the price Western men pay. To her, it's a month's salary.' She turned on the bedside lamp. Silhouettes passed by, formed shadow puppets against the curtains; we could hear the murmur of conversation. I placed a hand on her shoulder.

'It was great . . .' I said in a tone of incredulous wonder. 'It was really great.'

'Yes, she's very sensual, that girl. She was really good when she went down on me too.'

'It's strange, what sex costs . . .' I went on. 'I get the impression that it doesn't really depend on a country's standard of living. Obviously, depending on the country, what's on offer is completely different; but the basic price is always pretty much the same: the amount Westerners are prepared to pay.'

'Do you think that's what they call *supply-side economics*?'

'I've no idea . . .' I shook my head. 'I've never really understood anything about economics; it's like I have a mental block.'

I was very hungry, but the restaurant didn't open until eight o'clock; I drank three piña coladas at the bar while watching the pre-dinner entertainment. The effects of orgasm dissipated only slowly, I was a bit tipsy and from a distance all the reps looked like Nagui. Actually, they didn't, some of them were younger, but they all had something odd about them, a shaven head, a goatee or dreadlocks. They gave terrifying cries and from time to time grabbed members of the audience to force them onstage. Thankfully, I was too far away to be in any serious danger.

The bar manager was pretty tiresome; he was, for want of a better word, useless: every time I needed something, he simply waved contemptuously in the direction of the waiters. He looked a bit like an elderly bullfighter, with his scars and his small, contained pot belly. His yellow swimsuit hugged his penis very precisely; he was well hung, and he was determined to let it be known. As I was heading back to my table, having obtained, with extreme difficulty, my fourth cocktail, I saw the man approach one of the neighbouring tables, occupied by a compact group of fifty-something *québécoises*. I had already noticed them when they arrived: they were thickset and tough, all teeth and blubber, talking incredibly loudly; it wasn't difficult to understand how they had managed to bury their husbands so quickly. I had a feeling that it wouldn't be wise to let them go in front of you in the queue at the self-service, or to grab a bowl of cereal that one of them had her eyes on. As the ageing hunk approached the table, they shot him amorous glances, almost becoming women again in the process. He strutted extravagantly in front of them, accentuating his coarseness at regular intervals by gestures through his swimsuit, as though to confirm the physical existence of his meat and two veg. The fifty-something *québécoises* seemed thrilled by his suggestive company; their aged, worn-out bodies still craved sunshine. He played his part well, whispered softly into the ears of these old creatures, referring to them, Cuban fashion, as '*mi corazon*' or '*mi amor*'. Nothing more would come of this, that was clear: he was content to arouse some last quivers in their ageing pussies; but perhaps that was sufficient for them to go home with the impression that they had had a wonderful holiday. For them to recommend the holiday club to their girlfriends. I sketched out the plot of a socially aware pornographic film entitled *Senior Citizens on the Rampage*. It portrayed two gangs operating in a holiday club, one a group of elderly Italian men, the other of pensionettes from Quebec. Armed with nunchakus and ice picks, both gangs submit naked, bronzed teenagers to the most vile indecencies. Eventually, of course, they come face to face in the middle of a Club Med yacht; one after another the crew members, quickly rendered help-less, are raped before being thrown overboard by the bloodthirsty pensionettes. The film ends with a mammoth orgy of pensioners, while the boat, having slipped its moorings, sails straight for the South Pole.

Eventually, Valérie joined me: she was wearing make-up and a short, white, see-through dress; I still wanted her. We found Jean-Yves at the buffet. He seemed relaxed, almost languid, and desultorily informed us of his first impressions. His room was acceptable, the entertainment seemed a little intrusive; he had just been up by the sound system and it was almost unbearable. The food wasn't up to much, he added, staring bitterly at his piece of boiled chicken. All the same, everyone seemed to be helping themselves generously, coming back to the buffet again and again; the OAPs in particular were astonishingly rapacious – you'd almost have thought they had spent the afternoon exhausting themselves at water sports and beach volleyball. 'They eat, they eat . . .' Jean-Yves observed wearily; 'What else do you expect them to do?'

After dinner, there was a show where audience participation was once again called for. A woman of about fifty launched into a karaoke version of 'Bang-Bang' by Sheila. It was pretty brave of her; there was a smattering of applause. For the most part, however, the show was run by the reps. Jean-Yves looked as though he was ready to fall asleep; Valérie calmly sipped on her cocktail. I looked at the next table: the people gave the impression that they were a little bored but they applauded politely at the end of each song. Customer dissatisfaction with holiday clubs didn't seem to me too difficult to understand; it appeared to be staring us in the face. The clientele was made up of OAPs or people 'of a certain age' and the reps seemed to be trying to doing their utmost to take them to heights of pleasure they could no longer attain, at least not that way. Valérie and Jean-Yves, even I myself, in some sense, still had professional responsibilities in the real world; we were sober, respectable employees, each exhausted by routine worries, and suchlike. Most of the people sitting at these tables were in the same position: they were managers, teachers, doctors, engineers, accountants; or retired people who had once been employed in those professions. I couldn't understand how the reps could possibly expect us to launch ourselves enthusiastically into get-to-know-you evenings or song contests. I couldn't work out how at our age, in our position, we were supposed to have kept alive our sense of fun. At best, the entertainment had been designed to amuse the under-fourteens.

I tried to let Valérie know my thoughts, but the holiday rep had started speaking again; he was holding the microphone too close and it made a terrible row. Now they were performing an improvisation inspired by Lagaf, or maybe by Laurent Baffie; whichever it was, they were sauntering around carrying palm fronds while a girl dressed as a penguin followed them, laughing at everything they said. The show ended with the club anthem and some silly dances; a few people in the front row moved about half-heartedly. Standing beside me, Jean-Yves stifled a yawn. 'Shall we go check out the disco?' he suggested.

There were about fifty people, but the reps were pretty much the only ones dancing. The DJ played a mix of techno and salsa. Eventually, a number of middle-aged couples tried a salsa. The organiser with the palm fronds wandered between the couples on the dance floor, clapping his hands and shouting: *'Caliente! Caliente!'*; I got the impression they found him more embarrassing than anything else. I took a seat at the bar and ordered a piña colada. Two cocktails later, Valérie nudged me with her elbow, pointing to Jean-Yves. 'I think maybe we can leave him to it,' she whispered into my ear. He was talking to a very pretty girl of about thirty, probably Italian. They were very close, shoulder to shoulder; their faces inches from one other.

The night was hot, muggy. Valérie took me by the arm. The rhythm of the disco died away; we could hear the drone of walkie-talkies, guards patrolled the inside of the compound. Past the pool, we turned left towards the ocean. The beach was deserted. Waves gently licked the sand a few feet from us; we could no longer hear a sound. Arriving at the chalet, I undressed and lay down on the bed to wait for Valérie. She brushed her teeth, undressed in turn and came to join me. I pressed myself against her naked body. I placed one hand on her breasts, the other in the hollow of the belly. It was sweet.

8

When I woke up I was alone and I had a slight headache. I staggered out of bed, lit a cigarette; after a couple of drags, I felt a bit better. I slipped on a pair of trousers, went out on to the terrace, which was covered in sand – it must have been windy during the night. Day had only just broken; the sky seemed cloudy. I walked a few metres towards the sea, and spotted Valérie. She was diving straight into the waves, swimming a few strokes, getting up and diving again.

I stopped, pulling on my cigarette; the wind was a little chilly, I hesitated to join her. She turned, saw me and shouted: 'Come on!' waving to me. At that moment, the sun burst from between two clouds, lighting her from the front. Light gleamed on her breasts and her hips, made the foam in her hair and her pubic hair sparkle. I stood rooted to the spot for a second or two, conscious that this was an image that I would never forget, that it would become one of those images which apparently flash before you in the few seconds which precede death.

The cigarette butt burned my fingers, I threw it on to the sand, undressed and walked towards the sea. The water was cool, very salty; it was a rejuvenating experience. A band of sunshine glimmered on the surface of the water, running straight to the horizon; I held my breath and dived into the sunlight.

Later, we huddled together in a towel, watching day break over the ocean. Little by little, the clouds dispersed and the patches of light grew. Sometimes, in the morning, everything seems simple. Valérie threw down the towel, offering her body to the sun. 'I don't feel like getting dressed . . .' she said. 'A bit . . .' I ventured. A bird glided low, scanning the surface of the water. 'I really like swimming, I really like making love . . .' she told me again. 'But I don't like dancing, I don't know how to enjoy myself, and I've always hated parties. Do you think that's normal?'

I hesitated for a long time before replying. 'I don't know . . .' I said at last. 'All I know is that I'm the same.'

There weren't many people at the breakfast tables, but Jean-Yves was already there, sitting with a coffee in front of him, cigarette in hand. He hadn't shaved, and it looked as if he hadn't had much sleep; he gave us a little wave. We sat down opposite him.

'So, everything go well with the Italian girl?' asked Valérie, making a start on her scrambled eggs.

'Not really, no. She started telling me all about her job

in marketing, her problems with her boyfriend, how that was why she'd come on holiday. She got on my nerves, I went to bed.'

'You should give the chambermaids a go . . .'

He smiled vaguely, stubbed out his cigarette in the ashtray.

'So, what are we up to today?' I asked. 'I mean . . . well, this is supposed to be a discovery holiday.'

'Oh, yes . . .' Jean-Yves wearily pulled a face. 'Well, kind of. I mean, we didn't have time to get much set up. This is the first time I've worked with a socialist country; it seems it's a bit difficult getting things arranged at the last minute in socialist countries. Anyway, this afternoon, there's something involving dolphins . . .' He stopped himself, tried to be a little more precise. 'Well, if I've got it right, it's a dolphin show, and afterwards you can go swimming with them. I suppose you climb on their backs or something like that.'

'Oh yeah, I know,' said Valérie. 'It's crap. Everyone thinks that dolphins are these sweet, friendly mammals and stuff. Actually, it's not true, they live in highly structured hierarchical groups with a dominant male and they're really aggressive: they often fight to the death. The only time I ever tried swimming with dolphins, I was bitten by a female.'

'Okay, okay . . .' Jean-Yves spread his hands in a gesture of appeasement. 'Whatever the deal is, this afternoon there's dolphins for those who are interested. Tomorrow and the day after we're on a two-day trip to Baracoa; that should be pretty good, at least, I hope so. And then . . .' he thought for a moment; 'And then that's it. Actually, no, on the last day, before we head off to the airport, there's a lobster lunch and a visit to the cemetery in Santiago.'

A few seconds' silence followed this pronouncement. 'Yeah . . .' Jean-Yves continued, 'I think we fucked up choosing this as our destination.'

'In fact . . .' he went on after a moment's thought, 'I get the impression things aren't going too well at this resort. Well, I mean, not just from my point of view. Last night, at the disco, I didn't get the impression there were many couples getting together, even among the young people.' He was silent again for a few seconds '*Ecco* . . .' he concluded, with a gesture of resignation.

'The sociologist was right . . .' said Valérie, thoughtfully.

'What sociologist?'

'Lagarrigue. The behavioural sociologist. He was right when he said we're a far cry from the days of the sun worshippers.'

Jean-Yves finished his coffee, shook his head bitterly. 'Really . . .' he said disgustedly, 'I really never thought that one day I'd feel nostalgic about the days of the sun worshippers.'

To get to the beach, we had to suffer an ambush of people hawking shitty handicrafts; but it was okay, there weren't too many, and they weren't too persistent – you could get rid of them with smiles and apologetic waves of the hand. During the day, Cubans had access to the hotel beach. They haven't got much to offer or to sell, Valérie explained to me; but they try, they do their best. Apparently, no-one in this country could get by on just their wages. Nothing really worked: there was no petrol for the engines or spare parts for machines. Hence the sense of a rustic utopia which you noticed crossing the countryside: farmers working with oxen, getting about in horses and carts . . . But this was no utopia, nor some environmentalist re-creation: it was the reality of a country which could no longer sustain itself in the industrial age. Cuba still manages to export some agricultural produce like coffee, cocoa and sugar cane; but industrial output has fallen almost to zero. It's difficult to find even the most basic consumer products: soap, paper, biros. The only well-stocked shops sell imported products and you have to pay in dollars. So, everyone in Cuba gets by thanks to some secondary, tourist-related work. The privileged work directly for the tourist industry; the others try to get their hands on dollars, one way or another, in other services or through smuggling.

I lay down on the sand to think. The bronzed men and women weaving between the tourists thought of us purely as wallets on legs, there was no point in deluding oneself; but it was just the same in every third-world country. What was particular about Cuba was this glaring problem with industrial production. I myself was completely incompetent in matters of industrial production. I was perfectly adapted to the information age, that is to say good for nothing. Like me, Valérie and Jean-Yves knew only how to manage information and capital; they used their knowledge intelligently, competitively, while I used mine in more mundane, bureaucratic ways. But if, for example, a foreign power were to impose a blockade, not one of the three of us, nor anyone I knew, would have been capable of getting industrial production up and running again. We had not the least idea about casting metal, manufacturing parts, thermoforming plastics. Not to mention more complex objects like fibre optics or microprocessors. We lived in a world made up of objects whose manufacture, possible uses and functions were completely alien to us. I glanced around me, panic-stricken by this realisation: there was a towel, a pair of sunglasses, sun screen, a paperback by Milan Kundera. Paper, cotton, glass; complex machines, sophisticated manufacturing processes. Valérie's swimsuit, for example, I was incapable of grasping the manufacturing process which had gone into making it: it was made of 80 per cent latex, 20 per cent polyurethane. I slipped two fingers under her bikini; under the artificial fibre construction I could feel the living flesh. I slipped my fingers in a little further, felt the nipple harden. This was something I could do, that I knew how to do. Little by little the heat became sweltering. Once in the water, Valérie took off her bikini. She wrapped her legs around my waist and lay, floating on her back. Her pussy was already open, I smoothly pene-trated her, thrusting inside her to the rhythm of the waves. There was no alternative. I stopped just before I came. We came back to dry ourselves in the sun.

A couple passed us, a big black guy and a girl with very white skin, a nervous face and close-cropped hair, who looked at him as she talked, laughing too loudly. She was obviously American, maybe a journalist with the *New York Times* or something like that. In fact, looking more closely, there were quite a lot of mixed couples on the beach. Further off, two big blond, slightly overweight guys with nasal accents laughed and joked with two superb girls with coppery skin.

'They're not allowed to bring them back to the hotel . . .' said Valérie, following my gaze. 'There are rooms you can rent in a village nearby.'

'I thought Americans weren't allowed to come to Cuba.'

'They're not, in theory, but they travel via Canada or Mexico. In fact, they're furious that they've lost Cuba. You can see why . . .' she said pensively. 'If ever there was a country in need of sex tourism, it's theirs. But for the moment, American companies are subject to the blockade, they're simply not allowed to invest. In any case, the country will end up becoming capitalist again, it's just a matter of years; but until then, the field is open for Europeans. That's why Aurore doesn't want to give up on it, even though the holiday club is having problems: now's the time to get an edge on the competition. Cuba represents a unique opportunity in the Caribbean–West Indies zone.

'Yep . . .' she went on cheerfully after a moment's silence. 'That's how we talk in my line of work . . . in the world of the global economy.'

9

The minibus to Baracoa left at eight in the morning; there were about fifteen people on board. They had already had an opportunity to get to know each other and were full of enthusiasm for the dolphins. The retirees (the majority), the two speech therapists who took their holidays together and the student couple, naturally, expressed their enthusiasm in slightly different lexical registers; but all would have felt able to agree on the following: a unique experience.

Afterwards, the conversation turned to the features of the resort. I shot a glance at Jean-Yves sitting alone in the middle of the minibus. He had placed a notepad and a pen on the seat next to him. Leaning forward a little, his eyes half-closed, he was concentrating on getting down everything that was said. It was at this stage, obviously, that he hoped to glean a generous harvest of useful observations and impressions.

On the subject of the resort, too, there seemed to be a consensus of opinion among the members. The reps were unanimously considered 'nice', but the activities themselves were not very interesting. The rooms were good, except those close to the sound system, which were too noisy. As for the food, it really wasn't up to much.

None of those present took part in the early morning aerobics, or the salsa or Spanish lessons. In the end, what they liked best was the beach; all the more so as it was quiet. 'Activities and sound levels considered irritating', noted Jean-Yves on his pad.

The chalets received general approval, especially as they were far from the disco. 'Next time, we'll insist on a chalet!' a heavy-set retired man said emphatically; he was in the prime of life and evidently used to giving orders, in fact he had spent his entire career marketing the wines of Bordeaux. The two students were of the same opinion 'Disco unnecessary', noted Jean-Yves, thinking despondently of all the useless investment.

After the Cayo Saetia junction, the road got steadily worse. There were potholes and cracks which sometimes covered half the road surface. The driver was forced to zigzag continuously; we rattled around in our seats, pitched from left to right. The passengers reacted with shouts and laughter. 'It's okay, they're good-natured . . .' Valérie said to me quietly. 'That's the great thing about Discovery Tours: you can subject them to horrible conditions; to them it's all part of the adventure. In this case, it's our fault: for this kind of trip you need a four-wheel drive.'

Just before Moa, the driver swerved to the right to avoid an enormous rut. The vehicle skidded slowly and came to a halt in a pot-hole. The driver restarted the engine and revved hard: the wheels spun in the brownish mud, the minibus did not move. Desperately he tried several times, to no effect. 'Well . . .' said the wine merchant, folding his arms in a jovial manner, 'we'll have to get out and push.'

We got out of the vehicle. Before us stretched a vast plain encrusted with cracked brown mud, which looked unsanitary. Pools of stagnant water, which appeared almost black, were surrounded by tall grasses, withered and bleached. In the background, a huge factory of dark brick dominated the landscape, its twin chimney-stacks spewing out thick smoke. Rusted pipes ran from the factory and appeared to zigzag aimlessly through the middle of the plain. On the hard shoulder, a metal sign depicting Che Guevara exhorting the workers to the revolutionary development of the forces of production was itself beginning to rust. The air was pervaded by an appalling stench which seemed to rise from the mud itself rather than the pools of water.

The rut was not too deep and thanks to our concerted efforts we easily got the minibus back on the road. Everyone boarded the bus again, congratulated themselves. A little later we had lunch in a seafood restaurant. Jean-Yves consulted his notebook with a worried air; he hadn't touched his meal.

'With the discovery holidays,' he concluded after considerable reflection, 'I think we're off to a good start; but with the standard resort, I really don't see what we can do.'

Valérie observed him calmly, sipping her iced coffee; she looked as though she didn't give a fuck.

'Obviously,' he continued, 'we could just fire the team of reps; it would reduce our total wage bill.'

'That would be a good start, yes.'

'You don't think it's a bit radical as an idea?' he asked anxiously.

'Don't worry about that. Being a rep at a holiday club village is no education for young people. It makes them stupid and lazy, and anyway it leads nowhere. The only thing they're fit for afterwards is to be a holiday club manager – or a TV presenter.'

'Okay, then, I reduce the overall wage bill; but then again, they're not all that well paid. I'd be surprised if it saved us enough to be competitive with the German clubs. Anyway, I'll run up a spreadsheet simulation this evening, but I'm not convinced.'

She nodded in indifferent assent, something like: 'Go ahead and simulate, it can't do any harm.' She was really surprising me at this point, I thought she was cool. It's true we were fucking quite a lot, and there's no doubt that fucking is calming: it puts things in perspective. For his part, Jean-Yves looked ready to rush to his spreadsheet; I even wondered whether he was going to ask the driver to get his laptop out of the boot. 'Don't worry, we'll find a solution . . .' Valérie said to him, shaking him affection- ately by the shoulder. That seemed to calm him for a while; he quietly went back and took his seat on the minibus.

On the last leg of the journey, the passengers talked mostly about Baracoa, our final destination; they already seemed to know pretty much everything about the city. On 28 October 1492, Christopher Columbus dropped anchor in the bay, impressed by its flawlessly circular form. 'This is the most beautiful land human eyes have ever seen,' he had noted in his logbook. At the time, the region was solely inhabited by the Tainos Indians. In 1511, Diego Velazquez founded the city of Baracoa; it was the first Spanish city in the Americas. For more than four centuries, being accessible only by boat, it remained isolated from the rest of the island. In 1963, the con- struction of the Farola viaduct made it possible to establish a road link with Guantanamo.

We arrived at about three o'clock; the city stretched along the bay which did indeed form an almost perfect circle. The satisfaction of the group was universal and was expressed in appreciative exclamations. In the end, what all lovers of journeys of discovery seek is confirmation of what they've already read in their guidebooks. All in all, they were a dream audience: Baracoa, with its modest one star in the *Michelin Guide*, was unlikely to disappoint them.

The El Castillo Hotel, situated in a former Spanish fortress, dominated the city. Viewed from above, it seemed magnificent; but to be honest, no more so than other cities. In truth it was actually quite nondescript, with its seedy tower blocks of blackened grey, so squalid that they looked uninhabited. I decided to stay by the pool, as did Valérie. There were about thirty rooms, all occupied by tourists from Northern Europe, who all seemed to have come for much the same reasons. I first noticed two rather plump English women in their forties; one of them wore glasses. They were accompanied by two easy-going mixed-race guys, who were twenty-five, tops. They seemed comfortable with the situation, talked and joked with the fatties, held their hands, slipped their arms around their waists. For my part, I would have been completely incapable of doing this kind of work; I wondered if they had some kind of trick, something they could think about when they needed to get an erection At some point, the English women went up to their rooms while the two guys stayed and chatted by the pool; if I was truly interested in human nature, I would have struck up a conversation, tried to find out a bit more. Still, maybe you just had to jerk off properly, an erection could probably be a purely mechanical reflex; biographies of male prostitutes would undoubtedly have enlightened me on this point, but the only thing I had at my disposal was *Discourse* on the Positive Spirit. As I was leafing through the subsection entitled 'Popular politics, ever social, must above all become moral', I noticed a young German girl coming out of her room, accompanied by a big black guy. She looked exactly the way we imagine German girls, long blonde hair, blue eyes, a firm, pleasing body, big breasts. As a physical type, it's very attractive; the problem is it doesn't last: by the age of thirty there's work to be done, liposuction, silicone. Anyway, for the time being, things were fine, in fact she looked positively sexy – her suitor had been very lucky. I wondered whether she paid as much as the English women did, if there was a going rate for men as there was for women; here again research needed to be done, enquiries made. It was too exhausting for me, I decided to go up to my room. I ordered a cocktail which I sipped slowly on the balcony. Valérie was sunning herself, taking a dip in the pool from time to time, I noticed she'd struck up a conversation with the German girl.

She came up to see me at about six; I'd fallen asleep with my book. She took off her swimsuit, showered and came to me, a towel wrapped around her waist; her hair was slightly damp.

'You're going to think I'm obsessed with this, but I asked the German girl what black guys have that white guys don't. It's true, though: white women clearly prefer to sleep with Africans and white men with Asians. It's pretty obvious after a while. I need to know why, it's very important for my work.'

'There are white men who like black women . . .' I observed.

'It's not as common; sexual tourism is much rarer in

Africa than it is in Asia. Of course, tourism in general is rarer, to be honest.'

'What was her answer?'

'Standard stuff: black guys are laid-back, virile, they have a sense of fun; they know how to enjoy themselves, they're not hung up, you never have any trouble with them.'

The German girl's reply was banal, true, but it provided the basis for a workable theory: all things considered, white men were repressed Negroes searching for some lost sexual innocence. Obviously it in no way explained the mysterious attraction which Asian women seemed to wield; nor the sexual prestige which, by all accounts, white men enjoyed in black Africa. I sketched out the basis of a more complex, more questionable theory: generally speaking, white people want to be tanned and to dance like Negroes; Negroes want to lighten their skin and straighten their hair. All humanity instinctively tends towards miscegenation, a generalised undifferentiated state, and it does so first and foremost through the elementary means of sexuality. The only person, however, to have pushed the process to its logical conclusion is Michael Jackson: he's neither black nor white any more, neither young nor old and, in a sense, neither man nor woman. Nobody could really imagine his private life; having grasped the categories of everyday humanity, he had done his utmost to go beyond them. This was why he could be considered a star, possibly the greatest – and, in fact, the first – in the history of the world. All the others

– Rudolph Valentino, Greta Garbo, Marlene Dietrich, Marilyn Monroe, James Dean, Humphrey Bogart – could at best be considered talented artists; they had done no more than imitate the human condition, had aesthetically transposed it. Michael Jackson was the first to have tried to go a little further.

It was an appealing theory, and Valérie listened attentively as I explained it; I, on the other hand, was not entirely convinced. Did this mean that the first cyborg, the first individual to accept having elements of artificial, extra-human intelligence implanted into his brain, would immediately become a star? Probably, yes: but that actually had very little bearing on the subject. Michael Jackson might well be a star, but he was certainly not a sex symbol; if you wanted to encourage the sort of mass tourism that would warrant heavy investment, you had to turn to more basic forces of attraction.

A little later, Jean-Yves and the others returned from their tour of the city. The local history museum was chiefly devoted to the customs of the Tainos, the first inhabitants of the region. It appeared that they had led a peaceable existence, dedicated to agriculture and fishing; conflicts between neighbouring tribes were practically non-existent; the Spanish had had no difficulty in exterminating these creatures, who were ill-prepared for combat. Today, nothing of them remains apart from some minimal genetic traces in the physiognomy of a handful of individuals; their culture has completely disappeared, it might just as well have never existed. In a number of drawings made by the missionaries, who had attempted – more often than not in vain – to sensitise them to the message of the Gospel, they can be seen ploughing, or busying themselves cooking at the fire; bare-breasted women suckle their children. All of this gave the impression, if not of Eden, then at least of a slow pace of history; the arrival of the Spanish had speeded things up significantly. After the classic conflicts between the colonial powers who led the field at the time, Cuba gained its independence in 1898, only to fall immediately under American control. Early in 1959, after a civil war lasting many years, the revolutionary forces led by Fidel Castro overthrew the regular army, forcing Batista to flee. Considering that the whole world was forcibly divided into two camps at the time, Cuba had been quickly compelled to make overtures to the Soviet block and establish a Marxist-style regime. Deprived of logistical support after the collapse of the Soviet Union, now that regime was drawing to a close. Valérie slipped on a short skirt slit up one side and a little black lace top; we had time for a cocktail before dinner.

Everyone was gathered around the swimming pool, watching as the sun set over the bay. Near the shore, the wreck of a freighter slowly rusted. Other, smaller, boats floated, almost motionless, on the waters; it all exuded a powerful sense of decline. Not a sound drifted up from the streets of the city down below; a few streetlights flickered hesitantly into life. At Jean-Yves's table sat a man of about sixty, his face gaunt and exhausted, his expression gloomy; and another much younger man – no more than thirty – whom I recognised as the hotel manager. I had seen him several times during that afternoon moving nervously between the tables to make sure that everyone was happy; his face seemed to be ravaged by constant, needless worry. Seeing us approach, he got up quickly, brought two chairs over, called a waiter, ensured that the latter arrived without delay; then hurried to the kitchens. The old man at his side shot a cynical look at the swimming pool, the couples sitting at tables and, apparently, at the world at large. 'The poor people of Cuba . . .' he said after a long silence. 'They've nothing left to sell except their bodies.' Jean-Yves explained that this man lived nearby; he was the hotel manager's father. More than forty years before, he had fought in the revolution, he had been a member of one of the first companies to rally to the Castro uprising. After the war, he had worked in the nickel works at Moa, at first as a worker, then as a foreman, eventually – after he had gone back to university – as an engineer. His status as a revolutionary hero had made it possible for his son to obtain an important position in the tourist industry.

'We have failed . . .' he said in a dull voice; 'and we deserved to fail. We had great leaders – exceptional, idealistic men who put the good of the country before their own personal gain. I remember *comandante* Che Guevara, the day he came to open the cocoa-processing plant in our village; I can still remember his noble, honest face. No one could ever say that the *comandante* had lined his pockets, that he tried to get favours for himself or his family. Nor could it be said of Camilo Cienfuegos, or any of the revolutionary leaders, not even of Fidel. It's true Fidel likes power, he wants to keep an eye on everything; but he is disinterested, he has no magnificent properties, no Swiss bank accounts. So, Che was there, he inaugurated the factory, he made a speech in which he urged the people of Cuba to win the peace through production, after the war for independence; it was just before he went to the Congo. We could easily win such a battle. The land here is fertile, the earth is rich and well irrigated, everything grows in abundance: coffee, cocoa, sugar cane, tropical fruit of every kind. The subsoil is rich in nickel ore. We had an ultra-modern factory, built with help from the Russians. In less than six months, production had fallen to half its normal level: all the factory workers stole chocolate, raw or in bars, gave it to their families, sold it to strangers. It was the same in all the factories, all over the country. If the workers couldn't find anything to steal, they worked badly, they were lazy, they were always sick, they were absent for the slightest reason. I spent years trying to talk to them, to persuade them to try a little harder for the sake of their country: I met with nothing but disappointment and failure.'

He fell silent; the last of the day floated above the Yunque, a mountain peak mysteriously truncated in the form of a table, which towered over the hills and which long ago had made a considerable impression on

Christopher Columbus. What could possibly incite human beings to undertake tedious, tiresome tasks? This seemed to me the only political question worth posing. The old factory worker's evidence was damning: in his opinion, only the need for money; in any case, the revolution had obviously failed to create the *new man*, driven by more altruistic motives. And so, like all societies, Cuba was nothing more than a system painstakingly rigged so as to allow some people to avoid tedious and tiresome tasks. Except that the system had failed, no one was fooled any longer, no one was sustained any more by the hope of one day rejoicing in communal labour. The result was that nothing functioned, no one worked or produced the slightest thing any longer, and Cuban society had become incapable of ensuring the survival of its own members.

The other members of the tour got up and headed towards the tables. I racked my brain desperately for something optimistic to say to the old man, some vague message of hope; but no, there was nothing. As he so bitterly foresaw, Cuba would soon become a capitalist country again, and nothing would remain of the revolutionary hopes he had nurtured – only a sense of failure, futility and shame. No one would respect or follow his example, his life would in fact become an object of revulsion to future generations. He would have fought, and afterwards worked his whole life, completely in vain.

During the meal, I drank quite a bit and, by the end, I found I was completely smashed; Valérie looked at me a little anxiously. The salsa dancers were getting ready for their show; they were wearing pleated skirts and multi-coloured sheaths. We took our seats on the terrace. I knew more or less what I wanted to say to Jean-Yves; had I chosen an opportune moment? I felt that he was a little distraught, but relaxed. I ordered one last cocktail, lit a cigar before turning to him.

'You really want to find a new formula that would save your holiday clubs?'

'Of course I do, that's why I'm here.'

'Offer a club where the people get to fuck. That's what they're missing more than anything. If they haven't had their little holiday romance, they go home unsatisfied. They wouldn't dare admit it, they might not even realise it, but the next time they go on holiday, they go with a different company.'

'They can fuck all they like, everything has been set up to encourage them to; that's the basic principle of holiday clubs; why they don't actually fuck, I haven't the faintest idea.'

I swept the objection aside with a wave of my hand. 'I don't know either, but that's not the problem; there's no point trying to find out the causes of this phenomenon, always supposing the phrase actually means something. Something must be happening to make Westerners stop sleeping with each other; maybe it's something to do with narcissism, or individualism, the cult of success, it doesn't matter. The fact is that from about the age of twenty-five or thirty, people find it very difficult to meet new sexual partners; although they still feel the need to do so, it's a need which fades very slowly. So they end up spending thirty years of their lives, almost the entirety of their adult lives, suffering permanent withdrawal.'

Halfway along the path to inebriation, just before mindlessness ensues, one sometimes experiences moments of heightened lucidity. The decline of western sexuality was undoubtedly a major sociological phenomenon which it would be futile to attempt to explain by such and such a specific psychological factor; glancing at Jean-Yves, I realised however that he perfectly illustrated my thesis, so much so that it was almost embarrassing. Not only did he not fuck any more and didn't have the time to go looking, but he no longer really wanted to, and, worse still, he felt this decay written on his flesh – he was beginning to smell of the stench of death. 'But . . .' he objected after a long moment of hesitation, 'I've heard wife-swapping clubs are quite successful.'

'No, actually, they're doing less and less well. There are a lot of clubs opening up, but they close almost immediately because they haven't got the customers. As a matter of fact, there are only two clubs making a go of it in Paris, Chris et Manu and 2 + 2, and even they are only full on Saturday night: for a city of ten million people, it's not much, it's a lot less than at the beginning of the 1990s. Wife-swapping clubs are a nice formula, but they're seen as more and more passé, because people don't want to swap anything any more, it doesn't suit modern sensibilities. In my opinion, wife-swapping has as much chance of surviving today as hitch-hiking did in the 1970s. The only thing that is doing any business at the moment is S&M . . .' At that point, Valérie shot me a panicked look, she even gave me a kick in the shins. I looked at her, surprised. It took me a few seconds to work it out: no, of course I wasn't going to mention Audrey; I gave her a little reassuring nod. Jean-Yves hadn't noticed the interruption.

'Therefore,' I went on, 'you have several hundred million Westerners who have everything they could want but no longer manage to obtain sexual satisfaction: they spend their lives looking, but they don't find it and they are completely miserable. On the other hand, you have several billion people who have nothing, who are starving, who die young, who live in conditions unfit for human habitation and who have nothing left to sell except their bodies and their unspoiled sexuality. It's simple, really simple to understand; it's an ideal trading opportunity. The money you could make is almost unimaginable: vastly more than from computing or biotechnology, more than the media industry; there isn't a single economic sector that is comparable.'

Jean-Yves didn't say anything; at that moment, the band began the first number. The dancers were pretty and smiling, their pleated skirts whirled, amply revealing their tanned thighs; they illustrated my point perfectly. For a moment, I thought he wouldn't say anything, that he would simply digest the idea. However, after about five minutes, he said:

'It doesn't really work for Muslim countries, your idea . . .'

'No problem, you just leave them with their Eldorador Discovery. You could even steer them towards something much tougher, with trekking and environmental activities, a survivor kind of thing maybe, which you could call Eldorador Adventure: it would sell really well in France and in Anglo-Saxon countries. On the other hand, the sex-oriented clubs could do well in Germany and the Mediterranean countries.'

This time, he smiled broadly. 'You should have been in business . . .' he said half-seriously. 'You're an ideas man . . .'

'Ideas, yeah . . .' My head was spinning a little, I could no longer make out the dancers, I finished my cocktail in one gulp. 'I might have ideas, but I wouldn't be able to throw myself into balance sheet or budget forecasts. So, yeah, I'm an ideas man . . .'

I don't remember much about the rest of the evening, I must have fallen asleep. When I woke up, I was lying on my bed; Valérie lay naked beside me, breathing gently. I woke her as I moved to reach for a pack of cigarettes.

'You were pretty drunk back there . . .'

'Yes, but I was serious about what I was saying to Jean-Yves.'

'I think he took it seriously . . .' She stroked my belly with her fingertips. 'And actually, I think you're right. Sexual liberation in the West is over.'

'You know why?'

'No . . .' she hesitated, then went on: 'No, actually, not really.'

I lit a cigarette, propped myself up on the pillows and said: 'Suck me.' She looked at me, surprised, but placed her hand on my balls and brought her mouth towards me. 'There!' I exclaimed triumphantly. She stopped what she was doing and looked at me in surprise. 'You see, I say "Suck me" and you suck me. When actually, you didn't feel the desire to do so.'

'No, I hadn't thought of it; but I enjoy doing it.'

'That's precisely what's so extraordinary about you, you enjoy giving pleasure. Offering your body as an object of pleasure, giving pleasure unselfishly: that's what Westerners don't know how to do any more. They've completely lost the sense of giving. Try as they might, they no longer feel sex as something *natural*. Not only are they ashamed of their own bodies, which aren't up to porn standards, but for the same reasons they no longer feel truly attracted to the body of the other. It's impossible to make love without a certain abandon, without accepting, at least temporarily, the state of being in a state of dependency, of weakness. Sentimental adulation and sexual obsession have the same roots, both proceed from some degree of selflessness; it's not a domain in which you can find fulfilment without losing yourself. We have become cold, rational, acutely conscious of our individual existence and our rights; more than anything, we want to avoid alienation and dependence; on top of that we're obsessed with health and hygiene: these are hardly ideal conditions in which to make love. The way things stand, the commercialisation of sexuality in the East has become inevitable. Obviously, there's S&M too. It's a purely cerebral world with clear-cut rules and a prior contract. Masochists are just interested in their own sensations, they try to see how far they can plunge into pain, a bit like people who do extreme sports. Sadists are something else, they will take things as far as they possibly can regardless – it's a very ancient human propensity: if they can mutilate or kill, they will do so.'

'I really don't want to think about it again,' she said shivering; 'It really disgusts me.'

'That's because you've remained sexual, animal. You're normal, in fact, you're not much like Westerners. Organised S&M with its rules could only exist among cultured, cerebral people for whom sex has lost all attraction. For everyone else, there's only one possible solution: pornography featuring professionals; and if you want to have real sex, third-world countries.'

'Okay . . .' She smiled. 'Is it okay if I go back to sucking you off?'

I leaned back on the pillows and let it happen. I was vaguely conscious at that moment of being at the beginning of something: from an economic point of view, I knew I was right; I estimated that potential clients might run to 80 per cent of Western adults. But I knew that people sometimes find it difficult, strangely, to accept simple ideas.

10

We had breakfast on the terrace, by the swimming pool. As I was finishing my coffee, I saw Jean-Yves emerge from his room accompanied by a girl I recognised as one of the dancers from the previous evening. She was black and slender, with long, graceful legs, she couldn't have been more than twenty. For a fleeting moment, he looked embarrassed, then came over to our table and introduced Angelina.

'I've thought about your idea,' he announced straight off. 'What I'm worried about is how feminists will react.'

'Some of the clients will be women,' said Valérie.

'You think so?'

'Oh, yes, I'm sure of it . . .' she said a little bitterly. 'Look around you.'

He glanced at the tables around the pool: there were indeed a number of single women accompanied by Cuban men; almost as many as there were single men in the same situation. He asked Angelina something and translated her reply:

'She's been a *jinetera* for three years; most of her clients are Italian or Spanish. She thinks it's because she's black: Germans and Anglo-Saxons are happy with Latino girls, to them that's exotic enough. She has a lot of friends who are *jineteros*: their customers are mostly English and American women, and some Germans too.

He took a sip of coffee, thought for a moment:

'What are we going to call these clubs? We need to think of something evocative, something very different from Eldorador Adventure, but all the same, not too explicit.'

'I thought maybe Eldorador Aphrodite,' said Valérie.

'"Aphrodite" . . .' he repeated the word thoughtfully. 'It's not bad; it doesn't sound as vulgar as "Venus". Erotic, sophisticated, a little exotic: yes, I like it.'

An hour later, we headed back towards Guardalavaca. A couple of metres from the minibus, Jean-Yves said his goodbyes to the *jinetera*; he seemed a little sad. When he got back on to the bus, I noticed the student couple giving him black looks; the wine merchant, on the other hand, clearly looked as though he didn't give a damn.

The return trip was pretty gloomy. Of course there was still the diving, the karaoke evenings and the archery; the muscles tire, then relax; sleep comes quickly. I remember nothing of the last days of the trip, nor of the last excursion, except that the lobster was rubbery and the cemetery disappointing: this despite the fact that it housed the tomb of José Marti, father of the nation, poet, politician, polemicist, thinker. He was depicted in a bas-relief sporting a moustache. His coffin, bedecked with flowers, lay at the foot of a circular pit on the walls of which were engraved his most notable *pensées* – on national independence, resistance to tyranny, justice. Nonetheless, you didn't get the sense that his spirit still animated the place; the poor man seemed quite simply dead. That said, he was not an unpleasant stiff; you felt you would have liked to meet him, if only to be ironic about his rather narrow and earnest humanist; but it hardly seemed likely, he seemed to be well and truly stuck in the past. Could he rise up once more and galvanise his homeland to greater heights of the human spirit? One didn't really imagine so. All in all, it was a disappointment letdown, as indeed all republican cemeteries are. It was irritating, all the same, to realise that Catholics are the only people who have succeeded in creating a functional funeral system. It's true that the means they use to make death magnificent and affecting consists quite simply in denying it. Difficult to fail with arguments like that. But here, in the absence of the risen Christ, you needed nymphs, shepherds, tits and arse, basically. As it was, you couldn't imagine José Marti romping about in the great meadows of the hereafter; he looked more like he had been buried in the ashes of everlasting *ennui*.

The day after we got back, we found ourselves in Jean-

Yves's office. We hadn't slept much on the plane; my memory of that day is of an atmosphere of blissful enchantment, rather strange, in the deserted building. Three thousand people worked there during the week, but on that Saturday there were just the three of us, apart from the security guards. Close by, on the forecourt of the Évry shopping centre, a pair of rival gangs faced each other with Stanley knives, baseball bats and containers of sulphuric acid; that evening the number of dead would stand at seven, among them two onlookers and a member of the riot squad. The incident would be the subject of considerable debate on national radio and television; but at that moment we knew nothing about it. In a state of excitement which seemed slightly unreal, we set down our manifesto, our platform for dividing up the world. The suggestions that I was about to make might possibly result in millions of francs worth of investment or hundreds of jobs; for me it was very new and very unsettling. I felt a bit crazy all afternoon, but Jean-Yves listened to me attentively. He was convinced, he told Valérie later, that if I was given free rein I was likely to have a brainwave. In short, I brought a note of creativity while he remained the decision-maker; that was his way of looking at things.

The Arab countries were the quickest to deal with. In view of their absurd religion, all possible sexual activity seemed to be ruled out. Tourists who opted for these countries would have to content themselves with the dubious delights of adventure. In any case, Jean-Yves had decided to sell off Agadir, Monastir and Djerba, which were making too much of a loss. That left two destinations which could reasonably be classified under the category 'adventure'. The tourists in Marrakech would do a bit of camel trekking. Those at Sharm-el-Sheikh could observe the goldfish or take an excursion into the Sinai to the site of the Burning Bush where Moses had 'flipped his lid', to use the colourful expression of an Egyptian I had met three years earlier on a felucca trip to the Valley of the Kings. 'Admittedly,' he'd said emphatically, 'it's a very impressive rock formation . . . but to go from that to affirming the existence of the one God! . . .' This intelligent and often funny man seemed to have a fondness for me – probably because I was the only Frenchman in the group – as for some obscure cultural or sentimental reasons he nurtured a lifelong, and, by then, it has to be said, a highly notional, passion for France. In speaking to me, he had literally saved my holiday. He was about fifty, always impeccably dressed, very dark skinned, with a little moustache. A biochemist by training, he had emigrated to England as soon as he had completed his studies and had been brilliantly successful working in genetic engineering there. He was revisiting his native land, for which, he said, he still had great affection; on the other hand he could not find words harsh enough to revile Islam. Above all, he wanted to convince me, Egyptians were not Arabs. 'When I think that this country invented everything! . . .' he exclaimed gesturing broadly towards the Nile valley. 'Architecture, astronomy, mathematics, agriculture, medicine' (he was exaggerating a little, but he was an Oriental and needed to persuade me quickly). 'Since the appearance of Islam, nothing. An intellectual vacuum, an absolute void. We've become a country of flea-ridden beggars. Beggars covered in fleas, that's what we are. Scum, scum! . . .' (with a wave, he shooed away some boys who had come to beg for small change). 'You must remember, *cher monsieur*,' (he spoke five foreign languages fluently: French, German, English, Spanish and Russian), 'that Islam was born deep in the desert amid scorpions, camels and wild beasts of every order. Do you know what I call Muslims? The losers of the Sahara. That's what they deserve to be called. Do you think Islam could have been born in such a magnificent place?' (with genuine feeling, he motioned again to the Nile valley). 'No, *monsieur*. Islam could only have been born in a stupid desert, among filthy Bedouins who had nothing better to do – pardon me – than bugger their camels. The closer a religion comes to monotheism – consider this carefully, *cher monsieur* – the more cruel and inhuman it becomes; and of all religions, Islam imposes the most radical monotheism. From its beginnings, it has been characterised by an uninterrupted series of wars of invasion and massacres; never, for as long as it exists, will peace reign in the world. Neither, in Muslim countries, will intellect and talent find a home; if there were Arab mathematicians, poets and scientists, it is simply because they lost the faith. Simply reading the Koran, one cannot help but be struck by the regrettable mood of tautology which typifies the work:

"There is no other God but God alone", etc. You won't get very far with nonsense like that, you have to admit. Far from being an attempt at abstraction, as it is sometimes portrayed, the move towards monotheism is nothing more than a shift towards mindlessness. Note that Catholicism, a subtle religion, and one which I respect, which well knew what suited human nature, quickly moved away from the monotheism imposed by its initial doctrine. Through the dogma of the Trinity and the cult of the Virgin and the Saints, the recognition of the role played by the powers of darkness, little by little it reconstituted an authentic polytheism; it was only by doing so that it succeeded in covering the earth with numberless artistic splendours. One God! What an absurdity! What an inhuman, murderous absurdity! . . . A god of stone, *cher monsieur*, a jealous, bloody god who should never have crossed over from Sinai. How much more profound, when you think about it, was our Egyptian religion, how much wiser and more humane . . . and our women! How beautiful our women were! Remember Cleopatra, who bewitched great Caesar. See what remains of them today . . .' (randomly he indicated two veiled women walking with difficulty carrying bundles of merchandise). 'Lumps. Big shapeless lumps of fat who hide themselves beneath rags. As soon as they're married, they think of nothing but eating. They eat and eat and eat! . . .' (his face became bloated as he pulled a face like de Funès). 'No, believe me, *cher monsieur*, the desert has produced nothing but lunatics and morons. In your noble Western culture,

for which, by the way, I have great admiration and
respect, can you name anyone who was drawn to the
desert? Only pederasts, adventurers and crooks, like that
ludicrous colonel Lawrence, a decadent homosexual and
a pathetic poseur. Like your despicable Henry de
Monfreid, an unscrupulous trafficker, always ready to
compromise his principles. Nothing great or noble,
nothing generous or wholesome; nothing which has
contributed to the progress of humanity or raised it above
itself.'

'Okay, Egypt gets adventure . . .' Jean-Yves concluded
simply. He apologised for interrupting my story, but we
had to move on to Kenya. A difficult case. 'I'd be quite
tempted to put it in with "Adventure" . . .' he suggested,
having consulted his files.

'Pity . . .' sighed Valérie. 'Kenyan woman are very
pretty.'

'How do you know that?'

'Well, not just Kenyan women, African women in
general.'

'Yeah, but there are women everywhere. In Kenya,
you've got rhinoceros, zebras, gnus, elephants, buffalo.
What I suggest is that we put Senegal and the Ivory Coast
into "Aphrodite", and leave Kenya in "Adventure". In
any case, it's a former English colony, which is terrible for
its erotic image, but okay for adventure.'

'They smell good, the women of the Ivory Coast . . .'
I observed dreamily.

'What do you mean by that?'

'They smell of sex.'

'Yes . . .' he chewed unconsciously on his pen. 'That could be good for an ad. 'Something like "The Ivory Coast, the realm of the scents" – with a girl in a grass skirt sweating, her hair tousled. I'll make a note of it.'

'"And the nude slaves imbued with fragrance . . ." Baudelaire, it's public domain.'

'We'd never get away with it.'

'I know.'

The rest of the African countries posed fewer problems. 'In fact, in general you never have any problems with Africans. They'll fuck for free, even the fat ones. You just have to put condoms in the clubs, that's all; from that point of view they can be a bit stubborn.' He underlined PROVIDE CONDOMS twice in his notebook.

Tenerife took us even less time. The club's takings were average, but, according to Jean-Yves, it was crucial to the Anglo-Saxon market. You could easily throw together an adventure circuit with a climb to the summit of Mount Tiede and a trip on a hydroplane to Lanzarote. The hotel set-up was reasonable, it could be made viable.

We came to the two clubs which would be the chain's chief assets: Boca Chica in the Dominican Republic and Guardalavaca in Cuba. 'We could provide king-size beds . . .' suggested Valérie. 'Done,' said Jean-Yves immediately. 'Private jacuzzis in the suites . . .' I suggested. 'No,' he cut me off, 'We're strictly mid-market.' One thing led effortlessly to another, with no hesitations, no doubts; we would have to liaise with the resort managers to standardise the local prostitution rates.

We paused briefly to go for lunch. At that very moment, two teenagers from the Courtilières housing estate were smashing in a sixty-year-old woman's head with a baseball bat. I ordered *maquereau au vin blanc* to start.

'Have you got anything planned for Thailand?' I asked.

'We've got a hotel in construction in Krabi. It's the new, hot destination after Phuket. We could easily speed up the building work, it could be ready by January 1st. It would be good to have a high-profile opening.'

We devoted the afternoon to developing the various innovative aspects of the Aphrodite clubs. The central point, obviously, was authorised access for local prostitutes, male and female. Clearly, there was no question of offering to accommodate children; the best thing would be to restrict admission to the clubs to the over-sixteens. An ingenious idea, suggested by Valérie, was to list the single-room tariff as the basic catalogue price and to offer a discount of 10 per cent for double occupancy; to reverse, in short, the standard system. I think I was the one who suggested that we put forward a gay-friendly policy, and to circulate rumours that homosexuals accounted for 20 per cent of visitors to the clubs: that kind of information was enough to get them to come; and if you wanted a place to have an atmosphere of *sex,* they had it down to a fine art. The issue of the overall slogan for the advertising campaign kept us busy for some time. Jean-Yves hit on a solution that was basic and effective: 'Going on holiday: time to go wild'; but in the end, I got a unanimous vote for 'Eldorador Aphrodite: Because pleasure is a right'. Since the NATO intervention in Kosovo, the notion of rights had become very persuasive, Jean-Yves explained to me in a half-joking tone; but he was quite serious: he had just read an article on the subject in *Stratégies*. Every recent campaign based on the idea of rights had been a success: the right to innovation, the right to excellence . . . The right to pleasure, he concluded sadly, was a new one. In fact, we were beginning to feel a little tired. He dropped us off at 2 + 2 before heading home. It was Saturday night, the place was quite full. We met a really nice black couple; she was a nurse, he was a jazz drummer – he was doing well, he recorded regularly. He admitted that he spent a lot of his time working on his technique, all his time in fact. 'There's no secret to it . . .' I said a bit foolishly, but, strangely, he agreed; without intending to, I had hit upon a profound truth. 'The secret is there is no secret,' he said to me with conviction. We finished our drinks and headed up to the rooms. He suggested a double penetration to Valérie. She agreed, as long as I was the one to sodomise her – you had to take it very gently with her, I was used to it. Jérôme agreed and lay down on the bed. Nicole stroked his cock to keep him hard, then slipped on a condom. I pushed Valérie's skirt up to her waist. She wasn't wearing anything underneath.

In a single movement, she impaled herself on Jérôme's prick, then lay down on top of him. I spread her cheeks, lubricated her a little, and then started to fuck her up the arse with short, careful strokes. At the point when the head of my cock was completely inside her, I felt her rectal muscles contract. I stiffened immediately, breathed deeply, I had almost come. After a few seconds, I pushed in deeper. When I was halfway in, she started to move back and forth, rubbing her pubis against Jérôme's. There was nothing more for me to do; she started a long, modulated groan, her arse opened and I pushed into her up to the hilt. It was like sliding down an inclined plane – she came surprisingly quickly. Then she became still, panting, happy. It was not that it was particularly more intense, she explained to me later; but when everything went well, there was a point when the two sensations fused, it became something gentle and irresistible, like being warm all over.

Nicola had been watching us, fingering herself all the time; she was starting to get really excited and immediately took Valérie's place. I didn't have time to change my condom. 'With me, you can just go for it,' she whispered in my ear; 'I really liked to be fucked hard up the arse.' Which is what I did, closing my eyes to lessen the excitement, trying to concentrate on pure sensation. Everything went smoothly, I was agreeably surprised by my own stamina. She, too, came very quickly with loud, hoarse cries.

Then Valérie and Nicole knelt down to suck us off

while we talked. Jérôme was still touring, he told me, but he didn't like it so much any more. As he got older, he felt the need to stay home more, to look after his family – they had two children – and to work on his drumming by himself. Then he talked to me about new time-signatures, 4/3 and 7/9; to be honest I didn't really understand very much. Right in the middle of a sentence he gave a cry of surprise, his eyes rolled back: he came all at once, ejaculating violently into Valérie's mouth. 'Ha, she got me there . . .' he said, half-laughing, 'she got me good.' I felt I was not going to hold out much longer either: Nicole had a most particular tongue, large and soft, eager; she licked slowly, the ascent was insidious, but almost irresistible. I motioned to Valérie to come nearer and explained to Nicole what I wanted: she was to close her lips round my glans, rest her tongue and remain motionless while Valérie jerked me off and licked my balls. She agreed, closed her eyes, waiting for the ejaculation. Valérie started immediately, her fingers quick and vigorous: already she seemed to be back on top form. I spread my arms and legs as far as I could, closed my eyes. The feeling mounted with sudden jolts, like bolts of lightning, then exploded just before I ejaculated into Nicole's mouth. For a brief moment I felt almost concussed, points of lights flashed beneath my eyelids; a little later I realised that I had been on the brink of passing out. I opened my eyes with difficulty. Nicole still had the tip of my cock in her mouth, she sucked up the last drops of semen. Valérie had slipped her arm around my neck, she was looking at me tenderly, mysteriously; she told me I had screamed very loudly.

A little later, they drove us home. In the car, Nicole had another surge of desire. She slipped her breasts out of her basque, lifted her skirt and lay down on the back seat, laying her head on my thighs. I masturbated her thoughtfully, confidently, expertly controlling her sensations, I felt her hard nipples and her wet pussy. The scent of her sex filled the car. Jérôme drove carefully, stopped at the red lights; through the windows, I could make out the lights of the Place de la Concorde, the obelisk, then the Pont Alexandre III, Les Invalides. I felt good, at peace, but still a little energetic. She came as we neared the Place d'Italie. We went our separate ways after exchanging phone numbers.

Jean-Yves, meanwhile, feeling a little depressed after he had left us, had parked on the Avenue de la République. The excitement of the day had subsided; he knew that Audrey would not be home, but he was actually rather glad of that. He would run into her briefly tomorrow morning, before she went out rollerblading; since coming back from holiday, they slept in separate rooms.

Why go home? He pushed back in his seat, thought about trying to turn on the radio but didn't. Gangs of young people, boys and girls, went past on the street; they looked like they were having fun, at least they were yelling. Some of them were carrying cans of beer. He could have got out, mingled with them, maybe started a fight; there were many things he could have done. In the end, he would go home. In some sense he loved his daughter, at least he supposed he did; he felt for her something organic and potentially blood-stained for her which corresponded to the definition of the word. He felt nothing of the kind for his son. In fact, the boy might not even be his; his reasons for marrying Audrey had been rather minimal. For her, at any rate, he felt nothing more than contempt and disgust; too much disgust, he would have preferred to feel indifferent; at the moment he still keenly felt that she should be made to *pay*. I'm more likely to be the one to pay, he thought suddenly, bitterly. She would get custody of the children and he would be landed with huge alimony payments. Unless he tried to get custody of the children, unless he fought her on that; but no, he decided, it wasn't worth it. It was too bad for Angélique. He would be better off on his own, he could try to start a new life, which meant, more or less, find some other girl. Saddled with two kids, it would be tougher for Audrey, the bitch. He consoled himself with the thought that it would be hard for him to do worse, and that, at the end of the day, she would be the one to suffer as a result of the divorce. She was already no longer as beautiful as when he had met her; she had style, she dressed fashionably, but knowing her body as he did, he knew she was already over the hill. On top of that, her career as a lawyer was far from being as brilliant as she made out; and he had a feeling that having custody of the children would not help matters. People drag their progeny around with them like a millstone, like some terrible weight which hinders their every move – and which, as often as not, effectively winds up killing them. He would have his revenge later: at the point, he thought, when it had become a matter of complete indifference to him. For some minutes more, parked near the bottom of the now deserted avenue, he practised feeling indifferent.

His worries came crashing down on him all at once as soon as he had walked through the door of the apartment. Johanna, the babysitter, was sprawled on the sofa watching MTV. He hated this listless, absurdly trendy pre-adolescent; every time he saw her he wanted to smack her round the face, to wipe the expression off her nasty, sulky, careless face. She was the daughter of one of Audrey's friends.

'Everything OK?' he shouted. She nodded casually. 'Could you turn it down?' She looked around for the remote control. Exasperated, he turned the television off; she shot him a hurt look.

'What about the children, everything go alright?' He was still shouting though there was no longer a sound in the apartment.

'Yeah, I think they're asleep.' She curled up, a little scared.

He went up to the first floor and pushed open the door to his son's bedroom. Nicolas looked round at him abstractedly, and then went back to his game of *Tomb Raider*. Angélique, on the other hand, was sleeping like a log. He went downstairs, a little calmer.

'Did you bathe them?'

'Yeah . . . no, I forgot.'

He wandered into the kitchen and poured himself a glass of water. His hands were shaking. On the worktop, he saw a hammer. A couple of slaps wouldn't have been enough for Johanna; smashing her skull in with hammer blows would be much better. He toyed with this idea for a while; thoughts crisscrossed his brain rapidly, barely controlled. In the hallway, he noticed in terror that he was holding the hammer. He placed it on a low table, looked in his wallet for the taxi fare for the babysitter. She took it, mumbling thanks. He slammed the door behind her in a gesture of uncontrolled violence; the sound reverberated through the entire apartment, Something was clearly not right in his life. In the living room the drinks cabinet was empty; Audrey wasn't even capable of looking after that. Thinking of her, a wave of hatred coursed through him and he was surprised at its intensity. In the kitchen he found an open bottle of rum; that would probably do. In his bedroom he dialled in turn the numbers of three girls he had met on the internet: each time, he got an answering machine. They had probably gone out, fucking on their own account. It's true they were sexy, cool, fashionable, but they were costing him two thousand francs a night; it became humiliating after a while. How had he come to this? He should go out, make friends, spend less time on his work. He thought about the Aphrodite clubs again, realising for the first time that it might be difficult to get the idea past his superiors; there was a fairly negative attitude to sex tourism in France at the moment. Obviously, he could try getting a toned down version past Leguen, but Espitalier wouldn't be fooled; he sensed a treacherous shrewdness in the man. Anyway, what choice did they have? Their mid-market positioning made no sense up against Club Med – he would have no problem in proving that. Rummaging through his desk drawers he found the Aurore mission statement, drafted ten years earlier by the founder, and displayed in every hotel in the group:

> The spirit of Aurore is the art of marrying know-how, tradition and innovation with rigour, imagination and humanism, to attain a certain form of excellence. The men and women of Aurore are the repositories of a unique cultural heritage: the art of welcoming. They know the rituals and the customs which transform life into the art of living, and the simplest of services into a privileged moment. It is a profession, it is an art: it is their gift. Creating the best in order to share it, getting in touch with the essential through hospitality, devising spaces of pleasure: these are what make Aurore a taste of France throughout the world.

He suddenly realised that this nauseating spiel could just as easily apply to a chain of well-run brothels; maybe there was a card here he could play with the German tour operators. Defying all reason, Germans still thought of

France as the country of romance, of the art of love. If a major German tour operator agreed to include the Aphrodite clubs in their catalogue, it would mark a turning-point; no one in the industry had yet succeeded in achieving such a thing. He was already in contact with Neckermann over the sale of the North African clubs. But there was also TUI, who had turned down their initial approaches because they were already well established in the bottom end of the market; they might be interested in a more targeted product.

11

First thing Monday morning, he set about making some initial approaches. From the start, he was lucky: Gottfried Rembke, president of the board of TUI, was coming to spend a few days in France at the beginning of the month; Rembke would pencil them in for lunch. In the meantime, if they could put their proposal in writing he would be delighted to give it his careful consideration. Jean-Yves went into Valérie's office to tell her the news; she froze. The annual turnover of TUI was six billion francs, three times that of Neckermann, six times that of Nouvelles Frontières; they were the largest tour operator in the world.

They devoted the rest of the week to writing up a sales pitch that was as detailed as possible. Financially, the project didn't require substantial investment: there were some small changes in furnishings, the hotels would definitely have to be redecorated to give them a more 'erotic' feel –

they had quickly settled on the term 'friendly tourism', which would be used in all of the business documentation. The most important point was that they could expect a significant reduction in their fixed costs: no more sporting activities, no more children's clubs. No more salaries to be paid to registered paediatric nurses or windsurfing instructors; nor to specialists in ikebana, ceramics or painting on silk. After running a first financial simulation, Jean-Yves realised to his surprise that, allowing for depreciation, the annual costs of the clubs would drop by 25 per cent. He redid the calculations three times and each time got the same result. It was all the more striking because the catalogue rates he intended proposing were 25 per cent above the category norm essentially pegging the rates with those of the mid-range Club Med. Profits leapt by 50 per cent. 'Your boyfriend's a genius . . .' he told Valérie, who had just come into his office.

The atmosphere in the office at this time was a little odd. The clashes which had taken place on the streets of Évry the previous weekend were not uncommon; but the death-toll – seven – was particularly high. Many of the employees, especially those who had worked there longest, lived in the vicinity of the offices. At first they had lived in the apartment blocks that had been built at much the same time as the offices; later, as often as not, they had borrowed in order to build. 'I feel sorry for them,' Valérie told me; 'I really do. They all dreamed of setting themselves up out of town, somewhere peaceful; but they can't just leave now, they'd end up losing a chunk of their pensions. I was talking to the switchboard operator: she has three years before she retires. Her dream is to buy a house in the Dordogne; she's from there originally. But a lot of English people have moved there and the prices there now are outrageous, even for some miserable dump. And on the other hand, the price of her house here has collapsed, everyone knows that it's a dangerous suburb nowadays, she'd have to sell it for a third of its value.

'Another thing that surprised me is the second-floor secretarial pool. I went up there at half-past five to get a memo typed up: they were all on the internet. They told me that they all do their shopping that way now, it's safer; they go home, lock themselves in and wait for the delivery man.'

In the weeks that followed, this obsessive fear did not fade, if anything it increased slightly. In the papers now it was teachers being stabbed, nursery school teachers being raped, fire engines attacked with Molotov cocktails, handicapped people thrown through the windows of trains because they had 'looked the wrong way' at some gang leader. *Le Figaro* was having a field day: reading it every day, you got the impression of an unstoppable escalation to civil war. True, this was the run-up to an election and law and order was the only issue likely to bother Lionel Jospin. In any case, it seemed very unlikely that the French would vote for Jacques Chirac again: he seemed to be such an idiot it was affecting the country's image. Whenever you saw this lanky half-wit, hands clasped behind his back, visiting some country fair, or taking part in a heads of state summit, you felt sort of ashamed, you felt embarrassed for him. The Left, obviously incapable of curbing the rising tide of violence, behaved well: they kept a low profile, agreed that the figures were bad, very bad even, called on others not to make political capital of it, reminded people that when they'd been in power the Right hadn't done any better. There was just one little slip, a ridiculous editorial by Jacques Attali. According to him, the violence of young people on housing estates was a 'cry for help'. The shop windows of the Champs-Elysées, he wrote, constituted so many 'obscene displays flaunted at their misery'. Neither should it be forgotten that the suburbs were a 'mosaic of peoples and ethnicities, who had come with their traditions and their beliefs to forge new cultures and to reinvent the art of living together'. Valérie stared at me in surprise: this was the first time I had burst out laughing while reading *L'Express*.

'If he wants to get elected,' Jean-Yves said, handing her the article, 'Jospin would be well advised to shut him up until the second round.'

'You're clearly getting a taste for strategy . . .'

Despite everything, I too was beginning to feel anxiety gnawing at me. Valérie was working late again, it was rare for her to get home before nine o'clock. It might be wise to buy a gun. I had a contact, the brother of an artist whose exhibition I had organised two years before. He wasn't really part of the scene, he'd just been involved in a couple of scams. He was more of an inventor, a sort of jack-of-all-trades. He had recently told his brother that he'd discovered a way of forcing the new identity cards which were supposed to be impossible to fake.

'Out of the question,' Valérie said immediately. 'I'm not in any danger: I never leave the office during the day and at night I always take a cab home, regardless of what time I leave.'

'There's still the traffic lights.'

'There's only one set of traffic lights between the office and the motorway. After that, I take the exit at Porte d'Italie and I'm almost home. Our area isn't dangerous.'

It was true: in Chinatown, strictly speaking, there were very few assaults or rapes. I didn't understand how they managed it, did they have their own neighbourhood watch? In any case, they had noticed us as soon as we moved in; there were at least twenty people who regularly greeted us. It was rare for Europeans to move in here, we were in a very small minority in the building. Sometimes, posters written in Chinese characters seemed to extend invitations to meetings or parties; but what meetings? what parties? It's possible to live among the Chinese for years without understanding anything about the way they live.

Nevertheless, I phoned my contact who promised to ask around. He called me back two days later. I could have a serious piece, in very good nick, for ten thousand francs

– the price included a healthy quantity of ammunition. All I would have to do was clean it regularly to make sure it didn't jam if ever I needed to use it. I talked to Valérie again, who refused again. 'I couldn't,' she said, 'I wouldn't have the courage to pull the trigger.' 'Even if your life was in danger?' She shook her head, 'No . . .' she repeated, 'It's not possible.' I didn't insist. 'When I was little,' she told me later, 'I couldn't even kill a chicken.' To be honest, neither could I; but a man, now that seemed significantly easier.

Curiously, I was not afraid for my own sake. It's true I had very little contact with the barbarian hordes, except perhaps occasionally at lunchtime when I went for a walk around the Forum des Halles, where the subtle infiltration of the security forces (the riot squad, uniformed police officers, security guards employed by local shopkeepers) eliminated all danger, in theory. So I wandered casually through the reassuring topography of uniforms; I felt as though I was in Thoiry safari park. In the absence of the forces of law and order, I knew, I would be easy prey, though of little interest; very conventional, my middle-management uniform had very little to tempt them. For my part, I felt no attraction for this youthful product of the *dangerous classes*; I didn't understand them, and made no attempt to do so. I didn't sympathise with their passions nor with their values. For myself, I wouldn't have lifted a finger to own a Rolex, a pair of Nikes or a BMW Z3; in fact, I had never succeeded in identifying the slightest difference between designer goods and non-designer goods. In the eyes of the world, I was clearly wrong. I was aware of this: I was in a minority, and consequently in the wrong. There *had* to be a difference between Yves Saint-Laurent shirts and other shirts, between Gucci moccasins and André moccasins. I was alone in not perceiving this difference; it was an infirmity which I could not cite as grounds for condemning the world. Does one ask a blind man to set himself up as an expert on post-impressionist painting? Through my blindness, however involuntary, I set myself apart from a living human reality powerful enough to incite both devotion and crime. These youths, through their half-savage instincts, undoubtedly discerned the presence of beauty; their desire was laudable, and perfectly in keeping with social norms; it was merely a question of rectifying the inappropriate way in which it was expressed.

Thinking about it carefully, however, I had to admit that Valérie and Marie-Jeanne, the only two long-term female presences in my life, manifested a complete indifference to Kenzo blouses and Prada handbags; in fact, as far as I could make out, they bought any old brand at random. Jean-Yves, the highest paid individual I knew, exhibited a preference for Lacoste polo-necks, but he did it somewhat mechanically, out of habit, without even checking to see whether the reputation of his favourite brand had not been surpassed by some new challenger. Some of the women at the Ministry of Culture whom I knew by sight (though I regularly forgot their names, their job titles, even their faces, between each encounter) bought designer clothes; but they were invariably by some young, obscure designer who had only one outlet in Paris, and I knew perfectly well that they would not hesitate to abandon them if by chance they ever found a wider public.

The power of Nike, Adidas, Armani, Vuitton was, nonetheless, indisputable; I could find proof of this whenever I needed simply by glancing through the business section of *Le Figaro*. But who, exactly – aside from youths on housing estates – assured the success of these brands? Clearly there had to be whole sectors of society who were still alien to me; unless, more prosaically, they were bought by rich people in the third world. I had travelled little, lived little and it was becoming increasing clear that I understood little about the modern world.

On September 27, there was a meeting of the eleven Eldorador holiday club managers, who had come to Évry for the occasion. It was a routine meeting which took place every year on the same date, to assess the figures for the summer and consider improvements which might be made. However, this time, it had particular significance. Firstly, three of the resorts were about to change hands – the contract with Neckermann had just been signed. Secondly, the managers of four of the remaining villages – those which fell into the 'Aphrodite' category – had to prepare themselves to fire half of their staff.

Valérie was not present for the meeting; she had a meeting with an Italtrav representative to present the scheme to him. The Italian market was much more fragmented than those of Northern Europe. Italtrav might well be the largest tour operator in Italy, but its turnover was less than a tenth of TUI's; an agreement with them would, nonetheless, bring in valuable customers.

She came back from her appointment at about 7 p.m., Jean-Yves was alone in his office, the meeting had just ended.

'How did they take it?'

'Badly. I know how they feel, too; they must think they're next for the chop.'

'Are you intending to replace the resort managers?'

'It's a new project; we'd be better off starting out with new teams.'

His voice was very calm. Valérie looked at him in surprise: lately he had become more assured – and tougher.

'I'm convinced that we're going to be a success, now. When we broke for lunch, I was talking to the manager at Boca Chica, in the Dominican Republic. I wanted to be clear in my mind about something: I wanted to know how he managed to have 90 per cent occupancy regardless of season. He dithered, he seemed embarrassed, talked about team work. In the end, I asked him straight out if he was allowing girls to go up to the guest rooms; I had a hard time getting him to admit it, he was afraid I was going to put him on a disciplinary. I had to tell him that it didn't bother me at all, that in fact I thought it was an interesting initiative. At that point he confessed. He thought it was stupid that guests were renting rooms a mile away, often with no running water, and with the risk of being ripped off, when they had every comfort right there. I congratulated him and I promised him he'd keep his job as resort manager, even if he's the only one who does.'

It was getting dark; he turned on a lamp on his desk, was silent for a moment.

'For the others,' he went on, 'I don't feel the slightest remorse. They're all pretty much the same. They're all former reps, they joined at the right time, they got to have it off with anyone they wanted without doing a fucking stroke of work and they thought that becoming manager of the resort meant they could bum around in the sun until they retired. Their days are over – tough. Now, I need real professionals.'

Valérie crossed her legs and looked at him in silence.

'By the way, the meeting with Italtrav?'

'Good. No problems. He knew at once what I meant by 'friendly tourism', he even tried to make a pass at me . . . That's the good thing about Italians, at least they're predictable . . . Anyway, he promised he'd include the clubs in his catalogue, but he said we shouldn't get our hopes up: Italtrav has a strong presence because it's a conglomerate of a lot of specialised tour companies; in its own right it hasn't got a very strong image. In fact, it operates as a distributor: we can get on their list, but it will be up to us to make a name for ourselves in the market.'

'What about Spain? How far have we got?'

'We've got a good relationship with Marsans. They're much the same, except they're more ambitious: for a while now they've been trying to get a foothold in France. I was a bit worried that we'd be competing with their products, but apparently not, they think what we're doing is complementary.'

She thought for a moment and then continued:

'What are we going to do about France?'

'I'm still not sure . . . Maybe I'm being stupid, but I'm really worried about stirring up a moralistic press campaign. Obviously, we could do some focus groups, test the market . . .'

'You've never believed in that stuff.'

'No, that's true . . .' he hesitated for a moment. 'Actually, I'm tempted to do a minimal launch in France, just through the Auroretour network. Put ads in a couple of carefully targeted magazines like *FHM* or *L'Écho des Savanes*. But really, for the first stage, I want to focus on Northern Europe.'

The meeting with Gottfried Rembke took place the following Friday. The night before, Valérie made herself a cleansing mask and went to bed early. When I woke up at eight o'clock, she was already ready. I was impressed by the results. She was wearing a black suit with a short, tight skirt which hugged her arse magnificently; under the jacket, she was wearing a lilac blouse in lace, close fitting and, in places, transparent, and a scarlet push-up bra which showed off her breasts. When she sat opposite the bed, I discovered she was wearing black stockings, faded towards the top, held in place by suspenders. Her lips were emphasised in a dark, almost purplish, red and she had tied her hair up in a chignon.

'Does this do the trick?' she asked mockingly

'That does it *in spades*. Well, well, women . . .' I added, 'when you show yourselves to your best advantage . . .'

'This is my corporate seductress outfit. I put it on for you, in a way, too; I knew you'd like it.'

'Re-eroticising the workplace . . .' I muttered. She handed me a cup of coffee.

Until she left, I did nothing but watch her come and go, stand and sit. It wasn't much, I suppose, actually it was quite simple, but it did the trick, no doubt about it. She crossed her legs, a dark band appeared high up on her thighs, accentuating the contrasting sheerness of the nylon. She crossed them a little more, a band of lace was revealed a little higher up, then the fastener of the suspenders, the bare, white flesh, the curve of the buttocks. She uncrossed them, everything disappeared again. She leaned over the table: I could feel the palpitation of her breasts through the fabric. I could have spent hours watching her. It was a simple joy, innocent and eternally blessed; a pure promise of pleasure.

They were supposed to meet at 1 p.m. at Le Divellec, a restaurant on the Rue de l'Université; Jean-Yves and Valérie arrived five minutes early.

'How are we going to raise the subject?' Valérie asked

anxiously as she stepped out of the taxi.

'I dunno . . . just tell him we want to open up a chain of brothels for Huns . . . Jean-Yves gave a weary grin. 'Don't worry about it, don't worry about it, he'll ask all the questions.'

Gottfried Rembke arrived at 1 p.m. precisely. The moment he walked into the restaurant, handed his coat to the waiter, they knew it was him. The solid, stocky body, the gleaming scalp, the open expression, the vigorous handshake: everything about him radiated ease and enthusiasm; he was precisely what one imagined a head honcho, more especially a German head honcho, looked like. You could imagine him eagerly throwing himself into each new day, leaping out of bed, doing half an hour on an exercise bike before driving to the office in his spanking new Mercedes, listening to the financial news. 'This guy seems perfect . . .' muttered Jean-Yves as he got to his feet, all smiles, to greet him.

For the next ten minutes, in fact, Herr Rembke spoke of nothing but food. It turned out that he knew France very well, the culture, the cuisine; he even owned a house in Provence. 'Perfect, the guy's perfect . . .' thought Jean-Yves as he studied his *consommé de langoustines au curaçao*. 'Rock and roll, Gotty,' he added to himself, dipping his spoon into the soup. Valérie was wonderful: she listened attentively, her eyes sparkling as though charmed by him. She wanted to know where, exactly, in Provence, whether he had time to visit often, etc. She had chosen the *salmis d'étrilles aux fruits rouges*.

'So,' she went on without changing her tone, 'you'd be interested in the proposal.'

'The way I see it,' he said thoughtfully, 'we know that "friendly tourism"' – he stumbled a little on the expression – 'is one of the primary motivating factors of our compatriots when they holiday abroad – and, moreover, one can understand why, after all, what more delightful way to travel? However, and this is somewhat curious, up until now, no major group has actively taken an interest in the sector – apart from a number of attempts, all hopelessly inadequate, marketed to a homosexual clientele. Essentially, surprising as it may seem, we are dealing with a virgin market.'

'It's much discussed. I think that attitudes still have a long way to go . . .' interrupted Jean-Yves, realising as he did so that what he was saying was ridiculous. 'On both sides of the Rhine . . .' he concluded miserably. Rembke gave him a frosty look, as though he thought Jean-Yves was taking the piss; Jean-Yves hunched over his food again, determined not to say another word until the meal was over. In any case, Valérie was getting along brilliantly. 'Let's not project French problems on to the Germans . . .' she said, ingenuously crossing her legs. Rembke fixed his attention on her once more.

'Our compatriots,' he went on, 'forced to fend for themselves, often find themselves at the mercy of intermediaries of dubious honesty. More generally, the sector remains marked by rank amateurism – which represents a considerable loss of earnings for the industry as a whole.'

Valérie agreed eagerly. The waiter arrived with a *saint-pierre rôti aux figues nouvelles*.

'Equally,' he went on having glanced at his dish, 'your proposal interests us because it represents a compete reversal of the traditional view of the holiday club. A formula which was conceived in the 1970s does not correspond to the expectations of contemporary con-sumers. Relationships between individuals in the West have become more difficult – a fact which, needless to say, we all deplore . . .' he continued, glancing again at Valérie, who uncrossed her legs with a smile.

When I got back from the office at a quarter-past six, she was already home. I felt a twinge of surprise: I think this was the first time since we lived together. She was sitting on the sofa, still wearing her suit, her legs slightly apart. Staring into space, she seemed to be thinking of happy, gentle things. Though I did not know it at the time, I was witnessing the professional equivalent of an orgasm.

'Did it go well?' I asked.

'Better than well. I came straight home after lunch, I didn't even bother dropping into the office; I really couldn't see what else we could do this week. Not only is he interested in the project, but he intends to make it one of his key products as of next winter. He's prepared to finance printing the catalogue and an advertising cam-paign targeted specifically at the German market. He believes that, on his own, he can guarantee to fill all the existing clubs; he even asked whether we had any other projects in the works. The only thing he wants in return, is exclusivity in his own market – Germany, Austria, Switzerland and the Benelux countries; he knows that we've been in touch with Neckermann too.'

'I've booked a weekend,' she added, 'in a thalasso-therapy centre in Dinard. I think I need it. We could drop in on my parents as well.'

The train pulled out of the Gare Montparnasse an hour later. Quite quickly, as the kilometres passed, the accumulated tension faded and she was back to normal, that is rather sexual and playful. The last buildings of the outer suburbs disappeared behind us; the TGV approached maximum speed just as we came to the Plain of Hurepoix. A sliver of daylight, an almost imperceptible reddish tinge, hung in the air to the west over the dark mass of grain silos. We were in a first-class carriage arranged in small compartments; on the tables which separated our seats, small yellow lamps already glowed. Across the corridor, a woman of about forty, very upper-middle class but pretty stylish with her blonde hair tied up in a chignon, was leafing through *Madame Figaro*. I had bought the same paper and was trying without much success to interest myself in the financial supplement. For some years I had nurtured the theory that it was possible to decode the world, to understand its evolution, by setting aside everything dealing with current affairs, politics, the society pages and the arts; that it was possible to form an accurate image of the thrust of history purely by reading the financial news and the stock prices. I therefore forced myself to read the *Figaro* financial section daily, supplemented by even more forbidding publications like *Les Échos* or *La Tribune Desfossés*. Up to this point, my theory had remained impossible to judge. It was possible, in other words, that historic news was concealed within these editorials. with their measured tones, their columns of figures; but the reverse might just as easily be true. The only definite conclusion I had categorically come to: economics was unspeakably boring. Looking up from a short article which attempted to analyse the fall of the Nikkei, I noticed that Valérie had begun crossing and uncrossing her legs; a half-smile flitted across her face. 'Descent into hell for Milan stock exchange,' I managed to read before putting down the paper. I suddenly got an erection when I discovered she had found a way to take off her panties. She came and sat beside me, pressed herself against me. Taking off her suit jacket, she draped it across my lap. I glanced quickly to my right: our neighbour still appeared to be engrossed in her magazine, specifically in an article on the garden in winter. She too was wearing a suit with a tight skirt and black tights; she looked like a posh tart, as they say. Sliding her hand under her jacket, Valérie placed it on my penis; I was wearing only a pair of thin cotton trousers, the sensation was terribly precise. It was, by now, completely dark. I sat back in my seat, slipped a hand under her blouse. Pushing her bra aside, I encircled her right breast with the palm of my hand and began to stimulate her nipple with my thumb and forefinger. Just as we reached Le Mans, she undid my flies. Her movements were now absolutely brazen, I was convinced that our neighbour was missing nothing of our little game. As far as I'm concerned, it is impossible to resist masturbation by a truly expert hand. Just before Rennes I ejaculated, unable to suppress a muffled cry. 'I'll have to get this suit cleaned,' Valérie said calmly. Our neighbour glanced across, making no attempt to conceal her amusement.

Even so, at the station at Saint-Malo I was a little embarrassed when I noticed that she was boarding the same shuttle bus for the thalassotherapy centre; but not so Valérie: she even struck up a conversation with her about the various treatments. For myself, I've never really worked out the respective merits of mud baths, high-pressure showers and seaweed wraps; the following day, I was happy just to mess around in the pool. I was floating on my back, vaguely aware of the underwater currents supposedly massaging my a back, when Valérie joined me. 'Our neighbour from the train . . .' she said, all excited, 'she came on to me in the jacuzzi.' I registered the information without reacting. 'Right now she's alone in the hammam,' she added. I followed her at once, wrapping myself in a bathrobe. Near the entrance to the hammam, I took off my swimming trunks; my erection was visible beneath the towelling robe. I followed Valérie in, letting her make her way through steam so dense you couldn't see a couple of metres ahead of you. The air was saturated with a strong, almost intoxicating scent of eucalyptus. I stopped and stood still in the hot, whitish emptiness, then I heard a moan coming from the far end of the room. I untied the belt of my robe and walked towards the sound. Beads of perspiration formed on the surface of my skin. Kneeling in front of the woman, hands placed on her buttocks, Valérie was slowly licking her pussy. She really was a very beautiful woman, with perfectly rounded silicone-enhanced breasts, a harmonious face, a wide, sensual mouth. Unsurprised, she turned to look at me and closed her hand around my penis. I came a little closer, went behind her and stroked her breasts, rubbing my penis against her buttocks. She opened her thighs and bent forward, leaning on the wall for support. Valérie rummaged in the pocket of her robe and handed me a condom; with her other hand, she continued to masturbate the woman's clitoris. I penetrated the woman in one swift thrust, she was already wide open; she bent forward a little further. I was thrusting in and out of her when I felt Valérie's hand slip between my thighs, then close over my balls. Then she leaned forward and began licking the woman's pussy, with each thrust, I could feel my cock rubbing against her tongue. I desperately tensed my pelvic muscles at the point when the women came in a series of long, contented moans, then slowly I pulled out. My whole body was sweating, I was panting involuntarily, I felt a little faint and had to sit down on a bench. The clouds of steam continued to undulate through the air. I heard the sound of a kiss and I looked up: they were entwined, breast to breast.

We made love a little later, in the late afternoon, again that evening and once more the following morning. Such frenzy was a little unusual; we were both conscious of the fact that we were about to enter a difficult time, when Valérie would once more be stupefied with work, problems and calculations. The sky was an immaculate blue, the weather almost warm; it was probably one of the last fine weekends before the autumn. After making love on Sunday morning, we took a long stroll on the beach. I looked in surprise at the neoclassical, slightly kitsch hotel buildings. When we arrived at the far end of the beach, we sat down on the rocks.

'I suppose it was important, that meeting with the German,' I said; 'I suppose it's the beginning of a new challenge.'

'This will be the last time, Michel. If this is a success, we'll be set up for a long time.'

I shot her a doubtful and slightly sad look. I didn't believe in that line of reasoning: it reminded me of history books in which politicians declared that this would be the war to end all wars, the sort that was supposed to lead to a permanent peace.

'It was you who told me,' I said gently, 'that capitalism, by its very nature, is a permanent state of war, a constant struggle which can never end.'

'That's true,' she agreed without hesitation, 'But it's not always the same people doing the fighting.'

A gull took off, gained altitude and headed out to the

ocean. We were almost alone at this end of the beach. Dinard was clearly a very quiet resort, at least at this time of year. A labrador came up and sniffed us, then turned tail; I couldn't see its owners .

'I promise you,' she insisted. 'if this works as well as we hope, we can roll out the concept in lots of countries. In Latin America alone there's Brazil, Venezuela, Costa Rica. Apart from that we can open clubs in Cameroon, Mozambique, Madagascar, the Seychelles. In Asia too there are obvious possibilities: China, Vietnam, Cambodia. In two or three years, we can become an uncontested market leader; and no one will dare invest in the same market: this time we'll get it, our competitive advantage.'

I didn't reply, I couldn't think of anything to say; after all, it had originally been my idea. The tide was coming in; waves crashed on to the beach and died at our feet.

'On top of that,' she went on, 'this time we're going to insist on a decent share package. If it's a success, they can't possibly refuse. And when you're a shareholder, you don't have to fight any more: other people do the fighting for you.'

She stopped, looked at me, hesitant. It made sense, what she was saying, it had a certain logic. The wind was getting up a bit; I was starting to feel hungry. The restaurant at the hotel was excellent: they had impeccably fresh shellfish, and delicious, delicate fish dishes. We headed back, walking across the wet sand.

'I've got money . . .' I said suddenly. 'Don't forget that

I've got money.' She stopped and looked at me in surprise; I hadn't expected to say these words.

'I know it's not the done thing to be a kept woman,' I went on, a little embarrassed, 'but there's nothing forcing us to do things the way everybody else does.'

She stared calmly into my eyes. 'When you've got the money from the house, at best it'll come out to three million francs, maximum . . .' she said.

'Yes. That's right, something like that.'

'It's not enough, at least not quite. We need just a little more.' She began walking again and said nothing for a long moment. 'Trust me . . .' she said, as we stepped under the glass roof of the restaurant.

After the meal, just before heading to the station, we paid a visit to Valérie's parents. She was about to be submerged with work again, she explained; she probably wouldn't be able to visit again before Christmas. Her father looked at her with a resigned smile. She was a good daughter, I thought, an attentive and caring daughter; she was also a sensual lover, affectionate and audacious; and, if need be, she would no doubt be a wise and loving mother. *'Her feet are of fine gold, her legs like the columns of the temple of Jerusalem.'* I continued to wonder what exactly I had done to deserve a woman like Valérie. Nothing, probably. I observe the world as it unfurls, I thought; proceeding empirically, in good faith, I observe it; I can do no more than observe.

12

At the end of October, Jean-Yves's father died. Audrey refused to accompany him to the funeral; actually, he had been expecting as much, he had asked her only for the sake of propriety. It would be a modest funeral: he was an only child, there would be some family, very few friends. His father would have a brief obituary in the ESAT alumni newsletter and that would be it, the end of the line. He had hardly seen anyone recently. Jean-Yves had never really understood what had moved him to retire to this undistinguished area, rural in the most depressing sense of the word and to which, moreover, he had no ties. Probably a last vestige of the masochism which had dogged him more or less his whole life. Having been a rather brilliant student, he had become bogged down in a lacklustre career as a manufacturing engineer. Though he had always dreamed of having a daughter, he had consciously limited himself to only one child – in order, he maintained, to give the boy a better education; the argument didn't stand up, he earned a very good salary. He gave the impression of being accustomed to his wife rather than truly loving her; perhaps he was proud of his son's professional successes – but, truth be told, the fact was he never spoke of them. He had no hobby, no leisure activity to speak of, apart from breeding rabbits and doing the crossword in *La République du Centre-Ouest*. We are probably wrong to suspect that each individual has some secret passion, some mystery, some weakness; if Jean-Yves's father had had to express his innermost convictions, the profound meaning he ascribed to life, he could probably have cited nothing more than a slight disappointment. Indeed, his favourite expression, what Jean-Yves remembered him saying most often, what best encapsulated his experience of the human condition, was limited to the words 'You get old'.

Jean-Yves's mother seemed reasonably affected by her bereavement – he had, after all, been her lifelong companion – without really seeming to be shattered for all that. 'He'd gone downhill a lot . . .' she remarked. The cause of death was so vague that one might well have been talking about a general fatigue, or even despondency. 'He had no interest in anything anymore . . .' his mother said again. That, more or less, was her funerary oration.

Audrey's absence was, of course, noticed, but during the ceremony his mother refrained from mentioning it. The evening meal was a frugal affair – in any case, she had never been a good cook. He knew she would broach the subject at some point. Bearing in mind the circumstances, it was quite difficult to avoid the issue as he usually did, by turning on the television, for example. His mother finished putting away the dishes, then sat opposite him, her elbows on the table.

'How are things, with your wife?'

'Not great . . .' He expanded on this for a few minutes, getting ever more bogged down in his own boredom; in conclusion, he indicated that he was thinking of divorce. His mother, he knew, hated Audrey, whom she accused of keeping her from her grandchildren; actually, it was quite true, but her grandchildren weren't too keen to see her either. If things had been different, it's true, they could have become used to it; Angélique at least, in her case it wasn't too late. But it would have meant different circumstances, a different life, all things that were difficult to imagine. Jean-Yves looked up at his mother's face, her greying chignon, her harsh features: it was difficult to feel a rush of tenderness, of affection for this woman; as far back as he could remember, she had never really been one for hugs; it was equally difficult to imagine her in the role of a sensual lover, a slut. He suddenly realised that his father must have been bored shitless his whole life. He felt terribly shocked by this, his hands tensed on the edge of the table: this time it was irreparable, it was definitive. In despair, he tried to recall a moment when he had seen his father beaming, happy, genuinely glad to be alive. There was one time, possibly, when he had been five and his father had been trying to show him how Meccano worked. Yes, his father had loved engineering, truly loved it – he remembered his father's disappointment the day he had announced he was going to study marketing; perhaps it was enough, after all, to fill a life.

The next day, he made a quick tour of the garden, which, to tell the truth, seemed quite anonymous to him; it evoked no memories of his childhood. The rabbits shifted nervously in their hutches, they hadn't been fed yet: his mother was going to sell them immediately, she didn't like looking after them. In reality, they were the real losers in this whole business, the only real victims of this death. Jean-Yves took a sack of feed granules, poured a couple of handfuls into the hutches; this gesture, at least, he could make in memory of his father.

He left early, just before the Michel Drucker programme, but that did not stop him getting caught up, just before Fontainebleau, in endless traffic jams. He tried a number of different stations, and ended up turning off the radio. From time to time the queue moved forward a few metres; he could hear nothing but the purring of engines, the splat of solitary raindrops against the windscreen. His mood was attuned to this melancholy emptiness. The only positive element of the weekend, he thought, was that he would never have to see Johanna the babysitter again. The new one, Eucharistie, had been recommended by a neighbour; she was a girl from Dahomey, serious, worked hard at school. At fifteen she was already in two years from graduation. Later, she hoped to be a doctor, possibly a paediatrician; in any case she was very good with the children. She had succeeded in tearing Nicolas away from his video games and getting him to bed before ten o'clock – something that they had never been able to do. She was wonderful with Angélique, fed her, bathed her, played with her; the little girl obviously adored her.

He arrived at half-past ten, exhausted from the journey; Audrey was, as far as he could remember, in Milan for the weekend; she would fly back the following morning and go straight to work. Divorce was seriously going to cramp her lifestyle, he thought with malicious satisfaction; it was easy to understand why she should want to put off broaching the subject. On the other hand, she did not go so far as to feign any affection, any rush of tenderness; that was something that could be counted in her favour.

Eucharistie was sitting on the sofa, she was reading a paperback of *Life: A User's Manual*, by Georges Perec; everything had gone okay. She accepted a glass of orange juice; he poured himself a cognac. Usually, when he came home, she would tell him about the day, what she and the children had done together; this would last for a few minutes before she went. This time, too, she did so, as he poured himself a second cognac; he realised he hadn't been listening to a word. 'My father died . . .' he said, realising the fact again as he said the words. Eucharistie stopped abruptly and looked at him hesitantly; she did not know how to react, but he had clearly succeeded in capturing her attention. 'My parents were never happy together . . .' he continued, and this second observation was even worse: it seemed to deny his existence, to deprive him of a certain right to life. He was the fruit of an unhappy, mismatched union, something which would have been better if it had never been. He looked around him anxiously: in a few months at most he would leave this apartment, he would never again see these curtains, this furniture; everything already seemed to be fading, losing its solidity. He could just as easily be in the showroom of a department store after it closed; or in a photo from a catalogue, in something, at any rate, which had no real existence. He stood up unsteadily, walked over to Eucharistie and hugged the young girl's body violently in his arms. He slipped a hand under her pullover: her flesh was living, real. All of a sudden he came to himself and stopped, ashamed. She too had stopped struggling. He looked straight into her eyes, then kissed her on the mouth. She responded to his kiss, pushed her tongue against his. He slipped his hand higher under her pullover to her breasts.

They made love in the bedroom without a word; she had undressed quickly and then crouched on the bed, so he could take her. Even after they had come, they remained silent for some minutes and avoided mentioning the subject afterwards. She told him about her day again, what she and the children had been up to; then she told him that she could not stay the night.

In the weeks that followed, they did it again many times, every time she came over, in fact. He had more or less been waiting for her to broach the subject of the legality of their relations: after all, she was only fifteen, he was thirty-five; he could, at a pinch, have been her father. But she did not seem in the least inclined to see things in that light: in what light, then? In the end he realised, in a rush of emotion and of gratitude: in the simple light of pleasure. His marriage manifestly cut him off, he was out of touch; he had quite simply forgotten that certain women, in certain circumstances, make love *for pleasure*. He was not Eucharistie's first: she had already been with a boy the year before, a guy in his final year with whom she'd lost touch afterwards; but there were things she was unaware of, fellatio for example. The first time, he held back, was hesitant about coming in her mouth; but he quickly realised that she enjoyed it, or rather that it amused her to feel his semen spurt out. Usually, he had no trouble bringing her to orgasm; for his part it was immensely pleasurable feeling her firm, supple body in his arms. She was intelligent, curious; she was interested in his work and asked him lots of questions: she was almost everything Audrey was not. The universe of business was, to her, a curious, exotic world whose customs she wanted to learn; she would not have asked all these questions of her father, who, in any case, would have been unable to answer – he worked in a public hospital. In short, he thought, with a strange feeling of relatavism, theirs was a relationship of equals. Even so, he was lucky that his first child had not been a daughter; in certain circumstances he found it difficult to imagine how – and more especially why – incest might be avoided.

Three weeks after their first time, Eucharistie announced that she had met a boy. Under the circumstances it was best for them to end it; at any rate, it complicated matters. He seemed so desolate at the news that, the next time she came round, she offered to continue giving him blowjobs. In all honesty, he couldn't really see how that was less serious; but in any case he had more or less forgotten how he had felt when he was fifteen. When he got home he would talk for a long time about one thing and another; it was always she who decided on the moment. She would strip to the waist, allow him to caress her breasts; then he would lean back against the wall and she would kneel in front of him. From his moans she could tell precisely when he was going to come. She would then take her mouth away; with small, precise movements she would direct his ejaculation, sometimes towards her breasts, sometimes towards her mouth. In those moments she had a playful, almost childlike, expression; thinking back on it, he realised gloomily that her love life was just beginning, that she would make many lovers happy; their paths had crossed, that was all, and that in itself was a happy accident.

The second Saturday, at the moment when Eucharistie, eyes half-closed, mouth wide open, was beginning to jerk him off vigorously, he suddenly noticed his son popping his head round the door. He started, turned his head away; when he looked up again the child had disappeared. Eucharistie hadn't noticed anything; she slid her hand between his thighs, delicately squeezed his balls. At that moment, he had a strange sensation of immobility. Suddenly, it occurred to him, like a revelation, an impasse. There was too much overlap between the generations, fatherhood no longer had any meaning. He drew Eucharistie's mouth towards his penis; without quite understanding completely, he sensed that this would be the last time, he needed her mouth. As soon as her lips closed over him, he spurted several times, shoving his cock deep into her throat as shudders coursed through his body. Then she looked up at him; he kept his hands on the girl's head. She kept his penis in a mouth for two or three minutes, her eyes closed, running her tongue slowly over the head. Shortly before she left, he told her that they wouldn't do it again. He didn't really know why; if his son said anything it would surely do him a lot of harm when the divorce settlement was decided, but there was something else that he wasn't able to identify. He told me all of this a week later, in an irritating tone of self-reproach, begging me not to say anything to Valérie. I found him a little annoying, to tell the truth; I really couldn't see what the problem was. However, purely out of friendship I pretended to take an interest, to weigh up the pros and cons, but I couldn't take the situation seriously, I felt a little as if I was on Mireille Dumas' TV show.

From a professional point of view, on the other hand, everything was going well, he informed me with satisfaction. There had almost been a problem with the

Thailand club a couple of weeks earlier: there had to be at least one hostess bar and one massage parlour to cater for customer expectations. This would be a little difficult to justify in the budget for the hotel. He telephoned Gottfried Rembke. The boss of TUI rapidly found a solution; he had an associate on the ground, a Chinese building contractor based in Phuket, who could sort out the building a leisure complex just beside the hotel. The German tour operator seemed to be in a great mood, apparently things were looking good. At the beginning of November, Jean-Yves received a copy of the catalogue destined for the German market; he immediately noticed that they hadn't pulled any punches. In every photo the local girls were topless, wearing miniscule G-strings or see-through skirts; photographed on the beach or right in the hotel rooms, they smiled teasingly, ran their tongues over their lips: it was almost impossible to misunderstand. In France, he remarked to Valérie, you would never get away with something like this. It was curious to note, he mused, that as Europe became ever closer, and the idea of a federation of states was ever more current, there was no noticeable standardisation of moral legislation. Although prostitution was accepted in Holland and Germany and was governed by statute, many people in France were calling for it to be criminalised, even for punters to be prosecuted as they were in Sweden. Valérie looked at him, surprised: he had been odd lately, he launched increasingly frequently into aimless, unproductive ruminations. She herself coped with a punishing workload, methodically and with a sort of cold determination; she regularly took decisions without consulting him. It was something she was not really used to, and at times I sensed she felt lost, uncertain; the board of directors would not get involved, affording them complete freedom. 'They're waiting, that's all, they're waiting to see whether we fall flat on our faces,' she confided one day, with suppressed rage. She was right, it was obvious, I couldn't disagree with her; that was the way the game worked.

For my part, I had no objection to sex being subject to market forces. There were many ways of acquiring money, honest and dishonest, cerebral or, by contrast, brutally physical. It was possible to make money using one's intellect, talent, strength or courage, even one's beauty; it was also possible to acquire money through a banal stoke of luck. Most often, money was acquired through inheritance, as in my case; the problem of how it had been earned fell to the previous generation. Many very different people had acquired money on this earth: former top athletes, gangsters, artists, models, actors; a great number of entrepreneurs and talented financiers; a number of engineers, too, more rarely a few inventors. Money was sometimes acquired mechanically, by simple accumulation; or, on the other hand, by some audacious coup crowned with success. There was no great logic to it, but the possibilities were endless. By contrast, the criteria for sexual selection were unduly simple: they consisted merely of youth and physical beauty. These features had a price, certainly, but not an infinite price.

The situation, of course, had been very different in earlier centuries, at a time when sex was essentially linked to reproduction. To maintain the genetic value of the species, humanity was compelled seriously to take into account criteria like health, strength, youth and physical prowess – of which beauty was merely a handy indicator. Nowadays, the order of things had changed: beauty had retained all of its value, but that value was now something marketable, narcissistic. If sex was really to come into the category of tradable commodities, the best solution was probably to involve money, that universal mediator which already made it possible to assure an exact equivalence between intelligence, talent and technical competence; which had already made it possible to assure a perfect standardisation of opinions, tastes and lifestyles. Unlike the aristocracy, the rich made no claim to being different in kind from the rest of the population; they simply claimed to be richer. Essentially abstract, money was a concept in which neither race, physical appearance, age, intelligence nor distinction played any part, nothing in fact, but money. My European ancestors had worked hard for several centuries; they had sought to dominate, then to transform the world, and, to a certain extent they had succeeded. They had done so out of economic self-interest, out of a taste for work, but also because they believed in the superiority of their civilisation: they had invented dreams, progress, utopia, the future. Their sense of a mission to civilise had disappeared in the course of the twentieth century. Europeans, at least some of them, continued to work, and sometimes to work hard, but they did so for money, or from a neurotic attachment to their work; the innocent sense of their natural right to dominate the world and direct the path of history had disappeared. As a consequence of their accumulated efforts, Europe remained a wealthy continent; those qualities of intelligence and determination manifested by my ancestors I had manifestly lost. As a wealthy European, I could obtain food and the services of women more cheaply in other countries; as a decadent European, conscious of my approaching death, and given over entirely to selfishness, I could see no reason to deprive myself of such things. I was aware, however, that such a situation was barely tenable, that people like me were incapable of ensuring the survival of a society, perhaps more simply we were unworthy of life. Mutations would occur, were already occurring, but I found it difficult to feel truly concerned; my only genuine motivation was to get the hell out of this shithole as quickly as possible. November was cold, bleak; I hadn't been reading Auguste Comte that much recently. My great diversion when Valérie was out consisted of watching the movement of the clouds through the picture window. Immense flocks of starlings formed over Gentilly in the late afternoon, describing inclined planes and spirals in the sky; I was quite tempted to ascribe meaning to them, to interpret them as the heralds of an apocalypse.

13

One evening, I met Lionel as I was leaving work; I hadn't seen him since the 'Thai Tropic' trip almost a year earlier. Curiously, however, I recognised him at once. I was a little surprised that he had made such a strong impression on me; I couldn't remember having said a word to him at the time.

Things were going well, he told me. A large cotton disc covered his right eye. He'd had an accident at work, something had exploded; but it was okay, they'd managed to treat him in time, he would recover 50 per cent of the sight in his eye. I invited him for a drink in a café near the Palais-Royal. I wondered whether I would recognise Robert or Josiane or the other members of the group as easily – yes, probably. It was a slightly distressing thought; my memory was constantly filling up with information that was almost completely useless. As a human being, I was particularly proficient in the recognition and storage of images of other humans. *Nothing is more useful to man than man himself.* The reason why I had invited Lionel was not particularly clear to me; the conversation would obviously drag. To keep it going, I asked whether he'd had the opportunity to go back to Thailand. No, and it wasn't for lack of wanting, but unfortunately the trip was rather expensive. Had he seen any of the other members of the group again? No, none of them. Then I told him I had seen Valérie, whom he might perhaps remember, and that we were now living together. He seemed happy at this news; we had clearly made a good impression on him. He didn't get the chance to travel much, he told me; and that holiday in Thailand in particular was one of his fondest memories. I started to feel moved by his simplicity, his naïve longing for happiness. It was at that point that I did something which, thinking back on it even today, I'm tempted to describe as *good*. On the whole, I am not good, it is not one of my characteristics. Humanitarians disgust me, the fate of others is generally a matter of indifference to me, nor have I any memory of ever having felt any sense of solidarity with other human beings. The fact remains that, that evening, I explained to Lionel that Valérie worked in the tourist industry, that her company was about to open a new club in Krabi and that I could easily get him a week-long stay at 50 per cent discount. Obviously, this was pure invention; but I had decided to pay the difference. Maybe, to a degree, I was trying to *show off*; but it seems to me that I also felt a genuine desire for him to be able, even if only for a week, to once again feel pleasure at the expert hands of young Thai prostitutes.

When I told her about the meeting, Valérie looked at me somewhat perplexed; she herself had no memory of Lionel. That really was the problem with the boy, he wasn't a bad guy, but he had no personality: he was too reserved, too humble, it was difficult to remember anything at all about him. 'Okay . . .' she said, 'I mean, if it makes you happy; in fact he doesn't even have to pay the 50 per cent, I was going to talk to you about this, I'm going to get invitations for the week of the opening. It will be on January 1st.' I called Lionel the following day to tell him that his trip would be free; this was too much, he couldn't believe me, I even had a bit of trouble getting him to accept.

The same day, I received a visit from a young artist who had come to show me her work. Her name was Sandra Heksjtovoian, something like that, in any case some name that I was never going to remember; if I'd been her agent, I would have advised her to call herself Sandra Hallyday. She was a very young girl, wearing trousers and a tee-shirt, fairly unremarkable, with a roundish face and short, curly hair; she had graduated from the Beaux Arts in Caen. She worked entirely on her body, she explained to me; I looked at her anxiously as she opened her portfolio. I was hoping she wasn't going to show me photos of plastic surgery on her toes or anything like that – I'd had it up to here with things like that. But no, she simply handed me some postcards which she had had made, with the imprint ·

of her pussy dipped in different coloured paints. I chose a turquoise and a mauve; I was a little sorry I hadn't brought photos of my prick to return the favour. It was all very pleasant, but, well, as far as I could remember, Yves Klein had already done something similar more than forty years ago; I was going to have trouble championing her cause. Of course, of course, she agreed, you had to take it as an *exercice de style*. She then took a more complex piece out of its cardboard packaging: it consisted of two wheels of unequal sizes linked by a thin strip of rubber; a handle made it possible to operate the contraption. The strip of rubber was covered with small plastic protuberances which were more or less pyramid-shaped. I turned the handle and ran my finger along the moving ribbon; it produced a sort of friction which was not unpleasant.

'They're casts of my clitoris,' the girl explained; I immediately removed my finger.

'I took photos using an endoscope, while it was erect, and put it all on a computer. Using 3-D software I repro-duced the volume, I modelled the piece using ray-tracing, then I sent the co-ordinates to the factory.' I got the feeling she was allowing herself to be dominated a bit too much by technical considerations. I turned the handle again, more or less unconsciously. 'It cries out to be touched, doesn't it?' she went on with satisfaction. 'I had thought of connecting it to a resistor so it could power a bulb. What do you think?' To be honest, I wasn't in favour of the idea, it seemed to detract from the simplicity of the object. She was quite sweet, this girl, for a contemporary artist; I almost felt like asking her to come to an orgy some night, I was sure she'd get along well with Valérie. I realised just in time that, in my position, such a thing risked being construed as sexual harassment. I considered the contraption despondently. 'You know,' I said, 'I'm really more involved in the financial aspect of the projects. For anything to do with the aesthetics, you'd be better off making an appointment to see Mlle Durry.' On a business card, I wrote down Marie-Jeanne's phone number and extension; after all, she must know a thing or two about this whole clitoris business. The girl looked a little disconcerted, but even so, handed me a small bag filled with plastic pyramids. 'I'll give you these casts,' she said, 'The factory made a lot of them.' I thanked her and walked her back to the service entrance. Before saying goodbye, I asked her if the casts were life size. Of course, she told me, it was all part of her artistic methodology.

That same evening, I examined Valérie's clitoris carefully. I had never really paid it any serious attention; whenever I had stroked or licked it, it was as part of a more overall plan, I had memorised the position, the angles, the rhythmic movement to adopt. But now I examined the tiny organ at length as it pulsed before my eyes. 'What are you doing?' she asked, surprised, after five minutes spent with her legs apart. 'It's an artistic methodology . . .' I said, giving a little lick to soothe her impatience. The girl's cast lacked the taste and the smell obviously; but otherwise there was a resemblance, it was undeniable. My examination complete,

I parted Valérie's pussy with both hands and licked her clitoris with short, precise thrusts of my tongue. Was it the waiting that had stimulated her desire? More precise, more attentive movements on my part? The fact remains that she came almost immediately. Actually, I thought that Sandra was a pretty talented artist; her work encouraged one to see the world in a new light.

14

As early as the beginning of December, it was clear that the Aphrodite clubs were going to be a huge success, and probably a success on a *historic* scale. November is traditionally the most difficult month for the tourist industry. In October, there are still a number of late-season departures; in December, the Christmas period takes over; but rare, extremely rare, are those who consider taking a holiday in November, apart from some particularly hard-nosed and cynical senior citizens. Yet, the first results which came back from the clubs were excellent: the formula had been an immediate success, you might even go so far as to talk about a deluge. I had dinner with Jean-Yves and Valérie the night the initial figures came in; he stared at me, almost bizarrely, the results had so exceeded his expectations: taken as a whole, the occupancy for the month was 95 per cent, regardless of destination. 'Ah yes, sex . . .' I said, embarrassed. 'People need sex, that's all, it's just that they don't dare admit it.' All of this made us inclined to be contemplative, almost silent; the waiter brought the *antipasti*. 'The Krabi opening is going to be unbelievable . . .' Jean-Yves went on. 'Rembke phoned me, everything's been booked out for three weeks. What's even better is that there's been nothing in the press, not a line. A discreet success, as massive as it is confidential; exactly what we were aiming for.'

He had finally decided to rent a studio flat and leave his wife; he would not get the keys until January 1st, but he was a lot better, I sensed he was already more relaxed. He was relatively young, handsome and extremely rich: all of these things do not necessarily make life easier, I realised, a little alarmed; but they help, at least, in awakening desire in others. I still could not understand his ambition, the furious energy he invested in making a success of his career. It wasn't for the money I don't think: he paid high taxes and didn't have expensive tastes. Neither was it out of commitment to the company, nor from a more general altruism: it was difficult to imagine the development of global tourism as a noble cause. His ambition existed in its own right, it couldn't be pinned down to one specific source: it was probably more like the desire to build something, rather than to a taste for power or a competitive nature – I had never heard him talk about the careers of his former friends at the HEC business school, and I don't think he gave them a second thought. All in all, it was a respectable motive, not unlike the one that explains the advance of human civilisation. The social reward bestowed on him was a large salary; under other regimes it might have taken the form of an aristocratic title, or of privileges like those accorded to the members of the *nomenklatura*; I didn't get the impression that it would have made much difference. In reality, Jean-Yves worked because he had a taste for work; it was something both mysterious and clear.

On December 15, two weeks before the opening, he received an anxious phone call from TUI. A German tourist had just been kidnapped with a Thai girl; the kidnapping had taken place in Hat Yai, in the extreme south of the country. The local police had received a confused message, written in an approximate English, which expressed no demands – but indicated that the two young people would be executed for behaviour in contravention of Islamic law. For some months there had indeed been an increase in the activities of Islamic movements, supported by Libya, in the border area with Malaysia; but this was the first time that they had attacked people.

On December 18, the naked, mutilated bodies of the young people were thrown from a van, right in the middle of the main square of the town. The young girl had been stoned to death, she had been beaten with extraordinary violence; everywhere her skin was ripped open, her body was little more than a swelling, barely recognisable. The German's throat had been cut and he had been castrated, his penis and testicles had been stuffed into his mouth. This time, the entire German press picked up the story, there were even some brief articles in France. The papers had decided not to publish photographs of the victims, but they quickly became available on the usual internet sites. Jean-Yves telephoned TUI every day: up until now, the situation was not alarming; there had been few cancellations, people stuck to their holiday plans. The prime minister of Thailand made repeated reassurances: it was undoubtedly an isolated incident, all known terrorist groups condemned the kidnapping and the executions.

As soon as we arrived in Bangkok, however, I felt a certain tension, especially around the Sukhumvit area where most of the Middle-Eastern tourists stayed. They came mainly from Turkey or Egypt, but sometimes also from more hard-line Muslim countries such as Saudi Arabia or Pakistan. When they walked through the crowds, I could feel the hostile stares directed towards them. At the entrance to most of the hostess bars, I saw signs: 'No Muslims Here'; the owner of a bar in Patpong had even clarified his line of reasoning, writing in a decorative hand the following message: *'We respect your Muslim faith: we don't want you to drink whisky and enjoy Thai girls.'* The poor things were hardly to blame, in fact it was obvious that in case of a terrorist attack, they would be the first to be targeted. On my first visit to Thailand, I had been surprised by the presence of people from Arab countries, in fact, they came for exactly the same reasons as Westerners, with one slight difference: they threw themselves into debauchery with much more enthusiasm. Often, in the hotel bars you'd find them around a bottle of whisky at ten in the morning; and they were first to arrive as soon as the massage parlours opened. In clear breach of Islamic law and probably feeling guilty about it, they were, for the most part, courteous and charming.

Bangkok was as polluted, noisy, stifling as always; but I was just happy to be back. Jean-Yves had two or three meetings with bankers, or at some ministry, anyway, I only vaguely followed what was going on. After two days, he informed us that his meetings had been very conclusive: the local authorities were as obliging as possible, they were prepared to do anything to attract the smallest amount of Western investment. For a number of years, Thailand had been unable to alleviate its economic crisis, the stock exchange and the currency were at historic lows, government debt had reached 70 per cent of the gross domestic product. 'They're so deep in shit that they're not even corrupt any more . . .' Jean-Yves told us. 'I had to grease a few palms, but not many, nothing at all compared to what was going on five years ago.'

On the morning of December 31, we took the plane to Krabi. As we got out of the minibus, I ran into Lionel, who had arrived the previous evening. He was delighted, he told me, absolutely delighted; I had a bit of trouble stemming his torrent of gratitude. But, as I arrived at my chalet, I too was struck by the beauty of the landscape. The beach was immense, immaculate, the sand as fine as powder. Over a distance of thirty metres, the ocean veered from azure to turquoise, from turquoise to emerald. Vast chalk crags covered with lush green forests

rose out of the water as far as the horizon, losing themselves in the light and the distance, giving the bay a depth
that seemed unreal, cosmic.

'Isn't this the place where they filmed *The Beach*?'
Valérie asked me.

'No, I think that was at Ko Phi Phi; but I haven't seen
the film.'

According to her, I hadn't missed much; apart from the
landscapes it had nothing to recommend it. I vaguely
remembered the book, which tells the story of a bunch of
backpackers in search of an unspoiled island; the only clue
they have is a map drawn for them by an old traveller in a
shitty hotel on Khao San Road, just before he commits
suicide. First, they go to Ko Samui – much too touristy;
from there they go to a neighbouring island, but there are
still too many people for their liking. In the end, by
bribing a sailor, they finally arrive on their island, situated
in a nature reserve and therefore, in theory, inaccessible.
It's at this point that things start to go wrong. The early
chapters of the book perfectly illustrate the curse of the
tourist, caught up in a frenetic search for places which are
'not touristy', which his very presence undermines,
forever forced to move on, following a plan whose very
fulfilment, little by little, renders it futile. This hopeless
situation, comparable to a man trying to escape his own
shadow, was common knowledge in the tourist industry,
Valérie informed me: in sociological terms it was known
as the double bind paradox.

The holidaymakers who had chosen the Krabi Eldorador Aphrodite, at any rate, did not look ready to succumb to the double bind paradox: although the beach was huge, they had all chosen more or less the same area. As far as I had been able to make out, they seemed to conform to the expected breakdown of clientele. Valérie had the precise figures: 80 per cent Germans, mostly senior executives or professionals,10 per cent Italians, 5 per cent Spaniards and 5 per cent French. The surprise was that there were a lot of couples. They looked pretty much like the sort of swinging couples that you might have run into on the Cap d'Agde: most of the women had silicone-enhanced breasts, a lot of them wore a gold chain around their waists or ankles. I also noticed that almost everyone swam in the nude. All of this made me fairly confident; you never have any trouble from people like that. In contrast to a 'backpackers' paradise', a resort dedicated to wife-swapping, which only comes into its own when visitor numbers are high, is not paradoxical by definition. In a world where the greatest of luxuries is acquiring the wherewithal to avoid other people, the good-natured sociability of middle-class German wife-swappers constitutes a form of particularly subtle subversion, I said to Valérie, just as she was taking off her bra and panties. Immediately after undressing, I was a little embarrassed to discover that I had a hard on, and I lay down on my stomach beside her. She parted her thighs, serenely baring her sex to the sun. A few metres to our right was a group of German women who seemed to be discussing an article from *Der Spiegel*. One of them had shaved her public hair, you could easily make out her slender, delicate slit. 'I really go for that type of pussy . . .' Valérie said in a low voice. 'It makes you feel like slipping a finger inside.' I really went for them too; but to our left was a Spanish couple where the woman, by contrast, had a really thick, black, curly pubic bush; I could really go for that too. As she lay down, I could make out the thick, plump lips of her pussy. She was a young woman, no more than twenty-five, but her breasts were heavy, with large, prominent areolas. 'Come on, turn over on to your back . . .' Valérie whispered into my ear. I did as I was told, kept my eyes closed, as though somehow the fact that I could see nothing diminished the enormity of what we were doing. I felt my cock stand up, the glans emerging from its sheath of protective skin; concentrating purely on the sensation, the warmth of the sun on the mucous membranes was immensely pleasurable. I did not open my eyes when I felt a thread of suntan lotion trickle on to my torso, then on to my stomach. Valérie's fingers moved in short, light touches. The fragrance of coconut filled the air. At the point when she began to rub oil into my penis, I opened my eyes suddenly: she was kneeling by my side, facing the Spanish woman who had propped herself up on her elbows to watch. I threw my head back, staring at the blue of the sky. Valérie placed the palm of one hand on my balls, slipped her index finger into my anus; with her other hand she continued to jerk me off steadily. Turning my head to the left, I saw that the

Spaniard was busying herself with her own guy's penis; I turned back to stare at the azure. At the point when I heard footsteps approaching across the sand, I closed my eyes again. First there was the sound of a kiss, then I heard whispering. I no longer knew how many hands or fingers stroked and wrapped around my prick; the sound of the backwash was very gentle.

After the beach, we made a tour of the leisure centre; it was getting dark, the multicoloured signs of the go-go bars lit up one by one. Around a dozen bars arranged around in a circular piazza surrounded a huge massage parlour. In front of the entrance, we met Jean-Yves, who was just leaving, escorted to the door by a girl wearing a long dress. She had large breasts, pale skin and looked a little Chinese. 'Is it nice inside?' Valérie asked him.

'It's amazing: a bit kitsch, but very lavish. There are fountains, tropical plants, waterfalls; they've even put up statues of Greek goddesses.'

We settled ourselves on a deep sofa upholstered with gold thread before choosing two girls. The massage was very pleasant, the hot water and the liquid soap dissolved all traces of suntan oil from our skin, The girls moved gracefully: to soap us they used their breasts, their buttocks, their inner thighs: straight away Valérie started to moan. Once again I marvelled at the richness of a woman's erogenous zones.

After drying ourselves we lay down on a large, circular bed, two thirds of its circumference encircled by mirrors.

One of the girls licked Valérie, easily bringing her to orgasm. I knelt over her face; the other girl caressed my balls, jerking me off in her mouth. At the point when she felt I was about to come, Valérie motioned to the girls to come closer: while the first girl licked my balls, the other kissed Valérie on the mouth; I ejaculated over their half-joined lips.

The guests for the New Year's Eve party were mostly Thais connected in one way or another with the tourist industry. None of the directors of Aurore had come; the head of TUI had also been unable to get away, but he had sent a subordinate who clearly had no power whatever but seemed thrilled at the opportunity. The buffet was exquisite, a mixture of Thai and Chinese cuisine. The were crispy little *nems* with basil and lemongrass, deep-fried parcels of water spinach, prawn curry with coconut milk, fried rice with cashew nuts and almonds, an unbelievably delicious Peking duck which melted in the mouth. French wines had been imported for the occasion. I chatted for a while with Lionel, who seemed to be basking in contentment. He was accompanied by a ravishing girl from Chiang Mai whose name was Kim. He had met her in a topless bar on the first night and they had been together ever since. I could easily see what this big, slightly clumsy boy saw in the fragile creature, so delicate she seemed almost unreal; I couldn't see how he could ever have found such a girl in his own country. They were a godsend, these little Thai whores, I thought; a gift from heaven, nothing less. Kim spoke a little French. She had been to France once, Lionel marvelled; her sister had married a Frenchman.

'Really?' I enquired 'What does he do for a living?'

'He's a doctor,' his face clouded a little. 'Obviously, with me it wouldn't be the same kind of life.'

'You've got job security . . .' I said optimistically. 'Everyone in Thailand dreams of being a civil servant.'

He looked a me, a little doubtful. It was true, though, the public sector fascinated the Thais. It's true that in Thailand civil servants are corrupt; not only do they have job security, they're rich too. You can have everything you want. 'Well, I hope you have a nice evening   ' I said, making my way towards the bar. 'Thank you . . .' he said, blushing, I don't know what possessed me to play the man of the world at that moment; decidedly, I was getting old. I did have some doubts about the girl: Thai girls from the north are usually very beautiful, but sometimes they're a bit too conscious of the fact. They spend their time staring at themselves in the mirror, keenly aware that their beauty alone constitutes a crucial economic advantage; and as a result they become useless, capricious creatures. On the other hand, unlike some cool western chick, Kim was not in a position to realise that Lionel himself was a bore. The principal criteria for physical beauty are youth, absence of handicap and a general conformity to the norms of the species; they are quite clearly universal. The ancillary criteria – vaguer and more relative – were more difficult to appreciate for a young girl from a different culture. For Lionel, the exotic was a wise choice, possibly even the only choice. Anyway, I thought, I've done my best to help him.

A glass of Saint-Estèphe in hand, I sat on a bench to look at the stars. The year 2002 would mark France's entry into the single currency – amongst other things: there would also be the World Cup, the presidential elections, various high-profile media events. The rocky crags of the bay were lit up by the moon; I knew there would be a firework display at midnight. A few minutes later, Valérie came and sat beside me. I took her in my arms, put my head on her shoulder; I could barely make out the features of her face, but I recognised the scent, the texture of her skin. At the moment when the first rocket exploded, I noticed that her green, almost transparent dress was the same one she had worn a year before at the New Year's Party on Ko Phi Phi; when she pressed her lips against mine, I felt something strange, as though the very order of things had been upturned. Strangely, and without in the least deserving it, I had been given a second chance. It is very rare, in life, to have a second chance; it goes against all the rules. I hugged her fiercely to me, overwhelmed by a sudden desire to weep.

15

If love, then, cannot triumph, how can the spirit reign? All practical supremacy belongs to action.

Auguste Comte

The boat skimmed over the immensity of turquoise, and I didn't have to worry about what I was doing. We had left early in the direction of Ko Maya, sailing past the outcrops of coral and the immense chalk crags. Some of them had eroded to form circular islets whose central lagoons could be reached via narrow channels carved into the rock. Inside these islets the water was still, emerald green. The pilot cut the engine. Valérie looked at me, we remained silent, unmoving; moments passed in utter silence.

The pilot dropped us on the island of Ko Maya, in a bay protected by high rocky walls. The beach stretched out at the foot of the cliffs, it was about a hundred metres long, narrow and curved. The sun was high in the sky. It was already eleven o'clock. The pilot started up the engine and headed back in the direction of Krabi; he was to come back and pick us up in the late afternoon. As soon as he rounded the entrance to the bay, the roar died away.

With the exception of the sexual act, there are few moments in life in which the body exults in the simple pleasure of being alive, fills with joy at the simple fact of its presence in the world; January 1st was, for me, completely filled with such moments. I have no memory of anything other than that bliss. We probably swam, we must have warmed ourselves in the sun and made love. I don't think we spoke, or explored the island. I remember Valérie's scent, the taste of salt drying on her pubis; I remember falling asleep inside her and being woken by her contractions.

The boat came back to collect us at five o'clock. On the terrace of the hotel overlooking the bay, I had a Campari and Valérie a Mai Tai. The chalk crags were almost black in the orange light. The last of the bathers were returning, towels in hand. A few metres from the shore, entwined in the warm water, a couple were making love. The rays of the setting sun struck the gilded roof of a pagoda halfway up. In the peaceful air, a bell tolled several times. It's a Buddhist custom, when one has accomplished a good deed or a meritorious action, to commemorate the act by ringing a temple bell; how joyful is a religion which causes the air to resound with human testimony to good deeds.

'Michel . . .' said Valérie after a long silence, looking straight into my eyes. 'I want to stay.'

'What do you mean?'

'To stay here permanently. I was thinking about it as we were coming back this afternoon: it's possible. All I need is to be appointed resort manager. I've got the qualifications for it, and the necessary skills.'

I looked at her, saying nothing; she put her hand on mine.

'Only, you'd have to agree to give up your work. Would you?'

'Yes.' I must have taken less than a second to answer, without a hint of hesitation; never have I been faced with a decision that was so easy to make.

We spotted Jean-Yves coming out of the massage parlour. Valerie waved to him; he came and sat at our table: she explained her plan.

'Well . . .' he said hesitantly, 'I suppose we could manage it. Obviously Aurore are going to be a bit surprised, because what you're asking for is a demotion. Your salary will be cut in half at least; there's no other way of doing it given the other employees.'

'I know,' she said; 'I don't give a damn.'

He looked at her again, shaking his head in surprise. 'It's your choice . . . If that's what you want . . . After all,' he said, as if he were only just realising it, 'I'm the one who runs the Eldorador resorts; I've got the right to appoint whoever I like as resort manager.'

'So, you'd agree to it?'

'Yes . . . yes, I can't stop you.'

It's a curious sensation, feeling your life teetering on the brink of a radical change; all you have to do is stay there, do nothing, to feel the sensation. Throughout the meal I remained silent, pensive, so much so that eventually Valérie became worried.

'Are you sure this is what you want?' she asked. 'Are you sure you won't miss France?'

'No, I won't miss anything.'

'There's nothing to do here, there's no cultural life.'

I was already aware of this; inasmuch as I'd had occasion to give the matter any thought, culture seemed to me to be a necessary compensation for the misery of our lives. It was possible to imagine a different sort of culture, one bound up with celebration and lyricism, something which sprang from a state of happiness; I was doubtful – it appeared to me to be a highly theoretical proposition, and one which could no longer have any real significance in my life.

'There's TV5 . . .' I said indifferently. She smiled; it was well known that TV5 was in fact one of the worst television channels in the world. 'Are you sure you won't get bored?' she insisted.

In my life, I had known suffering, oppression, anxiety; I had never known boredom. I could see no objection to the endless, imbecile repetition of sameness. Of course, I harboured no illusions about being capable of getting to that point: I knew that misery is robust, it is resourceful and tenacious; but it was not a prospect that caused me the least concern. As a child, I could spend hours counting sprigs of clover in a meadow: in all the years of searching I had never found a four-leafed clover; I never felt any disappointment or any bitterness; to tell the truth, I could just as well have been counting blades of grass – all of those sprigs of clover, with their three leaves, seemed endlessly identical, endlessly splendid to me. One day, when I was twelve, I had climbed to the top of an electricity pylon high in the mountains. As I was going up, I didn't once look down at my feet. When I reached the platform at the top, the descent seemed complicated and dangerous. The mountain ranges stretched as far as the eye could see, crowned with eternal snows. It would have been much simpler to stay there, or to jump. I was stopped, *in extremis*, by the thought of being crushed; but otherwise, I think I could have rejoiced endlessly in my flight.

The following day I met Andreas, a German who had been living in the area for ten years. He was a translator, he explained, which made it possible for him to work alone; he went back to Germany once a year for the Frankfurt Book Fair; if he had queries, he made them via the internet. He'd had the opportunity to translate a number of American bestsellers – among them *The Firm* – which in themselves guaranteed him a healthy income; the cost of living here was low. Until now, there had been almost no tourism. He found it surprising to see so many compatriots descending on the place; he greeted the news unenthusiastically, but with no real displeasure either. His ties with Germany had in fact become very tenuous, despite the fact that his work obliged him to use the language constantly. He had married a Thai girl whom he'd met in a massage parlour, and they now had two children.

'Is it easy, here, to have . . . um . . . children?' I asked. I felt as though I was asking something incongruous, as if I'd asked whether it was difficult to acquire a dog. To be honest, I had always felt a certain repugnance for young children; as far as I was concerned they were ugly little monsters who shat uncontrollably and screamed insuffer-ably. But I was aware that it was something most couples *do*; I did not know whether it made them happy, at any rate they didn't dare complain about it. 'Actually,' I said glancing around the resort, 'with as much space as this, it might be feasible: they could wander between the chalets, they could play with bits of wood or whatever.'

According to Andreas, yes, it was particularly easy to have children here; there was a school in Krabi, it was even within walking distance. And Thai children were very different from European children, a lot less quick-tempered and less prone to tantrums. For their parents, they felt a respect bordering on veneration, it came to them quite naturally, it was part of their culture. Whenever he visited Düsseldorf, he was quite literally frightened by the behaviour of his nephews.

To tell the truth, I was only half convinced by this idea of cultural immersion. For reassurance I reminded myself that Valérie was only twenty-eight; in general, women don't get broody until about thirty-five. But, in the end, yes, if necessary, I would have her child; I knew the idea would come to her, it was unavoidable. After all, a child is like a little animal, admittedly with certain malicious tendencies; let's say, a bit like a small monkey. It might even have its advantages, I thought; eventually I would be able to teach it to play *Mille Bornes*. I nurtured a genuine passion for the game of *Mille Bornes*, a passion which remained, in general, unsatisfied; who could I invite to play with me? Certainly not my work colleagues; nor the artists who came to show me their portfolios. Andreas, maybe? I gauged him quickly: no, he didn't look the type. That said, he seemed serious, intelligent; it was a friendship worth cultivating. 'Are you thinking of moving here . . . permanently?'

'Yes, permanently.'

'It's better to look at it like that,' he said, nodding his head. 'It's very difficult to leave Thailand; I know that if I had to do it now, it's something I'd find very hard to deal with.'

16

The days passed with terrifying speed; we were supposed to go back on January 5. The night before, we met up with Jean-Yves in the main restaurant. Lionel had declined the invitation; he was going to watch Kim dance. 'I really like watching her dance almost naked in front of men . . .' he told us, 'knowing that later on, I'll be the one to have her.' Jean-Yves looked at him as he walked away. 'He's making progress, the gas man . . .' he noted, sarcastically. 'He's discovering perversion.'

'Don't make fun of him . . .' Valérie protested. 'I think I finally understand what you see in him,' she said turning to me; 'He's an endearing boy. Anyway, I'm sure he's having a fabulous holiday.'

It was getting dark; lights winked on in the villages around the bay. A last ray of sun lit up the golden roof of the pagoda. Since Valérie had informed him of her decision, Jean-Yves hadn't broached the subject again. He waited until the end of the meal to do so; he ordered a bottle of wine.

'I'm going to miss you . . .' he said. 'It won't be the same. We've been working together for more than five years. We've worked well together, we've never had a serious row. Without you, I would never have made it.'

Valérie didn't say anything. There was nothing to say; broadly speaking, it was true.

'Now,' he said thoughtfully, 'we'll be able to extend the formula. One of the most obvious countries is Brazil. I've also been thinking about Kenya again: the ideal thing to do would be to open another club, further inland, for the safaris, and leave the beach club as an 'Aphrodite' resort. One of the other immediate possibilities is Vietnam.'

'You're not afraid of the competition?' I asked.

'There's no risk there. The American chains wouldn't dare get involved in something like this. What I was a bit afraid of was the reaction of the French press; but for the moment, there's been nothing. It has to be said that most of our customers are foreign, from Germany and Italy – they're more relaxed about this sort of thing.'

'You're going to be the biggest pimp in the world . . .'

'Not a pimp,' he protested. 'We don't take a penny from what the girls earn; we just let them work, that's all.'

'Anyhow, there's no connection,' interrupted Valérie; 'they're not really part of the hotel staff.'

'Well, yes . . .' Jean-Yves said hesitantly. 'Here they're not connected; but I've heard that in the Dominican Republic the waitresses are only too happy to go upstairs.'

'They're doing it of their own free will.'

'Oh, yes, that's the least you can say.'

'Well . . .' Valérie extended a conciliating gesture to the world, 'don't let the hypocrites grind you down. You're there, you provide the framework, using the Aurore know-how, and that's all.'

The waiter brought lemongrass soup. At the neighbouring tables were German and Italian men accompanied by Thai girls, some German couples – accompanied or otherwise. Everyone quietly living together, with no apparent problem, in a general atmosphere of pleasure; this resort manager job promised to be pretty easy.

'So, you're really going to stay here . . .' Jean-Yves said again; clearly he was having trouble believing it. 'It's surprising; I mean, in a way, I understand, but . . . what's surprising is that you're giving up the chance of making more money.'

'More money to do what?' said Valérie emphatically. 'Buy Prada handbags? Spend a weekend in Budapest? Eat white truffles in season? I've earned a lot of money, I can't even remember where it's gone: yes, I've probably spent it on stupid things like that. Do you know where your money goes?'

'Well . . .' He thought. 'Actually, up to now, I think it's mostly Audrey who's spent it.'

'Audrey's a stupid bitch,' she retorted, mercilessly. 'Thank God you're getting divorced. It's the most intelligent decision you've ever made.'

'It's true, deep down she is very stupid . . .' he replied, unembarrassed. He smiled, hesitated a moment: 'You really are a strange girl, Valérie.'

'It's not me who's strange, it's the world around me. Do you really want to buy yourself a Ferrari cabriolet? A holiday home in Deauville, which will only get burgled anyway? To work ninety hours a week until you're sixty? To pay half of everything you earn in tax to finance military operations in Kosovo, or recovery plans for the inner cities? We're happy here; we have everything we need in life. The only thing the Western world has to offer is designer products. If you believe in designer products, then you can stay in the West; otherwise, in Thailand you can get excellent fakes.'

'It's your position that's strange; you've worked for years at the centre of Western civilisation, without ever believing in its values.'

'I'm a predator,' she replied calmly, 'a sweet little predator – my needs are not very great; but if I've worked all my life, it's only been for the cash; now, I'm going to start living. What I don't understand is other people: what's stopping you, for example, from coming to live here? You could easily marry a Thai girl: they're pretty, gentle, good in bed; some of them even speak a bit of French.'

'Well, um . . .' He hesitated again. 'Up until now, I've enjoyed having a different girl every night.'

'You'll grow out of it. In any case, there's nothing stopping you visiting massage parlours after you're married; that's what they're there for.'

'I know. I think . . . Fundamentally, I think I've always had trouble making the important decisions in my life.'

A little embarrassed by this admission, he turned to me:

'What about you, Michel, what are you going to do here?'

The response closest to the truth was probably something like 'Nothing'; but it's always difficult to explain that kind of thing to an active person. 'The cooking . . .' replied Valérie on my behalf. I turned to her, surprised. 'Yes, yes,' she insisted, 'I've noticed that from time to time you have vague creative aspirations in that area. It's just as well, I don't like cooking; I'm sure that here you'll be able to make a start.'

I tasted a spoonful of my curried chicken with green peppers; as it happened, I could imagine doing something similar with mangoes. Jean-Yves nodded thoughtfully. I looked at Valérie: she was a good predator, more intelligent and more tenacious than I was; and she had chosen me to share her lair. It is possible to suppose that societies are dependent, if not on a common goal, then at least on a consensus – sometimes described in western democracies as a *weak consensus*, by certain leader-writers whose political positions are very entrenched. As some-one of pretty weak temperament myself, I had done nothing to change that consensus; the idea of a common goal seemed less clear. According to Immanuel Kant, human dignity consists in not accepting to be subject to laws except inasmuch as one can simultaneously consider oneself a legislator; never had such a bizarre fantasy crossed my mind. Not only did I not vote, but I had never considered elections as anything more than excellent television shows – in which, to tell the truth, my favourite actors were the political scientists: Jérôme Jaffré in particular delighted me. Being a political leader seemed to me a difficult, technical, wearing task; I was quite happy to delegate whatever powers I had. In my youth, I had encountered militants, who considered it necessary to force society to evolve in this or that direction; I had never felt any sympathy or any respect for them. Gradually, I had even learned to distrust them: the way they got involved in popular causes, the way they treated society as though it was something they played an active role in, seemed suspicious. What did I, for my part, have to reproach the West for? Not much – but I wasn't especially attached to it (and I was finding it more and more difficult to understand how one could feel attached to an idea, a country, anything in fact other than an individual). Life was expensive in the West, it was cold there; the prostitution was of poor quality. It was difficult to smoke in public places, almost impossible to buy medicines and drugs; you worked hard, there were cars, and noise, and the security in public places was very badly implemented. All in all, it had numerous drawbacks. I suddenly realised to my embarrassment that I considered the society I lived in more or less as a natural environment - like a savannah, or a jungle – whose laws I had to adapt to. The notion that I was in any way in solidarity with this environment had never occurred to me; it was like an atrophy in me, an emptiness. It was far from certain that society could continue to survive for long with individuals like me; but I could survive with a woman, become attached to her, try to make her happy. Just as I turned to give Valérie another grateful look, I heard a sort of click to my right. Then I noticed an engine noise coming from the sea, which cut out immediately. At the front of the terrace, a tall blonde woman stood up, screaming. Then came the first burst of gunfire, a brief crackle. She turned towards us, bringing her hands up to her face: a bullet had hit her in the eye, the socket was now no more than a bloody hole; then she collapsed without a sound. Then I saw our assailants, three men wearing turbans, moving swiftly in our direction, machine-guns in hand. A second round of gunfire broke out, a little longer; the noise of crockery and broken glass mingled with screams of pain. For several seconds, we must have been completely paralysed; few people thought to take shelter under the tables. At my side, Jean-Yves gave a brief yelp, he had just been hit in the arm. Then I saw Valérie slide gently from her chair and collapse on the ground. I rushed to her and put my arms around her. From that point on, I saw nothing. The bursts of machine-gun fire followed one after another in a silence disturbed only by the sound of exploding glasses; it seemed to me to go on for ever. The smell of gunpowder was very intense. Then everything was silent again. I noticed that my left arm was covered in blood; Valérie must have been hit in the chest or the throat. The streetlamp beside us had been blown out and I could barely see a thing. Lying about a metre from me, Jean-Yves tried to get up and groaned. Just then, from the direction of the leisure complex, came an enormous explosion which ripped through the entire area and echoed around the bay for a long time. At first I thought my eardrums had burst, but some seconds later, in the midst of my daze, I became aware of a concert of dreadful screams, the genuine screams of the damned.

The emergency services arrived ten minutes later; they had come from Krabi. They went first to the leisure complex. The bomb had exploded in the middle of Crazy Lips, the largest of the bars, at peak time; it had been hidden in a sports bag left near the dance floor. It was a very powerful homemade dynamite device triggered by an alarm clock; the bag had been stuffed with bolts and nails. Under the force of the blast, the thin brick walls separating the bar from the other establishments had been blown out; a number of the metal girders which held up the whole building had buckled from the force of the blast, the roof was threatening to collapse. Faced with the extent of the catastrophe, the first thing the rescue workers did was to call for back-up. In front of the entrance to the bar a dancer crawled along the ground, still wearing her white bikini, her arms severed at the elbows. Nearby, a German tourist sitting in the midst of the rubble held his intestines as they spilled from his belly; his wife lay near him, her chest gaping, her breasts half torn off. Inside the bar a blackish smoke hung in the air; the ground was slippery, covered with blood seeping from human bodies and mutilated organs. A number of the dying, their arms or legs severed, tried to crawl towards the exit, leaving behind them a bloody trail. Bolts and nails had gouged out eyes, ripped off hands, torn faces to shreds. Some of the bodies had literally exploded from within, their limbs and viscera strewing the ground for several metres.

When the rescue workers reached the terrace, I was still holding Valérie in my arms; her body was warm. Two metres in front of me, a woman lay on the ground, her bloody face peppered with shards of glass. Others remained in their seats, mouths wide open, frozen in death. I screamed at the rescue workers: two nurses came over immediately, gently took Valérie and placed her on a stretcher. I tried to stand up, but fell backwards; my head hit the ground. It was then that I heard, very distinctly, someone say in French: 'She's dead.'

Part Three

Pattaya Beach

1

It was the first time for a long while that I had woken up
alone. The hospital in Krabi was a small, bright building;
the doctor came to see me in mid-morning. He was
French, a member of Médecins du Monde; they had
arrived on the scene the day after the attack. He was a man
of about thirty, a little stooped, with a worried expression.
He told me that I had been asleep for three days. 'Actually,
you weren't really asleep,' he went on; 'sometimes you
appeared to be awake. We spoke to you several times, but
this is the first time we've managed to make contact.'
Make contact, I thought. He told me, too, that the death
toll of the attack had been horrifying: at the moment, the
dead numbered one hundred and seventeen; it was the
most murderous attack ever to take place in Asia. A
number of the injured were still in a extremely critical
condition, considered too weak to be moved; Lionel was
among them. Both of his legs had been severed, a piece of

metal had lodged in the pit of his stomach; his chances of survival were remote. Others who had been seriously injured had been transported to Bumrungrad Hospital in Bangkok. Jean-Yves had only been slightly hurt: a bullet had fractured his humerus; it had been possible to treat him on the spot. Me, I was absolutely fine, not even a scratch. 'As for your friend . . .' the doctor said, 'her body has already been repatriated to France. I spoke to her parents on the phone: she will be buried in Brittany.'

He fell silent; he was probably waiting for me to say something. He watched me out of the corner of his eye; he seemed increasingly worried.

Towards noon, a nurse arrived with a tray; she took it away an hour later. She told me I really should start to eat again, that it was vital.

Jean-Yves came to see me sometime in the afternoon. He too looked at me strangely, a little sidelong. He talked mostly about Lionel; he was dying now, it was only a matter of hours. He had asked for Kim a lot. Miraculously, she was unhurt, but seemed to have got over it rather quickly: as he was taking a stroll in Krabi the previous evening, Jean-Yves had seen her on the arm of an Englishman. He had said nothing about this to Lionel, who didn't seem to harbour any illusions anyway; at least he had been fortunate enough to have met her. 'It's strange . . .' Jean-Yves said to me, 'he seems happy.'

As he was leaving my room, I realised that I hadn't said a

word; I really didn't know what to say to him. I knew perfectly well that something was wrong, but it was a vague feeling, difficult to put into words. It seemed to me that the best thing to do was keep quiet until the people around me realised their mistake; it was just a bad patch I had to get through.

Before he left, Jean-Yves looked up at me, then shook his head discouraged. It appears, at least this is what they told me immediately afterwards, that I talked a lot, all the time in fact, whenever I was left alone in the room; as soon as someone came in, I fell silent.

A few days later they transported us to Bumrungrad Hospital in an air ambulance. I didn't really understand the reasons for the transfer; in fact I think it was mostly so the police would have an opportunity to question us. Lionel had died the night before; crossing the corridor I saw his body wrapped in a shroud.

The Thai police were accompanied by an embassy attaché who acted as an interpreter; unfortunately, I had little to tell them. What seemed to most obsess them most was whether the attackers had been of Arab or Asian origin. I could well understand their preoccupation – it was important to know whether an international terrorist network had established a foothold in Thailand or whether they were dealing with Malay separatists – but all that I could do was repeat that everything had happened so quickly, that I had seen only shadows; as far as I knew, the men could have been of Malay appearance.

Then I had a visit from some Americans, who I think were from the CIA. They spoke brutally, in an unpleasant tone; I felt as though I was a suspect myself. They hadn't thought it necessary to bring an interpreter, so I couldn't understand most of their questions. At the end, they showed me a series of photographs, purportedly of international terrorists; I did not recognise any of these men.

From time to time, Jean-Yves came to see me in my room, sat at the foot of the bed. I was aware of his presence, I felt a little more tense. One morning, three days after we arrived, he handed me a small sheaf of papers: they were photocopies of newspaper articles. 'The board of Aurore faxed them to me yesterday,' he said; 'They made no comment.'

The first article, taken from the *Nouvel Observateur*, was headlined 'A VERY SPECIAL CLUB'; it was two pages long, very detailed, and illustrated with a photograph taken from the German advertising campaign. The journalist accused the Aurore group in no uncertain terms of promoting sex tourism in third-world countries, and added that, in the circumstances, the reaction of the Muslims was understandable. Jean-Claude Guillebaud dedicated his editorial to the same subject. Interviewed by telephone, Jean-Luc Espitalier had declared: 'The Aurore group, a signatory of the world charter for ethical tourism, in no way sanctions such activities; those responsible will be disciplined.' The dossier continued with a vehement but poorly documented article by Isabelle Alonso, from the *Journal de dimanche,* entitled: 'THE RETURN OF SLAVERY'. François Giroud picked up the theme in his weekly diary: 'Faced,' he wrote, 'with the hundreds of thousands of women who have been sullied, humiliated, reduced to slavery throughout the world – it is regrettable to have to say this – what do the deaths of a few of the well-heeled matter.' The terrorist attack in Krabi had naturally given the story considerable impact. *Libération* ran a front-page story in which it published photos of the repatriated survivors, taken when they landed at Roissy, with the headline: 'NOT SO INNOCENT VICTIMS'. In his editorial, Jérôme Dupuy singled out the Thai government for its lenient attitude to prostitution and drugs, as well as for its frequent breaches of democracy. As for *Paris-Match*, under the headline 'CARNAGE AT KRABI', came a full account of the 'night of horror'. They had managed to procure photos, which, it has to be said, were of pretty poor quality – black and white photocopies sent by fax – they could have been photos of just about anything, you could barely make out the bodies. In the same issue, they published the confessions of a sex tourist – who actually had nothing to do with the events: he was a freelance who operated mostly in the Philippines. Jacques Chirac had immediately made a statement in which, though he expressed his revulsion for the attack, he condemned the 'unacceptable behaviour of some of our fellow citizens abroad'. Speaking in the wake of the events, Lionel Jospin reiterated that a law existed to crack down on sex tourism, even when the victims were consenting adults. The articles which followed, in *Le Figaro* and *Le Monde,* wondered what means should be used to fight this plague, and the position the international community should adopt.

In the days that followed, Jean-Yves tried to get in touch with Gottfried Rembke by telephone; eventually, he succeeded. The head of TUI was sorry, truly sorry, but there was nothing he could do. In any case, as a tourist destination, Thailand was out of the question for several decades. Above and beyond that, the articles in the French press had had certain repercussions in Germany; it's true that opinion there was more divided, but the majority of the public nonetheless condemned sex tourism. Under the circumstances, he preferred to withdraw from the project.

2

I no more understood the reasons for my return to Paris than I had the reasons for my transfer to Bangkok. I was little liked by the hospital staff, they probably found me too inert; even in hospital, even on your deathbed, you are forced to play the part. Medical personnel like patients to put up a certain amount of resistance, to show a wilfulness which they can do their utmost to break, for the good of the patient, naturally. I manifested nothing of the sort. You could roll me on to my side ready for an injection and come back three hours later: I would still be in exactly the same position. The night before my departure, I banged roughly into one of the doors in the hospital corridor as I was trying to find the toilets. In the morning, my face was covered in blood, there was a gash above my eyebrow; I had to be cleaned, have a dressing put on. It hadn't occurred to me to call a nurse; in fact, I hadn't felt a thing.

The flight was a neutral period of time; I'd lost even the habit of smoking. By the baggage carousel, I shook Jean-Yves's hand; then I took a taxi to the Avenue de Choisy.

I immediately noticed that something wasn't right, that it would never be right. I didn't unpack. I walked around the apartment, a plastic bag in one hand, picking up all the photos of Valérie I could find. Most of them had been taken at her parents' in Brittany, on the beach or in the garden. There were also a few erotic photos that I had taken in the flat; I liked to watch her masturbate, I found her movements beautiful.

I sat on the sofa and dialled a number which I had been given to use in case of emergencies, twenty-four hours a day. It was a sort of crisis unit which had been set up especially to care for the survivors of the attack. It was based in a wing of the Sainte-Anne Hospital.

Most of the people who had asked to go there really were in a sad state: despite massive doses of tranquillisers, they had nightmares every night, every time there were screams, worried shouts, tears. When I met them in the corridors I was struck by their distressed, panic-stricken faces; they seemed to be literally eaten up by fear. And that fear, I thought, would end only with their lives.

For my part, more than anything, I felt terribly weary. In general I only got up to drink a cup of Nescafé or nibble a few biscuits; meals were not compulsory, nor were the therapeutic activities. Even so, I underwent a series of tests, and three days after my arrival I had an interview with a psychiatrist; the tests had revealed 'extremely weakened reactivity'. I was not in pain, but I did, in fact, feel weakened; I felt weaker than it was possible to feel. He asked me what I intended to do. I replied, 'Wait'. I showed myself to be reasonably optimistic; I told him that all this sadness would come to an end, that I would find happiness again, but that I had to wait a while. He didn't seem really convinced. He was a man of about fifty, with a plump, cheerful face, absolutely clean-shaven.

After a week, they transferred me to a new psychiatric hospital, this time for a lengthy stay. I had to stay there for a little over three months. To my great surprise, I met the same psychiatrist there. It was hardly surprising, he told me; this was where his surgery was based. Helping crisis victims was only a temporary assignment, something of a speciality in his case, in fact – he had already been on a committee set up after the bombing of the Saint-Michel RER station.

He didn't really talk like a typical psychiatrist, at least I found him bearable. I remember he talked to me about 'freeing oneself from attachments': it sounded like some Buddhist bullshit. Freeing what? I was nothing more than an attachment. Inclined to the transitory by nature, I had become attached to a transitory thing, as was my nature – none of this demanded any particular comment. Had I been inclined towards the eternal by nature, I went on, in order to fuel the conversation, I would have become attached to things eternal. Apparently his technique worked well with survivors haunted by fears of mutilation and death. 'These sufferings do not belong to you, they are not truly yours; they are merely passing phantoms in your mind,' he told people; and in the end, they believed him.

I don't know at what point I began to become aware of the situation – but in any case, it was only episodic. There were still long periods – in fact there still are – when Valérie is categorically not dead. In the beginning I could consciously prolong these without the slightest effort. I remember the first time I found it difficult, when I truly felt the weight of reality; it was just after a visit from Jean-Yves. It was a fraught moment; there were memories which I found difficult to deny. I didn't ask him to come back.

Marie-Jeanne's visit, on the other hand, did me good. She didn't say much, she talked a bit about the atmosphere at work; I told her straight away that I wouldn't be coming back, because I was going to move to Krabi. She acquiesced without comment. 'Don't worry,' I told her, 'everything will be fine.' She looked at me with mute compassion; strangely, I actually think that she believed me.

The visit from Valérie's parents was probably the most painful; the psychiatrist must have told them that I was going through a period of denial. As a result, Valérie's mother cried almost the whole time; her father didn't seem very comfortable either. They had also come to iron out some practical details, to bring me a suitcase containing my personal belongings. They imagined I wouldn't want to keep the apartment in the 13th arrondissement. 'Of course not', I said, 'of course we'll deal with that later.' At that point Valérie's mother began to cry again.

Life goes by effortlessly in an institution: there, for the most part, human needs are satisfied. I had rediscovered *Questions pour un champion*, it was the only show I watched, I no longer took any interest in the news. A lot of the other residents spent the entire day in front of the television. I wasn't all that keen, really: everything was moving too quickly. I believed that, if I could remain calm, avoid thinking as much as possible, matters would sort themselves out in the end.

One morning in April, I found out that matters had, in effect, sorted themselves out and that I would soon be able to leave. This seemed to me to complicate things rather: I would have to find a hotel room, create a neutral environment. At least I had money, that was something at least. 'You have to look on the bright side,' I said to one of the nurses. She seemed surprised, perhaps because this was the first time I had ever spoken to her.

There is no specific treatment for denial, the psychiatrist explained to me at our last interview; it is not really a disorder of mood, but a problem of perception. He had kept me in hospital all this time chiefly because he was worried about the possible risk of a suicide attempt – they are quite common in cases of sudden, brutal realisations; but now I was out of danger. I see, I said. I see.

3

A week after being discharged from hospital, I took a flight back to Bangkok. I had no particular plans. If we had an ideal nature, we could satisfy ourselves with the movements of the sun. The seasons were too distinct in Paris, they were a source of agitation, of insecurity. In Bangkok, the sun rose at six o'clock, it set at six o'clock; in the intervening time, it followed an unchanging course. There was, apparently, a monsoon season, but I had never witnessed it. The bustle of the city existed, but I couldn't clearly grasp the rationale behind it, it was more a sort of natural state. Undoubtedly all of these people had a destiny, a life, inasmuch as their incomes permitted; but for all I knew, they could just as easily have been a pack of lemmings.

I took a room at the Amari Boulevard; most of the guests in the hotel were Japanese businessmen. This was where we had stayed, Valérie, Jean-Yves and I, on our last visit; it wasn't really a good idea. Two days later, I moved to the Grace Hotel; it was only about ten metres down the road, but the atmosphere was noticeably different. It was probably the last place in Bangkok where you could still meet Arab sex tourists. They hugged the walls, staying holed up in the hotel – which had a discotheque and its own massage parlour. You spotted them in the surrounding alleys where there were stalls selling kebabs and long-distance call centres; but, further afield, nothing. I realised that without intending to, I had moved closer to the Bumrungrad Hospital.

It is certainly possible to remain alive animated simply by a desire for vengeance; many people have lived that way. Islam had wrecked my life, and Islam was certainly something which I could hate; in the days that followed, I devoted myself to trying to feel hatred for Muslims. I was quite good at it, and I started to follow the international news again. Every time I heard that a Palestinian terrorist, or a Palestinian child or a pregnant Palestinian woman had been gunned down in the Gaza Strip, I felt a quiver of enthusiasm at the thought that it meant one less Muslim. Yes, it was possible to live like this.

One evening, in the hotel coffee-shop, a Jordanian banker struck up a conversation with me. A man of amiable disposition, he insisted on buying me a beer; perhaps his enforced seclusion in the hotel was beginning to get to him. 'I understand how people feel, you know; you can't hold it against them . . .' he told me. 'It has to be said, we were asking for it. This isn't a Muslim country, there's no reason to spend hundreds of millions building mosques. To say nothing of the bomb attack, of course . . .' Seeing that I was listening to him attentively, he ordered another beer and become bolder. The problem with Muslims, he told me, was that the paradise promised by the prophet already existed here on earth: there were places on earth where young, available, lascivious girls danced for the pleasure of men, where one could become drunk on nectar and listen to celestial music; there were about twenty of them within five hundred metres of our hotel. These places were easily accessible. To gain admission, there was absolutely no need to fulfil the seven duties of a Muslim, nor to engage in holy war; all you had to do was pay a couple of dollars. It wasn't even necessary to travel to realise such things; all you needed was satellite TV. For him, there was no doubt, the Muslim way was doomed: capitalism would triumph. Already, young Arabs dreamed of nothing but consumer products and sex. They might try to pretend otherwise, but secretly, they wanted to be part of the American system: the violence of some of them was no more than a sign of impotent jealousy; thankfully, more and more of them were turning their backs on Islam. He himself had been unlucky: he was an old man now, and he had been forced to spend his whole life compromising with a religion he despised. I was in much the same boat: there would come a day when the world was delivered from Islam; but for me, it would come too late. I no longer really had a life; I had had a life, for a few months – that in itself was something, not everyone could say as much. The absence of the will to live is, alas, not sufficient to make one want to die.

I saw him again the next day, just before he left for Amman; it would be a year before he could come back. On the whole, I was glad that he was leaving; I sensed that otherwise he would have wanted to talk to me again. The prospect gave me a bit of a headache: I found it very difficult now to tolerate intellectual debate; I no longer had any desire to understand the world, nor even to know it. Our brief conversation, however, had made a profound impression on me; in fact, he had convinced me from the outset, Islam was doomed. As soon as you thought about it, it seemed obvious. This simple thought was sufficient to dispel my hatred. Once again I ceased to have any interest in the news.

4

Bangkok was still too much like a normal city, there were too many businessmen, too many tourists on package holidays. Two weeks later, I caught a bus for Pattaya. It had been bound to end this way I thought, as I boarded the vehicle; it was then that I realised that I was wrong, nothing in this story had been determined. I could easily have spent the rest of my life with Valérie in Thailand, in Brittany, or indeed anywhere at all. Growing old is no joke; but growing old alone is worse than anything.

As soon as I had put down my luggage on the dusty floor of the bus station, I knew I had arrived at the end of my journey. A scrawny old junkie with long grey hair, a large lizard perched on his shoulder, was begging outside the turnstiles. I gave him a hundred baht before drinking a beer at the Heidelberg Hof directly opposite. A few pot-bellied, moustachioed German pederasts minced around in their flowery shirts. Near them, three Russian teenage girls, who had attained a pinnacle of sluttishness, squirmed as they listened to their ghetto-blaster. They writhed and rolled about on their chairs, the sleazy little cocksuckers. In a few minutes' walk through the streets of the town, I encountered an impressive variety of human specimens: rappers in baseball caps, Dutch dropouts, cyberpunks with red hair, Austrian dykes with piercings. There is nothing lower than Pattaya, it is a sort of cesspit, the ultimate sewer where the sundry waste of western neurosis winds up. Whether you're homosexual, heterosexual, or both, Pattaya is the last-chance saloon, the one beyond which you might as well give up on desire. The hotels are distinguished, naturally, by different levels of comfort and price, but also by the nationality of their clientele. There are two large communities, the Germans and the Americans (among whom probably some Australians and possibly even some New Zealanders conceal themselves). You also get quite a lot of Russians, recognisable because they dress like rednecks and behave like gangsters. There is even an establishment intended for the French, called Ma Maison. The hotel has only a dozen rooms, but the restaurant is very popular. I spent a week there before I realised that I was not particularly attached to *andouillettes* or *cuisses de grenouille*; that I could live without following the French championship via satellite, and without leafing daily through the arts pages of *Le Monde*. In any case, I needed to find long-term accommodation. A standard tourist visa in Thailand only lasts for one month; but to get an extension, all you have to do is cross the border. A lot of the travel agencies in Pattaya offer a day return to the Cambodian border. After a three-hour trek in a minibus, you queue for an hour or two at customs, have lunch in a self-service restaurant on Cambodian soil (lunch is included in the price, as are tips for customs officials), then you start on your return journey. Most residents have been doing this every month for years; it's much easier than trying to get a long-term visa.

You don't come to Pattaya to start your life over, but to end it in tolerable conditions. Or, if you want to put it less brutally, to take a rest, a long rest – one which may prove permanent. These were the terms used by a homosexual of about fifty I met in an Irish pub on Soi 14; he had spent the greater part of his career as a designer working for the popular press and had managed to put some money aside. Ten years earlier, he had noticed that things were going badly for him: he still went out to clubs, the same clubs as always, but more and more often he came home empty-handed. Of course, he could always pay; but if it had to come to that, he would rather pay Asians. He apologised for this remark, hoped I would not infer any racist connotation. No, no, of course, I understood: it's less humiliating to pay for someone who looks nothing like any of those you have seduced in the past, who brings back no memories. If sex has to be paid for, it is best that, in a certain sense, it is undifferentiated. As everyone knows, one of the first things you feel in the presence of another race is that inability to differentiate, that feeling that physically, everyone looks more or less alike. The effect wears off after a few months, and it's a pity, because it bears out a reality: human beings do, in fact, look very much alike. Of course, we can distinguish between males and females; we can also, if we choose, distinguish between different age categories; but any more advanced distinction comes close to pedantry, probably a result of boredom. A creature that is bored elaborates distinctions and hierarchies. According to Hutchinson and Rawlins, the development of systems of hierarchical dominance within animal societies does not correspond to any practical necessity, nor to any selective advantage; it simply constitutes a means of combating the crushing boredom of life in the heart of nature.

So, the former designer was quietly living out the last years of his queer life treating himself to pretty, slender, muscular, dark-skinned boys. Once a year, he went back to France to visit his family and a few friends. His sex life was less frenetic than I might imagine, he told me: he went out once or twice a week, no more. He had been settled here in Pattaya for six years now; the profusion of varied, exciting and inexpensive sexual opportunities provoked a paradoxical calming of desire. Every time he went out, he was certain of being able to fuck and suck magnificent young boys who, for their part, would jerk him off sensitively and expertly in return. Confident of this fact, he spent more time getting ready to go out and he enjoyed these encounters in moderation. I realised then that he imagined I was in the throes of the erotic frenzy of my first weeks here, that he saw in me a heterosexual counterpart to his own case. I refrained from correcting him. He proved to be friendly, insisted on buying the beers, gave me a number of addresses for long-term accommodation. He had enjoyed talking to a Frenchman. Most of the homosexual residents were English; he was on good terms with them, but from time to time, he wanted to speak his own language. He had no real contact with the little French community which gathered at Ma Maison – mostly a crowd of straight, ex-colonial, ex-army thugs. If I was going to live in Pattaya, maybe we could go out together some night, no strings, obviously; he gave me his mobile number. I wrote it down, though I knew that I would never call him. He was pleasant, friendly, interesting if you like; but I simply wasn't interested in human relationships any more.

I rented a room on Naklua Road, a little outside the bustle of the city. It had air-conditioning, a fridge, a shower, a bed and some bits of furniture; the rent was three thousand baht a month – a little more than five hundred francs. I informed my bank of this news, wrote a letter of resignation to the Ministry of Culture.

There was nothing much left for me to do in this life. I bought a number of reams of A4 paper with the intention of putting the elements of my life in order. It's something people should do more often before they die. It's curious to think of all these human beings who live out their whole lives without feeling the need to make the slightest comment, the slightest objection, the slightest remark.

Not that these comments, these objections, these remarks are addressed to anyone in particular, nor intended to have any sort of meaning; but, even so, it seems to me to be better, in the end, that they be made.

5

Six months later, I am still here in my room on Naklua Road, and I think that I have more or less finished my work. I miss Valérie. If by chance it was my intention, when I began writing these pages, to lessen the feeling of loss, or to make it more bearable, I would by now be certain of my failure: Valérie's absence has never been more painful to me.

At the beginning of my third month here, I decided in the end to go back to the massage parlours and the hostess bars again. In principle, the idea didn't really fill me with enthusiasm; I was afraid it would be a total fiasco. Nonetheless, I managed to get a hard-on, and even to ejaculate; but I never once experienced any pleasure. It wasn't the girls' fault, they were just as expert, just as gentle; but it was as though I was anaesthetised. I continued to go to a massage parlour once a week, to some extent on principle; then I decided to stop. It was, after all, a form of human contact –

that was the drawback. Even if I didn't in the least believe that my ability to feel pleasure would return, it was possible that the girl would come, especially as the numbness in my penis meant that I could keep going for hours if I didn't make a little effort to interrupt the proceedings. I might get to the point where I wanted her to come, it could become an issue; and I didn't wish to have anything more to do with issues. My life was an empty space, and it was better that it remain that way. If I allowed passion to penetrate my body, pain would follow quickly in its wake.

My book is almost at an end. More and more often now, I stay in bed for most of the day. Sometimes I turn on the air-conditioning in the morning and turn it off at night and between the two absolutely nothing happens. I've become accustomed to the purring of the machine, which I found irritating at first; but I've also become accustomed to the heat; I don't really have a preference.

For a long time now, I've stopped buying French newspapers; I suppose that by this time the presidential elections have taken place. The Ministry of Culture, somehow or other, must be getting on with its work. Perhaps Marie-Jeanne still thinks about me from time to time, when she's working on the budget for an exhibition; I haven't tried to get in touch. I don't know what's become of Jean-Yves either; after he was fired from Aurore, I suppose he must have started his career again much further down, and probably in something other than tourism.

When your love life is over, life in general takes on a sort of conventional, forced quality. One retains a human form, one's habitual behaviour, a sort of structure; but one's heart, as they say, isn't in it.

Mopeds drive down Naklua Road, sending up clouds of dust. It is noon already. Coming from outlying districts, the prostitutes arrive for work in the downtown bars. I don't think I'll go out today. Or maybe I will, late in the afternoon, to gulp down a soup at one of the stalls set up at the crossroads.

When one gives up on life, the last remaining human contacts are those you have with shopkeepers. As far as I'm concerned, these are limited to a few words spoken in English. I don't speak Thai, which creates a barrier around me that is suffocating and sad. It is obvious that I will never really understand Asia, and actually it's of not great importance. It's possible to live in the world without understanding it: all you need is to be able to get food, caresses and love. In Pattaya, food and caresses are cheap by Western, and even by Asian, standards. As for love, it's difficult for me to say. I am now convinced that, for me, Valérie was simply a radiant exception. She was one of those creatures who are capable of devoting their lives to someone else's happiness, of making that alone their goal. This phenomenon is a mystery. Happiness, simplicity and joy lies within them; but I still do not know how or why it occurs. And if I haven't understood love, what use is it to me to have understood the rest?

To the end, I will remain a child of Europe, of

worry and of shame; I have no message of hope to deliver. For the West, I do not feel hatred; at most I feel a great contempt. I know only that every single one of us reeks of selfishness, masochism and death. We have created a system in which it has simply become impossible to live; and what's more, we continue to export it.

It's getting dark, the multicoloured fairy lights wink on at the entrances to the beer bars. The German OAPs settle in, placing their thick hands on the thighs of their young companions. More than any other people, they are acquainted with worry and shame, they feel the need for tender flesh, for soft, endlessly refreshing skin. More than any other people, they are acquainted with the desire for their own annihilation. It is rare to come across the vulgar, smug pragmatism of Anglo-Saxon sex tourists among them, that manner of endlessly comparing goods and prices. It is equally rare for them to exercise, to look after their bodies. In general, they eat too much, drink too much beer, get fat; most of them will die pretty soon. They are often friendly, they like to joke, to buy a round, to tell stories; but their company is soothing and sad.

I understand death now; I don't think it will do me much harm. I have known hatred, contempt, decay and other things; I have even known brief moments of love. Nothing of me will survive, and I do not deserve for anything of me to survive; I will have been a mediocre individual in every possible sense.

I imagine, I don't know why, that I will die in the

middle of the night, and I still feel a little anxious at the thought of the suffering which will accompany the severing of all ties with the body. I find it difficult to envisage the cessation of life as completely painless and unconscious; naturally, I know that I'm wrong. Nonetheless, I have trouble convincing myself of that fact.

The locals will find me a few days later, quite quickly in fact; in this climate, corpses quickly start to stink. They won't know what to do with me, and will probably contact the French embassy. I'm far from being destitute, the case will be easy to deal with. There will certainly be quite a lot of money left in my account; I don't know who will inherit it – the state probably, or some distant relatives.

Unlike other Asian peoples, the Thais don't believe in ghosts, and have little interest in the fate of corpses; most of them are buried in communal graves. Since I will have left no specific instructions, that is what will become of me. A death certificate will be drawn up, a box will be ticked in a registry office, far from here, in France. A few street hawkers, accustomed to seeing me in the area, will shake their heads. My apartment will be rented out to another resident. I'll be forgotten. I'll quickly be forgotten.